ADAMAS
FIRST LOVE

ADAMAS
FIRST LOVE

ANNE SMALLIDGE

Library of Congress Control Number:		2019917447
ISBN:	Hardcover	978-1-7960-6863-4
	Softcover	978-1-7960-6862-7
	eBook	978-1-7960-6861-0

Print information available on the last page.

Rev. date: 10/31/2019

To order additional copies of this book, contact:
Xlibris
1-888-795-4274
www.Xlibris.com
Orders@Xlibris.com
805061

CONTENTS

CHAPTER 1

Adama and Jola - The Twins

Adama

I hate being this young African girl stuck in this eighty year old white woman's body. How do I get out? How can this spirit of mine (or hers) escape? How did I get here in the first place? I don't understand any of it. I only understand that as time goes on, I am more and more restless to fly out of here.

At first, as I began to stir from a deep dreamless sleep, here in this white woman's body, as her spirit, I was not the only one. There were others in the darkness of herself. Like several butterflies in one crystalis, we were all coming and going. Some small, some fully grown. Some sighing deeply, then dissolving into a speck of light. Where did they go? I don't know. I never will. The speck of light is usually quite lovely. It is sparkling blue, then green, then gold, then disappearing. Now and then the speck of light is dull and grey, lying listlessly in a corner, then it, too, disappears.

Who were they? What mission did they follow? I'll never know.

All I know is I've got to get out of here because I think I'm driving this white woman crazy, whose body I serve as soul/spirit.

I know, at one point in my_life, I was a young African girl who played by the riverside nearby my village. Splashing along the sides in the muddy water I ran with my friends. We'd spend as much time as we could trying to catch the frogs and salamanders. We watched the bright green parrots in the trees. We'd gather nuts from the ground under the trees, and eat them with great joy. When I wasn't sweeping,or fetching water for mother's cooking, or when I wasn't carrying one of the babies on my back, I would be playing by the riverside. Very often however, I carried one of the babies of our compound.

My mother's name is Binta. She was the first wife of my father, Ebrima. They were married when she was fourteen and he was nineteen years old. Ebrima's mother and father chose Binta for Ebrima when they were just children. His family name is of the Mandinka tribe, as is my mother's. Our tribe had traveled from Mali many generations ago, down to this other land. The Gambia.

****

My mother, Binta, called me to come and bring the baby to her. Abduli was on my back, sleeping. I wondered why my mother wanted Abduli when he was sleeping. He was quiet and seemingly happy on my back. He wasn't hungry, or he would be awake, crying for Binta's breast. Binta had a few minutes with nothing to do, why would she want Abduli when she could be taking a rest without a baby at her breast or on her back? Yet, she was impatiently calling me to bring him to her. So I walked across the hard dry earth in the center of the compound to where she sat on the bantaba.

Abduli is my mother's, sixth baby, but the way she gazes at him you would think he was her first. She loves Abduli more than herself. Her mouth turns up, her eyes light up with softness, and she kisses him lightly every time she calls for me to bring him to her. My mother has had six babies and she is proud of each of them. She is especially happy when my father, Ebrima, comes to look at the baby. I guess she feels as if she has made Ebrima happy and proud, also, I guess babies are important to have. I am watching each of the three wives of my father and I see the jealousy. My other mothers are jealous of my Binta because she is the oldest wife and has the say of who cooks, who does the laundry, and who carries the water. She is in charge of the running of the compound. But, more than anything, she has been the only one who has given Ebrima babies. Sometimes, the other two wives don't appear to like my mother, but they hide it very well. My mother is always kind to the other two wives, Aimee and Haddi. But I have heard her tell her vue (women's group) that her husband, Ebrima, loves the youngest and, of course, the prettiest wife, Haddi, more than he loves her, or Aimee, the middle wife.

I watch all of this because I am a curious girl and am seeing what my life is going to be. I guess I should be happy and excited about growing up here in this village by the river, but I'm not sure. I am watching. I have never been any other place. I explore the bush surrounding our small village, and I play by the river. I followed the magic path to my friend's village only a few minutes away. Other than that, I have never been any place else. Elders tell us there are other places besides this village of ours, but I've never seen those places.

****

Binta took me to the bush last year when I was nine years old, along with many other girls and some of the other women from our village, and we lived there for six days. I don't remember some of the things that happened while we were there. I have a dark memory about some of what happened. I do remember the women teaching us about being a wife and mother. I actually knew most of it as I had been watching and doing much of the work of women since I was old enough to put a spoon on my head and go to the market for tomato paste refill. Or, to carry water from the well, or to carry babies, or to carry this, or to fetch that.

That time we were in the bush with our mothers and aunts we walked home through the bush early each evening to sleep in our own beds, but we were not allowed to go outside into the compound or village. We were always very tired anyway, and I was glad to get home to my room with my sisters. We were not allowed to talk to each other, but we whispered in the darkness.

The most confusing part for me of the six days we were in the bush was when the old ma cut me between my legs, and I cried, and it hurt.

My mother told me to be still, and not to cry. My mother held me tightly on the ground, lying there beside me, saying; 'shush, shush, it will be alright.' My mother said it would make me pure and clean for my whole life, this cutting between my legs. It hurt more than I can ever say, and all of us there tried not to be afraid and not to cry. But, we were and we did. It all had something to do with carrying babies inside our bodies. Something to do with the fact that our husbands will put the seed into our bodies and we will bring forth a baby sometime later. And we will be proud and should always submit to our husbands. And we will always honor him, and do his bidding. And we will love his other wives as ourselves.

I bled a great deal and it hurt to walk home that night. My mother helped me walk and she gently held me close to her, but she made me walk with pride beside her as we entered the village. The women had put herbs from the bush between our legs to absorb the blood.

It was during the middle of the six days in the bush when the cutting took place, and most of us began to heal within the second or third day of the cutting. One girl, Mia, did not return with us to the bush on the second day of the cutting, and I learned that she had died. No one said it had to do with the cutting. They said God took her. Why would God take a little girl? I am not supposed to ask or think such questions. I sometimes think I am not a good Muslim girl. I wonder too much. I am too curious.

The day we finally came home from the bush, we sang together in harmony as we entered the village. All of us walking through the corridors of our little village are singing a sweet gentle song about returning to our homes as pure women-to-be. I love to sing, but I felt as if my tears were very close to falling down my cheeks because I was no longer a little girl, but a cut near-woman.

My best friend, Tida, also came to the bush, as did my other vue (friends) Amie, Ningma, and Jola. We were all born the same year, and our mothers, also are best friends. Our compounds are in the same corridor of the Mandinka section in our village. We share the same well,which sits near the Chief's compound. Tida is the daughter of Chief Jammeh. Many families bear the name of Jammeh. It's an old traditional Mandinka name, as is Darboe. Darboe is my mother and my father's family tribal name.

When we returned from the bush we stayed in our own compounds, resting and healing from the cutting for a few days. Our mothers were so happy and proud of us that we tried also to be happy and proud. I cried at night. My sisters lay close to me and shushed me, gently, so no one would hear me. It's not what we were supposed to do, I guess cry from the cutting.

"You must not allow a boy or man to touch you until you are married to your husband. Then, only he should touch you," our mothers said this to us while we were in the bush. I was not happy to hear that because I liked to play the games the village boys and girls played in the late afternoon when our work was nearly done for the day. Games where we chased each other, tagged each other, and fell on the ground with each other. Could we no longer do that? And if so, why not? There was so much I didn't understand, so much that seemed ridiculous.

Tida did not seem as concerned about the new rules of our life as I did. She would shrug her skinny shoulders and say, "I'll touch the boys and the girls. No one will see me, anyway. They are all too busy. I'll touch you, too!" She pushed her hand against my chest and laughed, running away from me.

I chased her, my arms swinging like a tree on a windy day. Running and chasing. But I didn't touch her. I tried to remember if it was against the rules to touch girls.

Tida turned toward me, quick as a squirrel turns on the boys when they corner it. Her eyes flashed with fire. She pushed me again, and this time we fell onto dry, dusty earth, laughing all the while. She lay there on top of me, laughing. Quickly jumping up, she said, "There, see I touched all of you!" Then she ran down the corridor toward the other girls.

As I said before, Tida is the chief's daughter. Amie and Ningma are sisters to each other. They are of the Cham clan. And the other member of our vue is Jola, my twin sister. We love being twins because we can confuse our parents.

So that particular day, after Tida had pushed me down and landed on top of me, the five of us headed to the river, trying to run away from the compounds full of babies and work. Whenever we would run away to the river, we took the chance of getting into a lot of trouble. If one of our mothers could not find us after calling our name, or sending one of the other siblings to find us at one of the other compounds, and we were not visible, and there was work for us to do, then we suffered some serious pain. But, we were all used to the whippings by our mothers. It was part of the daily life in our village. Some mothers beat harder than others. Some mothers used the palm of their hands, like my mother did, which hurt badly enough. But some of the mothers used switches from the bush or big sticks from the firewood pile. Those mothers wanted their children to be nearby when they needed them to run their errands, and work, without having to call, and wait, or have to send someone to find their daughter.

We skipped through the magic path to the river. I was the best skipper. I was also the best tree climber. We never climbed trees in the village. Girls are not supposed to climb trees. Only boys. Don't ask me why.

As we skipped through the magic path to the river, we could hear the birds singing and see the red succulent flowers that jump out of the earth overnight during the rainy season. And this was the rainy season. Lushness was everywhere. Vines grew inches every day. Snakes liked to hide under the vines, so throughout the village, our fathers and brothers always kept the vines cut away. But, no one cut the vines away in the magic path to the river. We girls would push them out of the path, or snap them off with our hands, being careful to lift them off the ground before we stepped further. Then we would snap the vines off and throw them into the bush. If we found a snake lying there under the vines, we dropped the vine, screamed, and would ran home. Everyone in our village is afraid of snakes. Every rainy season someone in the village is bitten by a snake and when that happens, that person dies. Always. Snakes are very dangerous.

We called it the magic path because of the beautiful red succulent flowers that sprang out of the earth overnight. The only way a beautiful, big red blossom could pop out overnight is because it is magic. Other magic happens in the magic path, but no one except my vue knows of it.

We speak not of it to anyone. We are sworn to our faith not to mention it to anyone. Only our vue of five knows of it, and we will hide it in our hearts, forever.

We reached the riverside and sat for a minute on an old log that has been there many, many years. My father says his father sat on that same log when *he* was a boy, fishing. The log is so smooth I can nearly see myself in its shine. So, the five of us sat there, quietly looking out at the river. A peace came on us and we sat for several minutes before we began to squirm. Sitting is not our favorite thing to do. Our favorite thing to do is take all of our clothes off except for the one small piece of material, which covers our private, save-for-the-husband between our legs. And then, once all clothes are removed we jump into the shallow water, lie down, and pretend to swim. None of us know how to swim because we are not allowed to go further than our knees into the water. Our parents tell us there are monsters that live in the river. The monsters never come to the shore, but are waiting in the middle of the river to eat us. We don't really want to be eaten, so we play in the knee deep water, splashing and pretending to swim to the end of the river. I often wonder where the river ends or begins and what is it like up that river or down that river. Our fathers take their canoes and go around the corners to fish or trade with whoever it is they see. But I don't know what is beyond the corners of the river.

"I think the boys are watching us from behind the big tree," my twin sister, Jola, cried. We all screamed and pretended we didn't want the boys to be watching us. But it made the day even more exciting when they *did* follow us. We really didn't need the boys to follow us in order to have a good time by the river, but sometimes it helped.

The boys, three of them, stepped out from behind the tree, and we girls lay in the water on our stomachs, barely covered, but enough so they could see only our head and feet.

They carried their spears, going hunting. They slinked along, one in front of the other, on the path that led up the river and into the bush that surrounds the village. When the boys hunt, they walk in a single line, with their spears poised to throw, and they walk very quietly on their bare feet. They are careful not to even step on a branch or twig which would make a noise. They hunt anything that runs or flies. They bring rabbits, rats, squirrels, or doves, or any small bird that doesn't fly quickly enough to escape, back to the village. Then the boys build a fire and skin and gut whatever it is they've killed that day and eat it. We girls don't get any of it, nor do any of the other boys, or adults. It is their prize for their hunting skills.

Girls don't hunt. Don't ask me why not.

It was Binta's turn to cook for the people of our compound. All of us. She needed fish money from my father, Ebrima, who was nowhere to be seen. Binta needed the fish money now so she could go to the next village where fishermen sell the fish they have caught that morning. If Ebrima has not gone in his canoe to fish, or if he comes home from fishing without anything; then Binta has to go to the next village and purchase some fish. We have two goats, but they are saved for sacrifice on holiday celebrations. That is when we are expected to slaughter a goat or a cow, or a sheep, or, if nothing more, some chickens. But each day there needs to be something to add to the rice and sauce. Fish goes the furthest in a pot of rice for all of the people in our compound. It is less costly than cattle or goat or sheep.

"Adama," Binta called me. "Adama, go find your father. He knows I need fish money. He is hiding, I know. Go to the mosque. That is his favorite hiding place."

I always know Binta is really angry with my father when she sends me to the mosque to find him. His vue (men friends) sit across the street from the mosque, smoking, talking, and watching the people who come to the market, which sits beside the mosque. Usually, Binta will wait until Ebrima returns from his wandering to get the fish money, even if it makes her daily tasks more difficult. But, today I could tell she was not happy with my father.

I found him where he usually is, sitting on the old worn log by the market, across from the mosque. Surrounded by his vue, he was smoking a cigarette and laughing his raspy, deep laugh.

My father is 'too handsome for his own good,' my mother says. I think my mother is a very wise woman. I think if you are a woman in this place it helps to be wise.

"Binta wants you," I said as I quietly slid up beside him, not looking directly into his face.

Ebrima took my arm and pulled me over to him. "What does she want?"

"I guess she wants fish money," I said.

Ebrima's vue chuckled. All of them.

"Tell Binta I'll be home, soon," he turned me around toward the corridor that leads to our compound, and tapped me on my backsides.

I felt as if I might fly when my father tapped my back. His hands were firm and warm. I loved my father very much. I wanted to be one of his special children. It is good for fathers and mothers to have many children, so I didn't want to be the only child; but, I would like to have been the favorite among a few.

I skipped through the corridor around the corner to our compound,.

"Well, where is your father?" my mother snapped as soon as she spotted me rounding the corner.

"He says he will be here soon."

"Soon for Ebrima Darboe is not soon for me! I need to get fish money and go to Sanyang! I am tired of your father!"

My stomach felt as if it might flip over. My mother never spoke of my father in that way. What did that mean? 'Tired of your father?'

Was she going to throw him away? She could not do that. Wives can *never* do that. Wives never even *say* they will do that. Except my mother just did.

I tried to slip away from my mother, turning quietly away from her. I stepped toward our gate.

"Do not even think about it! Get this baby off my back and change his clothes. He is wet and messy. Clean him up and walk with him until he sleeps." Ya moi?!" (*'do you hear?'*)

Binta Darboe - Mother of Adama

My name is Binta Darboe and I am the first wife of Ebrima Darboe. On this particular day as I walk down the path that leads to the women's garden just outside the village I am thinking. It is a big garden where a few large trees grow, providing shade for the vegetables. The sun is very hot here in our village, and often vegetables, unless watered twice a day and provided with shade, will die on the vine. I go early each morning and water the vegetables before the sun becomes too hot. There are two wells dug by the old man who digs wells in our area. He wears ragged skins from some animal and is covered with mud and dirt all over his body. He lives in the bush, and comes out only when it is time for him to dig wells for the women's gardens. He also digs wells for the men's cash crop gardens of cassava and groundnuts.

I also go to the garden late in the afternoon, before I cook dinner for all of us, when it is my turn to cook. The days I cook are also the nights I go to Ebrima Darboe, my husband. When the other wives tease me about it being my turn to 'go' to him, I chuckle. It is difficult to be the eldest wife of a compound. It is difficult to be in charge of the other wives. Part of me knows I really need help in a compound full of work. But, if there was only me and Ebrima and our children I believe it would be possible to do all the work. We wives seem to like each other most of the time. Eating together around the communal bowl with the girls in the family. We work together in the gardens and they watch my children as if they were their own children. But after dinner, one of us will quickly wash up, put on a fresh, pretty dress, fix our hair, and that one will go to him.

I am older now, yet I still like being with Ebrima Darboe when it is my turn. We have much to discuss, as I am the oldest wife and am in charge of the women and children in our compound. Ebrima Darboe is the man and leads us all. He is the one who holds all the money when there is any. He decides all things, yet, because I am the eldest and first wife, I am second in command. Besides Ebrima should not have to be concerned about the daily chores and work of the compound. After all, he is the man. The leader. And, so, I am very pleased to be his second in command. I am actually the leader of many things that Ebrima is not even aware of and never will be.

****

Adama

I am ten years old and I am in love with a boy who I've known since we were born. I will not want to share him with anyone when I become old enough to claim him as my own! I am already planning how to convince my parents that we, he and I, should be married when the time comes. It's not impossible. We are of the same tribe, Mandinka. There is a history between the two families from many generations back. But, I know, because I've heard my parents talking about who I will marry, and it's not Modu Barrow, who I love. Modu and I were born on the same day, in the same corridor. The same mid-wife was supposed to help deliver us, but she could not be in two places at once. So my grandmother and aunt helped to bring me into the world, while the mid-wife was at the Barrow kunda delivering Modu. Our mothers are the best of friends. His mother's name is Fatou. Fatou Jammeh. Jammeh is also of the Mandinka tribe.

Fatou Jammeh and my mother, Binta Darboe, grew up together. Their parents chose their husbands for them. It is the custom.

Modu Barrow will not recognize me when we are all playing in the corridor. We play jump the stick and tag. Modu Jammeh will not look at me or touch me. But, I love him, and I know he loves me. Sometimes when we are alone together, by accident, like walking from the market mid-day, he will come upon me, and tap me on my shoulder, laugh and run. I will chase him, but he is much faster than I and he disappears around the corner and into his compound before I can catch up. If I ever catch him, I will tell him I love him and he has to marry me or I will die.

****

Jola - Adama's Twin Sister

My name is Jola, and I am the twin sister to Adama. She is my best friend and my twin sister. We confuse people all the time. I am not as brave as Adama is, though. One day we saw an owl on the magic path and Adama walked carefully up to the branch where it sat and spoke into its big white face. The owl did not move, nor did it look at her. It turned its head so far around, it looked as if the head was screwed onto its body. It looked directly behind itself. Then, it turned again and looked directly at Adama. Adama spoke to it saying the greetings in Mandinka. Adama says the owl returned the greetings to her, and told her a secret that Adama has never told me. The owl flew into the bush, but it's not the last time we've seen it resting on the same bush. I walk carefully past it, not looking directly at it. But, Adama always stops, greets it speaking quietly, and listens to the owl saying nothing. Adama talks to that owl quite often on our walks to the riverside. The owl is never there when the other girls go with us to the riverside.

Adama is a strange girl. In many ways she is part of me, so I guess I, too, am strange. I do not resent being a girl in this place, but I think Adama is not as content as I am. She tries to do some of the things only boys are allowed to do, but is always stopped by our parents. Our mother, Binta, says she's 'headstrong,' which means she is determined to do what she wants to do, I guess. Binta caught her climbing a tree on the path to the women's garden one day. That day, my sister, Adama, received a serious whipping. But, it's not the last time I've seen Adama climb trees. She does it now when she is sure no adults are around. I don't like to climb trees. I do like to play with our girlfriends who live in the same corridor. We play games in the sand of the road, making marks to skip and jump into and out of. We even jump over the stick that the boys set up with two sticks stuck in the ground and one lying across them nestled in the groove at the top. I do well with jumping. But, I don't climb trees.

Another thing Adama is not content with is the fact that she can't marry Modu, who she has loved since we all were born. I am the only one knows this. I think I know who my parents have chosen for me to marry, and I am looking forward to meeting this boy and his parents when the time comes. I know he is part of our tribe and lives in a village not far from here. His name is Ousmanie Touray. He is older than I am and I will probably not be the first wife. It is not all settled and arranged yet. It is what my parents want. This Touray family has cattle and a big compound.

"Not me!" my sister says. "I'm not going to be a *second* wife, or a *third* wife. I'm going to be the *first* wife, and maybe the *only* wife!"

I gasped when my twin sister said that. Why would she want to be the only wife and have to do all that work and be alone all day caring for all of the children by herself? Sometimes I don't understand my twin sister at all.

But, we are only ten years old and have a few years to grow up before we are married. I am happy to wait and see who is chosen for me. I hope I will like him and that he is good to me. That's what I hope. I hope to have many beautiful children for this man, whoever he is. It is God's will. Whatever happens, it's God's will.

The time we went to the bush with our mother and the other girls in our neighborhood, and their mothers and aunties, I was very worried. That first morning we walked into the bush, quietly. The sun was just beginning to peek up over the palm trees across the river. The river was pink. The sky was pink. The whole world was shining, clean and pink. It seemed we walked for a long time, deeper and deeper into the bush. The trees were close to the path, and we could hear rustling in the deepness of it. Animals lived in that place. But I knew our mothers and aunties would not take us where they could not protect us. Yet, it was scary. Adama held my hand as we followed Binta.

I don't remember much about being in the bush except for the lessons the aunties and mothers told us about being good wives and mothers. They taught us how to cook, and prepare food for the whole family. They taught us how to please our husbands. They taught us how to be good wives. To obey and please. They also prepared us for our husbands by doing a secret thing between our legs. It made us clean and pure and ready for our adult lives.

I think it hurt more than I wanted it to. I think I made myself pretend it was not happening. I think my mother held me very close to herself while the cutting took place. I closed my eyes and thought about the pinkness of the sunrise. Even so, it was difficult.

****

Jola Talks about Adama and Her Vue

Tida, Aimee, and her sister, Nygma, Adama, (my twin sister) and I lay on the straw mattress in Tida's room and whispered about the trip to the river when we saw the boys watching us. We lay there curved around each other, arms flung over legs. Sometimes pinching an ear or a nose, just to get a slap from the one who was pinching.

"If I'd had a stone, I'd have thrown it at them," my sister Adama said.

"Of course you would. You are always throwing stones. You are always looking for trouble." Tida, Adama's best friend (next to me) could say anything to Adama and get a way with it. They were best friends, forever.

"I am not! I just don't want to be watched from the bush by those stupid boys!" Adama whispered so loudly anyone could have heard her wherever they were in the compound. But, most of them were already sleeping. It was late and our parents knew where we were. We often slept together in the compounds of our parents.

"If the boys see us naked, the animals will eat us," Tida said.

"Tida, you are making that up," Adama said

"I am not. Mata told me that when we were at the bush. Don't you remember? Or were you crying too much to hear? You cried most of the time we were there. Cry baby!"

"I'll have to beat you," Adama said as she tried to unfold herself from entangled arms and legs and climb over the bodies there on the mattress.

The girls began to giggle and laugh and cover each others mouths so as not to be heard. Adama would never beat Tida, but they loved to pretend they were arch enemies, just for the fun of it. At the same time, they were holding Adama back from pretending to climb across them in order to beat Tida.

Adama says adults think that boys are more important than girls. Adama gets very upset when we talk about the fairness of being a boy and unfairness of being a girl. I really don't care. I think it's nice to have babies. And then, seven days later we have a naming ceremony where everyone in the village comes to watch as the baby receives his name. The Imam or the marabou shaves a bit of hair from each side of the baby's temple, to be buried later. And a cora player comes to play his beautiful music, and sing all during the day, and everyone in the village comes to greet us. The women cook huge bowls of rice and meat. Usually a cow or goat or sheep is slaughtered in honor of the new birth, and everyone has lots of meat to eat that day!

We dress in our finest clothes and always change at least once or twice during the day and evening. There is dancing in the evening. Drums beat and women dance. Some of the men dance also, but not as much or as often as the women. The men like to sit and watch the women dance like flying, crazed birds! It makes the hair on my arms stand up to watch the women dance their mad dance. They have too much fun dancing like wild women.

This is part of why I will be fine with growing up as a woman to become a wife, number one, or number two, or even number three. Having babies, celebrating the naming of those babies, getting material for the dresses we will wear, and going to the tailor who will make the dresses for me. I will look beautiful as a new mother. Or a not so new mother; or even as an older mother. I will look beautiful and please my husband. Whomever he may be.

****

Adama

Sometimes I want to run away and hide from the people in my compound, but I don't know where to go that they won't find me. The owl tells me I should be patient, that I will see many things in many lives, and in many places, eventually. Sometimes I don't understand what the owl is telling me. But, most of the time it is very clear that I am not always the same as the others around me. But maybe everyone thinks that about themselves. I am sure of this though no one in the village talks to an owl on her way to the river, except me.

The reason I want to run away from the people in my compound sometimes is because there are too many of us there. Too many babies, too many children, too many mothers, and one father who is very stern when he is in the compound, yet tries to be fair to all of us. My father is the father of twenty children. Their ages range from birth to twenty. My father is proud to have this many children. It makes him a real powerful man to father that many children.

One day I tried to run away when Binta called me to take the baby while she cooked. I was tired of taking the baby. I wanted to play in the street with the girls and boys who had managed to sneak away from their duties in their compounds, or had already finished their tasks for that moment.

I heard Binta call my name and I slipped around to the back of the house and hid behind the latrine. I sat on a stool and tried to be invisible. I continued to hear Binta calling and calling. I heard her tell Jola to go find me. Jola was carrying water, so Binta could not have her take the baby. Jola must have gone looking for me, but she didn't come to where I was hiding. I knew someone would come soon, so I went out the back gate of our compound and ran like a rabbit down the corridor lined with compounds on both sides as far as I could see until I came to the corner that led to the bush. The bush where the magic path leads to the river.

I rarely went into the bush alone. None of us girls go into the bush and onto the magic path alone. Nor did the boys. Even the boys, when going to hunt or fish, or just play by the river, would not go alone. We were taught to respect the animals of the bush and to respect the dragons of the river. But, this day I felt I must escape the baby. That is one reason I think I am not exactly like my twin sister, or even like the other girls in my vue. I really love my baby sisters and brothers, but I don't want to have to take care of them all of the time. Maybe the other children feel the same way I do, but we never admit it to anyone. It's like blasphemy;like the Imams tell us not to blaspheme. Not to say sinful words or think sinful thoughts. Like never to disobey our parents, and to always love our sisters and brothers. I do really try to do all those things. But, sometimes I just cannot!

So, I ran to the river all alone. When I stopped at the edge, I wondered what was on the other side. The river is quite wide and flows very rapidly. Across the river I saw monkeys in the trees, chattering, and swinging from branch to branch eating whatever monkeys eat. But, I have never been across the river. I would like to go there sometime. From where I stood I looked across the river, by myself and I felt strange and very alone. We don't like being alone. The people of our village. I know this to be true, because we are always close to one another. I think it's the way it's supposed to be, but, still sometimes I feel as though I will stifle if I can't see some more of what is around the corners of this place. Maybe there is nothing and that is why we are told not to go there.

As I stood watching the river I heard a branch snap behind me and jumped in surprise. Turning quickly to see what made a branch snap, I saw Modu, the boy I love, standing there with his spear held high over his head. He was looking up over and past my head; standing as still as a solid rock, he quickly swung his arm back which held the spear, and drove the spear over my head and up into the air. I heard branches crashing, and smashing over my head. Something made a deep thud just behind me on the ground. I swung around, quickly and saw a huge black catlike animal lying at my feet. A spear stuck out of its side, and its tongue stuck out from its mouth dragging on the ground. Its eyes were wide open, but there was no breath coming from its enormous mouth full of long, sharp teeth.

I screamed and shuddered as I looked at the huge black beast. He was beautiful in a terribly frightening way. But, he was dead. Killed by Modu, the boy I love.

Shivering from the top of my head to my bare feet, I felt as if I might not be able to stand much longer. I shook so hard my teeth were chattering.

"You were not looking up at the branches," Modu said. "This animal was about to spring on top of you. You should not be in this bush alone. Your mother and father will punish you when they find you missing, and not with your vue. Go home and tell them nothing. I will take care of this beast. Its coat will make a beautiful cover for my bed during the cold season. And my vue and I may even eat some of it. It will give us strong medicine and power. Go home now, Adama Darboe."

This secret stayed with me forever. This beautiful story of being followed and saved by Modu, the boy I love.

Amie - Second Wife of Ebrima Darboe

My name is Amie Cessay and I am the second wife of Ebrima Darboe. I was fifteen years old when my father and mother gave me in marriage to Ebrima. Ebrima is older than I, but I don't know how much older. I know his first wife, Binta Darboe was not happy when I came to live in her house. Binta loves Ebrima too much, therefore does not want a second or a third wife in her, or his life. She wants only Ebrima and her children here in this compound. But, it's too bad for Binta. Ebrima and my parents gave me to Ebrima, who is not a bad man as husband's go, I guess. He doesn't beat me, and he gives me fish money when it's my time to cook. He used to really like me to come to him on the nights when it was my turn to be with him. He was, playful then. He would speak baby talk to me and tickle me everywhere on my body, which made me laugh. I am never scared of him. I guess that is the way it is supposed to be when a person is married.

Since he took a third wife a few years ago, he is not as much fun when I go to him as he used to be. After he has eaten his evening meal with the boys and men, they all sit outside and chat for several hours, smoking, drinking tea, and chuckling, always chuckling. He wanders into his bedroom where I have been waiting for him in his bed for several hours, trying to stay awake so we can talk alone and in secret where we can play together and laugh and then do what it is he likes most to do.

But, lately he comes in to his bedroom where I am waiting, and he throws off his robe, sighs deeply, and flops down beside me. Often the talking and playful tickling do not take place. Often, he rolls over onto me and is done with it in a very few minutes. I am not happy with him when that happens. I lie beside him where he snores, and I am wide awake, and I think to myself, *What is happening to me*? He doesn't care about me any longer and I am stuck here, in this room, in this compound, in this life, and he doesn't care about me any longer. I will never be any prettier than I am now. But, Ebrima will never care because he now has his new wife, Haddy Badgie, who is young and 'fresh', as the men of the village say. You are young and fresh for a very short time in this place.

Binta Darboe, first wife to Ebrima Darboe is the leader of this compound. She is good to me, and she told me that she helped Ebrima choose me as his second wife. Another family wanted their daughter to be Ebrima's second wife. The father came to the compound many times to visit with Ebrima and Binta. After a few visits over a period of several months, the father, Momodou brought his wife and daughter. His wife's name is Oomie and his daughter's name is Araki. Araki was very young and could not become Ebrima's wife for several years, but the family wanted to establish an agreement with Ebrima that he would take Araki when she became 'fresh'. According to Binta, Ebrima was ready for a second wife right then and there. He did not want to wait for this girl Araki, no matter how beautiful she was. He needed for Binta to have another baby and therefore he needed a second wife for many reasons. So, that is how I came to be Ebrima's second wife.

And now Ebrima has three wives, and I am not the young, beautiful wife.

I am not liked by the other two wives, because I am too sick to do much of the compound work.

I cannot carry children full term any longer. Ebrima makes babies in my stomach and within a few weeks they come out, unready for life. The pain is severe as the baby comes out and I cry because of the pain as well as the fact I have lost yet another baby. Ebrima is quietly kind about this, but we don't speak of it. Binta cares for me during these times. She clucks and moves her big body around and wheezes her big breath and prays all at the same time as she freshens my bed, and helps me change my clothes after the baby has gone.

A few months after the new wife, Haddy has been with us, I am moved into the house where Ebrima lives, and where the boys rooms also exist. I have a separate living space directly beside Ebrima's private space. Because the other wives did not like it because I could not work, they did not talk to me. Also, they were afraid I was bewitched, and they did not want to become bewitched and unable to have babies, like me. They were not unkind to me. They simply did not recognize my presence. It was as if I were a ghost. They would look through me with no expression on their faces. The pains in my stomach became too severe to describe. That is when Ebrima moved me to his rooms at the other end of the compound away from the wives house. It was a relief to have my own room away from the daily lives of the other wives. I was too weak to do any heavy work, therefore the wives resented me. I did cook dinner for the boys and the Chief on the days that it was my turn. The wives had to cook their own meals for themselves and the girls during those two days of the week. I am sure all of this increased their dislike and resentment of me. I'm not at all sure what Ebrima will do about me, and my sickness, my condition. I am of no use to him in any way. I am sick, unable to eat enough to give me the strength I need in order to do the work necessary to do my share. I cannot carry his babies. I am useless to him and this family compound. These facts give me even more pains in my stomach. I do not know what to do.

Haddy - Third Wife of Ebrima Darboe

I came to the Darboe compound when I was seventeen years of age. Several years after Ebrima and my parents made the arrangements. My family lives in a village called Faraba, about a days drive from Jambanjeli. I miss my family and friends, but I love the people in the Darboe compound, especially Ebrima Darboe, my husband. Ebrima Darboe is much older than I am, but he is very handsome and young in body and heart. He loves me too much! He has a special name for me, which only I know. He whispers it to me when we are in his bed. I am very happy and excited when he whispers that name to me while we are in his bed.

When it is my turn to cook for everyone in the compound, twice a week, that is the time I can go to him, my husband, Ebrima Darboe. I can hardly wait to finish eating and cleaning up the cooking area. I jump up from where we wives and girls are gathered around the dinner bowl, and run to my room and wash my body. I make sure my braids are looking smooth and close to my head. I choose one of my newest dresses that Ebrima has given me permission to buy the material for. My heart actually races in my chest while I'm preparing to go to him. When I come out from my room and Binta Darboe is still cleaning out the rice bowl, and the oil which she loves is dripping through her fingers, she chuckles at me. Her eyes twinkle as she chuckles and says things like, 'She is going to her husband', or, 'She will be happy later tonight.' Binta Darboe is the first wife of Ebrima Darboe, and she is as good to me as she is to her children. She loves me like a child, I believe, although I know she always feels that she is number one to her husband, Ebrima Darboe. She chose me for Ebrima Darboe's wife. She knows my parents very well, and she brought them (and me) to meet Ebrima Darboe many years ago. Ebrima did not know that is was Binta's intent for me to be his wife, but it didn't matter, because once Ebrima looked at me I could tell he was happy to meet me. Eventually the arrangements were made, and that was three years ago since I moved here and became Ebrima Darboe's wife.

The only problem with our marriage is that I have given him no babies. This is a big problem. Especially because Amie, second wife to Ebrima has given him no babies either. This causes a big problem for me; even more than for Amie. Amie is ill and will probably be returned to her family in Gunjuir, soon. It has been too long they have been married without babies. I know Ebrima and Binta Darboe expected me to have a baby the first year I was married to Ebrima. And, now three years have passed with no new babies in the compound, except for Binta Darboe, who give Ebriima a new baby every other year once she can see no babies are coming from Amie or me. Binta Darboe is a baby maker.

I am afraid Ebrima will send me away, back to my family, also. First he will need to do something about Amie, before he sends me away. Binta Darboe has gone to her Marabou for help about this problem. Her Marabou tells her that I have probably been cursed by someone in the village, if not within our very compound. Binta and Ebrima talk about this problem on the nights she goes to be with him. Binta thinks Amie's Marabou has put a curse on me and that is why I can have no babies.

Adama

I walked down the magic path this afternoon alone. I wanted to be alone and to think. Usually I want to be with my vue, but today I wanted to be alone for a short time by the river. And in order to get to the river, I had to walk through the magic path. The owl was waiting for me on his usual perch. I stopped and looked directly at him. He turned his head, as he always does, rotating half way around his body, from his chest to his back. I looked at the back of his head for some time. He seemed to be ignoring me, or gazing at something interesting in the bush behind him. I continued to watch the back of his head, and his chest, and his mighty claws clutching the branch of his favorite tree. Then when I was beginning to fidget, and sigh, he rotated his head back so that his face was in its rightful place. He cleared his throat and said, "You know I am your guardian animal, do you not?"

"I do not know about that", I said. "My parents did not tell me about guardian animals. We are taught owls are like ghosts, and can take your soul away from you if they want to. That is why I am confused about your being here, and you speak to me, only. Why are you here? What do you want with me? Why am I not afraid of you as I should be?"

"You are not afraid of me, because I am your guardian animal. Everyone has one, but many times the person does not want to recognize or listen to their guardian animal. They will not hear him even when he speaks to them, therefore they are without a guardian animal who could tell them about their next life."

"What are you talking about?! Next life! I do not understand. Do you mean I will live another life after I die?"

"Exactly", Owl replied.

"I do not understand." I said.

"You do not need to think or worry about it. Your life, this life, will go on as if you had never heard me. You will live until you die. After you die, your spirit, you, will live another life, in another body. Maybe it will occur in another place, other than here in this land. I will be with you throughout this life, and try to be of help to you as you go through it. Then, your spirit will go on, even after this body you have today gives way to the earth."

I could not bare to hear any more from Owl. I was completely confused and disturbed. I shook my head and turned away from him. I walked away down the magic path toward the river. I did not look back and I willed myself to think no more about this strange Owl and his intrusion into my life.

Jola - Twin Sister

I watch her run and jump and climb and swing. I watch her staring at the stars while sitting at the back of our house. I see her dream. I can really see her dream. We are that close, she and I. We can really see each others dreams; hers and mine. Adama, my twin sister, and I are like one. I think we always must be together. However, I do not know what the owl and she have for a secret. She will not tell me that. And, I think when I cannot see her dream it is when it is about the owl. It is the only thing that keeps Adama and I separate.

Adama

Jola is sick. She is lying on our straw mattress. Her body shivering like leaves on the trees in the bush when the first rain is coming. At times she is nearly tossing off the mattress. Binta is holding her down. Binta is bathing her in cool water. Binta is sitting beside her crooning and clucking. Jola is not speaking, only groaning and sighing and moaning. And shaking, shaking, shaking. The Marabou has come, and he is reading the bones, which he pulled from a skin pouch. He has tossed them on the ground and reads them. He scoops them up in his cupped hands and blows into the them. He spits into his cupped hands, and shakes the bones again. His prayers are mixed with other intonations. He stays for a short time, puts the bones in the skin pouch, stands from a squatting position, puts on his flowing white robe over the thin strap undershirt. His wide glistening shoulders shine. He walks out of the room.

Binta follows him, leaving me with my sick sister, Jola.

Time goes slowly by and then Binta returns.

"Go eat your dinner, Adama. I will stay with Jola."

"Binta, I cannot leave her. I will stay with her. I am not hungry."

Jola's throat is full of bubbling sounds. I am afraid for her. Binta says, "Go out of this room and eat your dinner!"

I have a very bad feeling about Jola. I know part of me is in that room with Jola, suffering from the sickness with her. I cannot eat. The people of our compound are moving about silently. Amie is cooking this evening and she says nothing. She stirs the pot of sauce and rice. She lays the spoon quietly, without a cling or a clang. She pushes at the wood burning under the pot, using another stick of wood from the pile, with slow motion pushes. Even the sparks from her pushing do not snap and crack like they usually do. My siblings are sitting quietly waiting for their dinner to be placed before them in the one big pot which is for the men and boys; then one for the women and girls. The men's pot is on my father's verandah. The women's pot is inside Binta's rooms, on the other side of the compound.

The sun is setting over the lattice fence behind our houses and through the palm trees. It is a big red fire of a sun. Heat seeps from it, although we can feel the heat lessen as the red fired of a sun falls slowly off the earth. It falls, and still the beautiful colors remain, spreading out behind the trees. Orange, red, lavender, and green grace our horizon for the time it takes the chickens to settle under the house.

I slept beside Jola that night. I did not really sleep. My other sister, Mariama who is five years old, shares our bed and she slept all night. She does not want to recognize how sick Jola is. She is too young to realize Jola is very, very sick. We are all saying Jola will be better. Jola is better. Jola is breathing better this morning. This is what we are all saying.

Binta came in during the night and moved us all over to one side, so she could lie beside Jola. She kept a cool cloth on Jola's burning forehead and kept praying to Allah to attend to this sick child of his.

The next morning Ebrima, our father, brought one of the elders and the Chief to visit Jola. Ebrima and the two men stepped into our sleeping room, quietly sat beside Jola's bed and moved their beads around in their hands. One bead, one bead, one bead. Lips moving, one bead moving. Then they left.

After they left I lay there beside Jola and placed my arm across her chest. My face snuggled into her neck. I told her in our old secret language that she must get well. I told her that we had many, many things to do together, she and I. That we could be together always, no matter what, because we were from the same blood and stomach of our mother, Binta. I felt the tears come from my eyes and I saw tears come from Jola's eyes, even as her breath came raspy and gurgling, and then stopped.

Her breath stopped and her chest did not rise and fall, and her fingers did not twitch as they had. She there as quietly as a stone. As still as a silent night. I looked into her face, and saw a mask like the carvings that some of the elders make for celebrations. Cold, mask-like face of my twin sister, Jola. Binta ran in our room. Without anyone telling her that Jola was gone; she knew. She ran in screaming and wailing and throwing herself onto Jola. And then there was bedlam all around me. The other mothers came creaming, the little girls followed the mothers; the room was full of wails and tears and crying. I felt nothing, but an overwhelming, devastating sadness. I felt as if my body rose off the mattress where I had been lying beside Jola, and was hovering over the whole scene of crying, screaming people.

She was gone. My other self, my Jola, was dead and I was left alone.

For weeks it seems I didn't sleep. I tossed and turned. And I pushed my little sister, Mariama off the mattress, onto the floor, where she continued to sleep curled into a ball like an orange or a grapefruit. Mouth open and wet, soft sounds of sleep coming from her comfortable self. How I wished I could be Mariama. Snoring and dreaming of butterflies and soft clouds in the sky. I am here, on the mattress, now alone. Feeling the empty spot, indented as if Jola were lying there beside me. I reach for her, carefully, praying it has been a bad dream these past few weeks. I pray that Jola is really there beside me. Lying in this indented spot beside me. *Please, Jola do not leave me. You did not leave me, right?*

The sun rises and Mariama goes to relieve herself just outside our room. She returns and slides up onto the mattress. She sneaks into the indented spot of Jola and I slide my arm over her chest. I fall asleep when the dawn arrives.

CHAPTER 2

Modu Barrow

Three years ago Jola Darboe, twin sister of Adama Darboe died. Adama Darboe used to be a happy girl. She used to chase me down the secret path, and pretend she was chasing after her vue. They were supposedly near the riverside, where she was to meet them. They were never there. Once she arrived, and I came along behind her because she had chased me. Then she would punch me on the arm and splash her feet in the water, and run back through the secret path to the village. I know she did all of this just to be able to tease and play with me. I know Adama Darboe loves me and always has since we were born. It is going to do her no good, because I am spoken for. My parents have chosen the girl I am to marry. And, that is that. Even if I love Adama Darboe it would not matter. We could not be married; I could not give her babies, and I cannot touch her.

It really doesn't matter.

Adama Darboe is no longer a happy girl. She sits with her mother. They pick over the rice. They shell the ground nuts, or sit on the ground while the women braid one another's hair. She longs for her sister. She does not even speak or look at me, the boy she loves. I am sad for Adama Darboe. It has been too long since her sister, Jola, died, for her to be sad and thin, and nearly weak from loneliness. He mother, Binta Darboe has had two babies since Jola died. Binta's sadness has not gone away, I suspect, but she is very busy having babies, cooking for her family and going to the garden. She tries to keep Adama busy, helping with all the work that must be done, but Adama is too thin and weak to do much of the work. Binta speaks to my mother, Fatou Jammeh, about her concern for Adama Darboe. They both are afraid that the witches have taken her soul and sent it to be with Jola Darboe, her twin sister. I am hoping they are wrong because I find myself caring for Adama Darboe more than I should be. I worry for her. I want to see her running and playing and teasing me, once more.

I think tomorrow I will have my vue go with me to the bush and help me hunt and kill a young rabbit. Then we will take it to clean, cut it up, and cook it for Adama. That's what I will do tomorrow. Maybe that will make her eyes light up like they used to when she saw me, long ago, when we were young and Jola Darboe was still with us.

****

The next day Adama lies beside the cooking pot in the yard where the open kitchen stands. She lies on a colorful rattan mat which has been lain on by many family members in past years. She is curled in a fetal position with eyes half closed, gazing into the fire. Breakfast porridge is bubbling in the big pot. Binta Darboe is stirring the porridge, slowly, and wiping the tears from her eyes. The wood smoke causes Binta's eyes to tear. Children wander out from the various rooms of the compound; stretching their skinny arms up into the morning air, pushing fists into their eyes, scratching rumps, and heading to the latrine or behind the buildings to relieve themselves. Adama does not see them. The children are tired of trying to cheer Adama up, so they do not greet her any longer as they did the first few months after Jola died.

Wooden hand carved spoons are shared among the boys communal bowl and the same for the girls. They crouch at the bowls on the verandas by the rooms where they sleep. Sometimes sugar is available for the porridge, and sometimes there is milk. Other times only porridge is available and the children are grateful. Often they go to bed hungry and anxious for the morning porridge.

Binta reaches down, across the pot, and takes Adama's arm and carefully pulls her toward her. Binta props Adama up against her legs. Adam's head is leaning against Binta's lap, like a rag doll. Binta smoothes Adama's hair down against her head. The braids have come loose and must be re-braided today. Binta strokes Adama's face gently, once down, once up. She clucks and murmurs into Adama's face.

Binta will bathe Adama later. The other mothers will care for Binta's babies while she cares for Adama. Binta feeds Adama porridge, like a three month old baby is fed. Mouth opens reluctantly, food is dripping into her mouth and Adama swallows.

CHAPTER 3

Binta Darboe - Mother of Adama

I lost my beautiful daughter, Jola, and I swear I will not lose her sister, Adama. I pray to Allah every day that Adama will awake from her sleepless sleep, and become the lively, and fractious girl she used to be. I pray to Allah that he will give me the strength to care for her until she wakes from her dreaming. I have two new babies since our beautiful Jola passed away. I need to feed them and watch over them, in addition to caring for all of the people in this compound and not counting my most important task, caring for Adama Darboe, my sleeping daughter.

Even though she is ill, Amie Cessay, second wife of Ebrima Darboe, is very helpful cleaning and cooking and watching the children. She and Haddy Touray, third wife of Ebrima Darboe keep life flowing here in the Darboe compound while I care for Adama Darboe. They durect everyone to what must be done. Pulling water from the well, carrying it to the places it must go for washing the clothes, and in the shower rooms, and for the cooking. Carrying firewood from the bush to the compound and cutting it to fit the fire pit. Cleaning the sleeping rooms, sweeping the courtyard of the compound each day. All of this must be done daily, sometimes several times each day. Every morning and every late afternoon someone must walk outside the village to the women's gardens. plant, weed, water, and harvest.

I could never list all that must be done everyday here in this compound. It is why Amie and Haddy are still with us. If Jola had not died, leaving Adama half alive, sick, and needing constant attention, these wives would have been sent back to their family compounds. They had no babies. They were of no value to Ebrima Darboe or to me, for that matter. They were two extra mouths to feed. And what good is a woman who does not have babies? If women do not give their husbands babies after a few years of the marriage, it is believed that they have had a spell cast over them by witches. And they are sent back to their families before the other females in their husbands compound catch the spell that has been cast on these barren women.

Our Marabou, Ousamni Sanyang, has told us that the spell is no longer potent, and that they will do no harm here in the Darboe compound. They should stay to help me with this burden I carry. Our Marabou told me to kill one chicken, take two onions and six tomatoes, and give them to one of our elders here in the village. That is giving thanks to Allah for cleansing the wives who were bewitched.

My Jola passed, and my Adama is sick, and my two new babies need mothering. So, thanks to Allah, the wives are here to help me with this problem.

Amie Cessay - Second Wife of Ebrima Darboe

As long as I can go to Ebrima when it is my turn, and spend the night with him, I will be satisfied to be here in this compound. If I could not be with him, by myself those nights and have time for him to talk to me, to speak only to me, even if he's scolding me for something I did not do during the day that Binta had told me to do, even then I would be willing to listen to his voice and pretend he's telling me something sweet. For, if I am sent back to my family compound I will be in disgrace for the remainder of my life. My father will not be able to find a husband for me. For it is well known that a woman who is married and has had no children after five years, she is not eligible for marriage.

I do not know why I am unable to have babies. It is a mystery. But, I am a good mother to Binta's one year old, Mata. She is like my own child. The only thing I cannot do for her is give her milk from my breast. While Binta is nursing her, I care for Ishmial our three year old. But he is actually cared for by Haddy more than I. But, then sometimes I just sit beside Binta while she nurses Mata, and I'll help with picking over the rice, or braiding someone's hair, or I'll set up the iron; fill it with hot charcoals and press some clothes there on the veranda. But, whatever I do, I stay close to Mata, and I sometimes let a tear slide down my cheek just watching someone else feed the baby that is really mine.

There is an old man who lives in this village named Noah. He is quite handsome for an old man. He has broad shoulders and thick arms that are still very strong, I think.

He comes to the compound often to visit Ebrima. Noah had two wives. Both of these wives died within a few years of each other. They both died while giving birth to babies who lived only a short time He seems to be quite healthy and is always telling jokes. Laughing and telling stories to the children. He and Ebrima have attire (tea) almost every afternoon. They smoke their cigarettes and chat. I catch him glancing at me quite often, and then his eyes dart to another place away from me if he sees me looking towards him. I think he likes me and I don't mind that. It's nice to be admired, even though I cannot have babies. I am a pretty woman. I know that. I can see that in the one mirror that Ebrima brought home to us from the village where there is a big market.

I don't know what's to become of me. I am not nearly an old woman. I still long for a marriage that is good and whole. Ebrima is kind and considerate, but I know I am a big disappointment to him. When we are together at night he never makes love to me. He needs to save his seeds to plant babies. He doesn't want to contaminate himself by touching a person who may have been bewitched. It hurts my heart to have to live such a life. But, what am I to do? I console myself with Mata. My baby. My child. She is not Binta Darboe's baby. She is mine.

Haddy Touray - Third Wife of Ebrima Darboe

I think I will be sent back to my parents before Amie Cessay is because I am the third and last wife. Even though Amie has this stomach problem, now that she is caring for Mata, the stomach aches seem to be less severe and less frequent. She seems to think Mata is her own baby and she delivered her from her own stomach. Mata can hardly be left without Amie for one second. Except for the time Binta is breast feeding her, Amie is holding Mata. That's fine with me, because I don't want to be holding her, or any other baby for that matter. I am a young woman who does not carry babies inside her stomach, and as rarely as possible, on her back, or in her arms. I think Allah must have known I was not supposed to have babies, because I am not like the other women here, always clucking, and bouncing, and smiling and cuddling babies.

I care for Ishmial, Binta's three year old boy who is already acting as if he were the king of the world. He struts around and gets away with throwing a temper tantrum and then getting whatever he wanted. Every family has at least one Ishmial. A chosen one. Well, they can have him. It's not that I don't like Ishmial. Actually I do. but I just can't be bothered letting him get to me. I let him do whatever he wants, make sure he is not going to hurt himself by grabbing the only cooking knife in the compound, or hot coals from the cooking pit. Or not let him climb too high off the ground, or not wander too far out of the compound without some of the other children knowing where he is. I know I am responsible for him and I would feel badly if something happened to him. Amie loves Mata as if she were her own. It seems to have made her life almost full. But, I do not feel full at all. I was too young to marry Ebrima Darboe, or anyone, for that matter. Oh, I know, women are supposed to be happy to become a wife and mother, and be satisfied with our lives. For some reason I am not satisfied, and it is not because I don't have babies. It is because I do not like being a woman here in this compound, in this place.

I know what happens to women who are sent back to their family compounds, once it has been determined they will not be having babies. Many of them are sent to be trained to be clowns for the celebrations of the villages, for naming ceremonies, marriages, and feast days. All the women living in a certain area come together and learn how to dress as comical people, wearing feathers in their strange hats, big shoes, blowing whistles, pounding on buckets, dancing the chicken dance and collecting money for their food. When they dance they wiggle their butts in a disgusting, silly way. They sew plastic and tin onto their clothes. They act like simple minded people, and poke at one another, and trip one another. Everyone laughs at them, and they love it.

It may seem unbelievable but I would rather be a clown than live this half life I'm living now. I am an ungrateful person, I know. I don't belong in a compound with a man who will not touch me because I may contaminate his seed! Or with another woman who does not carry babies either. Or with a woman who is like the queen of all the village. Binta Darboe is like the queen of this village. I don't want to live here with all of this that makes me angry and sad. I would rather be a clown.

Although it makes me too sad to think of how much I loved Ebrima Darboe in the beginning years of our marriage. I still would be very happy if it could be like it used to be. Ebrima made me feel special. He loved me in every way.

****

One day when Modu, the boy who Adama loved, walked past the compound of Ebrima Darboe, on his way to meet his vue, he saw Adama sitting alone by the fire. He knew Binta must be someplace close by, but he hesitated at their gate. He was concerned that Adama was alone. She had been so ill, and vacant since Jola died that she was always being watched by someone, most often it was Binta. He leaned against the gate and whistled, softly. There was no reaction from Adama or anyone else who may have been within earshot of Modu's whistle. He crossed his legs, folded his long, skinny, tight muscled arms, and whistled again. Adama raised her head and looked up into the sky. She gazed through the trees, probably looking for a bird whose song was like Modu's whistle. This made Modu happy because Adama was reacting to a sound. Modu said quietly almost in a whisper, "Adama."

Adama dropped her head, closed her eyes, and began to rock back and forth. This frightened Modu. *What is wrong with this girl,* he asked himself. *Why is she acting so strangely? I know her twin sister died, but it has been over three years, and still she has not recovered.*

He quickly walked away from the gate of the compound. He met with his vue and they proceeded to the mosque. It was Friday, prayer day. He prayed the usual prayers. The Imam led the prayers. Men knelt, stood, and sat as the Imam said the prayers of the Quran. Women filled the back of the mosque also reciting the prayers.

As the time came to leave the mosque, and the men rose to leave, Modu lingered. Pretending to look for something he may have dropped, he lingered. And when he was there alone, he asked Allah to help Adama recover from her loss of her sister. Modu realized then that he cared more for Adama than he wanted to accept. They were born on the same day, and now were nearly fifteen years of age. But, he again reminded himself that his fate was already determined as far as a mate was concerned. His wife had already been chosen, so he must keep Adama as his close friend when she became whole again.

That very day, as he left his vue from an afternoon of sitting and chatting at the market, he passed by Ebrima Darboe's compound again. Binta Darboe and several other family members were moving about in the courtyard, near the outside kitchen area, or sitting on the verandahs. The children were playing, using an orange as their soccer ball. He looked for Adama, and she was there sitting on her mother's verandah, on a mat. Her back leaned against the wall of the house. Her head was nodding slightly. Her hair had been freshly braided and it looked as if she had just had a shower, with clean dendiko and fanno (top and skirt). Binta was sitting by the cooking pot. Modu stood by the open gate and cleared his throat, wishing for Binta to notice him and greet him. Binta glanced toward the gate and smiled broadly when she saw Modu standing there.

"Ah, Modu Barrow, I saw you at the mosque! You are on your way home?"

"Yes, I am going home. How are you, Mba Binta?"

"I am fine, Modu Barrow. And you are looking fine. But, look at my Adama Darboe! She is still not well. I am worried about her. She has not spoken since our Jola died. I do not know what to do with her. Go speak to her, Modu. Greet her!"

Binta Darboe had never said this to Modu before. 'Go greet her.' Modu was a bit startled, but it was no problem for him to go greet Adama Darboe. So, he walked into the compound and across the dry hard packed earthen courtyard, stepped up onto the veranda of Binta Darboe's house and stood before Adama.

Adama did not move. Her face was turned downward a bit, looking into the floor of the veranda. Modu shuffled his feet slightly. No reaction from Adama. Modu placed his hand in front of her face, offering a greeting shake. Adama did not move.

"Adama Darboe, I am here to greet you. Why do you not look at my hand and offer me your hand to shake? It is rude not to do this."

Adama did not move.

Modu moved his hand back, and stood erect. He put his hands behind his back, and said, "I am sorry you do not hear me. I came as your friend to greet you and wish you well. It is a nice prayer day."

With that, Modu turned around and left the compound.

"Come back tomorrow. I need your help, Modu. We must bring Adama back," Binta called.

Modu nodded as he left the Darboe compound. He was not sure if he would come back tomorrow. But he was haunted the remainder of prayer day, and even throughout the evening, when he sat with his vue just outside his family compound on the log that had been there for many years. He was haunted by Adama's head nodding as he stood before her. Her blank face, staring into the floor in front of her. His friend, who loved him, was in a perpetual daze. Half here, half some other place.

"I greeted Adama Darboe today, on the way back from prayer," Modu spoke to Suliman and Lamin, his main boys, his vue.

"Did she return the greeting?" Suliman asked, scratching his back with a long stick he'd picked on his walk from the farm.

Modu has dark velvety skin. His little ears lie close to his head. His almond shaped eyes are a dark brown, like melting chocolate. His very full mouth smiles often. He was leaning forward with his elbows resting on his knees. He scratched his head, sighed and said, "She does not speak."

"What is wrong with her? She has been like a bewitched girl since her sister, Jola died," Suliman said.

Lamin, the oldest of the three by nearly a year, tilted his head back against the fence. He had heard his parents discuss the condition of Adama.

"I have heard that when a person is a twin and one dies, the other who is left here, is never the same. He is missing part of himself. That is why Adama lost her speech and her will to live when Jola died."

The other two were quiet for some time after Lamin spoke.

"Does that mean that Adama will never be different than she is now? She will never speak or have the will to live?" Suliman asked.

"I don't know. I will listen to my parents and learn."

Modu stood, stretched, and moved away from Lamin and Suliman. He mumbled a good night to them, walked into his compound, straight into his room, and said his night prayers.

The next day Modu picked up his short handled hoe and stepped out of his room onto the veranda. His ragged pants cut off at midshin were loose and he kept them from falling with some old rope he'd found on the ground beside the market. He was heading to his father's cassava field just outside the village. It was on the opposite side of the village from the women's vegetable garden. It was a flat piece of land shaded by several mango trees. Cassava was his father's cash crop and the only income his father had. The cassava and sometimes the mangos could be sold at the local market. Sometimes a large agriculture company from the bigger towns would send a team of horses or oxen to collect a harvest of produce and then the families of the village would be extremely happy and secure for several months. Most often, what the women grew, and the men raised, would be their meals. They fished the river, and raised a goat or cattle, or chickens. Sometimes they would barter with each other for rice, corn, and millet.

Modu ate some of the rice from last night's meal, as he squat by the embers under the cooking pot. He washed his face and hands in the boys shower area. He picked up his hoe and headed toward the gate of his family compound. His mother, Fatou, watched him leave from where she sat inside her rooms. She waved at him through the door, quietly smiling at her oldest son, her favorite child.

Modu had only a few hundred feet to walk before he came to Ebrima Darboe's compound, across the wide dirt street. He crossed the street and slowed his pace as he came upon the gate that led into the Darboe compound. He glanced into the compound where only a very few people mingled and sat. It was still early. He could not see Adama, nor did he see Binta, so he walked on toward his father's cassava farm.

On his way home at mid-morning Modu stepped into Ebrima Darboe's compound and saw Adama sitting in the same spot she was yesterday when he tried to get her to greet him. He went to Amie Cessay, second wife of Ebrima Darboe, where she sat by the cooking pot. Amie stirred rice in the big pot. Tears streamed down her cheeks from the smoke. As she looked up she smiled at Modu. Wiping her cheeks with a piece of material, She coughed and greeted Modu with her smile and her free hand.

"Greetings, Modu. You have come. We are happy to see you. Go greet Adama. She is sitting there, like always. Saying nothing. Maybe you can get her to smile!"

Modu glanced over at Adama. He slowly turned and walked toward her. He stepped up onto the veranda. By now he was surrounded by young ones of the compound and the neighboring compounds. Hanging onto him, riding on his legs, they hounded him. Clinging to his legs, they laughed and hugged his thighs. Two little ones, maybe three years old, each clutched a hand as Modu pumped their little bodies up and down and moved slowly along toward Adama.

CHAPTER 4

Modu Visits Adama

Modu stood before Adama. From each arm and foot a child dangled. Giggling and wiggling, with bare feet and bare chests, they remained clinging to him. Adama stared into the veranda floor in front of her. Modu, looked down at her and said, "A sallam mali cum" (Greetings to you).

Then he said; "Look here, I have grown four young people from my feet and my hands! They are attached to me, and I cannot walk easily from now on!"

He pulled the two who were attached to his wrists and bounced them up and down several times. The little ones laughing hysterically. Heads thrown back and gasping for air in their wild, squealing laughter.

"And look here, I have grown two little ones onto my ankles. See how they are sitting on my feet, and I can barely move my legs because of the weight of these creatures!" And those two also laughed like small, wild jackals.

Modu moved his legs slowly, with great groans and sighs. The children by now were screaming with laughter.

A slight smile crept across Adama's face. Edges of her full lips tilted upward. Minutely, minuscule, tilting upward. Her eyes moved from the floor where she sat, further toward the feet of Modu and his attachments.

Even the children lessened their loud raucous laughter to a quiet giggle. To a quietness fit for the event. Modu's heart flipped. He held his breath and moved not an inch. The little ones did not move.

"Adama," Modu said in a very low voice, "What am I to do with these attachments that are so heavy and uncomfortable, when I want to take you for a walk to the river?"

Adama closed her eyes and put her head against the wall behind her.

"Adama, I am speaking to you. I am here with these attachments. Tell me what to do about that. I want to walk to the river. I want you to walk with me. I am speaking to you."

Adama rolled her head to the side, eyes still closed. She slid to the floor, curled into a ball and closed her eyes.

All four of the attached children looked up into Modu's face. They let go of his ankles and wrists. Modu turned away and walked out of the compound.

Binta Darboe - Mother of Adama

I watched as Modu was trying to reach Adama with his playfulness, and Adama began to smile. I gave a quick thanks to Allah for that smile. And for Modu. But, then Adama slid to the floor and rolled into a little ball, like a baby. She stayed in that position for the remainder of the morning. Only when she rose to go to the latrine at lunch time, did she move. My heart broke again when this happened. Is my Adama never going to improve from the loss of her sister, Jola?

Ebrima Darboe, father of Adama was standing at the gate about to enter our compound when Modu was nearly reaching Adama, with his light hearted game and the children's laughter. When Adama smiled, I saw Ebrima's eyes become wet. And then when Adama slid to the floor and closed her eyes, I watched Ebrima turn and walk away, out of his compound. I watched him go, and I watched Modu go, and I thought to myself, once more, we women are left here to face the problem.

Adama Darboe

It is not possible for me to hide here in my shell for many more moons. I am too sad to continue this, and I see how I am making others very sad. People who love and care for me are suffering because I too am suffering. I must realize that Binta Darboe and Ebrima Darboe and Ebrima's other wives are also suffering for the loss of my sister, Jola. It has been too long that I have been hiding in my misery. For the sake of the others I must begin to try to live. I am afraid to come out of this shell, but I must. When Modu, the boy I love, reached out to me these past two days it made my heart begin to move in my chest. Skip and beat, not just thump slowly as it has these past many months. How much I love him, only I will ever know. But, how am I to walk to the river with him knowing I will not be able to walk by his side the remainder of our lives? He cannot be my husband because his parents have chosen another girl for him. How am I to live through that? But, if I am to come out of this hidden shell, I can only do that by walking to the river with Modu by my side.

I will begin my new life tomorrow. I must take today to prepare myself for my new life. I must think of leaving this safe life of being half alive. Of sleeping through the day and night. Eyes opened, eyes closed always within myself. I am to move out of myself and let Modu, the boy I love, walk with me to the river.

****

Adama walked to the river many times during the days of her recovery. Modu, the boy she loved, walked with her nearly every day for several weeks. He would come after morning prayers and take her hand, pull her up from where she sat on a bench by the cooking pot, and smile. She would bashfully, eyes lowered to the earth, let him lead her out of the compound. Everyone who was awake and in the compound yard felt silent joy to see such a sight. Adama, clean and neat shyly walked with Modu out of the compound. Her hair braided into hundreds of braids clinging close to her head. Aime Cessay was the best braider of hair in the whole village. The girls and women of Ebrima Darboe's compound were known for sporting the most elegant cornrows in the village.

The first few days Adama could not go all the way to the river. She walked slowly down the lane, past the fenced-in compounds, turning right at the end of the dirt street which led into the magic path. The path to the river. The path where Owl roosted. Only the first few times of walking through the magic path Owl was not present. And Adama did not look for it or think about it. In fact she did not look at much of anything, only the path itself. Modu held her hand and remained silent. He nearly held his breath, wanting desperately for Adama to begin to react in some way show excitement being out of the compound for the first time in months. Or perhaps to show some sign of pleasure walking beside the boy she claimed to love. She moved her eyes from the path in front of her over to the bush beside the path. Red succulent blossoms burst forth on the floor of the bush; brilliant in color, shining, a sign of the rainy season. Modu hoped that Adama was looking at the blossoms.

"Do you remember these flowers, Adama?" he asked.

No answer. Just a silent girl walked with him.

They continued a few hundred steps, half way to the river, and Adama stopped. Pulling her hand from Modu, she turned around, facing the village and, as if sleep walking, headed for home. Modu watched her for a few seconds then he shrugged, also turned around and followed her back to the lane that led to her compound. He didn't try to catch up to her and walk with her. He only followed a few yards behind her. He felt sad and a little angry with this stubborn girl.

"What is the matter with you?" he said, in a low, unhappy voice. A bit of an edge of anger in his tone. "When are you going to wake up?"

Adama continued to walk and reached the main corridor, which led to her compound and turned toward it.

Modu followed her until she stepped into her family compound. He stood at the open gate, leaned against it, and waited for her to reach the spot where she had sat for all the these many months. She slid down onto the floor of the veranda and moved not an inch for the remainder of the day.

"She has come back," Binta Darboe said to Modu and anyone else who was present. "What will we do with her, Modu?"

"I will come one more day to take her to the river. But, I must go to my garden and work at the rice field soon. The rain is here, MbaBinta (mother Binta). I had hoped she would come alive enough to walk by herself if I took her one time to the river" Modu looked at Binta with a eyes heavy with sadness.

"Yes, Modu. You will come tomorrow and Adama will go with you," Binta looked toward Adama, scowled at her and grumbled. "Ya moi!?" (Do you hear?! "N moi." Modu said. He glanced over at Adama, said not a word, turned to the corridor and walked away. Thinking, I don't know why I even began to look at her there where she sat on the verandah two days ago. I have started something I did not need to start. I am a fool to even care about this girl. She has always troubled me, since we were babies. She was always following me, and bothering me, and tugging at me and trying to push me down. I know she loves me, but she cannot be mine, and especially now that she is such a mess. I will take her to walk one more time, and it doesn't matter if we get all the way to the river or not, I will wash my hands of this girl who sits and moans for months. She is pitiful and I will be done with her after tomorrow!

He turned into his compound and called for his sister to bring him his lunch.

CHAPTER 5

Adama Awakens

I am Adama Darboe and I have decided that at the age of fifteen years, I must come alive, again. My sister, my other half, my Jola, died some years ago, and I died with her. I felt her leave her body, with a lightness of feathers she moved out of her body, and I clung to the mat on the floor where we lay with our mother, Binta. I clung to the edge of the mattress, because I felt myself leaving my body, also. Lightly, like feathers, I began to leave this place, this body. I shut my eyes so tightly that my cheeks and lips scrunched up into a solid ball. I clung to the mattress and moaned like the cattle moan when lost in the bush. Binta held my sister to her solid body. Clinging to Jola, my mother cried out, and her vue heard. Her sister-friends, her vue came running from the surrounding compounds and they crowded into the room where we lay, and they fell to their knees and cried out in long loud moans. Some of them fell on us, crying and pulling at their hair. They held me down. They hugged Binta. They did not touch Jola, only looked at her there lying between Binta and me. And these women, these best friends of Binta never left our sides for seven days. All during the washing of my precious sister's body, all the time cooking and feeding the many who came to pay their respects, these sisters, this vue of Binta's did not leave.

I did not leave with my sister, nor did I stay. I was in another place of silence. I could not be alive without my sister, but I could not leave with her. So, for all this time I have been nowhere. Just no place at all. And, now I know it is time to awaken. To begin my new life, even though it cannot be what I want it to be.

Even though I know I will not have my sister, Jola with me; I also know I cannot have Modu, the boy I love, with me for the rest of our lives. His family has chosen a girl to be his wife, and I must accept that. But, I cannot. It is too difficult for me to accept. I must begin my new life now, this day, and we will see what is to become of it.

Modu at the gate

Modu did not intend to stop at the gate of Ebrima Darboe's compound this morning. He intended to pass on by and not even take one glance toward the gate. As he rushed past the compound, he used the middle of the wide dirt road instead of walking close by the Darboe compound. And that is when he heard a girl's laughter coming from inside. It was not the laughter of Binta, first wife of Ebrima. Nor was it either of Ebrima's other wives Amie or Haddy. He knew the sound of the laughter of all of these women, as well as the laughter of most every woman and man in this corridor. And Modu knew the laughter of young Miriama, Adama's younger sister. So, who could it be? He had heard that laughter before, but many years ago, and he could not even hope it was the laughter of Adama Darboe, the girl who claimed to love him. Even though he had sworn he would not continue to help Adama he could not walk past the compound without stopping by the gate to see if a visitor was there, laughing.

As he slowly peeked around the door of the open gate, Modu saw Adama sitting on the log beside the cooking fire. She was wearing a wrap and a blouse with many shades of red and orange splashed about like a sunset before the first rains. Her hair was braided in a swirling design which must have taken Amie all last evening, and late into the night to braid. Adama looked fresh and clean and shining. She was eating porridge and her eyes swung toward the gate. She saw Modu's face peering at her.

Modu quickly snapped his head out of her vision. And, he heard the laughter again. This time he knew it was Adama, and he stepped into the compound with a wide grin, showing his pleasure to everyone there.

The greetings were said, and only then did Modu glance shyly in Adama's direction.

"You are sounding happy today, Adama Darboe."

Adama looked up over her bowl of porridge as she drank the remaining drops of milk from the bottom, and blinked her eyes in a flirtatious flutter.

"Yes, Modu Barrow," she whispered, "I have decided to be happy, at last."

Binta Darboe smiled and nodded her plump head once quickly and firmly, and the other mothers smiled, and the children smiled.

Ebrima, father of Adama was not present.

Modu caught his breath and tried to remain cool and unaffected. But, inside his chest his heart thumped loudly. He hoped people could not hear his heart thumping the way he could hear it. What was happening to him that he was feeling this way simply because Adama Darboe fluttered her eyes at him? And more importantly, she was happy!

"I am happy that you are happy," he said. He stood uncomfortably in front of the group who were eating breakfast. His long skinny arms folded over his chest. He didn't know whether to leave, or stay a little bit longer, as was the custom.

"Come eat," Binta said to Modu, motioning him to sit beside her, as she pushed Miriama out of the way.

"Thank you, but I have just had breakfast at home. I am on my way to the market for my mother. I must bring her some tomato paste, but you are kind to offer."

"Well, it is good of you to come visit us. Adama Darboe is much improved. Will you take her to the river sometime soon?" Binta's robust body jiggled as she chuckled under her breath.

Modu looked over at Adama where she was licking the milk from the side of the bowl, and her lips turned up as she looked him squarely in his eyes.

"Well, I would like to walk her to the river if she will not turn and run back to her compound like she did the last time we tried that."

"Yes I will go," Adama started to get up from the log where she sat.

"Wait, Adama. You must wait until Modu does his errand for his mother, then he will return for you and you can walk to the river."

"I will go also," said ten year old Miriama, sister of Adama. She grasped Adama's hand, looking up at her big, new sister.

Adama gazed at Miriama and said nothing.

They walked to the river that day, Miriama between the two of them. None of them said a word as they passed through the forest leading to the river. It was the rainy season and the red succulent flowers graced the floor of the forest. They passed the tree where Owl used to sit. Adama cast a sidelong glance toward the tree, saying nothing. Did she remember the tree and Owl? Modu did not know of Owl and Adama's secret talks, so he did not even notice her glance toward that particular tree.

Mariama pulled her hands from the two of them and skipped several feet down the path, swinging her long arms freely. She twirled around and smiled at the two of them and then continued to skip, free and easy, like a floating butterfly.

When they came to the river, wide and calm, they sat quietly on the old log. Miriama walked to the water's edge and waded ankle deep, kicking the water into the air.

"How does it seem to be back here by the river? Modu asked Adama. When he glanced at her, he saw tears well up in her eyes. She drew a quick breath, wiped her eyes with the palm of her hands and smiled.

"It is good."

Adama's vue

Soon after Jola died, Adama's friends did not come as frequently to be with her as they had initially. Because Adama had not been there, nor here, nor any place. The girls could see her, they could touch her, they could talk to her; but Adama was not really there. After a few weeks of loyal visits, her friends, Tida, Aime,and Nygma came less often. They grew, they swam, they danced, they worked for their mothers, and played whenever they could escape their mothers' demands.

And they began to find boys less obnoxious and more interesting; more exciting, and more fun to be chased by, to be caught by and flung to the ground. Sometimes when they were flung to the ground by a boy, he would fall on them, and scramble to get up and off the girl. And, in the process his hand would fall on the girls chest or legs. It was all in good fun, and the girls knew it was not correct for them to allow this kind of fun, but somehow is was delicious when it happened.

Adama missed this part of growing up. She had been asleep; But, now her friends, her vue, saw Adama walking back into the village from the magic path with Modu, the boy she loved, and with Miriama. The girls had just returned from the well, carrying water to their respective compounds. Backs straight, a bucketful of water on each head, and surprised expressions on their young faces. They nearly dropped the buckets, and if they had, they would have been severely punished; but they did not drop their buckets of water. They screamed and started to run towards Adama; holding the buckets on their heads they ran toward her calling, "Adama!, Adama,! You are awake! God is good!"

The water splashed, but did not spill. The girls ran up to Adama and Adama looked at them as they ran toward her and she felt weak from so much happening to her this first day of being happily awake.

Amie Cessay - Second Wife

I am Ebrima Darboe's second wife, and now that Adama Darboe is well again, I will be sent back to my family. I am sure of that, and it is making me sicker than ever. I was able to stay here in Darboe compound and continue to be the second wife of Ebrima Darboe longer than I expected because Adama was so sick and Binta Darboe was in need of extra help caring for her. Also, Binta has delivered three more babies since the loss of Jola. Binta was responsible for giving babies to Ebrima because neither Haddy Touray, third wife to Ebrima Darboe, nor I were able to.

And now, I'm sure we will both be sent back to the villages of our families. I am grateful for the extra time I've had with Ebrima Darboe.

He has been kind, and he has been very sad over the loss of Jola; even though he has had three more children added to his big family, he still mourns the loss of Jola. I believe she was one of his favorite children.

Haddy Touray - Third Wife

I am the third wife of Ebrima Darboe, and finally I will be released to return to my family. It is not looked on as something to be proud of, being sent home and divorced from your husband because you are unable to have babies. But, I don't care. I am tired of trying to have babies when I know it is impossible for me. I have been to many marabous and I have prayed and I have done everything my mother has told me to do, and it is not to be. Ebrima no longer loves me. He no longer whispers my secret name when I am with him. We only sleep when we are in his bed. He is not unkind to me. But he treats me politely like a stranger. And I have lost my love for him. I miss the time when I loved Ebrima. I was happy and excited just to be with him. Just to think of being with him. But, time has made the Darboe compound a different place. Jola's death, Adama's sickness, and Aime (second wife) being very ill, but trying to help out, all of this has been different from the first few years when I was the young, pretty wife who everyone liked.

Except for Amie. And especially Ebrima Darboe.

Even Binta Darboe found pleasure in my presence. We laughed together while we worked in the garden. We would gossip with the other women. When we took our vegetables to the market to sell, we would sit in our stall by the side of the road leading to Sanyang and to Brikama.

We would laugh and joke with the women from the other compounds, talking about our men and our children.

I look forward to returning to my village. My mother says I should go to the village of the clowns. I will be a clown like some of the other women who can not carry babies in their stomachs. I think I will make a very fine clown. I will like living with women and no men.

****

Modu - the boy who Adama loves

I am not happy about what I must do today. It has been three weeks since Adama woke from her sickness and we have been together for our walk to the river nearly every day. Most often several of our young sisters and brothers come with us, but that is no problem. We are always many. Adama is once again a feisty, strong girl, full of life and a beautiful girl, soon to become a woman. I am not sure if her family has found a husband for her yet. Probably he will be someone in the Darboe clan, but, I do not know who it will be.

I do know that what I have to say to her today is going to be very difficult. Adama knows my family has chosen a wife for me, and what I must tell her today is that my parents have decided Mimuna and I must begin to spend time together, as is the custom. Mimuna will come tomorrow for a day visit. She will travel by bush taxi for an hour long drive. She will visit my whole family and sit outside on the bantaba with the girls and women. I will be sitting with the boys nearby. She may help my mother cook lunch. She may go to the market with some of my sisters to fetch something for cooking like tomatoes or onions. Sometime during the day I will sit with her in the compound yard. There will be younger siblings sitting there, also, and maybe one of the other mothers, or aunties. But, this will be the beginning of Mimuna and I becoming acquainted with one another, preparing for our marriage which will take place within a year or two.

Adama and Modu's news

When he came to collect me for our walk to the river Modu looked different. His face carried an expression I could not remember seeing before this. I smiled in his direction.

What a hot day it was. I didn't care how hot it was. Modu was there in our compound coming to fetch me.

Binta Darboe turned on her seat by the cooking pot and grinned her wide, round faced, grin. My mother has a beautiful smile. My mother,

Binta Darboe is a strong, big woman. 'Big in body and big in spirit,' I've heard my father, Ebrima Darboe say.

"You are here once more, Modu Barrow! Welcome! Greetings! I think Adama is ready for another walk to the river, right, Adama?"

I nodded my head and rose to meet Modu by the gate.

And now, here in my compound, preparing to walk with Modu to the river, I was happy and content, but Modu did not seem to be his usual self. He hung his head and looked at his feet intently. He spoke quietly.

"Are you ready?" he asked.

I started toward the gate of our compound, and said goodbye to my mother, Binta. And Binta, as usual with her smiling face said, "Goodbye, come back soon."

We walked to the river in silence. Modu said nothing and I said nothing. We walked past Owl's tree. We walked through the path with the red succulent blossoms hugging the green leaved earth. We walked until we reached the river, and there we sat on the old ancient log.

"You are very quiet, Modu Barrow," I said.

"Yes," Modu Barrow quickly responded.

Then he cleared his throat.

"My mother has invited Mimuna Cessay to visit our compound tomorrow. She will be here for just the day this time. You know Mimuna Cessay, right?" Modu turned his head toward me.

"I know Mimuna Cessay," I responded in a whisper.

"She will be here tomorrow," he replied.

I said no more. Modu said no more. We quietly returned to the village and Modu left me at the gate of my compound.

Modu's news to Adama

That night I could not sleep. My heart was aching. I was going to lose Modu-the-boy-I-love. The girl, Mimuna, would be here tomorrow in this village, in his compound learning how his family lives, how they cook, and where the women's garden is. They will take her to the women's garden, and my mother Binta's garden is directly beside Modu's mother's garden. We will be weeding and watering the garden at the same time tomorrow. I cannot bear to think of it. She will become part of his family and I will be here across the corridor where I can see them sitting on the bantaba in the compound. I cannot think of it, yet I lay here thinking of it. My heart is breaking.

****

Adama's vue

The next day, after Modu told Adama of Mimuna's upcoming visit, he did not come to the Darboe compound. His parents expected him to be in their compound until it was time for Mimuna to arrive. She would come on a donkey cart or a horse and buggy. Her parents had both a donkey and a horse, and whichever she comes on, it is unpredictable when she will arrive. One of her brothers or uncles will bring her and he will stay for the day also. In order to reach their family compound before darkness they must leave by mid afternoon. No one wants to be caught after dark in the bush between villages.

Adama was not expecting Modu to come to her that day. She only knew that she needed her vue, her friends to come to her. She called Miriama, her little sister, to her side.

"Miriama, come!" she called. Miriama was carrying fire wood from the bush. She was with Ishmial, her three year old brother who she was responsible for this morning while Binta Darboe was at the garden.

"I want you to go to Tida's compound and tell her to bring Amie and Ningma to me. I am needing them to be here. Go, find them for me!"

Mariama sighed, dropped the firewood beside the cooking pot, grabbed Ishmial by the wrist, and dragged him through the compound gate.

This morning it was Adama's job to build the fire for the cooking of lunch and to pound the rice. She would have her vue help her with the pounding instead of Mirama. That way she would be able to tell them of her problem. Of Modu, the boy she loves, and his visitor who would arrive today. They would listen to her and sympathize with her, and be angry with Modu, yet know that he had no control over this situation. But, even so, Adama was sad and broken hearted. Her vue was with her, listening to her grief. It seemed to them Adama was cursed. First, losing her sister who was half of herself and now, losing the man she would love forever.

"After we finish pounding the rice, let's run to the river and play in it! Can we all get away at the same time and go to the river?" Tida asked.

"We will go home to our own compounds after we help with the pounding, and we will help with the cooking, or whatever we are told to do, and then we will eat lunch. We will pretend to sleep during the resting time. When the sun gets to the other side of the high point of the sky we will quietly sneak out and meet at the crossroads on the path.

Is that not a good idea?" Amie Cham whispered to the girls.

"Yes, it is a very good idea. We must be careful not to be seen by anyone, or we will be in very bad trouble. Ya Moi?" Adama whispered.

They continued to pound the rice; only now they pounded with the strength it takes to truly pound rice. When they were whispering to one another standing around the mortar, no rice was breaking free of it's sheaths.

When Binta returned from the garden she found Adama and her friends pounding rice. Two were pounding, and the other two were winnowing the husks from the rice. Binta was pleased to see Adama working with her friends. She knew today was the day Modu-the-boy-Adama loved was expecting Mimuna, his intended to visit for the first time. Binta knew Adama would be upset about that, and she also knew Adama would be alright as time passsed All girls must accept the choices their parents make for them as to who they will marry. There was a time she wished she could have talked Ebrima Darboe into arranging the marriage of Modu-the-boy-Adama loved to Adama, but the only time she suggested it, a long time ago, when the children were less than five years old, Ebrima said it would not be possible. He had already made an agreement with the family of the boy who would be Adama's husband.

Binta worried that Modu's intended, Mimuna, coming to visit would set Adama back into her listless half alive state. It was happening so soon since Adama came alive, and thanks to Modu, Adama was once again herself. He was the one who brought her back to life, and now he was about to be taken from her. Oh, Binta was sure, after this day was finished, and Mimuna returned to her village, Modu would continue to come and take Adama by the hand and lead her to the river now and then. Men and boys were allowed to do almost anything they wished to do.

But, now Adama's girlfriends were coming to her rescue. *That is good*, Binta thought.

"You are all working together. That is good. Adama needs her friends to help her. I will tell your mothers that you all need time to go to the river after lunch. Once you have finished eating and you have done the work your mothers have told you to do you will go to the river. Ningma, I know you have a visitor in your compound, so if your mother needs you to be there we will understand. But, let me send a message to her and we will see. So, go on home now and help with the lunch. Come and collect Adama when your mothers release you. Ya moi?!"

"Yes, we hear you, MbaBinta," the three girls replied in unison. Casting sidelong glances, they scattered to the compound gate.

****

Owl and Adama

No one knows that I have seen Owl and spoken to him since I've awakened. I have left the compound through the back way during the middle of the day when everyone is resting, waiting for the worst of the heat to subside. Running like a rabbit in the bush, I reach the middle of the magic path where Owl's tree stands. Three times I have done this. The Owl is always there when I arrive, alone.

This is a very large, pure white owl. As tall as my two year old brother, Ousamani. Tall and full with huge, round yellow eyes. His ears are straight and point toward the sun.

Owl blinked twice, opened and closed his beak twice, then said in a low voice, "Do you have questions of me, Adama Darboe-who-sleeps-for-years?"

"Well, why are you speaking to me, only? What is your reason for speaking to me, and no other person in the village? I am not imagining this, but I do not understand why you are here only for me."

"Because you are a special person who has a spirit that has lived many, many, different lives. And I am your Spirit Animal who will continue to guide you through your next lives."

"I do not understand what you are saying to me. I have lived more than the life I am living now? How can that be? I do not understand."

"You do not need to understand anything more than the fact you are living this life in preparation of the next, and the next. Some people live only one life on this earth, yet some live many lives. You are one who has been chosen to live many lives in many places, and in many different eras. Do not worry about it, Adama. Just listen to what I have to tell you during these times we meet on this magic path. It will prepare you for this present, and your future lives."

I shook my head slowly, closed my eyes, opened my eyes, sighed deeply, and waved farewell to Owl.

Too many strange things were happening to me lately.

Adama and her vue run to the riverside

Adama kept busy in the compound until late afternoon doing the duties assigned to her. She only looked across the wide dirt street into Modu's compound one time, at mid- morning, and saw Mimuna sitting on the bantaba with Modu's mother and his sister, Ningma, one of Adama's best friends.

Sliding her eyes in the direction of Modu's compound she spotted the two girls and the mother, Fatou Jammeh sitting, not moving a muscle, staring into the day. Each of them in their own thoughts; swinging their legs. Bare feet crossed at the ankles crossed. Their hands rested in their laps, fingers loosely curled. It seemed to Adama the three were being very comfortable with one another. It seemed to her that Mimuna would be considered a part of the family immediately, as was the custom.

This was the time Adama told Mariama to go to her friends compounds and to tell them they must come to her immediately. It was midmorning after she had seen the three sitting at the bantaba across the street. She expected that mother Tida would have gone to the garden and the girls would go with her, but maybe Mimuna's arrival had occurred just a few moments ago, thus making it too late to go to the garden this morning. Maybe some of Tida's vue would do her work for her in the garden because they knew Mimuna was coming for the first visit to Modu-the-boy-Adama loved.

****

Adama was pleased to see Ningma enter the compound with her other friends when they arrived around mid-morning after Miriama had run to the two compounds telling them they must come to Adama.

"You were allowed to come and leave your company?" asked Adama.

"My mother said to me, 'Your terrima (friend) has been very sick, so you must go to her whenever she sends for you, until we know she is (Allah willing) truly well.'"

"Your visitor is here," Adama said.

"Yes, she is here until the end of this day. But, my mother is releasing me for part of the day to be with you, my best friend who has not been well, and is recovering, slowly."

And the day wore on, and Binta Darboe had commanded her vue to let their daughters, who are Adama's vue to come to be with Adama and to pound rice; then return to their own compounds and cook lunch. After lunch was cooked and eaten, then to allow the girls to go to the river with Adama. All because Modu-the-boy-Adama-loves is having his intended visit him there across the dusty street, in plain sight.

And that is the way the day went. Adama and her friends pounding rice. They giggled because they did not know what else to do. Their friend, Adama loved Modu, the boy across the street who was sitting with his vue on a bantaba in his compound, and his intended, Mimuna was sitting on the other bantaba with some of Modu's cousins. At times Adama would giggle instead of cry. Sometimes there is very little difference between giggling and crying. This was a very good example.

Or, another example of choosing between giggling or crying is when the girls and boys were playing in the street, jumping over the stick, and falling, and a stick thrusts into your foot and it starts to bleed and you want to cry from the hurt, but you know if you cry you will be sent out of the game, and told by the boys to *go home* and stop *crying like a baby!* That's another example of giggling instead of crying. Or when one of the boys teases you by pulling your hair and it seems he is being mean about it, and it hurts so much you want to cry, but you giggle instead because if you cry everyone calls you a baby, even the girls who are not your close friends.

Once in a while tempers flair and fists begin to fly. Sometimes it's boys against boys. Sometimes it's girls against girls, and sometimes it's a quick tempered girl reacting to a boy and the fists fly, and the dust flies, and a circle of children form around the fisticuffs. Within one minute it ends, and everyone giggles. Sometimes the bloodied one neither giggles or cries. Sometimes he or she is allowed to hold his or her bleeding wound and slink home to his room.

When you are punished by your father or mother, you cry silently so they will know you do not want anymore punishment. If you giggled at that time, you would end up crying loudly. It is not advisable to giggle when parents punish you.

****

They walked to the river. They ran to the river. They skipped to the river. The path was wide enough for two girls to walk side by side. Adama and Aime Cham led the way; hand-in-hand. Tida Cham and Ningma Jammeh, sister to Modu-the-boy-who-Adama loves, followed them. Swinging their clasped hands. Singing some of the songs their parents had taught them. Songs the parents of their parents had taught them. Tall palm trees line the wide path. The bush was not thick under the tall trees, only parched earth during dry season, and during the rainy season succulent leaves and brilliant red blossoms scattered about on the floor.

Shortly before they arrived at the riverside they became quiet and thoughtful. Perhaps the heat and a nearly full stomach made them sleepy. They walked silently and slowly through the remainder of the magic path. They played ankle deep in the water. Bare feet and legs splashing and kicking water onto each other. Holding up their long wrap-around skirts, showing their legs, not often shown. Laughing and squealing like monkeys or donkeys or just plan silly girls, they romped through the shallow edges of the riverside. Amie Cham pretended to dance a wiggle butt move and the girls giggled loudly.

Then all four of them wiggle butt danced in the water. Arms flying into the hot air. Knobby knees bending and flexing. Water flying. Girls giggling into loud laughter. Finally, flopping onto the ancient huge log.

An ant crawled along the old log with the glistening sheen toward Aime's hand and it commenced to climb onto her little finger. Not looking she brushed it off and continued to talk of the new material her mother had bought for a new skirt and top. The color was blue with green swirls like the river. It would be for prayer day after the fasting of Ramadan.

"My mother and I will have the same material and the same style. We will be very beautiful, I am sure."

"No more beautiful than me," Tida, her sister retorted.

"It does not matter," Adama said "You are the same. You both will be very beautiful."

Amie bent forward looking around Adama and stuck her tongue out at her sister, Tida. Tida rose from the log and swung past Adama toward her sister with her fists clenched.

She started to swing at Amie who was still sitting, but beginning to rise with her fists also clenched, preparing to hit her sister.

Adama and Ningma Jammeh each grabbed one of the sisters and held her closely, as the sisters tried to pull their arms free from the firm grip of Adama and Ningma.

"Whoa!" Adama and Ningma laughed as they held the two angry sisters. Dust flew as the scuffle continued. Aime and Tida tried to get loose from their captives. They thrashed and growled and spit, and finally gave up. Exhausted, they stood with their heads hanging.

Adama and Ningma released them and sat them down on the log. It was nearing late afternoon, and the heat did not lessen, and the girls knew they should go home now to their never ending work.

"Will your visitor be gone when we return?" Adama asked Ningma.

"I am not sure. She will need to be returning before the darkness arrives, of course. It will be soon, I am sure," Ningma replied, looking at her best friend, Adama, knowing that Adama hoped this girl,Mimuna, would be gone when they all returned to the village from the river. And most likely Adama would be wishing Mimuna would never return to their village. Ningma knew how much Adama loved her brother Modu, and how difficult it was to see him beginning the move toward the marriage of someone else.

That night Adama slid into bed beside her sister, Mariama who was sleeping with her mouth slightly open, breathing deeply and twitching like she was having a scary dream. Mariama moaned and moved her feet as if she were running. Her arms jerked slightly and quickly. Adama put her arm around Mariama's shoulder and curled up against her back. She lay her face on the back of Mariama's neck. A tear rolled down Adama's cheek and ran into her mouth. A second tear followed, and soon she was trying to swallow her sobs so she wouldn't awaken Mariama. She was glad the day was over. Mimuna had returned to her village with her brother. Adama hoped Mimuna would never return to this village again, but she knew that was a foolish wish.

CHAPTER 6

Ebrima Darboe and Haddy Touray

Their backs touched where they lay on the straw mattress in the heat of the small room of Ebrima Darboe. Adobe walls, white washed. No windows and a piece of bright red and orange material hung at the open doorway of his room. On the other side, his living room stood nearly empty of anything other than two stools, two wooden chairs with arms, and a prayer mat at the far corner. No breeze moved anything. A straw roof protected the small room from the night air and from the stars shining like stars shine nowhere else in the world. Brilliant, radiant, dazzling, sparkling, gleaming, shining, bright. Stars in Africa.

Ebrima could feel Haddy's back against his. Hot from the never ending heat of the season, yet stiff. Stiff from her anger and sadness, he guessed. Not soft, like Haddy could be. Like they used to be in this bed, not that many years ago. Haddy, his youngest, sweetest, and dearest wife. The girl who could make him happy by simply lowering her head and looking up at him through eyelashes as long as the legs of the spiders living in the straw roof.

Earlier that evening they had sat outside in the darkness on a wooden bench placed against his house. Their backs leaned against the wall warm from the day's sun. Two people fit perfectly on that old, smooth bench. Especially when two people sat closely, as did Ebrima and Haddy many times, long ago. Now they sat with a space between them. Legs folded, arms folded. Looking off into the night air. No words between them until Ebrima knew he must speak. Tonight was the night he planned at last to bring up the long awaited subject. He had decided this was the night. After talking with his first wife, Binta Darboe, several times in the past few weeks about the inevitable move, he had waited too long already to speak to Haddy Touray of her destiny.

"You no longer touch me," Haddy whispered through tears and a quivering voice.

"We have talked about this, Haddy Touray, too many times already,"

Ebrima tried a gentle whisper, for he did not want to hurt this barren woman. This woman who he had cherished since she came to him as a very young woman. A girl, really. And he had adored her youth, her humor, her beauty. He was sure she would bring him many children, all of whom would be as beautiful as she, or as handsome as he.

Binta Darboe had nearly promised him this would happen for him through this young, whimsical girl. Binta Darboe had seen how sad Ebrima was after several years when Aime Cessay, his second wife, had produced no children for him. Binta, his first and most loyal, strongest and wisest of all wives had helped him decide to take a third wife.

Now, how many years later, he lay beside Haddy trying to collect enough courage to tell her she must return to her family.

He rolled over onto his back and said, "Haddy, I must talk with you and you may be sorry I have spoken to you by the time I am finished, but it must be said."

Haddy rolled into a small fetal ball, and tried not to scream. Already sweating from the closeness of the room, her tears were greater than before.

"I will not talk about this. It will not happen. I cannot go away from you, Ebrima Darboe. Someone has placed a curse on me and I cannot have your babies. I think it is someone very close by, or even in our compound. You cannot be so cruel as to send me back to my family in disgrace only because this curse is preventing me from having your babies. Do not make me leave you. I beg of you."

Her voice trembled in a whisper in the darkness of the hot room.

"Haddy Touray, it is the only thing we can do. You know what agreements were made with your parents when they brought you to me. Most important they would give us land in Brikama, and next, you would give me children. If we are not blessed with children, the land will return to them, and you will return to them.

When my Jola died, and Adama became so ill for such a long period of time we needed everyone in the compound to be here to help with the work. You helped through the difficult time, and you were my wife in every way. Yet, still no babies came."

"You do not care that a curse has been put on me? You do not suspect someone in this very compound? Someone has gone to her marabou and asked him to send bad spirits into my body to poison me? Poison my womb so no babies can live in it? You know who hates me, Ebrima Darboe. You know who else in this compound brings you no babies! Why is she not being sent back to her family compound? Even if she is the one who puts a curse on me, you will keep her here, and send me away?"

Haddy was sobbing, and shaking so severely her arms and legs were twitching. Her face was wet with tears. Ebrima felt like a monster for making her so unhappy. He wanted to comfort her by putting his arm around her, but he knew it would be unfair to give her any hope of his giving in and allowing her to stay.

"Aime is leaving, also. She and I have talked about it. She is very ill, and wants to return to her family, so they can care for her and make her as comfortable as possible. You know both of you stayed longer than expected because we needed everyone here to help take care of Adama and the new babies who came these past few years."

Haddy's sobs subsided. She lay quietly, and loosened her tight fetal position. She rolled over onto her back and looked up at the straw roof.

"My mother and father will send me to the clowns village, you know. I will be entertaining as a clown at all the village celebrations. Does that shame you, Ebrima Darboe?"

"Why should it shame me? I am not the one who could not produce babies," Ebrima whispered.

"If women do not produce babies they have to be nobody. They are nobody. Sometimes I feel it is not fair to be born a woman."

Ebrima chuckled. She could still make him smile. He wished they could begin their lives again, and maybe whoever had put the spell on Haddy would not do it this time. And they would have many babies. But Ebrima is a wise man and does not allow himself to become too sentimental.

"When must I leave?"

"Your parents are coming on the next prayer day. They will go with us to the mosque, stay overnight here, and you will leave with them the following day," Ebrima covered his eyes with the back of his hands.

Haddy slid off the bed, walked to the end of the room, and lay on a piece of material on the floor for the remainder of the night.

The next day Ebrima went to Binta Darboe's house. Actually it was the wives' house, but Binta being the first wife claimed it to be her own. The other wives lived there, but Binta was the matriarch. Aime no longer lived in the wives' house because of her sickness. She lived in a room attached to Ebrima's and the older boys' house.

"Do you have a minute?" he asked. Binta was sitting on the veranda sorting rice in a winnowing basket. Plucking the small hard pieces from the clean pieces. The chaff would be winnowed after that. Tossing it into the air from the basket, and letting the breeze blow the chaff away.

"I always have a minute for my husband," Binta smiled and chuckled. Binta had become a very large woman in every way. She was the biggest woman in the village, and she was proud of herself for that. She was a beautiful woman with twinkling black eyes and a round face as black as her eyes. Her nose was broad and symmetrical to her wide mouth. She smiled often, and laughed a loud merry laugh.

Binta was secure in her place as the oldest wife and the only one who could bear children. She organized the compound and kept two or three girls who were not her children but who were 'given' to her to work for her, and in turn for her to feed, clothe, and provide a home. There was much to do in a large compound and some families were unable to care for all of their children. Ebrima and Binta were successful in the village. Their cash crops of cassava, ground nuts and citrus trees, in addition to a few chickens, a goat or two, and a sheep or two provided with enough to survive. At the women's collective garden, Binta grew tomatoes, peppers, and some greens. During the rainy season, rice was grown in the low lands outside the village. But never enough to last the year. Rice was their main food, and the rainy seasons were not lasting as long as they used to. So, now some rice had to be purchased, which was difficult.

The girls were never far from Binta, so when she needed them to run an errand ("Go to the market and fetch a scoop of tomato paste") they would be there to respond. They would run quickly, carrying a spoon made by the village smithy, on the top of their heads. Small bare feet, raggedy skirts, and tattered shirts running to the market.

"I spoke with Haddy Touray last night," Ebrima watched Binta as she carefully picked through the rice.

"You have come to tell me Haddy Touray is leaving this compound?"

"Yes, and now I must arrange for Aime's family to come and collect her before Haddy leaves. Do you think this is the way it must be done?" He sat on the porch steps near Binta.

"Why must she be the first to leave? Is it not correct for the youngest wife to go if they both must leave? Is that not the fairest way?" Binta plucked two tiny pebbles from the basket of rice and tossed them onto the ground. Three chickens fluttered, clucked, and dashed to the spot where they landed.

"I think there must be time between the two departures. I think Haddy's family should come this week as you have already arranged. They will come, as you have told them on prayer day and stay overnight. The next day they will take Haddy with them to their village."

Ebrima Darboe sighed deeply. He scratched his head and rubbed his face with both hands. "I will tell Aime that in two weeks she will go to her family. I think she will be relieved to go. She is so sick that I think she wants only to be cared for and to be near her medicine man, Sifou Jammeh. He gives her medicine from the bush that makes her sleep long periods of time."

"You will miss her," Binta said in a low, gentle voice.

"If it were you going, I could say I will miss you," Ebrima said with sad softness.

Binta nodded as she tossed a few kernels of rice to the chickens.

Ebrima Darboe stood, stretched, then letting his arms drop to his sides he turned and left Binta Darboe sitting on the porch alone with her rice and chickens.

****

Adama visits Owl

I left the house early that morning. I did not sleep all night, it seemed. I tossed and turned. Too many things were happening in our compound and in my life and that was why I could not sleep. Perhaps it was better to live my life as a sleeping girl. So something made me rise from my bed and leave Miriama and our little sister, Mata, sleeping. I slipped on my wrap-around skirt and slid out of our room,which faced the center of the compound but was close to the back of the yard. I wanted to go to the magic path. I wanted to go to Owl. I wanted to tell him how scared I was of all the changes taking place. He seemed to know many things.

I found him sitting on his usual branch. Daybreak was upon us. The village was about to awaken. The first call to prayer was just echoing throughout the corridors. Some fires were beginning to be lit. I could smell the pungent, newly lit wood.

****

"Adama Darboe, why are you out of the village before the light of day is safely here?" Owl shook his feathers, causing a clutter of white down to fill the air around him. I jumped, startled by the noise the owl made as he shook his whole big, round body.

"I could not sleep all night. I am sad about many things and do not know what to do to stop the sadness. When my sister, Jola died, I fell into a sickness of sleep, and I am worried that it will happen to me, again, with so many things happening that make me worry. People in our compound are leaving and I will miss them. People are coming into another compound that I wish would go away and never return."

The red sun was peeking through the forest casting beams of light.

"You are going to miss your other mothers, but they will always have you in their hearts and you will also carry them in your heart. Surely you will be able to visit them at times. Will you not?"

Owl put his yellow eyes on me, blinked twice and waited for my response. I wondered how he knew about Aime and Haddy leaving. Owl seemed to know everything about me. I wanted to understand how that could be. Owl always would say to me, whenever I asked him how he knew about something in the village or in my compound, "Don't worry, Adama, I am your spirit guide, therefore I know everything about your life; now and forever." It always startled me when he would say that to me.

I wanted to tell him about Mimuna visiting Modu the boy I love, and how he will be spending time with her until they are married. Maybe in two or three years they will marry, and I will lose him forever. I cannot even think about it without feeling a rock in my stomach and my heart feeling empty, lost, and abandoned.

How could I tell Owl about such a thing? How could I tell anyone such a thing except for my vue. My girls. My friends. They know everything about me.

They want to kill Mimuna. Really they do.

I say 'no' to them when they say we must go to the Marabou who is a very strong Marabou. This Marabou does not always give kind and forgiving directions to people. This Marabou puts spells on people. Spells that may seriously do damage to that person. Makes them barren, sick, sad, violent or crazy. Or even ill enough to make that person die.

But, I say to my girls, we will not kill Mimuna, nor will we go to the strong Marabou. We are too young to do anything like that. We must wait until we are older before we make decisions about the destiny of others.

"But, it will be too late to save Modu, the boy you love, from having to marry Mimuna. Then, what will you do? It will be too late for you to do anything except to be sad and lonely and marry someone you do not love." They say this to me, and I have no answer for them.

Owl looked at me as I was thinking these thoughts. He waited for me to finish my thoughts, and then, as if he had been reading these thoughts, he said.

"Modu and Mimuna will not marry for two more years. You will be here in this village. Modu will be here in this village. Mimuna will come to visit the Barrow compound sometimes often, sometimes not so often. You will be here all the time. Modu is there across the corridor from your compound. Life will continue as it has forever here in your village. You will see Modu, the boy you love, and he will see you. Do not worry about what will take place two years from now. Live the day. Live the next day. Know that you will understand what must take place as these times go forward, Adama Darboe. Know that you have a Spirit Guide who will be watching."

"You are my Spirit Guide, Owl?"

"Yes. I am here for you. One life is just a small, short part of your eternal lives, Adama Darboe. You are one of the chosen ones to travel through many years and lives and lands, but think only of today, and maybe tomorrow. The rest will come gradually. I will be with you. Now, return to your compound before they find you missing. Hurry!"

****

Haddy Touray

Haddy Touray waited for her parents to arrive at the market place where the wagons came down the lane from the other villages. It was prayer day and she expected them to arrive anytime during the morning. Ebrima Darboe had told her today was the day they would be coming and he had planned to wait for them there, himself, but one of his family members in Sanyang sent word for him to come and help them solve a problem they were having. A sonko (argument) was taking place and it was serious.

"You must go and wait for your parents, Haddy. I am called to help them at Sanyang. Bring your family back to the compound and wait in my rooms. Make them comfortable."

Binta Darboe was having her hair braided by her youngest girl on the veranda where Ebrima was talking to Haddy. Binta listened to every word said within hearing distance. It was her duty to make sure things were in order.

"Binta Darboe, 'ya moi', do you hear?" Ebrima spoke to the back of Binta's head.

"I hear", 'n moi'. She nodded her head once, quickly and with certainty.

****

Noah Camara

Noah Camara was fifty years old the summer when Amie Cessay was about to return to her family compound in Gunguir. Noah had admired Amie since she first came as a bride to live with Ebrima Darboe, his best friend. At that time Noah had lost one wife. She had died when trying to deliver a baby who was coming too soon. The baby was stillborn; and his wife Ningma Sambu died at the same time. For several weeks Noah was not able to sleep or eat.

Ningma was an energetic young woman who was feisty and quick to argue with Noah. Noah often was challenged by her quick temper and her inability to understand that she should not challenge her husband. Nevertheless, Noah cared deeply for this young wife of his.

He married Fatou Manny one year after he married Ningma Sambu because it appeared Ningma was not going to give him babies. And, as soon as he married Fatou Manny, (who was quite different from Ningma) Ningma became pregnant.

Within the year he married Fatou Manny, Ningma lost her baby and her life.

Fatou was gentle, submissive, and happy to be the wife of Noah Camara. Noah was a very handsome man with muscled arms as large as any man in the village. His chest was broad and hard; a few tiny black hairs sprung from the center of his chest. His waist and hips were slender and narrow, leading to his long and powerful legs. Fatou knew the women in the village admired his beauty. She saw them cast glances at him when he was near the well where he sometimes worked, digging a trench to direct the water from the street. The women would giggle and push one another, and whisper. They knew Fatou had this man, and they knew he was very much in love with Fatou. It was fun to push and laugh and giggle during the long, hot, hard working days.

Now Fatou had followed the same pattern Ningma Sanbou had. She became pregnant soon after their marriage and within the same year she delivered a full term stillborn baby boy, and then she died as a result of hemorrhaging. Noah had lost two wives in less than two years time.

This was many years ago. Noah never remarried, although he had many women who shared his bed in the secret pattern of widowers in this village. No one spoke of the afternoons when the women went to the gardens and, on the way, one of the women would 'catch up later' with her vue. The husband of that woman would be sitting at the mosque, or be working at their groundnut field, or traveling to the next village to fetch a tool or visit with a relative or his mistress. That woman would slip into Noah's back door, slide into his bed where he lay smoking and waiting, and in thirty minutes she would be on her way to the garden down the magic path.

****

Noah sat with Ebrima Darboe the night Aime Cessay was preparing to leave the next day. It was quiet in the compound. There was no moon that night, so people were settling down inside their respective rooms. Candles flickered dimly through the curtains hanging in the doorways. The chickens had crawled under the bushes. The dogs were stretched out in front of the verandahs, showing rib cages, and raw sores on their ears. A donkey brayed its long, honking, deadly sound. One of the babies in a nearby compound cried out, as if in pain.

"How is Binta Darboe, tonight?" Noah asked.

They both smoked, and leaned their elbows on their crossed legs.

"She is fine," Ebrima knew where this conversation was going as if he, himself were saying it.

"She will miss Amie Cessay," Noah said.

"Yes, I think she will," Ebrima replied.

"And, how about you? Will you miss Amie Cessay?"

"Yes, of course I will miss her. But, she is very ill, Noah. You know that. She needs to be cared for by her family."

"I pray Allah will give her peace of mind and the return of good health, Ebrima Darboe." Noah flicked his cigarette onto the dry earth and said goodnight to his friend.

Ebrima sat alone for a long time. He didn't want to go to his room. No wife would be there. Amie was leaving the next day and as the custom goes, the last night of a wife about to be sent home does not visit her husband.

Haddy Touray had left with her parents the week before. It was a difficult day for them all. The whole compound tried to carry on as if nothing unusual was taking place. But, the children of Binta Darboe were very sad to see their other mother leave. Haddy had been a young healthy *other mother*. She played with them, and sang to them and had special ones among them who she took as her own children. They cried with great tears and loud noises.

The other two wives fussed with the cooking pot and the fire. Trying not to show any emotion.

Aime was sad for herself. Aime knew in two weeks she, too would be leaving the Darboe compound. Part of her was relieved to be going to her family. But, Aime had spent many years in Jambanjelly, in this compound with a kind and loving husband, who cared enough to protect her from the two wives who were not really very good to her. They were not openly unkind to her. They merely ignored her most of the time. She did not do her share of the work because of her illness, and Ebrima was a kind husband who tried to be fair to his wives. It was not easy. So he brought Amie to his quarters where the boys also had rooms, and Amie was allowed her own two small rooms next to Ebrima's rooms.

And so, Aime Cessay was leaving on this day.

Noah Camara came to say goodbye to Aime Cessay. They walked to the street where her brothers sat on the donkey wagon piled with Aime's belongings. Two brothers looking very much alike, and looking straight ahead.

Ebrima stayed in his rooms as is the custom when a wife is going to her family. One of the husband's vue usually takes care of the final goodbyes for him. Noah Camara was more than happy to do this for his best friend. He not only wanted the honor of adhering to this tradition, but he wanted to let Amie know that he, himself was going to miss her too much.

He walked her to the wagon. Straggling behind the two of them, all the children of the compound, and several from neighboring compounds followed.

Binta Darboe stayed in her house, spilling great tears.

Noah took Amie's hand as they walked. He spoke in a very low, deep voice.

"I will come to Gunguir to see you, Amie Cessay."

"That will be fine," Amie whispered, as she slid onto the side of the donkey cart. She looked down into the dirt of the corridor, as she nodded for her brothers to start the donkeys on their way.

Great calls of sadness came from the cluster of children. Streams of tears ran down their dusty faces. Another mother was leaving them! What were they to do? An older sister, and now two mothers! How strange.

CHAPTER 7

Adama's Fourteenth Year

We went to the riverside nearly every day during the dry season, Modu and I. I had fourteen years of life and not one of those years did I not love Modu Barrow.

The times when Mimuna, his intended, came to visit for a day, and sometimes for two days and a night, we did not go to the riverside. I would have a headache and sleep many hours when Mimuna was there sitting on the bantaba in Modu's compound. Laughing and smiling and swinging her legs, and flirting with him and his vue. I slept many hours during those times.

My mother, Binta Darboe was dissatisfied with my actions when Mimuna was in the compound across the corridor. She would say to me, "Adama Darboe, I do not want you to be lying around here with a headache every time that girl comes to be with her intended. It is to be. You are not to be so foolish. You are to forget Modu Barrow. I am telling you this. Do you hear me?!"

And I would swing my legs off the seat beside her and the cooking pot and I would jump up and tramp my feet to my room and flop on my bed and cry and fall asleep.

Binta Darboe did not know what to do with me.

As soon as Mimuna left for her village, Modu would come to me. He would greet the people of our compound and go to Binta Darboe and extend his hand and greet her with sincerity. Binta would shake her head, laugh and say,"Modu Barrow, why are you here?"

And Modu would smile and say,"I would like to walk to the riverside with my friend, Adama, if you will allow me."

Binta liked this boy, and found it difficult to refuse what made me happy.I had had a long illness and I think Binta did not want me to become ill again.

One day as we sat on the log by the river and we had said goodbye to Lamin Badgie, Modu's friend, who was on his way to hunt with Suliman Samba, Modu moved closer to me on the log. Our bodies touched. Something in my chest began to make a loud noise, a thump thumping, and a ringing sound echoed in my ears.

Modu's hand rested on mine,his face appeared in front of my face and he placed his warm lips on mine for a very short time.

I did not move. I do not understand this, but my eyes closed during that very short time.

Modu moved back into the position we had been before. We sat quietly for a long time. My chest noise stopped and my ears stopped ringing.

"The river is moving very fast today," Modu said.

"Yes," I replied.

"We should return, Adama Darboe."

I said nothing. We rose and walked back through the magic path to our separate compounds.

****

As time went by in my fourteenth year of life, our two vues, Modu Barrow's vue and my vue, would meet at the field behind the mosque where we prayed during Tobaski. A huge tree stood in the middle of the field, alone, big and beautiful.

Thousands of bees lived in that special tree. Now and then, the bees would come flying out of their nest in that beautiful tree and swarm toward whoever was there beneath it. We would hear them coming even before we saw them. A huge humming sound filled the hot air. That is when we knew the bees were coming from the big tree. We rarely got stung by the bees. We learned to move really fast to avoid their sting. The tree was the home of the bees, and the tree was our very beautiful, huge tree with branches reaching toward every part of the sky. My father told me the tree was given to the village by Allah. Allah seems to be very generous.

I would go to Tida and Amie Cham's compound. Their compound was one of the largest in our village. Four round houses with straw roofs stood facing a dry space of earth in the center. One house was the Chief's rooms. One was for the wives, and the remaining two were for the children, and for visitors. Each building had a bantaba in front for sitting and visiting throughout the hot, sunny days.

I would call to anyone who was there when the compound seemed to be empty. Mata Cham would come from her room where she was resting during the heat of the day, and she would say; "Adama Darboe, you are here. Where is Binta Darboe?"

"She is at home, resting. I am here to see Tida and Amie. Can they come to the prayer ground for a short time before it is time for us to help with the cooking?"

Usually Mata would agree to let the girls go to the prayer ground for a short time until it was time to prepare the dinner meal. Rice, goat meat or fish, tomatoes, onions. Usually that was what we cooked in several different ways. But, always in a sauce and with rice. We all love rice because it fills our bellies.

During the time of our going to the prayer ground to meet Modu and his vue, many things happened. Not only did we play games like jump the stick, or kick the large grapefruits from one end of the prayer ground to the other, girls on one side, boys on the other, not only did we laugh and push and let the little ones play with us, but other things happened during that time when we played at the prayer grounds.

Sometimes one of the girls and one of the boys would disappear into the bush beside the prayer ground and no one would notice. No one would say "Where is Fatou?" Or "Where is Lamin?" Everyone continued to play the games, or wrestle or run around like hens and chickens. Sometimes Modu and I would walk away into the bush and sit under a tree for just a short time. We would not talk much. Always when we were ready to return to the prayer ground Modu would put his lips on mine, and then I would know it was time to return.

One day, as we were preparing to leave our place under the tree, Modu said; "I do not know what to do. My parents want me to marry Mimuna and I will do that. But, I do not want to be without you."

My heart stopped this time. It did not do the thump thumping; it actually stopped for a minute. Then, I said,"We can run away together."

I did not know I said such a thing. It came from my mouth, but I do not know where the thought came from. I wondered if Owl had placed the thought in my head.

Modu stepped back quickly. He looked at me with a surprised expression on his face. He scowled and wrinkled his beautiful wide brow. He folded his arms across his chest, pushed his hips out, and looked at me in consternation.

"I do not understand what you are saying. 'Run away.' "What does 'run away' mean?"

"I want us to go away together from this village. I want us to be together. Only you and me." I could not believe I was saying this to Modu, the boy I love. Yet, I wanted this more than anything in the world.

"But where would we go? What would our parents do to us? If nothing more, they would disown us, probably beat us to near death when they found us. And they will find us, Adama Darboe. You know that. Every one in this whole world knows everyone else. Our clans know all the other clans in the whole world. They will find us and return us to this place, and we will be in disgrace. You know that. Do you not?"

"If we run far enough away they could not find us. We could first go to Amie Cessay's compound in Gunjuir. It takes only a day and a night to walk there and she will hide us until we can catch a fishing boat and they will drop us off far from here. Amie is my other mother, you know that, and she is not happy about being sent back to her family compound. I know she will help us leave. She has brothers and uncles who are fishermen. Maybe they can help us find a place to live and you can fish with them."

"I cannot think of this now, Adama Darboe. We must go back to the prayer ground. And then we must go back to our compounds in order for you to help with the cooking. Do not speak of this to anyone, do you hear me? I need to think."

Modu took my hand and pulled me up from the log where I sat. He placed his forehead against mine, but did not place his lips on mine this time. I swallowed a lump in my throat. A tear sprang in the corner of each eye.

****

Mimuna appeared the next morning. Her brother, Seiney, carried her on his donkey cart. They would stay the night as it was a long and arduous journey on a donkey cart twice in one day.

Adama saw Mimuna and Seiney pass by her compound early that morning. She had just stepped out of the girl's room, and was about to go to the latrine when she first heard the wagon and then saw Mimuna and Seiney. She slid out of her house and around the corner to the back of the compound. She used the latrine and then ran like a deer down the wide back path, past the compounds and palm trees and fences. She ran to the magic path and to Owl. She ran so fast that she was out of breath when she reached Owl. She fell to her knees, panting.

"You come so early, and so breathless, little one. You have a serious problem, Adama Darboe, You must calm yourself and then you must share with me your problem."

Adama was kneeling on the ground, head touching the earth, gasping. She stayed in that position for several minutes, until her breathing was stable and her wet face was wiped with the back of her hand. The shirt she slept in was wrinkled and damp.

"Mimuna is here."

"For this you come earlier than the first call to prayer, wet from weeping? This girl, this Mimuna comes to your village often. It disturbs you that she comes, but it is not a new event and you have learned to accept being with Modu when Mimuna returns to her village. So, what is different this time?"

"I think you already know, Owl. I think you have put an idea into my mind," Adama slowly stood before Owl and looked at his big claws where they clung to a branch.

"I am interested in what you have just said, Adama Darboe. Tell me more."

Owl shifted from one claw to the other; lifting his body and shaking his feathers. The rising sun peeked through the palm trees where red dust reflected around Owl.

"I want to run away with Modu, the boy I love. I think you have put this idea into my head. It is a very strong idea and I don't think I could have made it on my own."

Owl ruffled his feathers once more, and made a deep rumble in his throat. "I do not put ideas such as this in my spirit child's head. If I advise something it will come directly from my voice, Adama Darboe. I give great thought to your lives, and to advise you to take such a risk would not be a thing I would do. I am telling you now, Adama Darboe, Modu Barrow will always be in your life. This life. Go home and remember that Mimuna will be returning to her home in a day or two. And, if it's your destiny to love this boy as you always have and seems you always will, so be it. Go now."

****

Modu Barrow left the village one day and did not return.

"Have you seen Modu today?" His father, Ousman Barrow asked Modu's mother, Fatou Jammeh. Fatu was sitting there on her verandah, picking over rice.

"No, I think he went to the farm to work on the ground nuts. Did you not send him there this morning?" Fatou frowned at her husband. "He left early, just after first call to prayer."

"Well, I just came from the farm, and no one has been there working all day. Have you not seen him all day since he left just after first prayer?" Ousman returned Fatu's frown with a scowl.

"I'll send Ningma to look for him. Ningma! Ningma! Come her!" She called over her shoulder toward the open gate. "That girl is never here to help me. I need to beat her. She runs around the village like she has nothing to do for work!"

"Ningma! Ningma!" Fatou called in her loudest voice while Ousman stood beside her, looking toward the gate; foot resting on the step near where Fatou sat. His caftan of pure white looked freshly adorned. Ousman Barrow was a fastidious man.

Ningma raced around the corner of the open gate. Sweating and panting, she came to her parents, looking weary of what was to come.

"I am here," she said in a whisper of anxiety and exhaustion from the running.

"Where is your brother?" both parents spoke.

"Modu?" Ningma asked innocently.

"You have another brother?" Fatou beat Ousman to the question.

Ningma grinned slightly and hung her head.

"No."

"Then, tell your mother if you have seen your brother, and if so, when and where you last saw him." Ousman folded his arms and looked menacingly down at his daughter.

"Where could that boy be? Go find Lamin Badgie and Suliman Samba. They will know where he is. Probably you will find him once you locate those two." Fatou poked at the wood under the cooking pot. She was cooking rice for the dinner meal.

****

Ningma left the compound and ran to find Tida and Amic Cham, her friends, the vue of Adama Darboe. She knew where Modu was because she knew where Adama Darboe was. She was sworn not to tell anyone where Modu Barrow was, as well as where Adama Darboe was. Her vue knew, and probably Modu's vue knew. None of them were to admit they knew that the two had gone.

CHAPTER 8

Mimuna - Modu's Intended

Mimuna's father, Abdulie Conteh, is the Chief of the small village of Jambur. Her mother, Ndey Camara, is a strong, happy woman. She has seven children, including Mimuna who is the third child. Ndey Camara is the eldest of three wives. She will have as many babies as it takes to maintain the control of her position as the eldest and healthiest child bearer of all. She's not sure how much she cares about this husband she has been given. But, that's really not the most important thing in her life. She often thinks about this as she designates tasks and responsibilities to the other wives and the children.

She is pleased that Abdulie was able to arrange the coming marriage of Mimuna to the Barrow clan in Jambanjelly as that family owns farm land as well as some parcels in the village itself. In the future the two clans will be even closer than they have been, and when babies arrive, they will be heirs to some of that land.

Mimuna seems to be alright about going to the Barrow compound, and her brother, Seiney,watches over her while they are there,' Ndey thinks.

"Mimuna! You will be going tomorrow to the Barrow compound, so wash your best fanno and dendiko (skirt and top). Also be sure you have laundered your brothers clothes for the trip. Ya Moi?" (do you hear?)

"I hear. But, Ma sometimes I do not think Modu Barrow wants me to visit." Mimuna pouted, thrusting out her lower lip like a very young child.

"Why do you say that?" Ndey asked. Smoke from the fire filled her eyes causing tears to flow as she stirred the goat meat cooking in the pot.

"He sits with his vue, or they all go out of the compound and do not return for a very long time. I visit with his sister and cousins, who I think do not like me very much. His mother gives me chores to do with the girls, but Modu only speaks to me when he has to."

"Maybe he is shy," Ndey ventured.

"Maybe," Mimuna mumbled as she walked toward the buckets. She would carry them to the well and fill them. Her job today was to do the laundry. Mimuna is fourteen, tall, thin, and angular. Her face is rather long, with a full mouth and a nose a bit large for her face. Her eyes are oval shaped and set far apart, they have a deep smoldering beauty. She wears a serious expression, and rarely smiles or laughs. Mimuna broods about her life, but has no idea how to change it. She sees what is written for her future and with reluctance, accepts her fate. In which case, she guesses someone other than Modu Barrow could be a lot worse choice to have to live with the rest of her life.

The next day Seiney spoke to Mimuna through the curtain at her doorway.

"Mimuna, get up. We will leave very soon. You are late rising. Why!? Your mother is angry with you. You had better get up and prepare to leave or we will be traveling in the mid-day heat. Hurry! You are too lazy!"

Mimuna yawned, stretched and moved slowly, rolling off the mattress feet first, onto the dirt floor. She slipped into the latrine, washed her body quickly; prayed at the verandah, and went to the cooking pot for left over rice from last night. Ndey glared at her menacingly.

"You are a lazy girl! If you didn't have to be on your way, I would beat you. There is no time for that. When you return this evening I will be waiting with a switch!"

Mimuna let tears slide down her cheeks for several reasons. First, she learned long ago, if you don't want a really severe whipping, you

cry before it even begins. Secondly, she was in no mood to take this trip to the Barrow compound and spend very little time with Modu, and lots of time with his unfriendly cousins and sister. How would she ever get to know if she even liked him if she had very little time with him? And lastly, she was crying because she was not feeling well today. Her stomach hurt and she felt very hot. Chills had caught her at times during the night.

"Don't even let me see those pretend tears, Mimuna Camara! I am tired of you! Eat your rice quickly and then go, prepare for your trip!"

Within an hour, Seiney pulled up by the compound gate with the donkey cart. It was a small wagon with one seat, room enough for two people. The old donkey had a sway back and a head hanging to the ground. Mimuna carried a bundle with a bowl of rice for the trip and a change of clothes. They would stop at any compound on the way for a drink of water.

When they arrived in Jambanjelly there seemed to be more people mingling around the center near the market and the mosque than usual. A little stirring of excitement permeated the air. Small boys were kicking sticks and stones in the road, at the center of the four corners. Little girls were jumping, and skipping and swinging each other around. Mothers were sitting on the huge roots of the old baobab tree, cleaning their teeth with chewing sticks while they watched their little ones.

Scincy stopped and spoke with one of the young men whom he had become friends with since coming to this village.

"Salam ali cum," he says, greeting the fellow.

"Ali salam mali cum," his friend responded.

"What is going on? It seems the village has come alive," Seiney said.

"Modu Barrow has been gone since yesterday and no one knows where he is."

"Really? He was not expected to travel and yet he is not in this village? Seiney asked his friend.

"Yes, he is not in this village. He is nowhere to be found. You will learn more about this when you go to the Barrow compound. Greetings, Mimuna Camara."

"Good morning," Mimuna responded with her eyes cast to the ground through the rickety boards of the donkey cart.

"I will go now," Seiney said, as he snapped his switch on the butt of the donkey. The donkey startled and jumped forward, slowing down as quickly as he started. Lumbering forward they reached the Barrow compound only a few compounds beyond the market and the mosque.

When they stepped down from the cart, Seiney tied the donkey to the entry fence. One of the young boys brought water for the donkey. It took long drawing swallows, emptying the bucket in minutes. Mimuna stepped into the compound and found the whole family walking toward her. Everyone shook hands and said the greetings. By this time Seiney had joined in the greetings. Ousman Barrow and Fatou Jammeh, parents of Modu Barrow, led the two visitors to Ousman's rooms, and invited them inside. Mimuna did not like any of this. She wanted to be home, working. She did not want to hear what was to be said. She did not care enough about any of what was happening to be involved with this drama, whatever it was.

"Greetings, once more," said Ousman, "We are glad you came to visit, however we have to tell you that Modu Barrow is not here, today. He has been missing since yesterday. We expect he has gone to the coast looking for work with some of the local fishermen there. We have family in Gunjuir, and he may have gone there. We expect he got work immediately, therefore did not have the opportunity come back and inform us of his new work."

Conversation continued speculating about Modu Barrow's disappearance. Nothing was said about the disappearance of yet another member of Jambanjelly. No one mentioned that Adama Darboe also was among the missing. If the two visitors had not stopped at the market on their way back to their village of Jambur they would not have learned about Adama Darboe's disappearance. But, they did stop at the market to purchase red peppers for their mother. And Adama Darboe's aunt was the only woman selling red pepper that day. And this aunt, Awa, knew these two people, as did everyone in the village.

"You are missing Modu Barrow. We are also missing Adama Darboe. We are praying for her return. We are praying that she was

not stolen by the witches; or that she didn't drown in the river. We are looking everywhere for her. She will come home, we are sure of that."

Neither Mimuna nor her brother, Seiney changed their expression. No surprise, no gasping, no expression of anger came from the either of them. Only the passing of coins for the red pepper, and a murmur of regrets that Adama Darboe was missing from her home.

It was a long and silent trip back to Jambur. Mimuna sat with her fists clenched in her lap. Slouched over her lap, her head nearly touched her knees. Her brother drove the donkey silently and steadily. His thoughts were his own.

CHAPTER 9

Running Away

Modu crept from his room in the ink black darkness of a new moon night. The village was still. It was 2 a.m. Between sunset and sunrise. Tonight was not a night of dogs barking. Only a donkey's bray broke the silence of the village. He carried his spear, a bundle containing his other set of cloths, and four biscuits he had stolen from the previous morning's meal. He slid around the back of the house and out through the broken fence leading to the lane surrounded by the bush. He was meeting Adama Darboe at the crossroads where the lane led to the river.

Holding her breath Adama crouched on the path, looking anxiously in the direction Modu would be coming. The sounds from the bush frightened her. Loud barks from the hyenas and baboons echoed through the thickness. And the constant screams of the tree frogs made her want to run back to her compound and jump into bed beside her sisters. Then she saw Modu creeping toward her, skinny legs, bare feet taking easy, quick, silent steps toward her. He hugged the side of the path, stepping carefully along it's edge.

Adama's heart thumped so loudly she was afraid someone would hear it. She, too carried a small bundle of clothing. She was shivering from fear and the cool night. She could not believe they were doing this.

When he reached her, he beckoned for her to follow him further down the path toward the river. They had planned how they could reach Gunjuir without being seen. They would walk in the tall bush that trailed next to the road leading to Gunjuir. They would stay out of sight of the road, following it closely in the bush. They planned on it taking them until mid-day to reach Adama's other mother, Amie Cessay in Gunjuir.

They walked two hours before they stopped to rest and drink from the river. They felt safer having put some distance between them and their families. Adama was shivering as she sat to rest. "Come and drink,." Modu spoke in a muted tone.

"I cannot get up. My legs will not work. I am very afraid, Modu. We should not have done this. I am very afraid," Adama started to cry in racking sobs. She lay on her side and curled in a tiny ball.

Modu rushed to her side. "Don't cry. I don't want you to cry. I cannot bear to see you cry. Adama you must stop crying." He touched her shoulder with quick, light taps.

Adama sat up wiping her face with the back of her hands. "I am trying."

"Come to the river and wash your face, and take a drink of water. You will feel better. We must continue on if we want to get to Gunjuir by mid-day. We will be moving on after we rest and have food at your Amie's house. She will help us with our next move. We cannot stay very long with Amie because you know the families will come looking for us in every direction."

"Modu, will we ever be able to go home?"

Modu looked at Adama bemused and perplexed. He shook his head and sat on the hard earth, knees jacked up, head in his hands. He sighed.

"What? What is the matter, Modu? Are you angry with me? Are you going to get up and walk away, leaving me here for the hyenas to eat? Do you hate me? Do you wish you could beat me, and marry Mimuna?"

"Adama, Adama, why are you asking me these questions when we have just begun this journey? We knew this would be a very difficult and fearful thing to do, but we knew also we could not be separated by anyone. Now, in less time than when darkness leaves and dawn arrives you are questioning our decision? We are young, but we have made a strong commitment to each other, so we must not act like children as soon as we become frightened and tired."

Adama turned to Modu and flung her arms around him. "I know what you say is always correct. I will follow you forever. Please forgive me, Modu. I am a silly girl who is scared, but I am ready to go forward now." She moved her arms from around his neck and placed her hands in her lap.

Modu sighed deeply and stood, taking Adama's hand he pulled her up. "Are we ready now? Is it better?" he asked as he touched his forehead to hers.

"Yes, let's go," Adama smiled slightly, enough for Modu to feel his usual softness toward this difficult girl.

He broke one of the biscuits in two and passed the larger half to Adama who was following him through tall reeds growing along the side of the road. Darkness began to show signs of a warm blue light as cocks began to crow. In a very short time they could see further than a few feet, and daybreak arrived. Colors of yellow, azure, and purple streaked across the horizon through the bushes and tall palm trees. Birds began to sing and flutter from the trees, calling to each other. Settling on limbs, they watched the young couple trudge through the thick bush.

The day wore on. They had left the path by the riverside because it led in a different direction from where they were going. Another path led into the bush toward what they guessed was the direction of the road. As the heat increased the two became extremely thirsty. Their mouths were parched. It was difficult to swallow. They began to feel weak and exhausted. It was mid-day and they were not nearly where they expected to be by this time. As they trudged along, sweating and gasping, they saw a small one house compound tucked inside the bush away from the road.

"Look, Adama! A house! There must be water there. Let us go cautiously and ask for water. We must be careful not to say who we are. Let me do the talking. Do you hear?"

It was a roundhouse made from the local red mud bricks, a thatched roof looked as if it was ready to be replaced. Limbs from the coconut and palm trees were scattered about the compound yard. The fire pit where the kitchen should be was without any pots or pans or spoons. There was a bantaba in disrepair leaning against the back wall of the house. No chickens or dogs or people were in sight.

Modu whispered to Adama, "Even if is no one is living here, a well should be a nearby."

They stepped onto a path which led to the house. It was a side path which led to a broken down latrine. They walked to the front doorway of the little house where there was no door attached, nor the usual curtain serving as a door. Modu peered in cautiously, and muttered, "Konk, konk. Is anyone home?"

The room was bare of furniture. No stools, no bed, no table. It was an empty, unused house. This rarely happened here in Gambia. People were always needing a place to live. This was highly unusual. But, Modu still was not sure that someone was not living here. Maybe a single man who was tending his cattle in the bush came here later on in the day.

"Let us find the well, Adama. Then we will decide what to do."

They walked gingerly into the one room, and cautiously viewed its tiny space. It had two windows, one directly beside the open door looking toward the path which led to the road. The road was not within sight, but close by. The other window looked toward the back of the house where a small clearing of hard earth stretched for about twenty steps before the palm trees began. The trees reached into the forest and beyond.

As they cautiously stepped out of the front door and around the little round house, their eyes searched for any sign of a well. Modu spied a dent in the ground at the edge of the back yard. He pointed to it, and Adama's eyes lit up at the possibility of water. It was a very deep well and appeared to be only partially filled with water. They lay on their stomachs, and reached down into the well, but could not touch the water.

"I will drop down into the well and fetch some water, but first I must find a container, said Modu He cast about, not even really knowing what he was looking for. A gourd, an old mug, or pot, or most likely, a coconut.

"Help me find a coconut, Adama."

Adama was still lying near the well. Her thirst was intense and she was more tired than she ever had been. Even when she was sick from the loss of her sister, Jola. Even when Mimuna was visiting Modu across the way and Adama wanted to sleep only. Never had she been this exhausted, or thirsty. She stood slowly and began to look for a coconut. There were plenty of coconuts in the trees, perhaps because they had not ripened enough to drop. For whatever reason, the coconuts remained in the trees.

"I will climb up and take one from the limbs," Modu said as he took a deep breath, spit into his hands and commenced to walk up the tree. Modu, like every boy in the Gambia had walked up coconut trees, and palm trees ever since they were very young boys. It was no problem for Modu except he was becoming weak from hunger and thirst. But with hands clasping around the trunk and feet clinging to the trunk, he walked up the tree, then selected a sizable coconut. He tossed it down to Adama, who deftly caught it.

Modu took the coconut from Adama as soon as he slid down the trunk of the tree. He searched for a stone, remembering the only stone he had seen there in the compound, by the fire pit.

He cracked the coconut in two. Half of it was split and the milk was lost. Modu drank the milk from the remaining half, stopping before it was all gone, realizing he must share with Adama this marvelous milk. Thanking Allah before she drank, Adama shook with gratitude as she finished the milk. Modu yanked the half shell from her and ran to the well. He lowered himself down into the well, slowly, hanging onto the edge of the rim. The meat from the coconut remained in the shell. Modu dared not try to remove it right then as he feared the shell would crack.

His feet did not touch the bottom of the well. He hung there, his elbows resting on the edge, his head peeking over the edge, he said to Adama, "I have to drop down into the well, it will not be far down. But, you must find a long limb from a strong tree and lower it down for me to climb up. Also, drop the coconut shell to me once I tell you to. YaMoi (do you hear me)?

"Oh, Modu, please do not do that. I am too afraid to be here alone, if you cannot reach the bottom of the well. What if it has no bottom? What if there are witches down there? Oh, Modu, do not leave me here. It's beginning to be late afternoon. Darkness will come soon. Come back out from that hole. Now!"

Modu moved his elbows from the side of the well and dropped down out of sight.

Adama dropped to the ground and covered her mouth with her hands to keep from screaming.

She heard a splash and sat up quickly, holding her breath.

"Modu?"

"I'm standing in the water. There may be snakes in this well, Adama, quickly get a long stick and pass it down to me. Go now! Be quick! I am moving about to keep from being bitten by anything! Quickly, Adama! Hurry!"

She rushed to the bantaba,which was falling apart, made of limbs from small trees. Breathing in shallow, sobs she ripped two pieces of the broken bantaba away and carried them, running to the well. The poles were nearly as tall as Modu, and she hoped they were long enough for him to use to climb out.

"I have these two sticks, Modu. I can see you. It is not too far, is it, Modu? Here, I'll show you the sticks," She passed one down to him. He reached up and took it.

"Now, pass me the other pole and the coconut shell and I will fill it first for my self, and drink from it, then I will pass a full one up to you. The water comes to the tops of my legs, so there is plenty here. I want to get out fast, Adama, but we must drink first."

After they both drank, Modu wedged the sticks against the further side of the well floor and pushed the other ends against the wall near the top of the well. He climbed up the sticks until his hands reached the edge of the well.

"Now, Adama, you must hold my hands and be strong enough to let me pull myself out of here. Just get into a position that will allow you to do that. Sit with your knees up and your feet braced, and give me your hands, now!"

"Ohhhh, if I drop you I will die!" Adama cried.

"No, if you drop me, *I* will die," Modu said.

She took his hands, one at a time, and braced herself just as he had instructed her, and he stepped onto the two sticks, walking up the wall of the well when the sticks were no longer available. He made one big dive onto the ground once he nearly reached the top of the well. He lay flat for a long time, panting, wet and dirty.

Adama moved over to where he lay and placed her cheek on his back, kissed it lightly, and then lay beside him. Exhaustion over took them and they slept for a time.

When Adama woke she could see the sun falling into the horizon. It was the sweetest time of the day for Adama. She loved having the day of work nearly finished and the quietness that surrounded the village at the time of the next to last call to prayer. Dinner would be cooking, and the smell would permeate the entire compound mixed with the smells of dinner from the compounds on both sides of theirs. And the little ones would be fussing for food and attention. Adama and the older boys and girls would be helping with the preparation of the evening meal and putting the children and animals to bed.

She sat up with a start and looked around for Modu. They were still many miles from Gunjuir and the sun was setting. Their plans were already going wrong. She called in a loud whisper. "Modu! Where are you?"

He stepped out from the house and walked quickly to her, crouching in front of her, he smiled broadly. "You slept soundly," he touched her cheek, gently. "Do you feel better? I have cut some coconut meat for us and it's in the house. Come see," he took her hand and pulled her up from the ground. His eyes twinkled.

As they entered the barren little one room house, Adama was surprised at what Modu had done while she was sleeping. He had fashioned a broom from straw he had found in the bush in back of the house where there had been a pen for some animal. He had swept the dirt floor clean. A bench made from the tumble down bantaba sat in the middle of the room. He had used vines to weave the poles together. They would use it as a table.

In the corner a bed of fresh leaves and vines rested. "We can use it as a bed tonight. We can cover the straw with our extra clothes." He had not released her hand. They stood just inside the little room and Adama felt shy, like a little child being introduced to a new home.

"Is it alright? We cannot travel any further tonight. We are too tired and may get lost as darkness is upon us soon. We can eat the coconut, and some remaining biscuit. I will take another trip into the well after I climb for more coconuts to provide us with food and containers for the water."

"Adama, I think Allah has provided us with this little house where we can rest and live for a bit."

Or my spirit owl, Adama thought. She did not share the thought with Modu, however.

A resting place

A day had passed since Adama Darboe and Modu Barrow were missing. Each of the families had remained hopeful that the two children would enter the village, either separately or together. Everyone in this tight knit village knew they were missing.

Ebrima Darboe and Ousman Barrow, fathers of the two children visited Chief Nuah Cham late evening of the first day they were missing. Three of the elders who sat with the Chief at all meetings were also present. The six of them sat on the front veranda on low wooden stools, legs crossed, leaning against the still warm cement wall. The Chief was making attire, tea, over the small charcoal fire. The men's caftans were fresh and neatly pressed.

"Adama Darboe is a strong headed girl. She is also aware of the consequences of her actions. I am surprised she would go this far. If she has run away intentionally, she knows she will be severely punished." It was difficult for Ebrima to say these words as he loved his daughter more than any of his children.

"We must think about finding the two of them," The Chief said. "They are wrong headed children who must be found before something serious happens to them. The river is too near to the children. The river can be a dangerous thing, as well as a thing we need in order to survive. What are your plans, Ebrima and Ousman? How and where are you going to search for them?"

"I know one place that Adama may go, and that would be to Amie Cessay who is now living in Gunjuir with her family," Ebrima said.

"Maybe the two of us should travel there tomorrow, Ousman."

Ousman nodded, as he smoked his pipe. Drawing in, he released the smoke slowly through one side of his mouth.

"But, would Amie not send them back to Jambanjelly? Would she let them stay with her knowing their families are worried about them?"

"We shall see, Ousman. Are you willing to travel with me? Maybe we can use Noah Camara's horse and wagon. It is more comfortable and faster than my donkey and cart." Ebrima looked toward his friend, Noah, the owner of the horse and wagon.

Noah had visited Amie several times in Gunjuir since she had left Jambanjelly. Her father liked Noah and knew him as very close friend of Ebrima, ex-husband of Amie. However, Ebrima was not aware of the visits.

"Certainly. We will go in the morning. I will accompany you both. We should leave after the first prayer in the morning," Noah said.

"So it is settled, the three of you will travel tomorrow to Amie Cessay's family in Gunjuir hoping you will find them there. You can inquire if anyone has seen them as you pass the other villages along the way," the Chief said.

****

The women in the Darboe and Barrow compounds finished their day's work and nestled into their respective rooms. Candles cast shadows and figures on the walls of the small, windowless rooms filled with iron beds and straw mattresses. Large baskets filled with tomatoes stood in one corner. Girls and women spoke quietly of the mystery of the missing young ones. Binta Darboe was sick with worry. She knew how fragile Adama Darobe was since the loss of her twin sister, Jola. Binta remembered Adama's long time of sleeping deeply, almost not here but neither was she there. Lost in the nether world Binta Darboe feared that Adama would slip into that place again. Also, she knew the danger of the bush, the wild animals, of the river and of the wizards and witches everywhere. She tried not to think of the dangers her daughter must be enduring. Such a crazy thing for the two young ones to do. *Could they not have done what was planned for them? Could they not have accepted the choices made for them by their parents? What was wrong with them? Fool hardy and reckless. Adama, always saying 'Modu, the boy I love.' How silly is that? What is this love thing she speaks of? We care for the people who are chosen for us by our parents, and we do what we must in order to make that a good thing, for our children and our clan. I shall beat her seriously once she returns in one piece!*

****

Noah Camara went to his compound that night worried about how he should handle tomorrow's journey. He would be driving his best friend, Ebrima Darboe, along with Ousman Barrow to Gunjuir in search of Modu Barrow and Adama Darboe. He would be taking them directly to Amie Cessay's family compound. His horse could go there with his eyes closed at this point. Noah and his horse went often to the Cessay compound. He was visiting Amie Cessay several times each week since she had been sent away from Ebrima Darboe's compound. He had always admired Amie Cessay and now she was a single woman. Although she was in a bit of disgrace as all women are who are returned to their family compound by their husbands.

Noah found delight in her company. She no longer was sick with stomach pains. She no longer suffered from the agony of cramps and sharp searing pains. She was free of all of that. Her appetite was excellent and she relished cooking for Noah and the whole family there at the Cessay compound. She had put on some weight, and her color was vibrant and flush. She laughed and flirted and sat very close to Noah when he visited Sitting close, of course, took a few weeks, but now it was natural, and her family liked to see Amie with a man. A woman without a man at the age of Amie was not natural, or healthy, or correct.

Noah knew why Amie was well and happy in the Cessay compound and why she had not been well or happy in the Darboe compound. He had observed what took place there in his friend, Ebrima Darboe's place. He could see how unhappy Aime was competing with two other wives. She became ill because she wanted to be Ebrima Darboe's only wife. Some women did not want to share their husbands. And, when Amie could not even give Ebrima babies, she was distressed and sad and eventually felt the other wives were picking on her. Noah knew Binta Darboe would not pick on anyone. Binta Darboe was a very fair and kind woman, and also she knew that her place was not threatened by any other woman. She was the first, and strongest, and the one with the babies. But, it didn't matter that Noah knew this fact, it mattered that Amie had become ill as the time went on and she was not having babies, and she was not doing as much work as she was expected to. So, Binta would speak in private to Ebrima who would speak to Amie about doing her share of the work.

Then she would become full of pain in her stomach.

And, then Haddy Touray, third and most beautiful and most flirtatious wife came along. Full of youth and vigor and beauty. Amie felt more intimidated. She would tell Ebrima the other two wives hated her and picked on her and chided that she didn't do her share of the work.

Eventually Ebrima moved Amie into the room next to his rooms, and separated the women. Amie ate dinner most of the nights with the wives, but she would quickly return to her room. The two remaining wives would give a sidelong glance to each other, and finish the bowl of rice.

Now, here Noah was taking Ebrima to find his child hopefully at Amie's home. He hoped it would not cause a problem for any of them. Noah wanted things to remain as they were. He did not want a problem with Ebrima, or with Amie's family. He fantasized that one day he might be able to marry Amie. He no longer worried about having babies. He wanted a nice looking woman to share his compound. How that would work, he could not imagine. But he clung to the fantasy.

****

It was the third day since Modu and Adama had run away. They were beginning to feel at home in this little house they had discovered in the bush, far enough away from the road that no one could see them. They could hear the donkey carts, horses, and folks passing on their way to Gunjuir.

The village of Gunjuir sits by the sea and the road ends at its center by a beautiful beach. Fishing boats line up on the beach when they are not at sea. Each morning men work together pushing the huge hand made boats over the sand and into the sea. The men roll the boats over enormous logs, cut from the forest, making it possible to move the heavy vessels. There will be one or two logs lined up between the boat and the water's edge. Two or three men will grab each side of the boat and heave it onto the first log, and then run it along the two logs, groaning and straining every muscle in their taut, stringy arms and torso. Once the boat has been rolled onto the two logs, and over the second log, someone runs to the end of the boat, removes that log and rushes it to the front of the boat which is facing the sea, and slides it under the bow. Until the front half of the boat is in the water and beginning to float this process continues. It takes a great deal of time and cooperation and energy. But it's the way it has always been done.

Gunjuir was Modu and Adama's next planned destination, but they seemed relaxed here, and rested.

"I found roots from a plant in the bush that will be very good to eat. I am getting tired of coconut, are you?" Modu looked down at Adama where she sat on a woven mat behind the little house. Her back rested against the wall, and she was shelling a few nuts that had dropped from a tree in the bush. Using one of the few stones available, she cracked the round, brown shells and placed the nuts in a neat little pile.

"Now that we have solved the problem of getting water from the well using vines and a coconut shell, and we are finding a small amount of food, I think I want to remain here, Modu, for a few days. Can we do that? Just you and me, and this little house?" Adama looked up at the boy she loved with big, solemn eyes and a bit of a wistful smile.

Modu crouched on his haunches facing Adama. "If I could catch a squirrel or bird with my spear we could have a feast," he touched her ankle and moved his hand away quickly.

"So we can stay for a few days? If anyone who is looking for us goes to Gunjuir they will not find us there, then they will go home. So, when we decide to continue on, they will have already been there. Is that not a good idea? I like our little house, Modu. It is good," Adama smiled into the little pile of nuts.

They sat by the fire which Modu had started by rolling a stick between his hands back and forth quickly, into a bunch of very dry grasses, at the height of the day when the sun was beating onto an open area behind the house. He fed the fire in order to keep it going until they ate. Blowing into it gently, he would add more dry grass and watch it flare up into the hot air. Now the sun was setting and they were roasting a tiny bird that got in the way of Modu's spear. He aimed at a squirrel and let his spear fly. A little bird dropped down onto the ground in the very same place where the squirrel had been. The spear consumed the little bird and split it in two. It's little legs sprawled out, and the reddish head flopped over into the dirt. The squirrel darted away. The little bird would be a bite for each of them, along with some of the nuts, and remaining pieces of coconut.

They ate slowly knowing there was not much food. Knowing they had survived three days away from their village, their home, their friends. Knowing they had found a home and food.

They washed their bodies, using as little water as possible, yet still enough to become clean. Being clean was very important.

They sat quietly on the mat for some time. Darkness surrounded them, tree frogs sang their loud intoxicating chirps and peeps, filling the warm night air. Now and then one of them would speak of a friend and what he or she did that made them laugh. Of a sister, or a brother, and how bothersome they can be at times. Sometimes the story would be so comical the two of them would giggle quietly into the night. And sometimes they would mention one of their dearest friends and there would be a few minutes of silence.

"I think I want to go inside to the mat and sleep," Modu said, as he stretched and yawned.

Adama would never say she wanted to go to sleep when she was able to sit here beside Modu, the boy she loved, and chat and laugh. But, then she remembered she could follow him into the little house and sleep there beside him.

"I think we should keep a small fire going so the animals will not come too close to us while we sleep. I will keep checking it through the night. You will sleep against the wall on the mat, so I will not disturb you when I rise to check it," Modu was smoothing the grasses and matt where they slept as he said this to Adama.

They lay on their backs looking up at the grass roof, listening to the night sounds of the bush. A full moon peeked through the wisps of the fine dry grass, twinkling like so many stars.

"Are you all right, Adama? Do you like it here?" Modu whispered as though someone might hear them.

"Oh yes, Modu, I am very happy now we have this little house to stay in. Maybe tomorrow we could walk into the bush and find more water. We are not that far from the river, are we? I do like it here with you Modu. Are you all right?"

There was no response from the boy she loved. She gasped, fearing what he would say next. Nothing came from him. Then she heard soft breathing and she looked over at him. He had fallen asleep there beside her. Adama smiled, touched his shoulder with one finger, and rolled over onto her side, closing her eyes.

He woke several times during the night and checked the small fire. Once he heard the breathing and low growl of what must have been a hyena. Modu carried his spear with him at all times. He knew animals recognized the danger of a spear therefore it was wise to always carry it.

The next day after washing, praying, and eating the remainder of the nuts, they headed into the bush. The path, probably made by monkeys, or the people who had once inhabited the little house, was like a tunnel, tall and narrow. The forest of tall palm trees lined the path. The leaves at the top reached across the well used path. A lacy sky shone through. Golden specks of dust cast a mystical light.

Adama walked directly behind Modu. Modu carried his spear prepared to use it in an instant. It was very still in that forest on this early morning. The sun peeked through the skinny trunks of the sky-reaching palm trees. The terrain of palm trees and semi darkness continued for some time. They both were cautious of snakes and spiders. They crept silently in bare feet. Then, as the sun rose and time passed,they noticed the trees were spaced farther apart, and bushes filled the areas where the palms trees had stood closely together. The light became more intense, and they could see what looked like an open area ahead of them. Where the path ended they entered a large field of tall golden grass. The grasses swayed gently like the feathers of an exotic bird. Surely a crop of some kind had been planted and harvested there at one time. It was a large, open space, surrounded by mango and cashew nut trees. Tall, lush fruit bearing trees with deep green leaves hugged the rectangular, unused farmland. It was serene in that golden place. They heard weaver birds shouting from the trees; the only sound. This meant to them that the river was not far from them. Weaver birds build their long hanging nests in trees by the river.

Modu reached his hand back toward Adama where she stood directly behind him. Adama's heart was racing in her budding chest. She saw mangos about to ripen, and cashews flowering. Lush, huge healthy trees ready to provide food for a long time to whoever was under them. And a field looking ready to plant. Seeds. They needed seeds.

Modu turned to Adama still holding her hand and whispered,"God is great."

Tears were filling Adama's eyes. She wiped them with the back of her slender hands.

"Why are there tears in your eyes, Adama Darboe?"

Modu dropped her hand. He put his fists on his hips and demanded; "Why? Why are you crying, now? Look before you, Adama Darboe. What do you see here?"

"I am sorry. It is just that I am too happy to laugh. I am so happy to see this place that I cry. I cannot explain it, Modu. I sometimes cry from happiness. That is what I am doing now," she hung her head and sniffed.

He took her hand, again, and pulled her to stand beside him in the path that entered the field. They stood for several minutes staring at the scene before them, each in their own thoughts. The sun was beginning to burn into the golden grasses. Even the weaver birds were not as noisy as they had been.

Modu and Adama stood each in their own thoughts, standing by the field of beauty and bounty.

"What shall we do now, Modu?" Adama Darboe asked the boy she loved.

"It is difficult to say, Adama. What do you want me to say? I am the man who must make the decisions, but you are the girl who must agree."

"Can we walk through the field and search the other side? Maybe we can find the water where the weaver birds live." It was Adama's idea.

Modu cleared his throat.

"I think we should go further than this place and explore the other side of the grasses," he said, with a thoughtful frown, corners of his mouth turned down.

"Yes, that is a very good idea," Adama murmured.

CHAPTER 10

Noah Camara and Aime Ceesay

The three men met at the Mosque for early morning prayer. Ebrima Darboe, father to Adama Darboe, Ousman Barrow father to Modu Barrow, and Noah Camara. Noah had hitched his horse and buggy outside of the Mosque, ready to leave directly from the first prayer. Breakfast consisted of left over rice from the night before. Each wife had warmed it for her husband in the early morning dawn. A brief goodbye was mumbled by the men as they walked out of their compounds.

Ebrima stepped onto the horse cart. A tiny smile passed over his full mouth. His closely clipped hair clung snugly to his head. A few white hairs sprinkled throughout. Ebrima's nose was small and wide at the nostrils. His eyes were black. The whites were tinted yellow, a sure sign of malaria having inhabited his body many times in the past.

Noah and Ousman were already sitting in the wagon. Noah at the driver's seat, and Ousman in the back of the wagon. Ebrima climbed into the passenger's seat beside Noah.

"Please bring Adama home with you, Ebrima Darboe," Binta Darboe said to Ebrima.

As they traveled down the dirt road the men spoke intermittently, observing a garden here, some monkeys there about to raid the garden. One of the compounds had a new building which Ousman reported was for the wives, because the previous rains had ruined the old one.

Besides, it needed to be larger because the man of the compound had taken on a third wife, and there were new babies being born nearly every year. The three men chuckled at that.

After nearly two hours they came to the tiny village of Jambu where they stopped to let the horse rest and drink. The road ran directly through the village, where small shops and compounds hugged the street. Bamboo fences enclosed the compounds. Trees were abundant in Jambu causing shade and comfort like a hen tucking her chicks under her wings. Men and boys sat on the verandas of the three small shops. Noah called to a young boy to go fetch water for his horse. A well was just around the corner in the lane leading further into the village. The men jumped down from the wagon and stretched. Ebrima lit his pipe as they wandered into one of the shops. Greeting the shopkeeper Ebrima and Ousman noted that Noah knew this man. They each greeted him, shaking his hand.

Noah inquired about Modu and Adama. Asking the shopkeeper and several people who were standing around if they had seen two young people passing through in the past day or two.

They shook their heads. No, they had not seen anyone they did not know. Yes, they would watch for them, and bring them back home to Jambanjelly and their families if they should see them.

The three men rested for a short time and drank water. Shaking hands with all the people, they climbed onto the wagon and headed down the road to Gunjuir.

Noah was secretly relieved that in the presence of Ebrima the shopkeeper did not make a comment about the frequency of Noah's trips to Gunjuir.

Each step Noah was making this day was a step of uneasiness. He did not want problems to arise between he and Ebrima, and he did not want to lose Amie, who he believed could make his life a happy one once again. Too many years had passed since Noah was a truly happy man. Now, he was on the verge of experiencing that joy again, and he did not want that chance spoiled.

It was nearly high noon when the horse and wagon entered the town of Gunjuir. Noah hoped that Ebrima did not notice how the horse automatically made a right turn into a narrow dirt lane where compounds lined each side. Fences made of natural sticks from the bush enclosed the compounds. Some compound had trees others were barren of trees and had only a few small houses scattered throughout.

The first person Noah saw inside the Cessay compound was Amie Cessay. She stood clutching one of the pillars held up the veranda roof. Her eyes were as wide as two full moons. Her mouth was open like an awestruck child looking at a konkaran; like the scary things used during the holidays. She stepped back from the pillar and slid into the curtained doorway.

Noah pretended not to see Amie. Ebrima was looking at the new cook house beside the main house. Ousman saw Amie, and called to her just as she was slipping into the house.

"Amie Cessay, hello. Aime Cessay, we are here to visit the compound. Come! Greet us!"

Amie stepped off the vernada and began to walk slowly toward the gate. Then her father, Momodu came around the corner of the main house and called loudly, waving his hand.

"Salam Mali Cum! Greetings! Jambanjelly is here! Welcome! It is good to see you all.! Come in and sit. Amie, get water for our visitors." He eagerly walked toward them with his hand extended and huge smile on his handsome, wrinkled face.

Noah felt immense relief, Momodou was going to make this visit pleasant. Praise Allah. From the corner of his eye he saw Aime carrying a gourd full of drinking water for the travelers. How lovely she was gliding toward them as if she floated rather than walked. How Noah loved feeling alive again. Excited and young.

The three of them took the water from Amie, one at a time; each with a different expression on his face. Ebrima, being the oldest of the three, although only a year or two older, was the first to receive the gourd. Amie cast her eyes to Ebrima's feet and Ebrima murmured a gentle greeting to his ex-wife. Amie whispered a brief response, and slightly curtsied. Ousman next reached for the gourd and greeted Amie with a broad smile and warm touch to her fingers as she passed the water to him. He was a mutual friend who could easily continue his friendship with both Amie and Ebrima. Amie looked quickly at his face, smiled and greeted him in the traditional lengthy greetings. Next came Noah. Noah tried earnestly to look neutral, unmoved, casual, but his heart was thumping in his chest like a teenager about to give away his first kiss. He was astounded at his emotional state when Amie was near him, yet he loved this feeling of aliveness. He mumbled a greeting not looking into her eyes, reached for the gourd and took it from her quickly. Amie stepped back and let him finish. Then accepted the gourd from Noah and turned toward the outdoor kitchen.

The visit lasted throughout the mid-day and into mid-afternoon. The three men explained what they were doing here in the Cessay compound. Ebrima explained how the two young ones had disappeared and the adults thought perhaps they had headed towards Gunjuir and the Cessay compound, knowing Amie might allow them to stay for a few days, and set them out on their next destination.

Amie was not present while the men sat drinking tea and chatting. Only the four men were on the veranda looking into the heat of the day.

"Surely, you must know if Adama and Modu came to us I would return them immediately to their parents," Momodou said to Ebrima.

"I know, Momodou, but we discussed the plans the children may have made, and one of them was that they may mistakenly think Amie would help them, in spite of them knowing that you are the head of the compound and therefore it would be your decision as to what to do."

"I understand, Ebrima. And I understand why you think Adama might come here asking help of Amie. She and Amie have always been close. But, we have not seen them and I believe if they were coming this way they would be here by now. I hope that when you return home you will find them there in their family compounds. And, I also hope you will not punish them too severely. We must remember when we were young and foolish."

Ebrima smiled sadly and nodded. He looked at Ousman and said, "Well, what do you think, Ousman? Should we leave before we are on the road in darkness? Let us go to the Mosque before we leave."

The three men rose simultaneously, each extending his hand to Momadou. Saying their goodbyes, they walked across the street to the Mosque with Momadou.

As they wended their way up the road to Jambanjelly, they passed not far from the path that led to Adama and Modu's little house.

Dusk was upon them when they finally arrived home. The families were waiting anxiously, hoping to see more than three on the wagon when they pulled into the corridor of the Darboe and Barrow compounds. Binta Darboe did not move from her seat on the wives' veranda. Looking up anxiously she sighed, then continued picking over the rice in the basket in her lap.

****

Early the next day Noah quietly left his compound using the donkey and cart, instead of the horse, hoping people would think he was going to his farm just outside the village on the south side going toward Gunjuir. He did not want to call attention to his journey. He hoped he could go and return without Ebrima and Ousman missing him.

He met only a few people walking toward their respective gardens or toward the next village to visit family. He nodded and continued on his journey.

He arrived in Gunjuir mid-morning and went straight to the Cessay compound. Amie was sitting on the veranda picking over the kale she planned to cook for dinner with rice and oil. When she saw Noah pulling up to the fence of the compound and tying the donkey to a hitch, she stood and walked brusquely toward him. With a soft smile she greeted him as he walked through the gate. They shook hands, and turned towards the verandah where she had left her work.

"You are here. I was happy to see you yesterday, and am surprised to see you again so soon. But, I am glad. Is something wrong? I there a problem? Come, sit." In spite of her concern she could not help but beam at Noah.

"I must find and greet Momadou before I sit. I will be back as quickly as I can, Amie Cessay. I did not sleep last night. I don't know why, but I knew I must come today to see you. It was strange yesterday."

She cast her eyes to the ground and murmured, "Yes, it was strange."

"I will return,." Noah said as his lanky body moved toward the next house where Momadou lived.

His greeting through the curtained doorway was returned by Momadou from inside where he was resting from the heat.

"Come," he spoke from his bed.

Noah stepped inside and sat on the only chair in the windowless room. A wooden chair and an iron double bed furnished Momadou's bedroom. Baskets pushed under his bed contained his freshly pressed clothes. His small agateware teapot and four small cups sat on a mat in the corner.

Momadou swung his legs off the bed and extended his hand to Noah.

"Welcome, once again, Noah. I am surprised to see you so soon. Is there a problem? Did you forget something? I hope all is well with you and your friends. Tell me, what brings you here?" Sitting there on his bed Momadou rubbed his head. Usually he was not that direct and to the point. It is not the custom to hurry into a conversation. But, Momadou was truly unnerved at Noah's hasty return to Gunjuir and his compound. Momadou was not a stupid man and he could see that Momadou was interested in his daughter, Amie, and that he came at least once a week to see her. He also realized that it was unusual to bring Amie's ex-husband with him yesterday, but it was justified. It came to Momadou that Ebrima must be unaware of Noah's frequent visits to Amie.

"My garden does not need weeding today, and it is a quiet day in Jambanjelly, therefore I thought I would take another trip alone to visit the Cessay compound. No other reason, except to briefly visit you and your daughter, Amie,who I enjoy being with. I hope this is appropriate, Momodou Cessay. I enjoy my visits to the people of your compound, and especially Amie Cessay."

Momadou smiled as he slowly shook his head.

"Noah Camara, we have known each other all our lives. I think you know there is no reason I would not want you to visit my daughter, Amie. Amie needs to have someone who will care for her. She is a woman who needs to be in a compound with a husband. I would hope that is what you have in mind for Amie. She is of an age, in fact past it, as are you, to be sharing a compound and I would hope, a marriage."

Noah looked to the floor, elbows on his knees. He sat silently for some time, then drew in a deep and long breath. He slowly let the air leave his lungs, and sat straight, clutching his knees. He looked at the wall in front of him, and slowly shook his head.

"Momadou, this comes sooner than I expected. This discussion I thought to take place later, but I will tell you I am pleased you have brought it to my attention. I can only say you are making me a very happy man; giving me permission to eventually marry your daughter, Amie. Will you speak to her at some point about this conversation? What does her mother, Mata, think of my visits?"

Noah's head was reeling from so much information and so many things happening in the past few days. He was wishing for time to be alone and sort through all of this.

"Mata is not happy that Amie failed at her marriage with Ebrima Darboe. She thinks Amie should have gone to a marabou to see to her problems. Mata things Amie was bewitched and could not have babies because of that. And whoever bewitched her asked for Amie to be barren and to suffer from constant stomach pain. Mata is not a patient woman especially when one of her daughters brings shame and disgrace to this compound."

"Our women are not very understanding at times," Noah murmured.

"Mata will be overjoyed to have Amie out of the compound and into a marriage of respect. And I realize it may take several moons before the ceremony actually takes place. Your visits can continue until you and Amie see fit to become man and wife. So be it. Mata will be very relieved to see this take place."

The two men sat quietly for several minutes. Finally, Noah stood, looked down at Momadou and stretched out his slightly knotted hands. Long fingers gnarled from many years of working in the fields. They shook hands.

"I'll go to Amie now and visit for a short time. I need to return before last prayer, Momadou. Thank you for this conversation."

Momadou stood and cupped Noah's elbow in his left hand as they shook hands.

Amie was sitting beside her mother, Mata, on the veranda, both staring at the door of Momadou's house.

Mata was a thin, tall Mandinka woman with a gaunt, tired face. She was the second wife of Momodou. But now, because Momadou's first wife had died from childbirth eight years ago, she was number one and the only wife of Momadou. The first wife, Haddy had delivered four living children. She had also delivered two babies who died before the end of their first week on earth. Mata had three children. In all there had been seven off-spring living in the Cessay compound. Several of the off-spring, including Amie were adults. Those who were still living in the compound were able to do much of the work. Some were married with children, filling the compound.

Mata greeted Noah and offered him a lunch of rice and sauce. It was nearly noon time, and Noah would be leaving soon. She was gracious and reserved, with a cool edge to her, unlike most of the people in the compound. Amie helped Mata fix the lunch for Noah. Amie and her mother had always been close, but Mata was not happy about the way Amie's marriage to Ebrima had ended. She considered it a disgrace to the compound. Amie being sent home because she could have no babies, and was always sick. This brought disgrace to the whole clan, Mata felt. She had seen Amie recover quite rapidly once she was back in her family compound. This did not solve Mata's problem of feeling embarrassed for Amie's failures. She knew that Amie would probably never have babies even though she was still not a really old woman, by any means. Yet, she was past the age most women had babies.

Mata was not very comfortable with Noah Camara's obvious attraction to Amie. Noah Camara was Ebrima Darboe's best friend and Mata knew well enough the total commitment and loyalty men had to one another. Especially those who had been in the same vue (group) since childhood. There would be repercussions. Surely there would be some strong emotions. She and Momadou had not discussed this issue yet. She knew they must do that sometime soon.

Mata's secret wish was that somehow Ebrima would take Amie back as his wife, now that she had improved in health and beauty. Maybe she could even have a baby, since she had been to their marabou in the Cassemas for treatment. For a week Amie had stayed with their marabou and had regained her health, and (pray Allah), her ability to have babies. Mata traveled with Amie on the journey and they stayed at the marabou's compound. He was Mata's family marabou and one of the most respected and wealthy marabous in Gambia and Senegal.

Amie watched Noah eat his lunch. Mata had gone off to do some other never ending chore. Amie looked out onto the open area of the compound yard. Dry, hard earth, old tired dogs and chickens scattered about. Noah finished the rice and sauce and rinsed his hands under the mug of water Amie poured for him.

He smiled at her as he waved his hands into the hot dry air. "Now, I will go. I am happy to see you two days in a row, Amie Cessay. I hope to return again, soon,." Noah reached to shake her hand.

Waving goodbye to several children of the compound who clustered around his horse and wagon, and to Amie, he made his way around the corner and onto the road that led to Jambanjelly.

On his return home, he stopped at the village of Jambu where his marabou, Buba Cham lived. He had been thinking he needed a juju made to protect him from anyone who may be wishing him bad will. Somehow he did not trust Amie's mother, Mata. Sometimes he wondered if she was putting something in the meals that she offered him. Many times when he ate her meals he would go home with severe stomach pain,. He would often be ill during the night and into a part of the next day.

"Buba Cham! Hello. Are you here?" Noah strolled into the quiet yard of the compound.

"Hello? Noah called. It was the middle of the day and people were either resting or at the market place.

Buba stepped out from his room. "Come in, Noah Camara. I am in my room in the heat of this day. Come, join me," Buba Cham smiled a broad, yet reserved smile. "You are coming from Gunjuir?"

"Yes. I stopped to speak with you on a personal matter. I need for you to make a juju for me," Noah was speaking in a low voice as they entered Buba's room through the curtained door.

"Sit. I will call for water. I am sure you are thirsty; it is a hot time of day for travel."

One of the young girls came with a gourd half filled with water. Noah drank it as quickly as his throat would allow.

Buba sat on a mat on the floor of his room. He had a small pile of minute animal bones beside him, a few kola nuts and several large semi-dried leaves neatly stacked. In the corner of his small room were several pieces of animal hide, some with the pelt remaining, some clear cured leather. Also heavy thread and a bone needle lay beside the cluster of his trade.

The men briefly exchanged the greetings, then Buba asked Noah what he could do for him.

"I need a juju made to protect me from someone who wishes to do me harm. I have been ill many times when I return from Gunjuir. I do not wish to accuse anyone in particular. I am concerned only with protecting myself from anyone who wishes me harm," Noah spoke quietly and solemnly.

"I will make this juju for you and you will return in three days to collect it. When you return I will explain in detail what it contains and what it will do for you. YaMoi?"

"N'Moi (I hear you)," Naoh replied. "I will come three days from now and collect the juju. Thank you, Buba Cham."

During that same night Noah woke with violent pains in his stomach. Stabbing, excruciating, rolling pains wracked his body for hours. Perspiration covered his whole body to the point of throwing his covers and sleeping kaftan from his bed. He rolled and squirmed and moaned until one of the daughters of one of his sons tapped on his door saying. "Pa, are you not well?"

"I need water, Tida. Water please!"

When she came with a gourd of water she found him shivering, and sweating, and writhing in his bed. He was shivering so severely his teeth chattered. She held him by his shoulders tightly as she guided the cup to his lips. When she touched him his skin felt as if he were on fire. Yet, he shivered.

When he had finished drinking, he fell back onto the bed, and she covered him. She sat for a short time by his bedside. Once he seemed to be sleeping, the shivering stopped. She placed the back of her hand on his forehead and he felt cooler to her touch. His stomach pains seemed to subside. When he began to snore quietly, Tida knew he was sleeping so she returned to her room.

As usual it took Noah a full day to recuperate from his stomach upset. This time it had been the most severe pain of any of the previous times. He was becoming more and more convinced that someone put a curse on him. He wondered who in that compound would want to poison him.

He was glad he would be going to Jambu in two days to collect the juju.

Ebrima visited Noah that afternoon.

"I've not seen you for nearly two days, Noah. We have heard nothing from the two run away children. Have you any new information since I saw you two days ago? Binta Darboe is frantic with worry," Ebrima looked at Noah with a worried, tired face.

"I have not been well, Ebrima Darboe. My stomach is giving me misery. I'm not sure if it's food that does not agree with me or if a curse has been caste on me. But, presently I am better. I am glad you came. I have heard nothing about the children, either. Yesterday I was in Jambu to see some of my friends and family. No one I spoke with has seen them."

Noah felt that he was not lying to his friend. Just telling him what would be acceptable for him to hear.

****

Modu finds seeds to plant

Ten days had passed since Modu and Adama left Jambanjelly. They had settled into the little house and fixed the well so the water could be pulled more easily. They had cleared the ground around the little house several feet so no snakes or spiders could hide in the growth of vines. They had stored a supply of coconuts in a corner of their one room. Now, since they had found the field, surrounded by mango trees and cashew nut trees, they had some food to rely on. Next they wanted to find seeds to plant in the field where a cash crop or vegetable garden surely had previously grown. More than anything, they wanted to find where rice grew. They hungered for rice. Nothing could fill the belly like rice. All meals were based on rice. Now they had many of the ingredients that would make a good meal; but not the rice.

Modu had wandered through the bush where he thought a small village might be. He wanted to find a garden where he could take some of the vegetables and dry their seeds for planting.

It was not very far from their little house. He took the narrow path leading to the field and mango trees, then walked directly through the middle of the field. There he found another narrow and nearly overgrown path. He was quite sure the little village stood in that direction. Sometimes when he and his vue ventured farther than they were supposed to while hunting they came across that little village. They never entered it, because they had their spears and did not want to disturb the people who lived there. His family indicated that the people of that little village were strangers from another country and preferred to live without interference. Something about being outcasts. He didn't understand and wanted only to find a garden near the edge of the woods.

In a matter of minutes, Modu could see a clearing, an open space, there in front of him where the path led. He crept cautiously through the path, ducking behind trees and peeking around them hoping to spot a garden near the forest, behind the compounds.

It was a tiny village of perhaps ten small round houses. They were situated in a circle, facing inward, forming a round courtyard. These were mud brick houses with straw roofs. In back of each building a small garden grew. Modu spotted eggplant, peppers, and tomatoes, and some things he did not recognize. His heart was racing. He could see no one in the village, but was sure there were people someplace nearby.

Suddenly he heard a baby cry, and soon a woman's voice, quietly shushing the infant. Then silence.

While wondering which garden was the closest to grab one of each kind of vegetable, he saw a young girl come around one of the houses and squat to relieve herself. She was perhaps ten years old. When she finished she seemed to be alert to something strange in her territory. She froze, then turned her head carefully toward the trees and path where Modu hid. He crouched behind the tree and held his breath. Waiting for a few minutes, he carefully peeked around the tree. No one was there, and without thinking for a second he raced to the nearest garden, yanked a handful of vegetables, not even caring or thinking what kind they were. Whatever they were would have seeds inside for planting, and that was all that mattered.

Modu furiously raced to the path without looking back. He ran for a long time until he was out of breath, and he fell to the ground, exhausted. He had wrapped the vegetables into his shirt where he held them. He lay on the path for several minutes regaining his breath and senses. Sitting up finally, he looked down at the vegetables wrapped in his shirt. Unfolding his shirt, he found two tomatoes, a few hot peppers, three okra, and a small yellow squash. Modu smiled a broad, beautiful smile. He had obtained a garden. The rainy season was coming any day now. These seeds would dry enough before planting to grow in a very short time. Now he could spend his days hunting for squirrels and game, while Adama planted and cared for the garden.

Modu caught his breath. What was he thinking? Was he planning to stay in this place for some time? Time to plant a garden, and hunt, and find a better source of water? What was happening to him? He could not think beyond this point. He sat on the path holding the vegetables.

I must think this through, Modu thought. *I cannot believe I ran away from my village and have brought dishonor to my family and to Adama Darboe's family. We may never be able to return to our family and village because of our thoughtless action. I am happy with Adama Darboe. She is the one I care for, but we have gone against our family and now we are left with only each other to suffer the consequences. I do not know what is to become of us.*

Modu sat in the path for some time, holding the stolen vegetables folded in his shirt. His heart had slowed to a normal pace. He was no longer sweating. He heard birds singing in the trees and saw the sun peek through the palm trees. His thoughts quieted and created a calm humming in his head. As he began to think of moving from where he sat on the path, his thoughts moved to Adama Darboe and that he should get up and go to her. She would be anxiously waiting for him. She would be worried about his safety. Adama Darboe always thought of him and his safety. Her whole life was wrapped into his. She had always loved him, even as a child, and Modu knew that. Modu liked that. He must get up now and go to Adama Darboe.

****

For Adama Darboe, this day that Modu left her to go and find seeds for planting was long and frightening. She pulled water from the well and washed her shirt and hung it on a branch to dry. Once it was dry she would wrap it around her waist so it would cover her private place, and then she would wash her fanno (skirt). After Adama washed and dried her clothes, she stood in the middle of the back yard and turned around in a full circle with her hands on her hips. Now what? She decided to take a stroll down the little path in the back of the house that lead to the open field where Modu had gone to explore further. She would go only a short distance. She was bored and lonely. She missed Modu. She missed her mother and her father, and her sisters and her brothers. But, mostly, she missed Modu.

She hummed a tune as she walked down the narrow, green leafy path until she stopped short at what she saw. On the left side of the path a huge mango tree grew. A branch of that tree stuck out nearly into the path, and on that branch sat Owl. Adama Darboe gasped. She stopped short and held her breath.

Owl spoke. "You do not recognize me, Adama Darboe? You do not recognize your spirit animal? I have found you, at last."

"Owl, how did you find me, and why do you follow me?" Adama stood in the middle of the narrow path, trembling."

"It is my duty to follow you and guide you. You have left a village full of worried people. Why have you done this thing, Adama Darboe? We had spoken of your love for this boy, Modu, yet we had not discussed your plans to do this foolish thing you have done."

"I could not endure the thought of Modu marrying Mimuna, so I begged him to run away with me, and he did. We had planned to go to Gunjuir and seek help from Amie Cessay, then we found this little house down the lane, and we love it. Now we may stay here for a time. We are hungry, but managing. I am not sure how long we can go on this way, Owl."

"Do you remember the conversation we had not long before you left the village? I want you to think back on that and return tomorrow to talk with me about what you remember of it. Now you must go back to your house, because Modu is very close by. Go, child!"

Adama whirled around and flew as quickly as a weaver bird toward the little house. Her clean clothes flapped around her ankles and waist. Her bare feet skimmed the earth as she flew home to the little house. She fell onto the mat at the back of the house. Adama had woven this mat a few days earlier using reeds from a wet area in the bush near the open field. The mat was large enough for the two of them to lie on throughout the night. During the day she pulled it out to the back of the house where they spent many hours sitting, their backs against the wall of the little house, chatting, fixing coconut and any other food they could find.

She sat now looking down the lane where she had found Owl, and where Modu would be walking toward her very soon. And there he came. Always her heart leaped when she saw him coming toward her. Adama never wondered if this was how all people felt about another person. It never occurred to her that she had a never ending, forever-love for the soul of this boy, an unusual and rare emotion. She only knew that she had no control over this attachment and love she was born with. It was that way.

He dropped the vegetables onto the mat in front of her, and stood looking down at her with a broad smile. He folded his arms across his chest, and puffed it out like a rooster about to crow.

She marveled at the vegetables and they spoke of how she would use a small area of the field to plant the seeds, but first they must find or make a tool to dig with.

"Your spear would not work?" Adama asked.

"No. It is not strong enough, or the correct shape, and besides I will be using it to hunt while you are working in the garden. I will search for a stone that may be suitable for digging."

Adama was feeling not as strong as she had been when they first ran away. She also knew Modu was looking thinner than usual and tired more easily than before. They were not getting enough food, and they knew it.

Adama cut the vegetables open and pulled the seeds out, separating them from the fiber. She then cleaned them using a gourd filled with water. Once rinsed, she pulled them out from the water and spread them onto a corner of the mat so they would dry for the remainder of the day.

Before they went to bed, Adama wrapped the seeds in a broad leaf and strung some pieces of another broad leaf and wound it around the large leaf where the seeds nestled. She put the packet between the two of them so no animal would take them.

She woke late in the night aware of the moon looking in at them through the only window in the little house. The night sounds of the bush were loud and anxious. She had a feeling something was not safe. Then she heard the foot steps of a lightweight animal walking inside the little house. She opened her eyes and looked into the face of a huge rodent standing not more than two feet from her. The rat froze when he saw her face so close, with her eyes open. Adama reached behind her and grabbed Modu's arm in a fierce clutch. Modu groaned. Adama dug her fingers into his arm, not daring to release her stare at the animal the size of one of the village cats.

"What is it?" Modu was wise enough to whisper.

"You have to move slowly and kill this beast that is looking me in the eyes, she whispered to Modu.

Modu always had his spear beside him when he went to bed. He moved only his arm in the direction of the spear, grasped it, rose with the greatest of caution from where he lay, to a standing position before the rodent took his eyes away from Adama's.

Modu swung the spear up over his head and thrust it down in a matter of a second, into the belly of the animal, who squealed, and tried to run with the spear dangling. His feet ran into the night air for a matter of minutes, slowly coming to a final stop.

"He wanted the seeds," Modu said, as he picked up the spear and looked at the monster skewered there. "This will be a good meal."

Adama nodded, lay back on the mat and reached for the packet of seeds, which lay safely between her and where Modu had been lying.

The next day they cooked and ate the rodent. Modu had skinned and gutted it before he returned to sleep. He had strung it up over their heads above the sleeping mat where it could not be reached by another animal without stepping on them first. It was a gamble whether to entice a hyena into their house or to go without meat that they longed for. They built a little fire next to their mat inside the little house in order to keep the animals away. They took turns staying awake while the other slept in short naps. As soon as the sun rose they brought the fire outside and built it stronger in order to cook the rodent and have a feast for the first time. Only a few skinny birds had provided them meat; the rest had been coconut, mangoes and oranges. Not enough to provide them with the strength they needed to continue there in their little house.

CHAPTER 11

Staying for Awhile

"Would you like to walk with me through the path? You must be very quiet as we hunt."

"Yes. Let us go before the day becomes too hot," Adama said as she stood, brushing dust from her back. She was showing bones through flesh now. Her knees were like the knobs on bamboo.

The path led directly from the little back yard. Modu had cleared the back yard the day they had arrived. It was a narrow path lined by tall trees with limbs touching high above it. It was like a tunnel of quietness. Their bare feet fell silently and carefully as they crept along. Modu held his spear ready. Adama followed stepping into Modu's footprints precisely. Once Modu stopped abruptly, causing Adama to bumped into his back. Modu turned around, looking disturbed, he motioned for her to go. *Go back to the little house.* he scowled and pointed toward the house. Adama stood stark still, frozen, motionless. Modu turned back to his stealth-like creeping, never looking back to see if she was returning as he had commanded. Adama turned slowly and crept back toward the little house. Tears slid down her cheeks and she tried desperately not to sob. Owl watched her coming his way, and ruffled his great white feathers.

"You ran into Modu's back while he was trying to be quiet in his hunting. He did not like that, did he Adama Darboe?"

"Owl, sometimes you are not very kind to me. I did not intend to hit Modu's back. I am trying to be a grown up, and yet am only a girl. You say you are my guide, but sometimes I think you are my devil."

"Guides are not always what one wants them to be. I am trying to help you see that you two are destined to experience many circumstances that will be difficult in this life and in many others. I simply pointed out to you one of the less hurtful and dangerous actions you are and will be having, the two of you. Now, go back and wait for Modu Barrow to return to you, hopefully with something for the two of you to have for dinner. Go well, Adama Darboe," Owl spun his head around slowly, viewing his domain.

Adama left without saying a goodbye to Owl. Sometimes she was not happy having a guide. She wondered if her other friends had a guide. She didn't ever ask, and now she could not, because she was alone with only Modu, the boy she loved. She could definitely not ask Modu, because he never mentioned seeing Owl when they walked past him on their many strolls along the path. Times when she walked directly behind Modu she would see Owl sitting on his special limb so close by that one could nearly reach out and touch him.

CHAPTER 12

Four Weeks in the Little House-

The rains came and the seeds were planted. Row by row they were neatly planted at the edge of the field nearest the trail leading to the little house. The seeds sprung out of the red earth like hungry baby birds reaching for mothers beak where food hung. The seeds flourished in the rain and Adama tended them twice a day, weeding and cultivating them using a hand made hoe from a stone shaped like an arrow. Modu had found the stone one day while hunting for squirrels near a large mound of earth in the middle of the bush. He brought it home along with a stick strong enough to serve as a handle. Adama clapped her hands and danced toward him as he strutted down the path toward her. He passed the stone and stick to her and she grasped it to her breast. She said 'abarrake', meaning thank you. Then she proceeded to pull strands of bark from a dry tree trunk making string to wrap the stone onto the stick. It worked and served her well for the first two or three weeks of planting and weeding.

During those weeks they struggled to survive alone there in the little house, without their families and without much food. Adama and Modu lost much weight from their already skinny frames. They began to feel weak simply from daily activity. Modu hunted every day, and usually brought home a small bird, or rodent, or squirrel. After skinning, gutting, cleaning, and roasting it, there remained only a small portion of meat for the two of them. They lacked a pot to cook a sauce, so the meat and coconut was nearly all they had to eat. Now and then they found a ripe mango or citrus, but it made them ill if it was not ripe enough. This left them even more weak and hungry.

One day when the vegetables were nearly ready to harvest, Modu found an abandoned bucket. He thought it strange finding a bucket, though very rusty and with a few small pin holes in it, to be left by anyone in their right mind. There are many uses for a bucket. But, perhaps the original owner had become wealthy enough to leave this old bucket there in the bush. So, Modu brought the bucket home to Adama. Now they would bev able to cook a sauce using tomatoes, onions and some other vegetables they had growing in the garden. But, they had no rice, and they had no oil.

They sat on their mat looking at the bucket where it stood beside the pile of vegetables Adama had brought as the first harvest. They sat with their knees flexed against their bodies and their arms folded across them. They rested their chins on their folded arms. Tears flowed down Adama's hallow cheeks, but she didn't sob. Modu cast a sidelong look toward her crying eyes. He said nothing.

That night Adama became very hot, full of fever. Sweat poured from her body and she thrashed about, hitting Modu when he was near her. Then, in a few minutes she became very cold, and shivered madly into Modu's arms. He held her tightly as her teeth chattered. He felt her body heating rapidly. All night, Adama was full of fever, then freezing coldness took over. She was not conscious, nor was she sleeping. She called out and her eyes rolled back into her head. Modu clutched her tightly, and murmured softly into her ear, "There, there my girl. There, there."

By sunrise she fell asleep, having had frightening dreams, and crying out into the little house. Modu, all the time holding her and shushing her, murmuring, "Hush, Adama, people may hear you." But, Adama did not hear Modu.

She was in a different place.

All the next day Adama had a fever but slept soundly. Modu kept forcing her to drink as much as he could pour into her mouth. The following night her body was full of heat and cold, heat and cold. She dreamed of creatures coming into their little house and eating both of them.

On the third day Adama woke with a cool body and eyes which could focus and see clearly. She looked at Modu as he entered the room. He had stepped out into the back of the house to stretch his tired body, to look at the sun rising, and to think. What was he to do with his sick girl? What if she did not survive? Even though they were both taught not to think such negative thoughts, he could not help it.

He looked down upon her where she lay, weak and thin and barely able to move, but a least the fever had broken. He smiled. "You are here." he said.

She beamed a tiny smile and reached her arm to him, and he took it, and sat beside her. "You have been very, very ill, Adama Darboe."

"I know. I am better now, but I don't think I can sit up. I am not strong, Modu Barrow. I am not well enough to do anything. What shall we do?" Her eyes where pools of yellow and brown. Water caressed them. Her full mouth had cracks from the dryness of her illness. Her sunken cheeks used to be full and shiny. Now, they were not.

He was very quiet for some time. He stroked her arm and her face. He sighed, and lay beside her. "I too am weak, Adama Darboe. It is not easy, what we are trying to do. And it is too late to try to get to Gunjuir. We are too weak to walk there. I think we must go home and face our families. They will be very angry with us, and will punish us severely. But we have no choice."

Adama turned her head away from Modu. She did not like what she heard coming from his mouth. She knew however he was telling her the truth. She also knew that if they were able to get home they would be punished in many ways by their families, and the whole village for some time. But, then they would eventually be forgiven by everyone. The thing she did not even want to think about was that Modu would be marrying Mimuna. Her tears returned, crashing into her tired, sick head. But she nodded yes as she turned her head back toward Modu who had continued to stroke her arm. She rested her head on his shoulder for some time.

****

"We will sleep here, tonight. Tomorrow we will go to the road and begin our journey back home. Perhaps someone will let us ride on their wagon. And we can ask for food from the people on the way." Modu said this to Adama as he prepared to go to the bush and hunt. It was the second morning since Adama's fever had left her. She was still weak and hungry. She nodded her head in response to Modu's words. He stopped at the doorway and looked down at her where she sat on the inside matt.

"Will you be all right?

She nodded, hanging her head, yet peeking over at Modu as he prepared to leave.

"Your are sad," he said.

"I will be all right. Come back to me," she whispered as he stepped out the door.

He nodded quickly and moved on toward the path.

She stayed there on the mat for what seemed a long time. Then she went to the well and pulled water using all her energy. She rinsed her body and her skirt and blouse, letting them dry while still on her body. The heat was intense and it didn't take long for the ragged clothes to dry.

She wandered down the path toward her garden. Also, toward Owl. She wanted to see Owl.

He sat on the same branch where she always found him. He ruffled his beautiful white feathers, and settled them into his impressive body.

"You have been absent from this lane, Adama Darboe. What kept you from your garden and from our visits?"

"I have been very sick, Owl. I am hardly able to walk this far from the little house. I came to seek your advice, Owl."

"What is your question?" Owl asked as he watched Adama sit on the path.

"I must rest," she said as she folded her legs under herself, and hung her head.

"You are still ill," Owl said.

"Owl, Modu says we must return to our village and our parents. He says we cannot survive completely alone without help from others.

He says we are too weak to stay here or to carry on to another place as we had planned in the beginning."

"And what do you want from me? Are you asking my advice concerning the return to your village?" Owl sounded stern.

"Yes. I am afraid to return to our parents. The punishment will be very severe. The village people will shun us and we will be like outcasts for some time. I will not be able to see Modu. His family will quickly arrange the wedding to Mimuna, and my life will end."

Adama was exhausted having quickly recited all of her most fearful thoughts to Owl.

"Tell me, Adama Darboe, what has this experience taught you? Why did you urge Modu to run away with you? How well did you think about the whole adventure? What have you gained from this? Did I warn you about this plan?"

"You ask too many questions at one time, Owl. I am too tired to even remember them all. I know Modu is becoming tired of the burden I have become. I know he loves me and I will always love him. I know I am most responsible for the misadventure. I want to go home to my mother, Binta Darboe. She will protect me after she has punished me. I know that. But, Owl, will I lose Modu forever? I cannot bear to think that!"

"Remember what I told you some time ago? You will live many lives and in those lives you will lose Modu, and you will regain Modu, and he will be in several places with you in your many lives. I cannot tell you about this very life you are living now. You must continue it by having faith in yourself."

Adama pulled herself up from where she lay on the path using nearly all her strength and turned toward the little house. She did not speak to Owl. She turned her back on Owl. She could not bear to hear any more of his truths. She heard Owl sigh as she continued down the path.

CHAPTER 13

The Long Walk Home

They woke as the sun rose. They lay on their backs not speaking. Looking up through the straw roof, neither of them wanted to take on the day. They both wanted to stay in that place, in that position, forever. They wanted their bellies to be full, and the shade to protect them from the sun, and for the people to be there with them but not bothering them. Just there. Assuring them they were all right. Not to worry.

Modu drew in a deep, rasping breath. It filled his lungs, and stayed there in his chest for a few seconds, and then he slowly released it. Rolling over onto his side facing the room, his back toward Adama, he stood quickly and stretched, groaned and walked outside.

Adama lay with her eyes still on the straw roof, hardly blinking. She did not even react to Modu's sigh and moving out of the room. Their lives were about to change in scary ways. She could not grasp it all. All she knew was she was going home to Binta Darboe, and she was losing Modu Barrow, the boy she loved. With all her heart.

****

Noah Camara was heading back to Jambanjelly from his first overnight visit at the Cessay compound. It was mid-morning as he passed Jambu, half way between Gunjuir and Jambanjelly. By now the people in Jambu who knew Noah Camara were aware of his frequent visits to Gunjuir.

Now that he had had the conversation with Amie's father, Momadou Cessay about his feelings for Amie, it was safe for him to travel up and down, as well as visit overnight in that compound. He slept in the 'strangers' house where visitors slept when visiting.

As he passed Jambur, and left it behind, he was thinking about his garden that he must water this day. He looked at the road up ahead and saw two figures walking very slowly toward Jambanjelly. They appeared to be young adults, a boy and a girl. They looked as if walking was not something they were comfortable doing. They looked a bit ragged and unkempt. In fact they looked thin and weak. Noah nearly fell off the seat of the wagon when he finally realized he was looking at Modu Barrow and Adama Darboe. He could not believe his eyes. His heart started thumping wildly and energy came upon him. He snapped his whip at the horse, and yelled for it to speed up. The horse reared and started to trot at a faster pace.

Adama and Modu turned to see who was coming.

"It is Noah Camara, Adama," Modu held Adama against him. She was having a difficult time walking. She had become faint two times since they had begun their journey toward home. They had no food or water with them. The sun beat mercilessly on their uncovered heads. Now, they stood by the side of the dirt road watching Noah drive the horse toward them. They stood there looking and feeling dejected.

Noah pulled up directly in front of the two. He looked down at them and felt like laughing for glee, and crying from relief, but most of all he felt like taking the whip and laying it on each of them. He did none of these things, instead he stepped down from the wagon, extended his hand, and greeted them both briefly. He then took Adama in his arms and lifted her onto the wagon. He laid her on the boards of the wagon. He reached around to Modu and pushed him up to sit beside her. He said nothing more. He simply passed them two oranges which Amie had given him for his trip back to Jambanjelly, and they received them gently. They sucked the juice from the oranges and remained quiet and relieved and fearful of what was about to come.

As Noah approached the outskirts of Jambanjelly, he turned his head toward them.

"I will take the back road into the village and enter the corner where your family compounds stand. You both will wait while I enter the compounds, find your parents, and bring them to you. Do you understand?"

They nodded their heads in unison. Shivering slightly Adama reached for Modu's hand. He sat close to her where she lay. He looked down on her and smiled a tender smile. He took her hand and held it.

Noah stepped down from the wagon seat and disappeared into the Darboe compound.

"I am losing you, Modu. My heart is breaking. Will you ever forgive me for bringing this on the two of us?"

"It will always be in my heart. This time we have been together. I will be here across the way. We will see each other. I promise," he whispered to her. They heard voices coming close by, muted voices. And then both Ebrima Darboe and Binta Darboe appeared from around the fence. Binta began to wail and she reached her huge arms over the wooden side board of the wagon and grabbed her daughter and tried to pull her out of the wagon, clutching, pulling, crying, tapping her back in pretend beating. Ebrima stood as if he had been struck dumb. Motionless, he stood directly behind Binta and watched her scramble and flutter and cry and pretend to beat her daughter. Finally, he stepped between Binta and his daughter. He lifted her from the cart and began to turn toward the back door of the compound. He looked at Modu with a fierce scowl and said, "Go home."

Modu started to move, but Noah shook his head, and said, "Ebrima take your daughter to your rooms. I will take this boy to his compound."

Ebrima made a low grunt in his throat and walked toward the back fence door. Binta clung to Adama, crying and laughing and saying through the tears and weeping, "I will have to beat you, you know, Adama Darboe."

Adama looked through her tears and reached her skinny arm to her mother's face. Ebrima looking forward, gritted his teeth, and marched into Binta Darboe's rooms. He bent down on one knee and rolled

Adama onto one of the beds. While still there on his knee he said a brief prayer of thanks to Allah for returning his headstrong, sick, skinny, bad girl.

****

Noah motioned for Modu to sit next to him on the wagon seat. Modu sat as tall as his tired, weak body would allow.

"You will do the same as we did at the Darboe compound. We will swing around to the back of your compound and you will wait until I return with you parents. Do you hear?"

"I hear," He whispered, as he watched Noah step off the wagon and disappear around the corner into the compound. He sat there bewildered. He was tired and weak and surprised at himself for having taken this journey. How on earth did he ever come to this? He knew he was in big trouble, and his life would never be the same. He would miss that stupid little house and the path that led to the open field, and most of all, he would miss Adama.

Noah was the first to appear around the corner of the fence, then Fatou Jammeh, mother of Modu, peeked around the fence showing only her questioning face. Eyes wide, and wrinkled forehead showed first. Her eyes locked onto Modu's face and she fell to her knees and burst into tears. Ningma Jammeh, Modu's sister, and one of Adama's best friends fell upon her mother and hugged her back. She looked up at Modu sitting there in the wagon. Modu tried to climb down from the seat of the wagon, and he felt as if he had a weight tied around his waist. He struggled to stand and step down. He nearly fell off the wagon and with great effort he walked toward his weeping mother and sister. They both reached for him and covered him with their tears and their hands and with kisses and their wailing and their laughter. Now, Ousman, father of Modu, appeared and stopped in his tracks at what her was seeing. His son was being consumed by the mother and sister. Ousman took cautious steps toward the three of them and pulled the group apart one from the other. The women held their arms out, reaching for Modu. Ousman placed one hand around the skinny upper arm of his son and led him into the compound. With very little said, Ousman marched him into his house and pulled the curtain across the door.

Fatou stood outside the drawn curtain of Ousman's room, and called, "Do not hurt that boy. He is weak and ill. Do you hear me, Ousman Barrow?!"

"Leave, Fatou. Go to your work. I will take care of this boy," Ousman's deep voice carried through the cloth curtain and into Fatou's ears. She turned, still weeping and went to her work.

****

By now the village is alerted. When the women began to wail it is heard at least in the next few compounds. Then, people peek around the corners and see Noah with his wagon, and the women of the compounds where the two young ones had been missing for some time are wailing. It does not take too long to figure out what has happened. So, everyone comes to see what is taking place. The fathers of the two compounds stand guard of their place and sit with those who come to inquire about the children returning. They are assured the young ones are alive and not injured. The crowds are informed Modu and Adama are not ready to see anyone and may not be for a few days. The people remain for a short time in the two compounds, then return to their own chores, anxious to hear the story of Modu and Adama.

CHAPTER 14

Two Months Returned

They rested in their respective compounds. They slept in their respective beds with their siblings. They ate in their respective compounds with their families. They gained strength and weight and muscles.

Eventually Adama was allowed to go to the garden with her mother, Binta Darboe. And, eventually Modu was allowed to leave the compound with his father to the farm where the cassava was nearly ready to harvest and take to the market.

Their vues were allowed to come and sit with them in their respective compounds. But, the two, Adama and Modu were not allowed to go outside their compounds for two weeks. However, Mimuna was summoned to come visit the Barrow compound a few days after the missing two had returned home.

Mimuna sat on the bantaba with Ningma, sister of Modu, and sometimes Modu could be seen sitting with her on the bantaba, which was visible to the Darboe compound. Adama did not look across the way when she knew Mimuna was there visiting.

Adama was trying to mend her heart. She counted the blessings she had. Her sisters and brothers, her mother and father. Her vue. Food. Shelter. Everything she could conjure up in her mending heart that she could be thankful for. She did a great deal of praying to Allah during that time when she returned to her village.

That second day after Adama had arrived, her mother stepped into Adama's room with a switch from the bush. Adama had slept for twenty four hours, nonstop. She awoke when she heard her mother move the curtain aside from the door and step into the room.

Adama gasped and rubbed the sleep from her eyes. She pulled the bed cover over her head and began to cry when she saw the switch in her mother's hand. Binta pulled the cover from her daughter and rolled Adama over onto her stomach and switched her bottom and back several severe cracks. Adama wailed. Binta switched again and again while Adama cried loudly. And then it was over.

Binta bent down and spoke in a low, severe voice into her daughter's ear. "Now, you will never do such a stupid thing again. Now, you will grow and obey the elders of this compound and village. You did a callous and dangerous thing. Never again! Ya Moi?!"

In a quivering tiny voice Adama replied, "N Moi," I hear.

****

Modu's punishment was much more severe. His father and two of the elders, part of Ousman's vue, took Modu to the bush and severely beat him with whips made to use on the donkeys. He came home bleeding with gashes on his back, which his mother healed using her ointments made from plants in the bush.

His father said only, "I did not raise you to go against my will. You know what you will do. You will marry Mimuna, and you will not ever go to be alone with Adama Darboe. Ya Moi?'

Modu, head hanging, being held up by the two men, in order to stand said, "N Moi." I hear.

****

Modu Barrow

I am trying to keep my mind on the things that I am expected to do each day, and not allow myself to think back to the days Adama

Darboe and I were living in the little house together. No matter how difficult a struggle it was for us, no matter how hungry and lonesome for our family and friends we were, I can only think of being together, she and I, in our little house. I think time will take some of that thought away from me. I do not see her at all. She is across the corridor from me, but may as well be many miles away. Our parents are determined that we will not see each other. Mimuna comes to our compound and I am polite to her. She is a good girl. She knows we will be married sometime in the future. Maybe sooner than expected because our families want it settled and done with. I do not want to rush into this marriage. I am not ready to be a husband. Unless it is to be the husband of Adama Darboe, I am not ready to be married.

****

Ousman Barrow entered Ebrima Darboe's compound one day about two months after Modu and Adama had returned to the village. The two men had been together on several occasions since the young ones returned, but this visit was for a special reason.

"Just in time for attire," Ebrima said. "Come, sit." The charcoal burner was beginning to show orange heat just beneath the black coals. A small bright blue Aladdin lamp-like tea pot sat on the coals, heating the tea.

"I have come to inform you of Modu's impending marriage. Because our two children were together for some time without their parents, I feel it is only fair that you are told of this upcoming occasion. We hold no fault on either of these two foolish young ones," he chuckled, as did Ousman. "But, I feel it is fair to inform you that by the next full moon Modu and Mimuna will be married and she will come to live in our compound."

"Good. That is as it should be. That is your family's plan. Thank you for informing me of this happy occasion. It will be a wonderful celebration, I'm sure."

Tea was sipped. Cigarettes were smoked. Other elders arrived and stories were told. Another day in the corridor of the Darboes and Barrows.

****

Adama Darboe

I walked to the Owl early this morning. I could not wait another day to talk with my spirit guide. Binta Darboe told me as we winnowed the rice while sitting on her verandah in the afternoon heat that Modu and Mimuna were to marry before the next full moon. She told me it was to be, and that I had known always, that it was to be. She told me I must not think about it, or be sad about it, or be angry about it. She told me it was the way it was, and to accept it. It was the will of Allah. Binta said all of this in a steady, low, firm, loving voice. I winnowed rice very rapidly as she told me.

Binta looked sidelong down at me and said, "Ya Moi?" Do you hear?

I replied in a quiet, yet shaking voice, "N Moi" I hear.

We spoke no more. Once the rice was all winnowed, Binta heaved her big body up and went to her room for rest time. I crept into our girls room and curled into a ball, trying desperately not to cry. I did not want to spend my life crying. I wanted to stop it somehow. I did not go to Owl because I was afraid he would tell me what I already knew. Therefore, I waited for two more weeks before I went to him.

Two weeks later

One day Mimuna and her brother brought a wagon full of her possessions to Modu's compound. That day Mimuna moved into the Barrow compound. This was the beginning of the wedding event. It would be a few days of such events before the wedding was finalized.

I went to Owl on that day when the wagon passed our Darboe compound gate. It was full of pots and pans and a bed and boxes of material and her clothes. I saw it all. I felt it in the middle of my stomach. I ran to Owl.

"I am surprised you took all this time, Adama Darboe, to come to me. What have you to say?" Owl stretched and ruffled his feathers.

"Mimuna is moving into Modu's compound today. The wagon filled with her possessions passed our compound this morning. Mimuna was on the wagon, also. I am trying to be calm about this, Owl, but I have other worries that are stronger than this wedding."

"I know, Adama Darboe, and what are you going to do about that?"

"You know?" I was stunned. I stared at Owl with wide eyes and gaping mouth.

"Yes, I know. There is nothing I do not know about you, Adama Darboe."

I was not sure Owl was speaking of the same thing I was, so I waited a moment. Then I said, "What do you know about me? Is it the same thing I am worrying about? Tell me Owl, please."

Owl looked at me and said, "There is a new life growing within you, Adama Darboe, and that is what you have come to talk about. Am I not correct?"

I collapsed onto the path and did not move or cry. I was not certain that a baby was there inside me, because I was afraid to speak of it to anyone. I knew it was time for me to be bleeding two times without it happening, and I knew from the time we were in the bush learning about being a woman, we had been taught about the bleeding and the baby's coming. If we did not bleed that was the way we could tell after a few months a baby would be coming in a few big moons.

And now Owl, my spirit guide, has said it: *There is a new life growing within you. Son of Modu Barrow. How could I get up from this path and continue on? Return to the compound and pretend nothing was wrong?*

Owl spoke again. "You will go back to your compound and wait. I cannot tell you what you are waiting for beyond what you already know. This is all a continuation of your life, your growing, your being brave. This is your life, Adama Darboe."

"Owl, sometimes I am not sure why you have chosen me to guide. It is a mystery to me. What am I to do with Modu's baby inside my stomach and he is marrying Mimuna very soon? What am I to do? I am in enough trouble with the people of my compound and the village. I will be in total disgrace with everyone, including Allah. I will be cast away. What will become of the baby?"

"I have told you to go home to your compound, and wait. You will know what to do when it is time," Owl sounded more stern than usual.

"But, my mother must be told. I must tell my Binta Darboe. She has always helped me when I am in trouble. Can I not tell Binta Darboe?"

"I see you sharing this news with Binta Darboe, but you must wait until Modu Barrow is married to Mimuna. That will be very soon. You will tell Binta Darboe when the final celebration has been executed."

"Oh, I wish I was dead! Why am I alive and having to deal with all these awful problems? I want to die, Owl. Please help me!"

"You are acting like a weak girl. You are not a weak girl. You are to walk away from this place. Go home and do as you are told. Then, next week you may tell Binta Darboe of your problem. She will help you. Now go!" said Owl.

Adama turned around abruptly and ran as fast as her skinny legs would carry her. She sobbed as she flew over the path. Tears ran down her lovely cheeks and onto her neck. She ran until she reached the corridor where her compound sat. She stopped there, wiped her face using the hem of her skirt, sniffed, and wiped her eyes. She entered the compound and went directly to her room, hoping no one had seen her.

CHAPTER 15

The Wedding

The morning arrived with a hint of the day's heat. A hazy mist swept through the forest surrounding the village. A greenish yellow light cast a mystical hue. Cocks crowed, donkeys brayed, and Adama rolled over facing the whitewashed wall of the girls' bedroom. Her sister Mariama poked her in the back and said, "Get up. It's your turn to carry the water and bring the fire to flames."

Adama did not answer.

Mariama poked her sister once more. She shook her shoulder gently. Adama did not move.

"I know you do not want this day to arrive. But it has and it is here, and you will have to do your chores and attend the wedding."

Mariama rolled over and fell back to sleep. Mariama was tired of her sister, Adama, getting all the attention and always in some sort of turmoil. Mariama loved her older sister, but she seemed to be continually causing problems in their compound and village.

Moving the curtain at the door, Binta Darboe stuck her head into the girls' bedroom. In a low, hushed voice, she said, "Adama Darboe, get up and come to help with the breakfast. I do not want a problem with you today. There is a celebration taking place across the way, and you know it. You will join our family in attending the celebration and you will not cause a problem. Now, get up and go fetch the water for the cooking. Now!"

Binta Darboe pushed the curtain across the door and marched back to her place by the coals from last night's fire. It needed prodding and more wood to start a good flame in order to warm the left over rice.

****

One of the first steps into the marriage took place in Mimuna's family compound a week after Modu had returned to his village. Ousman's brother, Landing, uncle to Modu, had traveled to the village of Chief Conteh, Mimuna's father. He carried with him a small satchel full of kola nuts. These kola nuts were the traditional item presented to the father of the future bride, should it be agreed upon. It had been agreed upon many years ago that Mimuna and Modu would marry. Now, this next step into the process was to present the kola nuts to the father. After that in a matter of weeks or months the ceremony would take place, usually at the family compound of the boy.

****

By midafternoon people began to pass the Darboe compound at a steady pace. Two teenage boys ambled by, one dressed in a bright blue caftan and one in green that matched the sea when a storm is about to come. Then several younger boys straggled along in a cluster wearing bright shades of orange, yellow, green, blue, and muted red like a garden full of flowers, rarely seen in this part of the world. Not enough water to nourish anything that cannot be eaten; but, these boys, these with their bare feet and clean caftans and shaved heads were beautiful enough to be a garden full of flowers.

Old women with head wraps matching their grand dendikos and fannos carried huge pots full of rice and sauce on top of their head wraps, tottering to the wedding.

The teenage girls flittered along the corridor, chattering, bouncing, showing off their eyes by using charcoal from coals of the fire. Black eyebrows even blacker with black shadows dusted along the eyelid. Smoldering beauty on the young girls. They had made red dye from the roots of the plants in the bush for their pouting lips, and their naturally lovely faces peeked through it all. They knew their turn was coming soon. They would have the chance to have a special day. A wedding, some good food, and music to dance by. It would be their day. The only other time in their lives to be the center of attention would be the day their baby received his or her name. A Koolio. A naming ceremony. Then she would have a new dress, and the day would be centered around her and her baby. There would be music, much rice, and gifts of money from the villagers. The rest of their lives would be full of work. Not much other than that. But, ah, the day of her wedding was to be very exciting and special!

The gate to the Barrow compound was wide open and during the late morning into the afternoon the whole village passed through it. People mingled. Some sat on benches, which were borrowed from the compounds surrounding the Barrow compound. They were placed around the front of the houses that faced the center of the yard where the celebration would occur. Women were pounding rice at the back of the wives house, in the kitchen area. Cooking took place there when plenty of room was needed for the preparation of special celebrations. The vue of Modu's mother had brought their pestles and mortars for pounding of the rice. A goat was to be slaughtered very soon in the center of the yard where folks were sitting, waiting. A blessing would be said by the Imam offering a prayer of thanks to Allah for this feast about to be received.

The compound became very still as Modu's father led the goat out in the center of the yard. It was white with large splotches of black covering its back. Two members of Ousman's vue accompanied him as he led the goat into the yard. After Ousman had lifted the goat and pushed it onto its side, one of the men passed Ousman a long knife. The goat thrashed a short time and then laid its head onto the hard earth and did not try to move. Ousman took the large knife and made a clean sweeping cut across the goat's throat. Blood seeped out from its neck, running over and into the earth. The goat's life drained from it, and it became motionless; dead. Those gathered smiled and prayed in low voices. The goat would be cooked in a sauce of tomatoes, onions, hot peppers, and rice.

****

Mimuna, the girl about to marry Modu, spent the morning and into the afternoon out of sight with the sisters and cousins of the compound. They lay on the beds in the girls room and chatted. They ran errands for the adults; *Go to the market and fetch a cube of magi and a spoonful of tomato paste. Go to Njie compound and get the biggest pot they have, we need one more. Go to the mosque and find your father. He should at least be in this compound.*

The girls ran the errands and talked and giggled and inspected their new dresses just collected from the tailor in Brikama, late the day before.

Modu and his vue walked with their spears into the bush that morning. They didn't speak of the festival about to take place that very afternoon. No mention of Modu's marriage ceremony about to be completed was even mentioned. They joked about simple things, like someone burped at prayer time in the mosque and was ushered out by his father. How angry the father was and how embarrassed the boy, Abduli, was. They imitated the burp, and laughed at how silly he looked when his father yanked him out of the mosque by his ear. They speared a big fish and said how great it would be in the rice. They didn't mention how great it would be in the rice for the wedding. No mention of the wedding. The boys continued their life as if it were another day in the village.

By midafternoon Modu's vue appeared dressed in great finery. Beautiful caftans of colorful, embossed material covered their bodies shoulder to toe. Six of them entered the compound looking as if they owned the village, let alone the compound. Proud, looking a bit pompous, grown boys about to lose one of their vue to marriage. Unless they could ignore it for awhile. Pretend it's just another celebration of some sort. Not a marriage. Yet, it was, and they knew it.

The drummers came and the women danced during the last part of the day. The boys and men watched them and spoke among themselves, and ate the rice when it was brought out in huge iron vessels. Several pots were placed in front of the men where they sat in clusters. Five or six men sat around each bowl eating the fine meal. The boys waited until the men were nearly finished and were beckoned to join them at the bowl. They raced like little rabbits running from the village dogs. All of them squeezing between the men for their turn at the bowl.

Modu and his vue ate at the far end of the veranda of his father's house

The girls including Mimuna were the last to eat along with the women.

Dusk found some of the people leaving for their homes. The boys went out of the compound to a dance taking place on the other side of the village. A Koolio was happening and some special drumming was taking place. The drummers at the Barrows compound finalized their music just before dark and the women were finished with their dancing. They needed to carry water for the cleaning up, to wash the pots and pans for the next morning. The children were falling asleep on benches and floors. They needed to be carried into their beds or back to their compounds.

****

Mimuna waited for Modu in his room, which was now their room. Fatou, mother of Modu, carried a kerosene lamp into the room as she led Mimuna there.

"Ousman has gone to collect Modu. He will be here soon. You will be alright until he comes? Your clothes are here. There is plenty of water in the jardinière in your bathing area. You must be very tired. We are happy you have come to live with us. I want you to feel as if I am your second mother."

****

Adama went to the wedding with her sister Mariama. She went just in time to watch the girls and women dance. She did not see Modu. She danced one short dance because her vue pulled her into the middle of the group and insisted she dance with them. Adama felt the music rising in her arms and legs. She moved with the other girls and women, stepping in and out of the cluster in the center of the circle. She began to forget who she was and where she was. She danced the frenzied, wild dance of the Mandinka tribe. Arms flung out on both sides, bending forward, stamping feet, moving wildly. She felt like she once was as a little girl coming to a celebration of joy and excitement. Then she looked up into the face Mimuna dancing there beside her. Adama didn't realize Mimuna was dancing. She stumbled, caught herself, and picked up the beat in an instant. She eased herself from the center, gradually to the outer sphere of the circle, and stepped out of the circle.

She slid out of the dim, unlit compound. She quietly eased herself through the compound gate and ran across the road to her empty compound. She ran into the girls bedroom, fell onto her bed, and sobbed racking heartbreaking tears.

CHAPTER 16

Another Problem for the Darboe Compound

Adama walked toward the room where her mother Binta rested. She feared what she must say. Her young hands clenched in fists. Her shoulders hunched as if she was about to pull her head into them, like a turtle does when afraid. Tuck it in like a turtle hiding from its prey. She had to do this now. She had to tell her mother about her problem. She did not know what else to do. She could no longer think of running. She had done that once very recently and it had brought her to this. It had brought her to losing Modu, the boy she loves, and to bearing his child. Running was not an option.

"Binta," Adama whispered into the curtain hanging at the doorway.

"Hmmm?" Binta rasped out a snore as she turned her big body toward the doorway. "What?"

"I need to talk with you, alone, Binta. I am coming in."

"I am trying to rest, child. Come later. I am very tired."

"Please, mother. I am needing to tell you something while you are alone, and you are not often alone. Please, may I speak with you now?" Adama was stepping into the dimly lit room. Her mother rubbed her eyes and continued lying on the mattress filled with hay from the open field.

Adama tiptoed quickly across the hard packed dirt floor and crept up onto the bed beside Binta. Her legs hung, feet not touching the floor. The iron bed was high off the floor. She folded her hands in her lap and stared into them. Pulling in a deep breath she held it there for awhile before releasing it.

"I am in trouble, Binta Darboe. I don't know what to say about it."

"Child, you have already said it. You are in trouble. Do you expect me to guess what your trouble is? I do not have time to play games about your trouble. Your next words will be telling me what troubles you. Ya Moi!?"

"N Moi," she replied. "I have not seen my blood coming for two moons and I am afraid of what that means. I fear a seed has been planted in me and my blood is helping the seed to grow." She slid off the bed and lay on the dirt floor beside Binta's bed. Covering her head with her arms, she held her breath, waiting. Cringing, she waited for a reply from Binta.

Binta heaved her body to the edge of the bed, reached down where her fractious daughter lay, and pulled her up by one arm to the point of looking this girl in her wet, weeping face.

Binta spoke in the voice Adama feared the most. Low, quiet, deep rumbles.

"Once again you have managed to disgrace us. I have lost my patience with you. You are a bad seed. You have not made us proud once since your sister died. She is gone and you are here, and you do nothing but give us worries and shame," Binta released Adama's arm which left her falling rapidly to the ground. She smacked the earthen floor and once more covered her head.

Binta stood, looked around the room, marched to the back door where the fenced in wash and toilet area stood. She poured a bucketful of water over her head. She shook her head and grabbed a fanno (skirt) hanging from the fence. She covered her massive body with the cloth and marched back into her room.

"Are you still here?!" she asked the fallen child who had not moved an inch since Binta had left the room. "I don't want to see you in this room, or any other place for the remainder of this day. Leave me, *now*." she whispered in her most menacingly low voice.

Adama crept back to her room and curled into a fetal ball, hardly breathing.

Binta slammed pots, barked orders to every child and adult who was within her sight, and left everyone in the compound wondering what was causing Binta to be so unlike her usual kind, caring self.

The next day Ebrima came to the fireside where Binta sat in her usual place of cooking. He sat beside her. She did not even cast a sidelong look at him. He crossed his long legs, stared into the fresh fire and cleared his throat. "We seem to be alone for a short time. Do you wish to tell me what is causing you to be so worried?"

"I know I must do that. But, I do not know how to tell you this news. It frightens me to tell you."

"What could be so bad that you could not share it with me, your husband?" Ebrima asked.

"We must speak of this tonight when I come to you. It is too serious to talk about here when others may at any moment walk through the gates. Please be willing to wait just until tonight, Ebrima. It is a very big problem."

Ebrima sighed, took his pipe from his mouth, and tapped in on the side of the log where they sat. "All right I will wait until then. I'm sure it concerns Adama because I have only seen her once today, and she looks very unhappy."

Binta shrugged and did not reply.

That night Binta anxiously entered the house of her husband, Ebrima Darboe. It took a great deal to make Binta Darboe anxious, but she dreaded what she must discuss with him. Binta found Ebrima already in his bed with a cigarette between his fingers, and an arm behind his head, as he looked toward the door.

Binta sat on her side of the bed. She wore her loose sleeping gown. Blue with green swirls of batik material. Her body was round and full. She looked into the floor, not showing her face to Ebrima.

"Well?" Ebrima said.

"I do not know how to begin this," Binta sighed

"Say what you have to say. We can not discuss it until you say it, Binta Darboe."

"I know. It is what took place while Adama and Modu were together those weeks.," she ducked her head into her chest.

Ebrima lay smoking quietly. He looked at the ceiling. He delayed reacting. He did not trust himself to say the next thing. Finally he looked at Binta's back and said, "Are you telling me that Adama is with child?"

"She says it has been two moons since she has seen her blood.," Binta whispered.

"And Modu is married. Just last week Modu has become a husband," Ebrima sounded stunned, at a loss. "Why did Adama not tell us before the wedding took place?"

"I do not know. Would it have made a difference? Would you have expected Ousman to cancel the wedding of his son if this had been revealed to him earlier?" Binta wisely inquired.

"Probably not," Ebrima said. "And now we have a daughter without a husband and a baby coming within six or seven moons. I must think for a day or two before I can decide what we should do. You must also think about this. Adama will be in disgrace, as we will be, if she has this baby without a husband. It cannot and will not happen here in this village. You know that, Binta Darboe. We must think about what can be done. In the meantime you must punish your daughter for disobeying, once again. What has made this child so unruly I will never understand. Although she is one of my favorite children, I do not understand her."

Binta lay carefully beside Ebrima, facing the wall, with her back toward Ebrima. Ebrima patted her shoulder and rolled over facing out toward the living space of his room. The sounds of sleep filled the room within a short time. Sleep rests the mind.

****

Two days after Binta and Ebrima has talked about the problem of Adama Darboe, Binta came to Ebrima during midday resting time. She entered his room after a quiet knock outside his door. He said, "Yes?"

Binta replied "I want to talk with you now."

"Come." Ebrima lay shirtless on his bed. The heat of the day was heavy and exhausting. His chest shown wet with sweat.

"I have a plan that may work for everyone," Binta said as she sat on the only wooden bench in the room. Back resting against the whitewashed wall.

"I'm listening.," Ebrima murmured.

"I know you are still going to Haddy Touray's compound and visiting her. I know she wants you to come to be with her, and she still misses this compound very much. I know you are not ready to be finished with her, but not ready to decide what to do about her. The reason I am saying this is because Haddy Touray and Adama Darboe have always been close to one another, and Haddy has never had a child and if Haddy's family allowed Adama to stay with them while she has this child, it may work out well."

"And then what?" Ebrima inquired. "Then, when this child is born without a father, what is to become of it and Adama?"

"I have had a few thoughts about that, also. None of them are complete, but there are possibilities. What if Haddy takes the child and brings it up as her own? What if you allow Haddy to return to this compound once the child is born and people will think it belongs to the two of you? After all, people know you go to her and stay with her in her room. Adama will stay out of sight as much as possible while living there in that compound, and people do not need to know she is with child; she can hide that with loose cloths. And, Haddy looks pregnant all the time. She is a big bellied woman.," Binta chuckled at her own words. Ebrima smiled.

"What excuse would we use by sending Adama to the Touray compound in Haddy's village?" Ebrima wondered allowed.

"We need say nothing more than she has gone to visit Haddy, and help her with her garden."

A silence settled between them.

"I will think on this for a day or two. Then we can talk once again," Ebrima looked directly into Binta Darboe's eyes, which is not often done between man and woman. Only when there is a deep, lengthy affection, one for the other. Binta lowered her eyes first, turned, and left Ebrima's room.

****

Three days passed. Adama was quiet and in her room most of that time. She came out only to do her chores and run the errands directed by Binta. Only once she had gone quietly in the early morning to see Owl. The sun was rising, casting misty colors through the forest.

"You are very early, Adama Darboe. What brings you here at such a time?" Owl seemed to Adama to be even larger than the last time she had seen him some days ago. The rising sun created a halo around his pure white feathers, shining like brilliant gold. Adama shielded her eyes from the radiant light.

"My parents are planning my future and I am very fearful of what that may be. You seem to know everything about my life and future, Owl. Can you help me with this? Can you tell me what is to become of me and the baby inside me?" Adama squatted on the path in front of Owl, head resting in her hands, she looked down into the earth before her.

"Look at me, Adama Darboe. You must know by now I will not direct you or tell you what will be your future. You are to learn and experience that as you go through this and other lives. I will be here to listen and give thoughts to you, but I will not tell you what is your future."

"What can my parents do about this child within me? Already Binta has beaten me. Not too hurtful, and I knew that must happen. Now, the next decision is unknown to me. What can they do!?"

"How are you feeling about this child you carry?" Owl asked.

Adama was surprised at the question and realized she had not thought of it as a real living child within her. She had not allowed herself to think of it as a baby with arms and legs and needs. She squatted there, nearly stunned at the question. She now realized she must think about this living being inside herself. Until now it had been something causing her the lack of her monthly bleeding, a problem and a scary situation.

"How do I feel about this child? I do not know how I feel about it. It is here in my belly and will continue to grow and will someday, a few moons away come out of me, and I will be even more in trouble than I am now."

Owl frowned, "So you cherish this child within you?"

"Cherish? How can I cherish something I have not seen and do not know?"

"Then, I guess your answer is *no*," Owl said.

"I did not say that, Owl. Sometimes I feel as though you are tricking me with your questions."

"So, now you are beginning to understand, I hope, why I am your spirit guide. I ask questions to help you on your journey. Questions that are difficult, but necessary to think about and to learn from, and eventually answer."

"I can only wait and see. I want to see Modu Barrow, the boy I love. I long to see him, Owl. Please tell me it is alright if I follow him to the ground nut field when he is there weeding. I want him to know he has planted a seed in me."

"Adama Darboe, you have not been listening to me, I fear. What have I just finished telling you about your spirit guide?" Owl ruffled his beautiful pure white feathers until they made the noise of leaves rustling.

"That you lead me to learn from my mistakes. That you do not tell me of my future or what I should do or should not do. I am going home. "Goodbye, Owl," she stood and whirled around heading down the magic path toward home.

CHAPTER 17

Adama Marries a Stranger

Adama sat on the bed between Binta and Ebrima one evening during the rainy season. She shivered, yet it was not a cold day. Her body was cold with anxiety.

Ebrima cleared his throat and started to speak. "Adama," he said in a low serious voice, "You know that you are unable to stay in Jambanjelly because of your situation, do you not?"

Adama ducked her head further into her chest.

"Therefore we are taking you to Haddy Touray's compound in Sukita. You will live with her and the people of her compound. There is a plan beginning to form in our minds about what is to become of you in the future, but for now you will go to Haddy Touray."

Adama was stunned. Although she had no idea what her parents planned to do with her and the child within her, going to Haddy Touray's compound was not one of the possibilities. Tears began to roll down her cheeks. She sobbed in quick gasps. She said nothing. Silence was in that room. No one seemed to know what to say next. In a few minutes Binta drew in a breath and said, "Haddy will be good to you, you know."

"How long must I stay?" she asked in a quivering voice.

"We cannot say, because we have not, as yet, decided," her father spoke firmly with a sadness around the edges.

****

Several days preceding this meeting with Adama, Ebrima had traveled to Sukita to visit Haddy. Recently he had been going to be with Haddy on a weekly basis. Their relationship had rekindled, although it had never really died. Haddy was feeling much conflict about her love for Ebrima and also her strong affection toward this woman, Tida. She tried not to think about it, yet it burned within her when she and Tida were together in the fields working. Singing and dancing, and eventually sleeping together in the women's room. Touching one another in places that only men were allowed to touch. She tried not to think about it.

On this particular day when Ebrima came to visit Haddy she came toward him clapping her hands and smiling a broad, joyful smile. Ebrima tried not to look too pleased, but he found it difficult. After all, Haddy was his youngest, and favorite wife. Not counting Binta, of course. She was his oldest, yet the strongest and wisest of them all.

"You have come! That is good! Welcome!" Haddy led him to her father's rooms, and left the two men sitting on the veranda.

"I will be speaking with your father for some time, Haddy. Please allow us to be alone for awhile."

Haddy knew it was her duty to detain others from joining the two of them until told otherwise. She was very excited about this talk between her father and Ebrima. Perhaps Ebrima was asking her father if she could return to the Darboe compound. Although it would mean leaving her family compound where she was happy. And it meant leaving all the women who were teaching her how to be a Kanylenga and were becoming very dear friends. But, most of all to leave Tida made her feel a deep longing she was not familiar with. How could she go without the times they were together? Something she could not understand. What happened to her when she was with Tida? Tida with her warm arms around her while they slept meant as much to Haddy as when Ebrima held her. She could not think about it. It was too difficult.

For a short time Ebrima and Ebe Touray sat quietly as they intermittently asked for their family and friends.

"Ebe, I have come to speak to you about a problem I have concerning my daughter, Adama. You know our Adama. Her twin sister, Jola (may

Allah watch over her soul) passed on some time ago, and Adama was very sick after that unfortunate incident. For months she did not speak or do anything. Then she began to improve to the extent of a full recovery. I'm sure you are aware that she and Modu Barrow ran away together, and were missing for some time."

He paused, giving Ebe time to respond. "Yes, I am aware of that. And am pleased they returned to their families. You must have been very worried while she was missing." Ebe's small frame was erect and alert where he sat there on the bench.

"We were very worried, and happy when they returned, even though very angry at the two young ones for the anguish they caused the families, and in fact, the whole village. They were duly punished, I can assure you. But, this leads me to what I have to inform you and the favor I am to ask of you.," Ebrima shifted his position and lit a cigarette.

"I am listening."

"As you know, Haddy and I have been married for many years. And, as you know no babies were born during that time. That is why she came back to your compound. I have come to find it difficult not being with her. I hope you understand that, Ebe."

"I understand the problem both you and Haddy have. I am glad you come to be with her. Haddy is your wife until you want that to be changed. I see no signs of that, Ebrima. I know Haddy is very sad that no babies come to her. I feel she would like to be in your compound. But, I will tell you she seems to be happy here, back in her family compound and making friends with the women of the garden."

"Yes. But this leads me into the real problem, which I hope you will consider helping me with. Back to Adama. She has a very serious problem and will not be able to stay in Jambanjelly for several big moons. Binta came to me with this suggestion to consider. She reminded me of what good friends Haddy and Adama always were. She suggested that perhaps Adama could come and live in this compound and be part of it; helping with the work of the compound, and finally be finished with her problem here when the time comes."

Omar did not move. He sat still, hardly breathing. He stared into the heat. After a few minutes of silence he looked toward Ebrima, "I have many questions to ask, but I do not want to interfere into the private affairs of your compound, Ebrima Darboe."

"I realize that usually women of the compounds settle these issues, with the permission of the men, but we are in a bit of a different situation, I feel. I do not want to cause undue worry and problems on certain friends who perhaps should be informed and involved. Do you understand, Ebe?"

"I'm not sure I do."

"Let me ask you this, Ebe. What if in a few moons from now an infant is born in your compound and it could be known as Haddy's baby? Who would question if this baby is ours? Everyone knows we are together as husband and wife. Correct? Then, Haddy could bring 'our' baby back to the Darboe compound and live with all of us happily, with this new infant."

"Who will feed this child?" Omar's voice was subdued and cautious.

"There are always nursing mothers within two compounds of any place. You know that, Omar."

"And what of your daughter, Ebrima? What will become of Adama? She will carry the milk without the baby. Will she too be expected to nurse someone else's baby knowing her own baby is living in her family compound? And what of the father of this infant? Is he not across the way from his child, not knowing it is his? Or will he know in his heart it is his newborn baby? And will he not wonder where the real mother of this child is? There are too many unanswered questions to this problem to be solved this easily, Ebrima. Usually the parents of both young ones help decide the fate of the mother and child. Let us talk about it tomorrow before you leave. The tea is brewing and I see some of the men coming down the lane to join us."

****

The next morning when Ebrima left Haddy, he went to Ebe's rooms and knocked at the doorway.

"Come," Ebe was still resting from his night's sleep.

"Good morning, Ebe. Sorry to disturb you so early in the morning, but I must be on my way back to Jambanjelly I think we need to talk before I leave."

"Yes, sit Ebrima."

"I found our talk last evening very helpful, Ebe. However, Binta and I need to make decisions quickly under the circumstances. Can you share with me what you feel the people of your compound are willing and able to help us with?"

"Perhaps you should return to Jambanjelly and share with Binta Darboe what we discussed last evening. Then we can continue our discussion as soon as possible." said Ebe.

"Thank you, Ebe. I will be on my way and will return within a few days."

Haddy walked Ebrima to his donkey cart and stood as Ebrima mounted the cart and flipped his whip over the old donkey's back. He murmured a quiet goodbye to Haddy as he rounded the corner onto the dirt street leading to the road to Jambanjelly.

Haddy stood watching Ebrima leave her once again. She was very anxious throughout the night after Ebrima fell asleep there beside her. She thought surely he would talk to her about what he and Ebe had discussed the previous evening. But, now he was leaving her, with no hint of what the two had discussed.

****

Ebrima spoke to Binta that evening of his return from Sukita. He relayed the concerns Ebe had placed before him and Binta nodded her head many times. Yes, yes, she heard the concerns and had wondered how they should deal with the Barrows. Modu's parents. Their long time friends and neighbors. It took Ebe Touray to bring this to their attention. This fact that they were about to be grandparents, also. Grandparents of the same child.

The Darboes thought of this for two days. It seemed very awkward to go to the Barrows and speak of this. It was very difficult. The idea of sending Adama to the Touray compound and passing the infant off as Haddy's baby seemed not to be the answer when they thought about keeping this news from the Barrows.

"Should you take her to one of the women who will make it go away?" Ebrima asked in a very nearly inaudible voice.

"We have never done that in all of our clan's history, Ebrima."

"I know," he answered, sighing as he leaned forward over crossed legs.

"During the night I thought of the Badgies and our planning with the marriage between Mariama when she comes of age to one of their boys. Should we go to them? Perhaps they will agree to allow this boy to marry Adama instead of Mariama?"

Binta took a deep breath and straightened up. She looked directly into the center of the yard where a mother hen led six new chicks toward the shade of a mango tree.

"If we arranged that marriage should we go to the Barrows first, or should we go forward with the marriage and an early birth of the baby?" Binta asked.

"I truly believe the Badgies will agree to this arrangement. Mariama's husband to-be is old enough to be Adama's husband. The other boy, Buba, could be Mariama's intended. He will be a good age for Mariama when she is of age. The Badgies have been wanting to join our family for many years, as you know. Let us think of this tonight and decide tomorrow. If we do arrange with the Badgies, I think we should let the baby be an early birth for Adama and her husband, Mustafa. The Barrows need not be involved with something they have no control over. Modu and his wife, Mimuna, should not have this problem put upon them."

Ebrima sat silently for a long time. Binta stood, walked toward the cooking area and sat in her spot.

****

The next morning after early morning prayer, Ebrima came to Binta's room and entered without knocking, which is the custom, husband to wife. Binta had dressed and was about to go outside and stoke up the fire in order to warm the rice from the previous night's meal.

"Binta, I am prepared to go to the Badgies this morning. I will bring the kola nuts in case the family is ready to accept the engagement of the two young ones. We will plan the program at that point. I think you should not say anything to Adama until I return with firm news," Ebrima stood from the bench next to the door and waited for Binta's reply.

"I will prepare your rice immediately, Ebrima. This is a good plan. I am praying the Badgies will be in agreement. The marriage must take place very soon. YaMoi?"

"NMoi," Ebrima stepped back into his room to prepare for his journey to Brikama, the home of the Badgies.

****

Mustafa Badgie, twenty years old, sat on the edge of the veranda floor, feet on the ground. His father and mother sat behind him on a bench, their backs leaning against the wall of the house. They sat quietly for some time.

Finally his father, Momadou, spoke. "It will take place the day after prayer day. The Darboes will bring the kola nuts and it will be the beginning of the ceremony."

Mustafa dug a hole with his heel into the hard earth. He sat hunched and resistant. He grunted deeply in his throat.

His father spoke in a harsh voice to him, "You will speak in a voice of respect, Mustafa Badgie."

"I hear you," Mustafa replied. "But, I do not even know this girl. I thought it would be Mariama who I would marry sometime in the future. Not this girl, Adama, who I have never met. I am not ready to be married, mother," he turned his head, quickly, beseechingly toward Arake.

"The Darboe family is an honest and decent family. Part of our tribe, Mustafa. We will not question why they are requesting a speedy wedding. We only know you should be pleased that we will become part of the Darboe family. You will be a good husband to this girl, Adama. YaMoi?"

Mustafa stood abruptly and walked away, not replying to his mother and without saying goodnight to either of his parents. He walked out of the compound and slammed the gate. He found his vue at the corner where they sat every night. He grabbed a cigarette from Abdou and plunked down beside him.

"What is happening to you, Mustafa? Why are you so angry?" Abdou asked.

"Would you not be angry if you were just told by your parents you were to be married within a short time to a girl you have never seen?"

"I would not be happy. But, it happens, you know. Who is this girl? Why the hurry?" Abou asked.

"It doesn't matter. None of it," Mustafa stood. Tall with wide shoulders and long thin legs. He was brutally handsome. Midnight black skin with high cheekbones. Almond shaped eyes and irises of green and brown speckles. His hair was tight curls hugging his perfectly round head.

"So, what are you going to do?" Abdou asked.

"*Do?* What *can* I do? I have been told I will marry this girl. There is nothing I can do except marry her. I will marry her. Sex her. And continue my life as it is. I will work on the farm, no more and no less than I already do. I will sit with my vue at night time. And the good part is I will have one more woman to take care of me."

"What about Ndey?" Adou asked.

"What about her? She isn't marrying anyone, is she? I will still go to her. She's my girl," Mustafa bent over and laughed at his own brazen wit.

****

And, the kola nuts were delivered the next week by Adama's uncle Boubakar. The first step into the marriage ceremony. The wagon carrying her belongings was carried to the Badgie compound the day before Adama was brought there in a donkey cart with her father. The ceremony was to take place that very day. A small celebration with only the immediate families and neighbors to come and to partake of the rice and sauce. A drummer and a flute played while a few young girls and women danced. A fire lit the center of the compound, and the children ran about like moths flitting in and out coming too close. Dipping in and out, challenging their fate.

And then it was over, and Adama was led by Mustafa's mother to his room and left sitting on his bed alone.

She curled up on the side of the bed. She wore a white night gown her mother had their tailor make just three days ago. The material was embossed with tiny holes scattered throughout. She looked very beautiful and vulnerable.

She fell asleep before Mustafa came in. This evening was the first time she had ever seen him. He only looked at her once that she was aware of. He sat beside her during the specified time for them to be recognized as married. They did not touch nor did they look directly at each other.

When he came to their room, he removed his clothes except for his trousers and threw himself onto the empty side of the bed. He lay on his back and stared at the ceiling. Adama remained curled up with her back to him. A fist was jammed against her mouth. She hardly dared to breathe.

In a few minutes, Mustafa drew in a huge gulp of air and at the same time pulled Adama over onto her back and threw her gown over her head. She wanted to scream but dared not. She drew her knees up as Mustafa was about to get on top of her. They struck him in his middle and knocked the wind out of him. This infuriated him and he slapped her face hard. He took both of her wrists and held them on each side of her head. He fell onto her and tried to enter her, but she thrashed about, throwing her head back and forth. Throwing her hips back and forth. Mustafa slapped her once again and she went limp. He then entered her.

When she came to Mustafa was asleep. The side of her face hurt and when she touched it she realized it was swollen. She hurt between her legs, and knew he must have entered her while she was unconscious. She wept there beside this man she was destined to live with. She wept for a long time. Silently. Alone.

She thought of Modu the boy she loves and tried to will him to come and rescue her. She knew this was not to be.

CHAPTER 18

Adama Finds Owl

Mustafa woke realizing someone was in his bed. Turning toward the person sharing his bed, he remembered he had a wife, and her name was Adama, not Ndey, and he had hit her twice across the face last night. Their wedding night. And he had entered her while she was not awake. He felt angry and disturbed at the same time. Angry because this situation was not his fault. He was put in a position where he lost control and did this thing. Beating a wife is not unusual, but one usually can wait for some time after their wedding night to do so. Anyway, she was not a person he knew or cared about and besides, she resisted him, which is against everything he had ever been told. How dare she resist the advances of her husband?! *Especially* on their wedding night.

He swung his feet off the bed and stood abruptly. He stepped into his fenced in back yard to relieve himself and splash water on his face from the jardinière. He went back inside, and chose a bright red batik from his basket of well pressed shirts. Without so much as a glance toward the bed, he walked out onto the veranda and looked toward the fire and cooking pot where his mother sat, directing the young ones to fetch water and fire wood.

With her gentle voice, Arake said, "Good morning, son. You are up early. How is your wife?"

Not looking directly at Arake, he mumbled some inaudible words and walked out of the compound. He went toward the field where he and his father were working the groundnuts, but he didn't continue the path to the farm. Instead, he took the narrow path to the left. A stick fence lined the pathway, separating the compounds. Several people greeted him over the fences in their early morning voices. He returned the greeting, curtly. Walking rapidly, straight in posture, marching toward Ndey.

Entering the compound, he was greeted by Ndey's mother who was about the leave to go to the women's garden for early morning weeding and watering. Ndey stepped out of the girls room just as Alimata, mother of Ndey, looking startled, spoke to Mustafa. "You are here, Mustafa. E sama, (good morning)," she looked slightly surprised and attempted a smile. "How is your wife?"

"Good morning" Mustafa said grudgingly. He stood just inside the gate. He slouched a bit and shifted. "I have come to greet Ndey and your family," he hung his head, not knowing what to expect from Alimata, mother of Ndey.

"Ndey's father is at the mosque and will probably not return for some time as he usually meets with his friends after prayers for a visit. I will tell him you were here. Now, Ndey and I are on our way to the gardens. Thank you for coming, Mustafa. Greet your family for me. I wish you and your wife a long life filled with many children." She turned away from him, picked a huge agate basin filled with the usual needs for the time at the garden, and lifted it to her head.

"May I speak with Ndey, please?"

Alimata, turned to look at him. Holding the weighty load on her head with one hand she said, "I will stand here while you speak with Ndey, Mustafa."

Standing in the same spot by the fence, he looked past Alimata directly at Ndey. "Greetings, Ndey. I am glad to see you. I hope you are well."

He turned abruptly, swinging his whole body in one move, he marched out of the compound. He walked past several compounds before he stopped and placed his forehead against the fence, then banged it mightily again and again.

****

Adama stayed in the room until mid-day when Arake, mother of Mustafa, stepped inside looking concerned. "Adama, are you awake? It is the middle of the day, and we are worried about you."

Adama hid her head under the material that covered her. "I am all right. I am very tired," she spoke in a quivering voice.

"I want you to clean yourself and come for porridge. The children want you to join them for porridge, now."

Arake stepped into the room, walked to the bed and pulled the cover away from Adama. A gasp came from Arake when she saw the side of Adama's face. Black and blue and swollen. "Did you fall, Adama?"

Adama nodded her head. "Yes." she replied.

"Come, let us bathe you and put cool water on this face," Arake led Adama to the back yard where the bathing area and jardinière stood. Tender hands helped Adama wash herself and finally bringing her into the room she dressed her in fresh clothes. Arake sat Adama down on the bed and placed a cool wet cloth on her cheek. Arake murmured sweet soothing sounds as she put the compresses on her new daughter in- law's battered face. "You must be more careful of where you walk in this new home, Adama. You may trip easily over roots of trees or over steps entering our rooms.YaMoi?"

"N Moi", Adama replied to this new, kind mother.

Adama ate a bit of porridge with the children of the compound, and once the children had watched her they tired of the newness, and went on to play in the corridor.

She looked down the narrow path that led to the women's gardens. No one was in the compound. The women had gone to the garden and the men were either at the groundnut fields or in the village chatting with each other. She decided to stroll down the pathway. It was so much like the magic path at home that led to the river it made her homesick. She wanted to find Owl. She walked cautiously through the path lined with tall palm trees, which met at the top, creating a tunnel. Red earth covered the packed lane. Silence reigned as she tiptoed down that path. Her heart began to thump as she neared a tree with low branches nearly reaching into the path. She heard a ruffling of feathers and she knew Owl was nearby. She felt a joyful lifting of her heavy heart. Even her painful cheek felt better. Owl stepped off the limb at the back of the trunk and onto the limb at the front of the tree. He stood in his regal manner. Huge eyes gazing at Adama.

"You have an injury, Adama Darboe. I am sorry to see that."

"I am married to a man I have not even spoken to, yet been beaten by and taken advantage of. I am in a strange village in a strange compound and I have no way to escape this."

"You are going through a great deal of unhappiness and pain, Adama Darboe. I am sorry to see this. I know you will survive this piece of your life. I know you will be a stronger woman as you go through this phase."

"Sometimes I don't even know why I look for you, and you always are nearby, yet you are unable to make my life better, less troublesome, less hurtful, Owl."

"Life it full of good and evil. Full of hurts and happiness.

"What am I to do with this cruel man who is my husband? I do not want him. I am helpless. I am lost and afraid," Adama looked pleadingly at Owl.

"You must decide how to live in that compound. You must find your allies and spend time with them. There are always good people wherever one lives, Adama. Find them and be worthy of their friendship. Do you think you can do that for now?" Owl asked.

"Already I have felt the friendship of Arake, Mustafa's mother. She helped me this morning when I awoke feeling full of pain and misery. I am sure she knew Mustafa beat me, but she did not say that. However, she was kind to me and helped me. I think she will be a good mother-in-law."

"Good, then that is your first move toward living with protection and kindness in the Badgie compound. And, remember everyone has some good in them. Even your new husband, Mustafa has goodness hiding inside. Try to find that goodness; for his sake and for yours. But, do not let your strength be taken from you by anyone. Now go back to your new home and be brave, Adama Darboe," Owl blinked his eyes and lowered his eyelids halfway looking as if he may fall asleep any minute.

"I have a baby in my stomach that belongs to Modu, the boy I love. I will say that to myself many times each day. It will make me stronger. It is part of me and Modu," Adama spun around and ran toward the compound, not wanting to hear any response from Owl for fear it would be words she could not bear to hear.

CHAPTER 19

Modu Asks for Adama

Modu woke thinking of Adama. He had dreamed about her and, waking from the dream he thought, *I wonder how Adama is. I have not seen her since she went to Sukata to marry.* He swung his legs from the bed and resolved he would go to the Darboe compound as soon as he washed, prayed, and ate a bit of porridge. He had to admit Mimuna made very good porridge.

He greeted the people in his compound as he stepped out into the unending sunshine. Nodding to his mother and Mimuna, he sat on his veranda and waited for the porridge to be brought to him. Mimuna walked toward him carrying a gourd full of her special porridge. Smiling timidly she curtsied and passed him the bowl.

After he had eaten he stood, and without a word stepped through the gate onto the street. He had not been in the Darboe compound since his marriage and was not sure how he would be treated. However, he felt anxious about Adama. And, he truly missed that girl. He thought of her many times each day. The times they lay in their little house on the straw mattress talking, laughing, playing and finally making love. How he missed that. The freedom of it. Not having to be quiet. Not having to be totally covered with some kind of clothing or material. To be free of the rules of the family was as wonderful as it was difficult.

He shook his head trying to bring himself back to this morning and how he was to deal with Adama's parents. As he opened the gate to the Darboe compound, he spotted Binta Darboe sitting on the log by the kitchen fire. She was stirring into a large iron pot. *Probably porridge*, Modu thought.

"E Sama, (good morning) Binta Darboe," Modu smiled broadly. He liked Binta Darboe. She was like a second mother to him. He had known her from the day he was born. He spent hours in that compound from the time he was able to toddle across the corridor and into the Darboe compound. Now, much had happened to their lives, but he was still a neighbor and a part of the family in many ways.

"Modu Barrow, come in and sit with me," Binta beamed at him and patted the shiny log beside her. "Here, we have to talk."

Modu advanced toward her quickly and with thankfulness. Binta was still her kind, forgiving self. He sat beside her and looked at the porridge in the steaming pot.

"You look in good health, Modu. Your wife must be treating you well. Is she a good cook? Does she press your trousers so they look perfect?" Binta was teasing him slightly, with a twinkle in her eye.

Modu hung his head and grinned. "I am well and my wife is fine, also. Thank you for asking."

"But you have not come to speak of you and your wife, I suspect," Binta glanced at Modu as she wiped tears from her eyes caused by smoke from the fire.

"I dreamed of Adama last night and it made me wonder how she is doing in her new home with her new family and husband," he suddenly felt a huge lump in his chest and he felt dizzy. He wiped his forehead with the sleeve of his shirt. Taking a deep breath he was able to contain himself.

"Are you alright, Modu? You are looking ashen." Binta filled a gourd of water from the bucket sitting next to her and passed it to him. He drank thirstily and said "Thank you Binta Darboe."

"You are thinking of Adama Darboe. She is fine. She is married and living in her husband's compound. She will not be coming to Jambanjelly for a visit for several moons, I think. But, it is alright you have asked for her. You should go to your mother's marabou to inquire about the dream. You know how important that is, Modu, am I not correct?"

"You are correct, Binta Darboe. I will do what you advise and I will now go to the farm to help with the ground nuts. Thank you for your advice."

He left, trying to walk as a young, strong man should. It was difficult.

Watching him leave, Binta Darboe shook her head and sighed. How unfortunate this whole matter is. These young ones with problems too big for them to solve. They must go forward with their lives and let Allah be praised.

Binta Darboe stirred the porridge.

CHAPTER 20

Mustafa Badgie

Adama had been living in the Badgie compound three weeks before she looked at her husband, Mustafa. They lay on the same bed each night. Backs barely touching. Never intentionally touching. Quickly, impulsively jerking away from each other if an ankle or a wrist brushed against the other.

Mustafa wanted nothing of this girl who was foisted on him. Not that boys were allowed to choose their mates, but this arrangement was a total surprise and he did not understand what happened. He had hoped that his family would eventually relent and allow him and Ndey to marry. But, now it mattered not. He was married in great haste. He could not understand it, and he felt not only angry, but helpless.

This girl, Adama was not unattractive. In fact, she was quite beautiful, with dark, smooth skin, and eyes that peeked through long black, curly eyelashes. Her body was small with lovely breasts that pushed out against her blouse. Her hips and bottom were plump. The boys liked to watch girls with hefty bottoms move down the lane. But, aside from how she looked, she was not an agreeable girl; not willing to even try to forget the way he treated her on their wedding day. He didn't want her to treat him in any way. He wanted her out of his life, but he knew that was not to be. So, he was doomed, never to speak to or look directly at his wife; and he guessed he could not beat her at least for a while, or his mother would talk to his father about it. His father was not one to approve of mistreating women. His father was a gentle man, not like many of the men in this village who beat their wives on a regular basis. His father would make his life more difficult than it is now if he knew that Mustafa had beaten Adama.

Even after the wedding between Mustafa and Adama he was able to meet with Ndey in the bush behind the groundnut farm at least one day between each prayer day. Ndey would walk to the well between the women's' garden and beyond Mustafa's father's groundnut farm. She carried a bucket to fill at the well for watering the tomatoes, peppers, and okra. Mustafa would be hoeing the groundnuts, watching for her to pass by on the path that led to both the gardens and to another small village into the bush. Once she passed, he would wander toward the outer edge of his farm, and then quickly glance for passers by. If no one was on the path or working on his father's farm land, he'd sneak quickly into the thick bush and trees. Ndey would walk into the bush beside the path that led to the garden and they would meet there in the middle of the forest; crash into each other and quietly laugh pulling at each others clothes. Ndey would place her hands against a tree, arms straight, bending at the waist, legs spread, standing, they would make love. Quick and harsh.

He would have her no matter what. He cared for this feisty, easy girl. She loved to betray her parents, and she loved to make love in the bush with him. It was more fun now than it had been before Adama. Ndey knew he didn't care about this Adama. And, anyway, he could be married off to three girls, Ndey knew she was the one he really lusted for. Love was a made up word. Love was for the meek and obedient. Love was ridiculous. Ndey didn't care if they were caught and beaten. Or if she became pregnant. She only knew life in this village was tiring, and the same thing, day in and day out, and she was going to make it so when she got up in the morning something different and exciting would happen. At least, now and then. She knew Mustafa cared for her more than she cared for him because she was exciting to him. She dared to show him her whole naked body. She would let him touch her in her 'private place' and it excited her. He would take her nipples in his teeth and tickle them with his tongue and she would wrap her legs around his waist. Ndey would reach into his trousers and pull at him. Rub against him until he pushed her onto the ground. She would sit on him and rub herself against him. She never let him do anything to her she did not want done. She was in charge and Mustafa loved her for that. No other girls would let him do anything close to what Ndey allowed. Ndey was a bad girl, thought Mustafa, and he would love her forever.

This day, after he had finished with the sex by the tree, and he pulled his trousers up and she dressed, they stood for a short time, looking at the ground between them.

"Does Adama do that for you?" Not that she cared. Not that she even thought about it very often.

"No. I have not ever spoken to her."

Mustafa reached into her blouse and squeezed her breast. She slapped his hand away.

"What if I don't let you sex me ever again because you love this Adama?" Ndey asked with a pouting mouth.

"I will send her back to Jambanjelly to her parents."

"Good. Let's go before we are caught. In a few days we will meet again. Right?" She looked back as she lifted the bucket to her head and walked toward the women's garden.

"I will be looking for you in a few days, Ndey. You are the one. You know that." Mustafa turned back through the bush to the groundnut field.

****

Mustafa walked with a swagger, shoulders swaying and legs strutting. He moved fast, with ramrod straight stature. His vue (friends) called him 'Boss'.

He teased all the girls in the village. Some of them liked his teasing and would flirt, swaying their righteous bodies as they skirted past him at the market place where he and his vue staked out a spot on one of the four corners of the square. Donkey and pony carts trotted by, some parked by the side of the road. Sanyang was a village where there never was any hustle or bustle. There was, however, an undertone of voices buzzing throughout the lazy air. Voices from the compounds surrounding the village square filled the humid air. Women's voices echoed from the market where cement stalls stood under a corrugated roof. Stalls full of tomatoes, hot peppers, onions, magi cubes, greens and, in season, papaya and bananas. Women wore bright dresses and head wraps to match. However they were dressed they looked fresh, bright like a bed of flowers. Voices came from the people leaving the mosque, which sat on one of the four corners of the village center. Humming low deep sounds from the men. The whole village buzzed with sounds of voices. Like loud bees, they hummed.

This day, Mustafa sat with his vue on their designated sitting place and watched the people, donkey carts, and especially, the girls go by.

Fatamata walked past the boys, smiled seductively and swung her hips impressively.

"Hey! Fatamata Touray, you have a big bum, and I will get it one day!" Mustafa spoke in a voice loud enough for anyone within a few feet to hear. And Mustafa did not care. Mustafa was the boss and he would say and do what he wanted.

Fatamata continued on her hip swinging way, carrying a huge bundle of laundry on her head. She looked back toward him and grinned.

Masanneh, Mustafa's main man, looked at him grinning, yet quizzically. "How many women can you handle, Boss?"

"As many as I care to," Mustafa punched Masanneh on the arm and they began to wrestle with not too much enthusiasm for it was mid-afternoon and the heat was all consuming.

CHAPTER 21

Mustafa and Adama

It was four moons since Adama had been transported to and left at the Badgie compound. She had grown to like Arake, her new-mother-in law. She also enjoyed the little ones who were always under her feet. She helped care for the babies, and played with the older children. Her father-in-law was not often around and if he was, he would be entertaining his old friends with tea and chatting. He did keep his groundnut farm well tended, and some of his sons went with him to care for it. Mustafa went with his father, reluctantly, but rather faithfully.

Mustafa and Adama slept in the same bed, but were yet to touch one another. They sometimes acknowledged one another with a greeting consisting of a curt grunt, and now and then brushed past each other with a slight touch of skin.

One morning as Mustafa headed toward the door leading to the veranda, Adama nearly bumped into him as she too was leaving the room. They both stopped abruptly. Adama looking into his chest, Mustafa, breathing onto the top of her head. They froze. Neither moved. They both stepped back. Then they looked at each other and a small grin tickled their lips. Mustafa stepped out onto the veranda.

Adama stepped back and sat on the edge of the bed. Where did that grin come from? Something in her chest was thumping. She shook her head, and rose to go for porridge and work.

Days passed and life continued filled with loneliness for her family and for Modu, the boy she loved.

One night as she lay in the bed beside Mustafa she felt a flutter within her belly like she had swallowed a butterfly and it was trying to find a comfortable place to light. It went away and she fell asleep.

That same night she felt a hand rest on her belly. Of course it was Mustafa's hand. Why was he putting his hand on her? At the same time, the butterfly moved again. Mustafa's hand jerked very slightly, as if he was surprised to feel a butterfly in her stomach.

Adama pretended to be asleep. She turned onto her side hoping Mustafa's hand would slide from her hip. But, Mustafa allowed his hand to remain on her hip. Adama, carefully reached for his hand, lightly held it and placed it back on his side of the bed.

Mustafa drew in a deep breath of air and rolled over facing the wall.

Adama's butterfly was very active that night.

****

A few days past. On this particular day, Adama finished her work in the compound. After she had gone to the garden for weeding, she returned by way of the path where Owl lived. Adama had not been to see Owl for two weeks. She was a bit put out with him, and his unsatisfactory answers to her dilemma.

But, now she *had* to see Owl. She dared not ask anyone else about the butterfly in her stomach. Her mother, Binta Darboe, was expected to visit Adama one of these days, as her father-in-law, Momadou had been to Jambanjelly for a visit and returned with greetings from the Darboe compound. Momadou said Binta Darboe was coming within two prayer days to visit her daughter, Adama. Adama was very happy to hear that news. Yet, she could not wait for the arrival of her mother to ask about the butterfly.

It seemed Mustafa was as curious as she was about the butterfly, and she had actually let him leave his hand there more often than she thought she should. It was comforting to feel a human hand on her. Her loneliness was deep.

So, now she must find Owl and ask him about the butterfly.

"You are here, Adama Darboe. Welcome. How is your life in the Badgie compound?" Owl blinked and ruffled his feathers with a mighty shake.

"Owl, I am here because I have a butterfly in my stomach and I don't understand how it got there, and if it even should be there. Can you tell me how to get it out?"

"Oh my, you need to be asking Arake Badgie such things, you know. She is your elder and your mother now. She will be able to answer this question for you."

"I cannot ask this question. I am too afraid it may be a spell cast on me and Arake will suspect the worst. She may think I am a witch or that I have a witch around me. I dare not mention this butterfly to anyone other than you. And another strange thing is happening to me." She drew a circle with her toe in the dirt path.

"Yes?" Owl asked.

"I am letting Mustafa put his hand on my stomach where the butterfly lives, and he likes that."

"I don't understand, Adama Darboe. Is this a problem? Are you asking me to reply with an answer to something I'm not sure is a problem?"

"Oh, Owl, you know what the problem is. I do not care for this man who is my husband, and who is in my bed, and who beat me the one time we touched, and who has several girls in the village, one whom he loves. I do not know what to do about any of this. Mostly, I need to know how to get the butterfly out of my stomach."

"You have not forgotten that you have a baby in your stomach, am I correct, Adama Darboe? And while you were learning to be a good wife and mother, the women taught you about carrying babies and delivering babies, and caring for babies once they come out. They must have told you that babies begin to move around inside your stomach before they come out into the world. Right, Adama Darboe?"

Adama was silent for quite some time. She seemed to be thinking seriously. And soon, Owl noticed her expression change from a frown to a look of awareness.

"Is the butterfly my baby?" she asked Owl.

"I would guess it is. But, it is not a butterfly, it is a real baby who is growing inside you so it will have all the parts a baby must have in order to live here where we live, in this place." Owl crooked his head to one side and looked intently at Adama. "Do you understand, Adama Darboe?"

"Yes." She looked down at her stomach, touched it lightly, and smiled a gentle smile. "I am going now, Owl. Thank you."

She spun around and ran toward the Badgie compound. She had a plan.

That night Mustafa and Adama lay on their backs said by side. She felt the butterfly. It not only fluttered, it kicked. Adama slid her hand from where it lay on her belly and reached Mustafa's hand lying on the sheet between them. She placed his hand on the kicking butterfly.

For a short time his hand lay flat on her stomach with Adama's hand holding it there. The butterfly kicked. Mustafa gasped.

"Whoa!" he chuckled. "What is in there, Adama Darboe?!"

"I think you put it there. Remember the night of our wedding? You were angry with everyone, including me. I think you put a baby in there then, Mustafa Badgie," she felt calm and in control for the first time in a long time.

Mustafa did not remove his hand even after Adama moved hers, and rested it on *his* stomach.

He was silent. He moved his hand in circles around the slightly protruding stomach of Adama.

Adama moved her hand in circles around Mustafa's taut, flat stomach.

For many long minutes, they caressed the stomachs of one another, and fell asleep doing just that.

CHAPTER 22

Adama's Child is Born

Mustafa paced the veranda of his father's house. His father sat smoking a cigarette and smiling. He shook his head and chuckled as he watched his son nearly race back and forth from one end of the veranda to the other. He paced rapidly back and forth; looking over at the women's house where the old ma and several of the compound women were attending Adama. Mustafa was not reacting the way men customarily do when one of their wives is in the process of delivering a baby. They usually sit quietly with their vue and chat and smoke and pretend nothing is different from all of the other afternoons of their lives. Only when one of the women comes to announce the arrival of a baby does the man recognize something has taken place. But, Mustafa has become a changed young man these past few moons. It seemed to Momadou that a short time after Adama came to live in the compound, Mustafa was a far easier man to live with. He no longer defied his parents; or ran off to meet the other women he always ran with. He helped with the farming without being pushed out of the compound by his mother or Momadou.

At first, when Mustafa and Adama were married, Mustafa was very angry and more difficult to manage than even before. But, it seemed after the third or fourth moon he began to spend time with Adama, sitting with her on one of the compound bantabas, with some of his vue or some of his siblings. Sometimes Momadou would watch Mustafa tease

Adama and play with her as if the two of them were children. Adama was beginning to show a stomach protruding at that time, and the people of the compound were aware that a baby would be coming sometime. Momadou assumed Mustafa's changed behavior was due to the fact he was soon to become a father. And now the time had arrived and Mustafa was beside himself with concern and worry. And excitement.

Inside the women's room, Adama squat on the floor where a piece of material had been spread. She wore a dendiko (loose shirt) and nothing else. Her body shone with sweat, she moaned and covered her face with her hands. She panted. Arake, her mother-in-law, sat beside her on the floor bathing Adama's face with cool water, cooing and crooning softly.

"Why is my mother not here?" Adama cried.

"We have sent for her. You will go with her to your compound once the baby comes. We should have taken you there earlier before your pains began. Now, it is too late, little Adama, but she will bring you there with the baby in a few days, so you can stay until the koolio (naming ceremony)," Adama winced in pain and breathed quick, anxious breaths.

Two hours later when Adama was not sure she could pace any longer or squat another second, a pain grabbed her and sent her into a crouch; water gushed from her and a head appeared. The women took positions as automatically as they had done for generations. The baby dropped into the hands of the old ma, and Adama held onto the arms of the two women who stood on each side of her. She looked around her shoulder as Arake reached over Adama's shaking shoulder and passed the baby to her. The women helped Adama to the bed where she lay with her baby at her breast. A healthy boy.

The women bathed Adama, and the old ma took the placenta, wrapped in a large leaf, walked to the yue tree in the far corner of the back yard, and buried it. She then returned to the room where women fussed over the baby, and the mother; folding pieces of material, laughing, reliving the birth, and gathering dirty laundry.

The old ma then took the baby to the back yard for his initial soothing ritual bath. She sat on the bottom cement step and stretched her legs out, and placed the boy on his back, his head at her ankles, his fat legs and feet nearly reaching her knees.

He lay on her legs. He was relaxed and calm. Facing old ma, he looked up at her with a face of sweet acceptance. Old ma had a basin of sun warmed water on the ground by her feet. With oil she massaged his arms, fingers, legs, toes, belly, shoulders, at which time she flipped him over and repeated the process on his back. The baby lay totally enthralled to be there. To be entering a world that would treat him with such a soothing, caring touch.

Adama slept for three hours while the women and girls cooed at the new member of their clan. The baby was wrapped in swaddling clothes and beamed out at all of them. He fell asleep as they all fondled and squeezed him. Once his mother woke, Arake gave him to Adama to nurse and to check all parts of her son to ensure he was well and whole.

Mustafa entered the women's room a few hours after the child was born and beamed down at the bundle sleeping there beside Adama. The two parents greeted briefly and Mustafa gazed at the boy, never taking his eyes away. A self-satisfied smile tickled his full mouth.

"He is big," Mustafa murmured.

"He is, yes.," Adama replied.

"I will go now, Adama Darboe. Rest. Is the baby taking your breast?"

"A small bit.," Adama spoke shyly with her eyes cast to the bottom of the bed.

"Mustafa?"

"Yes?" Mustafa has turned, preparing to leave the room.

"When will my mother come, and when will I go to her compound?"

"I do not know these things. Arake can tell you,." he turned and left the room.

Mustafa came several times each day to gaze at his son. He would visit with Adama shortly, pleasantly, then be on his way, returning to check on his child two or three more times each day. He was bursting with pride. He was now a man. He could make a son. When they had the koolio he would name him Lamin but he would be called *Mustafa-boy*. Lamin traditionally is the name of the first born in each family.

****

Binta Darboe arrived late that evening after darkness had fallen on the village. She had hired Lamin Darboe to bring her to her daughter using his horse and wagon.

As soon as Lamin Darboe stopped the horse, Binta jumped down from the seat beside him where she sat during the drive. She was anxious and upset that Adama had not been brought to the Darboe compound in time for the baby to be born there. She would speak to Momadou Badgie about that! And Arake, wife of Momadou should have urged her husband to allow her to take Adama to her parents compound. Why had they not informed her that the baby might be coming soon? Then Binta Darboe stopped and thought about the timing of this birth. And she knew she should be careful how she handled this situation. She must observe how the Badgie's were reacting to the newborn.

Binta had not seen her daughter, Adama for several moons, since she had been brought to the Badgie compound to marry Mustafa Badgie. Adama was very happy when Binta entered the room. Adama held her baby who was nursing hungrily. He slurped and snuggled into Adama's body. A mass of jet black ringlets covered his head. One of the women had oiled his hair so it sparkled like black diamonds. His eyes were wide open and he suckled with great gusto. He moved his eyes toward the grandmother who was converging on him. A big, vital grandmother placed her hand on his forehead and wept.

"Momma," Amada reached her free hand to her mother, grasping a piece of her dendiko (shirt) she pulled Binta to her. The three of them were tangled in a mix of tenderness for a short spasm of love.

The baby wriggled and burped, and looked away from the nipple long enough to gaze at his new grandmother. A very new baby yet able to study a different person in his midst.

Binta thought, 'Oh, belie, he does look too much like the Barrow clan. We will hope no one notices this.'

****

The next day after Binta Darboe came to fetch her daughter and grandson, they prepared for the short journey home. Adama and the baby would stay for two weeks and during that time the koolio would take place. The naming ceremony, the celebration of all new babies in Gambia.

As Adama climbed onto the front seat of the donkey cart, she looked down at Mustafa who passed the baby to her. They exchanged glances of shy affection.

"I will come soon," he said to her.

"Yes," she replied, knowing those words meant nothing concrete. An empty promise, a half wish, a hopeful prayer. In a world of total uncertainty promises are not dependable.

****

Adama had not seen Owl since the baby was born and she longed to speak with him, to share with him the news of her new life. Of how once a baby comes your whole life revolves around him, and how love comes easily to everyone around this new life. How happy she is even when she knows Modu, the boy she loves, is the father of this precious gift, she must protect him against any danger or misunderstanding. That for the safety of this precious gift, he must be accepted into the Badgie clan as the son of Mustafa, who has become more gentle and ready to be a proud father.

Adama had so much to talk about with Owl and she did not know how she could get away down the path to find him. Now she was on her way to Jambanjelly, and she was excited and anxious to go. But, Owl may not be there. She needed his help with the problem of saving this most valuable life in her world from harm of any kind. All she could do this day, and a few more in the future, was to pray that no one notices how her baby resembled the Barrow clan.

CHAPTER 23

Adama and Baby Visit Her Family

Adama's little sister Miriama, showing the beginnings of young womanhood, budding breasts pushing through a worn bright green cotton shirt, greeted Adama with tears of joy and clapping of hands.

"You are here! You are here! Let me see the baby. Here, give him to me. He is mine! Now you have no baby! This one is mine!"

Miriama reached up to the front seat of the wagon where Adama sat holding her child. Willingly she passed him down to Miriama. Adama's eyes filled with tears as she watched her siblings running from all directions, coming to greet her. Miriama walked slowly toward the women's house, cuddling the child. She sat on a bench in the shade on the veranda. Brothers, Momadou, Ishmial, Ousamanie, and little sister Mata surrounded Miriama, anxious to gaze on Adama's new son.

Binta chuckled and walked into her room to bathe and change from her traveling clothes to her working dendiko and fanno.

Adama sat beside Mariama as she greeted her brothers and sisters. She took the baby when he began to stir and snuggle into Mariama's chest looking for his lunch. Mariama and the children smiled and watched Adama bring him to her breast. The little ones began to tire of all this and gradually moved on to other activities. Mariama sat watching her big sister, who was now a mother.

"Your vue is coming to greet you later today, when they finish watering the garden. They are excited to see this boy. You are the only one who is married, you know."

"I know. I am waiting to see them It has been a long time since I have been with my vue." Adama watched as her father walked toward her, coming from the mosque. His smile was gentle and full of warmth. He did not look at the baby. His eyes were only on his daughter, Adama. His favorite, yet most difficult of all.

Ebrima touched her shoulder and said the greetings. Only then did he look at his grandson. His eyes filled with tears, and he looked away for a quick time to wipe them away. He sat beside Adama on the bench and gazed at this new miracle for what seemed to be a full afternoon. Adama also looked down on her son and jiggled him slightly while he slept.

"He is a big boy."

"Yes," Adama replied.

"His naming ceremony will be the day after prayer day," Ebrima said as he rose to go to his veranda and prepare for his afternoon attire (tea drinking) with his vue.

****

Late that afternoon when the girls returned from watering the women's garden, they bathed and ate lunch, then gathered at Tida and Amie Cham's compound. They walked through the village toward the Darboe compound.

Sitting inside the girls room Adama's vue shyly looked down at her baby boy where he lay on the bed, sleeping.

"You are here," Tida Cham said.

"Yes. It is good to be here in the Darboe compound. I have missed them all too much. I have missed you, also, too much."

"How was it, having a baby?" Nigma Jammeh asked. "When the women have their babies in my compound it sounds as if there is great pain.

"It is difficult.I was full of pain. I was afraid. I wanted Binta, and she was not there. I did not like having this baby. It hurt too much."

All three girls made humming sounds in their throats, in sympathy for their friend.

"But, if we do not have babies it is not good," Amie Cham muttered.

"Yes, it is not good. We must have babies," Ningma Jammeh, sister of Modu Barrow replied. "Modu's Mimuna is having a baby in a few moons. We are all happy that a new baby will be in our compound."

Adama said nothing. She tried not to react to this news Ningma had just dropped in the midst of her vue's first meeting in months. Her joy was being drained from her.

"Amie and I are having dresses made from the same material for your baby's Koolio, Adama," Tida said.

Looking toward Ningma, she asked, "Will your mother purchase the same material so we can come as Adama's vue, all dressed the same?"

"Maybe," Ningma replied.

"I will ask Binta if I can have the same material, also, then we will surely be the most important vue attending my baby's Koolio.," Adama brightened a bit, trying not to think of Modu.

"When is your husband coming?" Ningma asked. "What is he like? Is he handsome?"

"I guess he will be here the day of the koolio. I'm not sure when that will be. Ousman says after prayer day, but I'm not sure which day that will be. Binta will tell me before the sun goes down today, I believe.

My husband's name is Mustafa Badjie. He may be handsome, but he does not act like a good husband much of the time. He is improving since the baby arrived. I like him a little more now than I did when we were first married. I did not like him at all then."

"Why? Did he beat you?" Ningman asked, nonchalantly.

"Why do you ask me such a thing?" Adama was surprised to hear that question coming from her friend.

Ningma shrugged, "I don't know. Men beat women. I would not like a husband if he should beat me. I thought that may be a reason for not liking him."

"I am liking him better now," Adama spoke in a quiet voice.

"Good," her vue spoke in unison.

****

The next day, Fatou Jammeh, mother of Modu, the boy Adama loves, came to greet Adama and her new baby. She came into the compound and went directly to Binta's veranda where three women were picking stones from rice in winnowing baskets. They looked up and shouted greetings to one another for some time.

"Come, sit. We have plenty of stones to pick for everyone!" Binta joked.

"I've come to greet the new baby and his mother. Where are they?" Fatou asked.

"Adama is bathing him in her room. Go in and greet her. Three days coming we will be having the koolio. It will be a nice celebration. We expect the people of your compound to join us, of course."

"I will help with the cooking," Fatou replied as she headed toward Adama's room.

As Fatou greeted Adama, her eyes were searching the bed where the baby would be having his bath. She spotted him there in a basin of tepid water in front of Adama. His plump arms and legs moved about lazily. He stared up at his mother with black oval shaped eyes, through long, curling eyelashes. He wore a quiet, quizzical expression. Staring directly into his mother's face, his mouth was a serious pout.

Fatou gasped and stepped back one step before she caught herself. She stopped; regained her composure, took a deep breath, yet could not take her eyes off this child whom she had seen before many years ago. A duplicate. An exact replica of her own child. Of Modu Barrow, years ago. She pushed it back into her mind and stepped forward to greet Adama.

****

On the second day that Adama was back in her village, early morning, and as the sun was barely rising, she tapped Miriama on the shoulder. The baby slept soundly there between the two of them. "Miriama. I must go to the latrine. If the baby cries, give him the sugar tit. I will be back directly. Do you hear? YaMoi?"

"Yes. Go. I am here. He is sleeping well," Miriama seemed awake enough for Adama to leave the baby with her.

She very quietly slipped out of the compound and went to the magic path. Her heart was pounding as she reached the tree where Owl usually was waiting. He was nowhere to be seen and she called in a whisper.

"Owl?. Where are you? I must speak with you. Come out from behind the tree. Please, Owl."

He stepped from the back of the tree and stretched his claws as he placed them on the branch.

"Adama Darboe returns. How are you and where is your baby?'

"Oh,Owl, you do not know what my life has been since I last saw you!"

"And, why do you say that, Adama Darboe? I think I know you have been away in a strange village, a strange compound, and have become married to a man who is not your choice for a husband. Although, you are beginning to care a bit for him, because he adores his son whom you have given him. Am I not correct in all that I have just shared with you?"

Adama sighed. "Yes. You are always correct, Owl. However, it does not make my life any less difficult. I have just learned Modu, the boy I love, is going to become a father. Mimuna is giving him a baby. I am across the way from him now and cannot see him. His mother came yesterday to see the baby, and I am sure she recognized her son in my baby's face. She nearly dropped to the floor when she looked at him, before she could stop herself from showing her surprise."

"What do you want from me, Adama Darboe?" Owl asked.

"I want you to let me have Modu, the boy I love."

"And how do you imagine I can do such a thing?"

"Are you not a witch?!" Adama asked, half knowing the answer.

Owl did not respond to that question. He sat silently there until Adama could be silent no longer.

"I know you are not a witch, Owl. You are my spirit animal. You want me to grow and learn from my mistakes. You want me to think about what happens when one does a certain act. I am trying to do all of that, and I am learning to be careful of what I do or think. But, can you talk to me about what is going to happen to me now, and in the near future? Please?"

"Yes, that is what spirit animals do. I am happy to see you, Adama Darboe. I think you will find me in a nearby path in your new village soon. You will be returning there. You will be living with your husband and caring for your son. You will learn to like it there and to be part of the Badgie compound. You will try to be a good wife, and your husband will treat you decently. Your husband loves another woman, you know."

"I know," Adama quietly responded.

"But, he cares about you and 'his' son, which is helping him to become a better person. A better man. It is part of your mission to help him with that."

"That is unfair! Why should I have to help him to become a better man? When is someone going to help me to be, or do anything? It is always me who has to help, help, help!?" Adama threw herself on the ground in front of Owl.

Owl did not respond. Owl sat for long minutes on the branch while Adama sobbed on the ground. Great tears streaming down her soft face. After a few minutes the tears subsided, and she looked up at Owl. He shook his head and said, just before he disappeared:

"I think there is a baby waiting to be fed."

CHAPTER 24

The Koolio

Fatou, mother of Modu, pondered over the laundry. The water had been pulled from the well by the girls who continued on to the garden. This morning Fatou was left to do the laundry. She wanted to be alone, she needed to think about the baby across the way. Adama's baby boy, the image of her son, Modu when he was an infant. The exact image of her son, now grown, now about to become a father. For the second time? What else was she to think? The timing left no question. Modu and Adama had been together for many, many days, and nights. They returned and were regaining their lives here in their family compounds. Then, suddenly, with very little discussion, Adama was sent to be married to someone who was not familiar to the folks in Jambanjelly. They knew of the Badgies but they were not a family who came to visit often, or had developed close relations here. For what other reason would the Darboes have made an agreement with the Badgies that Adama marry their son?

She wanted to talk with someone about this, but she hesitated to share it with the usual people she discussed problems. Certainly it could not be her husband, Ousman Barrow. He would be too upset at the possibility to be of any help to her. He would be trying to solve the problem in ways that would cause more trouble. She knew Ousman, a man of honor, and one who dealt harshly when traditions were broken. And, her best friend, Binta Darobe, mother of Adama, mother of the infant causing the concern would not be able to discuss this issue. Any of her other vue should not be told of her concern until the Darboe family shared it with their friends, which Fatou felt certain was not going to happen. This baby would always be known as the son of Mustafa Badgie. Somehow this made Fatou very sad. *'He is my grandson, and I know it., But, why did the Darboes not come to us with this situation, and allow us to help solve the problem? We are their friends and close neighbors. We could have worked it out with them, somehow.'*

As she thought this through she remembered the time Modu and Adama returned to their village, and that in a very short time after that Mimuna and Modu were married. Adama most likely was just beginning to know she was with child. Fatou recognized that perhaps the Darboes did not want to cause a big problem for the families of those two young newlyweds. She also thought of the gossip it would cause throughout the village. A baby before a marriage is a challenging problem.

She began to dunk the pieces of laundry into the huge wash tub filled with water. Modu walked toward her from his and Mimuna's house. He had already been to the groundnut farm to weed before the sun became too hot. He looked ragged and tired and it was still morning. After a shower and breakfast, he would look like his usual handsome self. He greeted his mother and sat beside her on a log.

"E Sama, Ma."

"E Sama, Modu. Porridge is by the fire."

"I need to ask you a question, Ma," he looked into the big washtub.

"Yes?" Fatou stopped scrubbing the shirt, it dangled wet and dripping over the huge tub like soggy trees after a rain storm. She looked at her son.

"I am told that Adama Darboe is here in the Darboe compound and her son is with her."

"You are correct. Yesterday I went to visit her, and saw the baby boy. The naming of the baby will take place in a few days at the Koolio. Why do you ask?"

"I would like to greet her, but I do not know if it is permissible to do so," Modu ducked his head submissively.

"I think you must go to your father first. If he permits you to go, then you should go to Ebrima Darboe and ask his permission, also. Ya moi?

"N moi", Fatou sat with her son for a good length of time as she scrubbed clothes and Modu ate porridge. Both sat in silent thought. Finally, Modu stood and went to find his father.

Ousman Barrow watched his son, Modu striding toward him from across the dry packed courtyard and the cooking area where his wife, Fatou sat. They greeted each other in the usual lengthy morning ritual. Modu sat beside his father looking out onto the courtyard of the compound. A few orange trees were scattered around the edges of the fenced-in area creating treasured shade.

"I have come to ask permission to go to the Darboe compound and greet Adama Darboe. She is here for the Koolio for her new baby boy, and I would like to say hello to her. Fatou advised me to come to you, first."

"I have no problem with this, but first you must go to Adama's father, Ebrima Darboe. If he grants permission I will agree," Ousman drew in on his pipe.

They sat silently for several minutes. Modu's brow wrinkled in deep thought. He pursed his ample mouth and drew in a long breath. His father continued to smoke his pipe as he waited for his son to either leave or say what was causing such consternation.

"Well, what is detaining you from your visit to the Darboe compound, son? Do you have other concerns you need to discuss with me?" Ousman was anxious to go the noontime prayer at the mosque.

"No, da, I will go now," Modu stood and walked toward the gate. He stepped out onto the wide, dirt street. Dust from the dry earth puffed up, then settled onto his bare feet. He stepped through the gate of the Darboe compound. His mind was not settled. He felt uneasy. What would he say to Adama? How long had it been since they had seen each other? It had been a long time for him to be without seeing Adama Darboe. Now he would see her with a new baby boy. He felt very nervous as he entered the Darboe compound in search of her father, Ebrima Darboe. It was quiet in the compound. Only Ebrima and a neighbor were visible where they sat on his veranda, chatting. Modu walked up the three cement steps that led to the bench where the two men sat.

"Greetings.," he said as he shook hands with each of his two elders, touching his heart after each handshake. He sat on a stool nearby quietly waiting for the neighbor to leave in order for Modu to ask permission to greet Adama. It was a matter of long minutes before Noah left. Ebrima and Modu sat several more minutes before Modu asked his question.

"Ebrima Darboe, I am here to ask permission to greet your daughter, Adama Darboe, who I understand is here with her new baby boy."

Ebrima sat still. He allowed a length of time to lie between them. He needed to think this through. He also wanted this boy to have time to be uncomfortable. After all, he was the cause of this situation. Even though Ebrima felt close to this boy, he was also very angry with him for taking Adama away and bringing her back in such a condition.

"Why do you wish to see her?"

"Adama has been my friend since childhood. You know we did a very thoughtless deed several months ago and caused much concern and worry to our families and friends, for which we both are sorry. But, it has not changed my feelings toward Adama as a friend," Modu hung his head as he spoke.

"You have a wife who is about to have your child," Ebrima looked at Modu sitting there in submissiveness as all young people should do when speaking to their elders.

"Yes," he responded, but did not quite understand what that had to do with Modu greeting Adama.

"Well, keep that in mind when you visit your friend Adama, and her son. Now go."

A bit confused, Modu rose and excused himself. He walked toward the girls' house where he assumed Adama would be. Binta Darboe stepped out of the girls house just as Modu took the first step onto the veranda.

Binta, who loved Modu nearly as much as she loved her own children, greeted him with a hearty smile.

"You are here to see Adama. Have you asked her father, and your father before you enter?" she asked in a gentle voice.

"Yes. It is alright," he said

Binta pulled the curtain at the door aside and stuck her head into the room, "You have a visitor, Adama."

Adama was nursing her son as she sat on the bed, the only furniture in the room. She was fondling his feet as the baby suckled, gazing into her face with intense huge black eyes. Adama's gaze was as intense as the yet unnamed baby boy.

Adama was startled to hear her mother's announcement, and quickly looked up as Modu entered the room. Binta stayed and watched as Modu glanced at the two of them where they sat on the bed. She saw Modu's eyes change as he looked at Adama, a happy, excited glance; and then Modu looked down in her lap where his son lay. The yet unnamed boy pulled away for his mother's breast long enough to look at the shadow Modu was creating. He stared directly into Modu's eyes, and Modu tried not to react. Even though his whole being was screaming to react. Modu looked into the face of himself.

He looked up at Adama quickly. A soft glance of affection and sadness.

"He is here."

"Yes," Adama whispered. "Modu, you are here. How are you? It has been too long since I have seen you. Are you well?"

"Adama Darboe. You are here also. You have a son. And you have a husband. How is that?" Modu stood over the two of them, looking lost; his long arms dangling at his side. His wide shoulders drooping slightly. Dressed in torn trousers and shirt from the farm work, and tears in his eyes.

Binta ducked out through the curtain at the doorway. She stood on the other side of the curtain on the veranda and stared into the heat. She had just watched two people being torn into pieces. And a beautiful little one on his way to a life unknown. *Yet a life like any other boy in any village in this place,* she thought.

Binta stayed on the veranda by the curtained doorway. She had seen what these two young ones could do in their passion for one another and she was not about to allow something like that to happen again. She heard their conversation, then stepped back into the room smiling and laughing as Binta was prone to do.

"Modu, you will be a father soon! Mimuna will be a mother soon. She is feeling well, and working in the garden yet. She cooks good porridge, I hear! You are a lucky man to have such a wife," Binta busied herself around the room, collecting a bowl for bathing the baby and finding a piece of material to wrap him and to dry him. She snatched the baby from Adama and excused herself as she went to the back wash area.

"Adama, find Miriama for me. We need an onion from the market. Ours from the garden are not yet ready." Binta called as she stepped out of the back door.

"I must go now, Adama Darboe. Binta Darboe, I will see you both soon.," Modu stepped out of the curtained front door and disappeared.

And now Adama Darboe sat alone on the bed. She felt bewildered and stunned. She had not seen Modu Barrow, the boy she loved, for months, and had missed him during the whole time. Now, here she was in her room alone. She could not even process what had just happened. She felt overwhelmed with emotion and sadness. He will never be able to claim this unnamed boy as his child. Even though when he looks into his face he looks at himself! Tears rolled down Adama's cheeks. She sat for sometime alone. Then she realized she must find Miriama for Binta Darboe.

****

Mustafa Badgie arrived in Jambanjelly early the day of the Koolio with his parents and a large contingency from Sanyang. They arrived in donkey carts, horse and buggies, and some by walking several hours since early morning. With bundles on their heads, the children and women carried changes of clothes, rice, sugar, tomatoes, onions, and pestles for pounding. By the time they all arrived, the cooking was well underway. The women had congregated at Binta Darboe,s back yard kitchen and commenced to prepare the sauces, pound the rice, make the munkoo, sweet sugar balls, and chagree, a sweet porridge made of rice and sugar. And panketoes or pancakes.

The Badgie group entered the Darboe compound, greeted everyone, unloaded their supplies and clothes, and joined the pounding, cooking, and chatting.

The men sat on the veranda, moving only when the call to prayer reached their ears.

Mustafa, after greeting the elders of the compound, went to greet Adama who was inside the girls' room. He stepped into the room gingerly moving the curtain to one side and peeking into the room. "Asalam Mali Cum," he called in a low voice.

He spotted Adama sitting on the bed with the baby on her lap. The unnamed baby glanced toward the door. He was naked, his fat legs moving casually, lazily. He stopped moving and stared at the new person coming toward him. He looked at his mother. He looked at the new person, and then began to search for Adama's breast.

Mustafa kneeled down on the hard dirt floor in front of Adama and the baby. His gaze was gentle, soft as the breeze during the dry season. Adama was touched to see Mustafa in a state of grace. She reached toward him and touched the top of his head. Mustafa glanced up quickly and met her eyes. At the same time the unnamed baby grasped Mustafa's finger and pulled it to his mouth. He sucked on the finger, then pulled it from his mouth, looked at it doubtfully and dropped it. Nuzzling his mother chest he searched for the source. The two grown ups softly chuckled.

"Will you come back with us tomorrow?" Mustafa asked.

"I think my mother intends for me to return with your family. She tells me often, it is my home now," Adama gazed at her son as she spoke.

"It is your home, now. You will come home with us tomorrow," Mustafa stood and lingered for a short time, staring down at his son. He turned toward the door.

"I am going to greet the people now," he said no more. Stepped out of the room and disappeared. Adama sighed and looked down at this beautiful infant lying in her arms.

Binta Darboe entered the room carrying a new dress for Adama, and fresh material in which to wrap the baby.

"I must go and attend to the cooking. Mariama will be with you and the baby until it is time for the ceremony. The two of you will be having lunch here with the rest of your vue. Your auntie will hold the baby while you sit beside her with your head covered. Noah Camara will cut the hair from the baby's head and will whisper the name of the baby."

"Mother, must I return with the Badgies tomorrow?" Adama looked pleadingly at her mother. Her heart was thumping in her chest as she looked at her Binta. *It is too lonely to be there*, she thought.

****

Guests began to arrive by noon. Dressed in their finest dendikos and fannos; men and boys in their caftans. Bright golds, and vibrant blues, white, and greens of every shade possible. Some of the women and girls had carried a second outfit for the evening dancing and feasting.

The kora player arrived and set up his instrument in the center of the courtyard on a large animal hide. His name was Abli from Gunjuir. Abli was the best kora player in the area, and he sang stories ancient as the earth. The kora, a twenty-one-string instrument with a huge gourd resonator, sent beautiful delicate music into the air. The evening would find the drummers beating loud and frantic sounds for the dancers.

Sweet porridge was distributed by the young girls of the nearby compounds to those who had already arrived. The porridge was scooped into small calabashes used as bowls. Spoons made from smaller gourds were passed to each guest. Folks gratefully partook of the first treat of the day.

The guests shook hands as they entered. They walked along the circle where people sat chatting extending their hands in greeting. Each person who entered did the same thing. It was the custom.

The kora player greeted people of the two villages as the day commenced, singing tales of each clan. In about an hour munkoo, sweet balls made of sugar and rice, were passed around by young girls, mostly girls from the compounds in the Darboe ward, the Mandinka section of the village.

Adama's vue had arrived and were dressing in the girls room. Tida and Amie Cham wore dresses of bright blue satin with embossed silver around the neck and bottom of the dendiko. They had braided their hair close to their heads the night before. Making V-shaped designs diagonally over their heads. New, large looped earrings of silver graced their ears.

Ningma Jammeh (sister to Modu Barrow, the boy Adama loved) was taller than the other two members of Adama's vue. She was strikingly slender with a long, elegant neck. Her skin was black as the night. She wore a gold satin one piece caftan with slits up each side to her knees.

"But, I thought we were going to dress the same this time," Amie Cham said as she watched Ningma pull her dress out from her basket.

"My mother chose this material. If I argued with her I would end up with something ugly. I tried to suggest she speak with your mother about the material she was purchasing for you, but she was stubborn and in a hurry." Ningma shrugged as she removed her everyday dress and commenced to pull the new gold dress over her freshly braided hair of elegant circle design.

Miriama was about to take the baby from Adama so she could take her shower and change, but the baby began to cry and suck his fists. Adama settled onto the bed and allowed him to nurse.

"He is a hungry baby," Ningma said. "He looks like another baby I know. But, I can't remember who," she continued to pick through her basket looking for her gold loop earrings.

Just after noontime, a goat was dragged into the middle of the courtyard by Ousman Barrow, friend of Ebrima Darboe and Momadou Badgie, father of Mustafa Badgie. The kora player stopped playing, and watched as the goat braced his feet only to be yanked by one man using a rope tied around its neck, and pushed on its rump by the other. Legs braced, it made no sound, only used all his strength to prohibit the inevitable. Ousman reached down under the goats belly and flipped him over onto his side and held it down. A knife was run across his throat as people made a murmuring sound as if the wind was winding down from a driving rain storm. Blood ran out onto the dry earth and seeped into the sand, leaving a large circle of dark red. The blood turned black and dried swiftly from the intense heat. While the goat slowly died a prayer was recited by the Imam. This sacrifice is part of the naming ceremony, a sacrifice to Allah. The meat was cut and added to the rice and sauce for the meal to be enjoyed by all those attending this gathering.

As the day wore on, the cooking of the rice and sauce was completed so the women were able to take their baths and change into their party dresses. By this time, it was mid- afternoon, and nearing the time for the actual naming to take place.

Noah Jammeh, best friend to Ebrima Darboe, arrived and sat with Ebrima on his veranda. Ebrima had asked Noah to perform the actual naming.

Noah went to Mustafa where he stood with some of his vue who had come to the ceremony. He shook Mustafa's hand. The two had never met. "I am chosen by Adama Darboe's father, Ebrima Darboe, to give the baby his name, so I must hear it from you."

The two stepped inside Ebrima's room and each sat on a stool. Facing each other, knees nearly touching, Mustafa told Noah he had chosen his infant son's name to be Lamin, as nearly all first sons of the Mandinka tribe are named.

"But he will be called Mustafa-boy from this day forward."

Mustafa said as he cupped his hands on his knees. He grinned at Noah and sat as tall as his body would allow, towering over Noah.

"What he is called from this day forward will not matter to me. I need only to know the true name of your son in order to announce it here at this very serious Koolio," Noah did not especially like this young man and he could not understand why.

Mustafa stood and shook Noah's hand before he stepped out onto the veranda.

In the meantime, Adama and her Auntie had walked through the back of the girls' house to the rear of the big house belonging to the women. There they entered the back door, walked through the center room where many of the women, including Binta Darboe, stood waiting for the baby to pass through to the verandaa

"Put the veil on now before you walk out there," Binta grabbed Adama's shoulder and slipped a netting of dark green over Adama's head and face. Auntie held the baby and walked solemnly, as she had for many naming ceremonies. Adama was trembling as her mother covered her head and face. This was a very important day for her and her son.

Adama's mother, Binta Darboe had purchased a lime green satin piece of material and had the tailor design a dress of elegance and sweeping style for her daughter. Her hair had been braided with v-shape designs. Large gold earrings hung from her ears. Her round face was radiant, almond shaped eyes peeked through the netting.

Noah stood on the veranda waiting for Auntie and Adama to step out and sit on the mat placed on the verandah floor. The kora stopped playing as the women sat. The baby slept peacefully in the arms of his auntie. Noah stepped to the side of auntie and said several prayers from the Koran. He reached into the folds of his deep blue caftan and pulled out a small knife. He cut a piece of hair from each side of the baby's forehead. He then whispered the name of the baby in his tiny ear. Then, reaching to the sky, he announced the name of the baby.

"May we all praise Allah. This baby is to be known as Lamin Badgie from this day forward."

"Amin, Amin," the people answered.

The kora began to play. The drummers commenced to beat their drums and people clapped their hands. Lamin Badgie was named.

CHAPTER 25

Adama Returns to Her Husband's Compound

The day following the Koolio, Adama woke early and crept to the magic path. Mariama opened one eye when she heard her sister quietly slide from the other side of the bed. Mustafa-boy slept peacefully between them, sucking his fist.

"I'm going to the latrine," Adama whispered. "Don't worry if I am gone for some time. If the baby cries bring him to me."

Mariama nodded and closed her eyes.

Adama ran in her bare feet down the magic path. Like a deer, she raced toward Owl, and found him sleeping on the big limb that bent out toward the path. His huge eyes opened as he heard her footsteps there in front of him. He blinked slowly, closing and opening his yellow eyes in a motion as slow as a spider spinning a web.

"Adama Darboe has returned to her parents village. What brings you here?" Owl asked in his deep owl voice.

"Oh, Owl you know why I am here. Why do you play games with me? You know more about me than I know about myself. You know my son had his Koolio yesterday and has received his name. I am sure you know he has a name that is not correct. You know his real father saw him yesterday and recognized him as his son as surely as I saw it. You know that his real father, Modu, the boy I love is going to become the father of a second child any time now. You know that Modu's mother

194

recognized my son as her grandson. You know everything, so do not pretend!" Adama gasped and knelt before Owl.

Owl perched, quietly gazing down at Adama where she knelt, head bent to the earth. Bereft. Owl shook his big, feathered head. This girl is always bereft. Owl spoke, "Adama Darboe, look up here and listen to me."

With tears in her almond-shaped eyes she looked up at Owl. Spots of dappled sun shone golden on her face. She remained kneeling. She felt exhausted. Her breasts were full and she knew Mustafa-boy was waking.

"You have a healthy, handsome infant. A boy. You have parents who love you in spite of the problems you have given them for the past few years. You have sisters and brothers, friends and relatives by the score. You now have two compounds you are a part of. You have food, and shelter, and I repeat, an infant who will depend on you for many years to come. You are growing up, you are a woman. You must stop agonizing about this boy you love. All in good time, you will be with him."

Adama stared at Owl. She wiped the tears from her eyes with the palm of her hands. She did not take her eyes from Owl as she slowly rose to stand before him. She said nothing, just gazed at him with a quizzical expression of awe. She dared not say more. She had heard more than she had even hoped for. She dared not hope for any more.

All in good time you will be with him.

"I must return. My milk tells me Mustafa-boy is searching for me," she turned slowly, looking over her shoulder at Owl as she took the first steps away from him and toward her baby. She knew she was going to her new home. She knew she must settle into the Badgie compound and be the wife of Mustafa Badgie, and the mother to her beautiful boy who was not Mustafa Badgie's.

He is mine. He belongs to me and Modu, the boy I love.

As she returned, she glanced at the red succulent blossoms pushing up from the darkened forest. The best place of all to see the red blossoms was here along the magic path.

She heard a rustling sound coming from deeper in the forest beyond the red flowers, behind the thick large leaves of the lush tropical trees. She suspected an animal was foraging there, and she was not afraid, but remained alert. Animals abound in the forest near the village. One needed only to watch and listen for all the sounds and sights of the place where they were. Then you would decide how to react, once you truly knew what was there out of sight, then coming into view.

He stepped out from behind the foliage and looked at her. Modu, the boy she loved, looked pleadingly at her, yet did not move toward her. Adama stopped walking and stared at him. Her breasts were beginning to leak the milk for their child. She stood stark still, and said; "You are here."

"Are you leaving today?" he asked.

"I think I have to go today. I have to go to my baby now, Modu."

"To *our* baby.," he said.

"The milk is coming. I have to go," she looked into his eyes with the saddest look Modu had ever seen on anyone. Even the times when they were together alone in their little house and she was ill. Even then she did not look as longingly sad as she was looking at him now.

"Then go. But, know that I know this baby you are about to feed is *my* baby."

She nodded, solemnly glancing at him as she began to run toward her son.

****

Adama crept into her room through the back door where the latrine and wash area stood enclosed by a stick fence.

Mariama cuddled Mustafa-boy while he sucked on a piece of cloth soaked in water and a bit of sugar. Mariama scowled at Adama as she entered their room. "I looked for you but did not want to alert mother. Where have you been? What kind of a mother deserts her son when he is hungry? The only way I could stop him from crying is to give this to him," Mariama passed the baby to Adama where she sat on the bed beside the two of them.

Mustafa-boy transferred from the sugar cloth to his mother's breast as ferociously as a baby bird grabs worms from it's mother's beak. A stillness settled onto the room. Mariama looked at the two of them, mother and child. She stood and left the room through the back door to take her first bath of the day.

Adama looked into the open eyes of her son and smiled as he suckled, "I saw your father just now."

The baby stopped sucking, pulled away and stared at Adama. For a second only, he stared directly into her eyes, then nuzzled for his milk. Again, eyes closed, he drank until he was full. He fell asleep and Adama carefully placed him in the middle of the girls' bed.

A little later, Adama went looking for her mother. When Binta was not visible in the compound courtyard or in the kitchen area, she would often be in her room. Adama carried Mustafa-boy on her back. His head full of black curls bounced gently.

"Ma Binta, e sama" Adama spoke as she entered the room and saw Binta sitting on the iron post bed sorting a large tub of small tomatoes. Mariama, and Mata, their young sister sat on the second bed, helping Binta with the sorting.

"E sama to you, Adama Darboe. Where did you go off to and leave your sister with your hungry infant?" Binta Darboe looked very unhappy. Her scowl was always like a thunder cloud dark and menacing. Her big face had wrinkles across the forehead and her full mouth was drawn down in a perfect reverse curve. Edges reaching to the bottom of her face.

"I went quickly for a walk down the path toward the river, but not all the way. MaBinta, I am leaving this day for another home. Am I not? Will I not miss this compound, and this family and the places I love the most? I am sorry, Ma. I was wrong." She plunked down beside her mother and hung her head, dejectedly.

Binta looked at Adama's back and placed her lips on the loose black curls of Mustafa-boy.

"He is your son to care for and I will not be there to tell you what you must do. You will listen and obey the lessons that Arake will teach you. She is a good woman and will treat you as her own daughter. But, you are not to wander off down paths of loneliness. Ya Moi?" Binta tossed several small tomatoes into a huge galvanized tub.

"N Moi," Adama murmured. "When am I leaving, Ma?"

"This morning. Arake and Momadou have had breakfast already and are visiting some of their relatives in the village here, then they will be leaving. You must be ready when they come for you. Your husband has been here looking for you. You must be ready to answer his questions. He did not seem very pleased to find his son in the care of a young girl such as Mariama."

"Was he not to marry Mariama before I was told I must marry him?"

Binta Darboe glared at Adama. "You are such a difficult girl," she growled. "You become a big problem, then you challenge me with this nonsense of being told who you must marry! I will not miss your difficult ways. I leave them up to Arake and your husband!"

"But Ma, I will miss you. I do not want to go back to that place. I feel like a stranger, and I miss my vue and I miss my sisters, and brothers and father; but most of all I miss you. Ma, I am sorry for all of what I have done. Please don't make me go!"

The room was uncomfortably silent for several minutes. Mustafa-boy slept, peacefully while Mariama sat with her slender hands folded in her lap. Her head bowed to her chest. She felt like weeping for her sister. She loved and missed her sister. She also loved this new baby very much.

"I will go to my room and prepare for the journey back to Sanyang and the Badgie compound," Adama rose and left her mother and sisters.

As she stepped up onto the veranda of the girls' room she saw Mustafa, her husband, striding toward her. Rushing as if he were going to a soccer match. He looked perplexed as he marched toward Adama.

"Where did you go without our son?" he demanded.

"He is here, on my back," Adama indicated, turning half way around, in order for Mustafa to see the infant snuggled into his mother's back.

"Do not make me any more angry than I already am, Adama Darboe. You know well what I am talking about! Did Mariama not tell you that I came to inform you we must prepare for our journey back to Sanyang? And I find you are missing. You left our baby here hungry and upset. That is *not* good."

Mustafa grabbed Adama's forearm and yanked her toward him. He squeezed her arm fiercely. His fingers reached deep into her firm upper arm. He held his grip and put his mouth into her ear and whispered loudly; "Do not *ever* leave our baby alone again, ya moi?

Adama's eyes were closed, mouth held in a tight grimace. Her arm felt as it were in a metal vise. It was a burning pain radiating up her neck. Hardly breathing, she nodded.

Mustafa pushed her away, snorted like an angry bull, and stepped off the veranda.

****

Modu the boy she loved had been walking past the open gate of the Darboe compound having gone to the market after returning from his walk down the magic path. He glanced through the open gate hoping to get one last look at Adama Darboe before she left for Sanyang. That is when he saw Mustafa holding Adama's arm in a forceful grip, and he saw Adama's face in a grimace of pain, and he saw Mustafa whispering into the ear of Adama with his head pressed against Adama's. He stood transfixed. Frozen like a statue, he stood with one leg about to step forward, one arm holding the side of the open gate. Stunned, he could not move. He then saw Adama, with closed eyes, nod in agreement of some kind.

Mustafa stepped off the veranda. As he stepped down, Mustafa noticed Modu watching him. Mustafa nodded to Modu, and walked in the other direction, towards Ebrima Darboe's house.

Modu remained there by the gate for a few moments waiting and hoping that Adama would see him before she went into her room. She did not look anyplace except down at the floor, wiped tears from her eyes, and stepped into her room.

Modu felt an anger that he could not remember ever feeling before. Heat began to radiate into his face and arms. Something in his chest was thumping like the sound of a drum. He needed to see if Adama was alright before she left for Sanyang. The thumping was making him breathe rapidly.

He walked around the fence outside of the Darboe compound toward the back of the buildings, and carefully stepped into the wash area of the girls room. He silently slid along the outside wall of the girls room, the wash area just outside of the back door. He stood flush against the wall beside the door of the girls room. He listened for any sound from inside the room where Adama had stepped. He heard her quietly sobbing. He peeked quickly around the open door of her room and in an instant could see her sitting there holding their baby, rocking back and forth, sobbing.

He could not stand it any longer. He whistled the delicate sound of a tiny bird. It used to be their private whistle when they were living together in their little house.

Her sobbing stopped. Like a startled deer, she snapped her head up straight and listened again.

Modu whistled once more.

Adama turned her head toward the familiar sound and rushed on bare quiet feet toward the back door.

It frightened her when she saw Modu, the boy she loved, standing there. For now she was aware that her husband could become a violent man with very little cause. "Modu, what are you doing here?"

"Adama Darboe, I saw what your husband just did to you. I was looking through the gate. I saw him grabbing your arm," He looked down at her arm and saw the dents already darkening into vile bruises.

Modu looked into Adama's eyes and sadness was everywhere.

"Modu, you must leave now. I am in more danger by you being here."

"I will speak to your parents about this, Adama Darboe."

"I am going back into my room now. Goodbye, Modu."

She stepped into the dimly lit room and began to pack her basket with clothes and a bag of rice.

****

When he entered his family compound across the way, Modu heard a woman's moan coming from the vicinity of his rooms. He looked toward his father's house and saw his father, Ousman Barrow sitting with two of his father's vue, smoking. Ousman was looking toward Modu, and once he seemed sure Modu was looking toward him, Ousman nodded. *I think Mimuna is giving birth,* he thought.

He walked toward his father's house and stepped up onto the veranda, greeted the three men and squatted beside them. No one spoke. The men smoked. Another moan came from Modu's room.

"Who is with her?" Modu asked his father.

"Your mother and Isatou. They have gone to fetch Binta Darboe."

Modu sat with the older men for an hour. He began to fidget and pace. The men chatted about the peanut farm, and the cassava farm, and the dry season, and the rainy season, and the price of it all. Finally, his father said, "Modu, go find your vue and we will fetch you when it is time. You are not good pacing here."

Modu walked away. He found his boys sitting at the corner by the market. They already had heard that Modu was about to become a father. In a village one knows these things.

Several hours passed. During that time he and his vue watched the people at the market come and go He had seen the Badgie clan leave town on three donkey carts. Included was his son and Adama. He looked up at the wagon passing him not five feet away. He caught a quick glance of Adama's eyes on him. His return gaze was full of sadness.

Modu returned to his compound for lunch and to learn any news about Mimuna and her labor. He found the men eating lunch on his father's veranda so he joined them. They were very quiet, and he noted several women moving in and out of his house. He heard Mimuna cry out. He heard several women shushing with calming voices. The cries now were unremitting.

The men finished their lunch and pulled out their tobacco.

The young girls who were doing the cooking this day cleared the big bowl from the mens' area and disappeared into the cooking area.

When the sun began to lose its strength and afternoon was ending, a woman's cry came loud and anxious from Modu's room where Mimuna lay. Then the second time it was more a scream than a moan. It was not Mimuna's voice that was screaming. Then Fatou, mother of Modu came out of the house and beckoned for Modu to come. She looked wretched and tired and in anguish. Modu stood, looked at his father for guidance and his father motioned with his head to go to his house where Mimuna lay. By now the loud voices of several crying women were heard coming from the room. Modu was nearly collapsing by the time he reached his house. He stood at the open doorway and looked about wildly. There he saw Mimuna lying motionless. She did not breath. She was completely still and without life. On her chest lay a motionless infant wrapped in cloth, with only its face and head exposed. It too was without life.

Modu fell onto the bare dirt floor beside the bed and wept. He reached up and clutched Mimuna's hand. His mother took his shoulders and pulled him up. She placed her arms across his back and led him to another room. He was shaking and sobbing and he bent forward as if he might fall to the ground any moment. There, his mother, Fatou, laid him down onto a mat, patted his shoulders, ran her hand over his forehead, touched her lips to his head, and left him. She had things she must do.

****

Adama felt a chill run across her back as the sun set that day they returned to Sanyang. She looked anxiously at her baby to be sure he was alright. She smiled lovingly at this gift Modu the boy she loved had given her. No matter how many bruises she received from Mustafa, she would remain strong because of this gift from Modu.

She rode in a donkey cart with Arake, mother of Mustafa, and one sister, Fatumata. Abduli, brother of Mustafa, drove the donkey cart. It was a nice day with heat,but not unbearable. There were monkeys in the trees near the narrow dirt road. Running through the branches they chattered and followed the donkey carts. Leaves and grass were still thick and green as the dry season had not yet peaked. Sometimes a monkey would throw a bunch of leaves down on the people in the wagons. And they would brush the leaves from their clothes and continue on. The monkeys would scream as if laughing, and follow the donkey over the path.

The rainy season had just passed. Now and again, an opening through the trees revealed a small cluster of round houses with straw roofs, proof of people living and farming their land in the bush. A child or two would run out to the side of the road and shyly wave to the donkey carts as they passed.

They arrived as the sun was meeting the horizon, and the women moved quickly to their houses in order to start a fire for cooking supper. It would be porridge, this day, as they did not have time before dark to pound rice and cook a full meal. Everyone was tired from the celebration and days travel.

Adama slept in the women's house with Arake, Fatumata, and Ndey. She would go to Mustafa's room three nights a week. It was the tradition. So when the man took another wife, the schedule would be already in place. She was relieved that this night was not one of the nights she was to go to him. She hated him too much to think of lying in his bed.

Arake looked at Adama's arm that evening as the two sisters, Arake and Adama, ate their porridge using small gourds. She took Adama's arm in her large gentle hand and clucked her tongue in distress.

"You must never make a man angry. It is too dangerous. You must learn how to obey the man and please him always. Ya Moi?"

"N Moi," Adama replied.

CHAPTER 26

Modu Has Lost a Son

Several weeks passed since Mimuna and her infant son died. Two villages mourned their loss. The same day they died, before the sun set, the two were buried. Her baby was buried with her. They were washed and wrapped in white cotton cloth. They were gently laid onto a wagon and pulled by the family donkey to the cemetery where they were buried in the Barrow family plot.

The drums had alerted Mimuna's family in Brikama to come immediately to Jambanjelly Mimuna's mother was already there helping with the birthing of her daughter's son. She was there also to bathe her dead daughter and grandson before they were wrapped in white cotton.

Mimuna's family was able to reach the cemetery just as Ousman Barrow's vue was lifting Mimuna and her baby from the donkey cart and laying them carefully into a shallow grave. No stones or markers were to be seen. Only an open barren plot of land designated the burial spot, the cemetery. Once laid to rest, and covered with soil, a large flat piece of timber covered the freshly dug earth.

Modu did not sleep for several nights. His mind was full of confusion. His loss of this young woman who was becoming part of his life cut deep into his heart. His loss of a son was overwhelming. A son is the most significant achievement a man can ever accomplish. It proves his seed is strong. Having many sons indicate a man is virile and strong and powerful.

I still have a son, but I cannot claim him. I wonder if this is why I lost this other son. I wonder if this is why I lost Mimuna. My sin is great, I fear.

As time passed, Modu went back to being a young single man doing what young, single men of Jambanjelli do; work in the cassava gardens and groundnut fields. They sit on the corner of the street near the mosque and market. They attend the celebrations of the village.

His vue helped him through his loss. Soccer helped him through his loss. His faith helped him through his loss. Yet, Modu never forgot that in the village of Sukita, his living son was with the mother, Adama Darboe. He longed to see them both.

Adama Darboe heard the news of Mimuna Conteh, wife of Modu the boy she loved. The news had come to that village only a few days after the actual death of Mimuna and the infant. Adama was at a loss as to how she should feel. Up until now death was shared with the whole compound and village. A joint mourning rushed through the entire place. Everyone knew how to feel and what to do. Adama wept for the young woman, Mimuna for the loss of her life and the loss of the infant son. The first night she heard this news she shivered as she lay in bed shared with her baby and her husband, Mustafa Badgie.

"What is wrong with you?!" Mustafa snarled at her, as he reached for the baby and lowered him onto the blanket lying beside the bed on the floor. Adama clutched the baby to her, making it impossible for Mustafa to take the baby. "What are you doing? I am to put him on his blanket so I can get into this bed. Stop being so difficult, or I will have to get angry with you. And, you know what that means.!" Mustafa yanked Mustafa-boy from Adama's arms and placed him on the blanket on the floor. Mustafa-boy slept on. Adama continued to lie curled into a ball on her side, hugging her breasts.

Mustafa, lay on the bed and said, "You are a stubborn girl, but somehow I like you." He patted her bottom and chuckled. Adama, facing away from him, closed her eyes and pushed her fist against her mouth.

****

Adama wanted to go home to Jambanjelly and share the mourning of the Barrow family with her family. She wanted to see Modu and comfort him. She longed to hold him and pat his back and say *I am so sorry, Modu.* But she could not. She would not be allowed or encouraged by any of the families to return to Jambanjelly after just being there for the Koolio of Mustafa-boy. She thought of Modu every day. She thought of his wife and baby, both dead and lying in the earth. She wondered if Modu the boy she loved was thinking of his other son and of her. If he was thinking of them, *what* was he thinking about them? She longed to know the answer to all of these questions that were tossing around in her head.

Arake, mother of Mustafa, watched Adama closely those first weeks that Adama was with them. She knew this baby, Mustafa-boy was not the son of her Mustafa. In her heart she had known this from the beginning. No one had said so outright, but she remembered the conversation and agreement she and her husband, Momadou had made with the Darboe family. They only intimated why there was a great need for Adama to be married immediately, and they were asking a big favor of them to allow Mustafa and Adama be married as soon as possible. Now this baby came sooner than expected. Mustafa was so overjoyed to become the father of this infant boy that no one wanted to spoil his joy.

Besides, what good would it do to make an issue of it? Here was a new baby entering the world and everyone seemed to be alright with the situation as it is. Why cause problems unless necessary?

****

Fatumata, sister of Mustafa, stood in the doorway of her brother's room. She came to visit Adama who was resting with Mustafa-boy as he nursed. On the days Adama was to be with Mustafa for the night, Adama could spend time in his room, if she desired.

Fatumata was the same age as Adama and they were fast becoming friends. Fatumata loved her new nephew, Mustafa-boy and often helped with his care.

"You are sleeping?" she whispered as she entered the curtained doorway.

"No. Come in. This little boy is always hungry. He is sucking the life out of me," Adama smiled down at her son.

"Yes. I can see he loves to eat. Can I take him to the well when I go to fetch the water, soon? Musakebba is bringing her sister's baby and we are pretending they are our babies. We are pretending we will meet our husbands for a party after we fetch the water." Fatumata's body was short and well proportioned. She had plump, round arms. Her hands were small with chubby fingers. All in all there appeared to be a luscious firmness about her.

"You are anxious to be married?" Adama asked.

"Of course. Who is not anxious to be married and have a party?" Fatumata looked bemused at Adama's question.

"I guess most everyone," Adama replied.

"Were you not excited to marry Mustafa? He is quite handsome and is loved by many girls, you know," Fatumata pulled the baby away from Adama as soon as he had finished nursing and was nodding off.

"No I didn't know he is loved by many girls. I do not go out of this compound, except to the market, so I do not know the people of this village. What girls love my husband? Who are they?"

Fatumata was placing Mustafa-boy on her back, leaning forward, while Adama lay him there. Fatumata wrapped a cloth around the baby and pulled it to her front where she tied the ends just over her breasts. Mustafa-boy slept on. His little head barely visible over the wrap.

"Oh, lots of the girls in the village love him, but Ndey Seiny is the one who owns him. She is his favorite. Did you not know that girls in this village really love your husband?" Fatumata grinned down at Adama as she checked to be certain Mustafa-boy was safely tied onto her.

"I just told you I know nothing of this village, Fatumata. Does he seriously love these girls, or does he flirt and play with them only?"

"Only Ndey is the one he loves. They sneak away into the bush almost every day. You know how boys are, Adama Darboe. They all have more than one girl. But, you are the wife and the mother of his son. These other girls are just what men do. I do think Ndey will never let him go, though. She does not like the idea of you."

"That is unfortunate. She will have to adjust to it, I think. I am here and so is his son!"

Fatumata laughed as she stepped out onto the veranda.

Adama lay on their bed thinking about this latest conversation and of her reaction to the news of Mustafa's girlfriends. Why did she care who Mustafa was with? She cared very little about this man. Why was she feeling anger about these women? She rolled over and fell asleep.

****

Ndey Seiny stepped out from behind a tree by the path and blocked the way for Mustafa. "Where do you think you are going?" Ndey challenged.

"I am looking for you. I was told you wanted to talk to me. What is this all about? I thought we were not to be seen together for awhile. Why are you telling my vue that you want to see me?"

"Oh, do not worry about your stupid vue. You know they will not tell anyone about you, no matter what you do. You are their leader, right?" Ndey was tall and slender with taut muscled arms. She always wore four tiers of cowry shells strung on twine around her long beautiful neck. Her posture was regal with long legs sticking out from her ankle length wrap-around skirt of many colors. She had a large oval shaped head with ears fitting tightly against it. Her hair was cropped short. Most girls wore their hair in corn rolled braids, but Ndey liked hers short and hugging her head.

"So, what do you want? Are you wanting me to lean you against this tree, right here on this path?"

Ndey pushed against his chest with both her strong arms, and Mustafa fell back just enough to set him off balance. He grabbed her wrists as he was falling backwards and yanked her to his chest and slapped her. She staggered back, tripping over a root growing at the edge of the path she caught herself from falling and stood, holding the side of her face with both hands.

Ndey held her hand against her cheek where Mustafa had slapped her. It was stinging and hurtful. She looked wounded and surprised. Although Ndey and Mustafa had arguments, he had never struck her.

"I came to be with you. I do not see you as often as we used to be together. I will go now. I will not bother you from now on.," she turned towards the village and left Mustafa standing on the path.

Mustafa watched her walk away holding her hand against her cheek. He watched for some time before he started down the path toward the village. He was thinking about what a problem women could be. He was not happy being tied to a wife, but it was not really that difficult if the women would behave and let him think. He did love being the father of a son, however. And, his wife Adama was really not that bad. She was trying to do what he expected of her and was a very good mother. Also, she was not resistant to his love making as he had expected her to be. Until he could have a second wife, which would not be for some time, he would like to keep Ndey happy, too. She was his true partner, no matter how much they fought, and made up, she was his soul partner. He guessed his parents would never allow her to be his wife, and maybe that was all right. Ndey would always be his best girl.

****

Next, he went to find Masanneh, one of his boys. One of his vue wanted to speak with Mustafa concerning a money-making deal. Only the two of them were to be present. This made Mustafa very curious. It was rare that only two of the four met, especially when it seemed to be a secret venture.

They met behind the mosque at the edge of the prayer ground in an open, dry field where one huge tree spread its ancient limbs over the center of the field.

"What is so important and secret that you want to meet me only, Masanneh?" Mustafa rolled some tobacco in a piece of brown wrapping paper. Looking up at Masanneh with one eye squinting against the smoke of his first exhale, he waited for Masanneh to respond.

"I have learned of a way we can gain much money, Mustafa. Much money."

"So. What might that be?" Mustafa's attention was with Masanneh now. Mustafa wanted money like everyone else in the village. Money was not very available in the village. Only exchanging commodities and favors were how the people made their way. Mustafa wanted money to buy things from the shops in Brikama when he was able to get there. He wanted to buy ready made clothes from the piles at the market place, which were shipped in from other parts of the world. And he wanted cigarettes already rolled, and jewelry to give the girls, and food from the street shops. He wanted to smoke the ganja he had tried several times with his vue. They had swapped their shirts they had purchased in Brikama for enough ganja to share and enjoy. The word was that if you smoked enough ganja you could make love all night long. Mustafa knew Ndey would be happy about that. He stopped, at that point and thought, *I wonder if Adama would like that.*

"So, what do we have to do in order to acquire all this money?" Mustafa asked.

"A group of boys from the village have been rustling cattle from the Fula men where they keep them in the bush. They steal only three or four cattle at a time, and lead them to the Casamance where they get a great deal of money from a group of men who wait just over the border. These boys came to me asking if one or two of our vue wanted to help, as they can expand their business if they can find some trustworthy boys to help."

"Why would they come to you and not some of the other boys in the village? What made them think we would not report them to the Chief?" Mustafa asked.

"One of them is my cousin, Lamin Cooley, and he knows I would not report him even if we said no to his offer."

"How dangerous is it? It must be done during the night. It must take hours of leading the cattle through darkness to reach those who are waiting. And then hours to return home after the delivery of these cattle."

"I want you to come and meet Lamin and discuss this with him. He will be at my compound this evening. His vue works two or three times a week driving the cattle to the destination. If we agree to work with him, we will go with the boys already working in order to learn how it is done. Will you at least come tonight and meet with him?"

"I will be there. Tell Lamin I will come to your compound tonight after the last prayer. Now, I have to go to the groundnut field. My father is waiting for me. I will see you this evening. I'm not sure about this program, Masanneh, but I will consider it once we have talked with him."

With that Mustafa rose from the log and walked toward his father's groundnut field.

****

That night they sat in a corner of Masanneh's family compound. Small houses were lined along three sides of the compound, facing the center. At the fourth side, a tall natural fence with a gate allowed an entry from the street. It was a dark, moonless night, and the boys had built a small fire of twigs outside by Masanneh's room. It was at the far corner of the compound. They sat under a huge orange tree, which stood a few feet from his house. They sat on stumps around the small fire and discouraged the children from clustering around them by the fire. They grunted at the young ones and told them that they had business to discuss. Several small boys sat a few feet away from them, watching them. Wanting to be them.

Lamin Cooley had come for an overnight visit with Masanneh's family, especially to discuss his business proposition.

"We have been leading three or four cattle through the bush to the Casamace border which takes three hours. We select the cattle who stray from the herds and are grazing close beside the forest where we are watching them."

"But, what about the Fula men, where are they? Are they not watching their cattle carefully?" Mustafa asked Lamin.

"They become casual as the night goes on, and they often are seen with their heads dropping to their chests. Napping. We, in the meantime are selecting the stray cattle, and cautiously moving them into the bush and away from the sight of the Fula men. There are usually four or five men and twenty or thirty cattle. Many times the men do not miss the cattle until daylight. By that time we have nearly reached the border."

Lamin was about the same age as Mustafa and Masanneh, with fiery black eyes, and hair hanging in loose ringlets over his head and down his forehead. He was very tall and wiry. He sat leaning forward, elbows on his knees, looking directly, excitedly into the faces of the two young men.

"It is a guaranteed way to make money. The men at the border are with large amounts of cash and once they inspect the cattle they pay us well. We are paid per head. We divide the money equally among each man. I take an extra commission as the leader. If you agree to do this, we will all work together, which means we can increase the number of cattle or nights of work, thus earning more money."

"And, if we are caught by the Fula men, they will beat us to death, right?" Mustafa asked, already knowing the answer.

"But, they won't catch us. We have been doing this for many moons now and have never even been chased by those lazy Fula men. All they know to do is sit around and keep the cattle in one place. You don't have to worry about the Fula men. If we all work together,we will be fine."

"But, what do they do about answering to their bosses? The owners of the cattle they care for? What do they tell them when cattle are missing?" Mustafa asked.

"The Fula men know how to fool their bosses by lying about the number they went with to the bush a few moons before. The bosses have to believe the Fula men when they tell them that the hyenas or the lions ate some of the cattle, or that they became sick and died, or that they fell into the river and drowned. The owners are angry and threaten to fire the Fula men. But they cannot depend on anyone other than the Fula men to care for the herd, and stay out in the god forsaken bush for long periods of time like the Fula men will do. Everyone knows the Fula men love cattle and want to be with them and want to care for them. It is a strange thing. But, it is a *real* thing."

"Are there several groups of Fula men with cattle in the bush in order to take that number each week?"

"Yes, between Jambanjelly and Gunjuir into the bush there are many small groups of cattle belonging to the rich men of the villages. My vue knows where all of them are moving and staying and moving again. I have a few of my boys who do the spotting and the movement and they inform me which group we should take on any given night." Lamin clasped his hands together close to the fire and his face showed great excitement.

Mustafa and Masanneh stared into the fire.

"Well?" Lamin asked.

"Mustafa, let us try this by going one night with Lamin's vue and watch how this is done. We can watch everything, and decide the next day or two if we want to be a part of it." Masanneh was very anxious to participate in this clandestine adventure. He was thinking that even if Mustafa decided not to do it, that he would anyway.

Mustafa drew in a deep breath and sat tall on his stool. He held the breath and puffed out his chest, then slowly exhaled.

The small boys who were sitting apart from the three men watched anxiously awaiting the response from Mustafa.

"Then if you want to give it a try, Masanneh, I too will explore the possibility of being part of it. I need to know how much we are paid for each trip before we agree to do this dangerous work. Also, what do your families think your vue is doing on all these night absences, Lamin?"

"We tell them we are staying at friends at different villages, or at a celebration on the other side of the village and sleeping with some of our own vue. You know how that works, Mustafa. We are always staying over with one another. Our families have enough to think about without worrying about their grown sons. Right?"

"I guess you are right. So, Lamin Cooley, we will meet you when you take your next trip to the Casamas. Inform us when and where we should meet you and we will be there."

Mustafa stood and extended his hand to Lamin.

"I will contact Masanneh soon. You will be glad you made this decision, Mustafa," Lamin smiled broadly.

Mustafa nodded as he said goodnight. He walked to the house of Masanneh's father and stepped up onto the veranda where the elders sat quietly chatting and smoking their tobacco. He shook the hands of the each of them and wished them good night. He then left the compound to return to his family.

CHAPTER 27

Cattle Rustling

Mustafa-boy's first birthday was celebrated in the Badgie compound with a big party. Drummers came from Brikama and the women danced. A goat was slaughtered, and a sauce was made and, the goat meat was added to be poured over the rice. Nearly everyone in the village dropped by to celebrate. Lately, the Badgie family appeared to have plenty of food. The buildings in the compound were always in good repair and the children had clothes from the market that were sold in piles on the street in Brikama. Good, ready-made, used clothes from other parts of the world. No one questioned where the money was coming from. At least no one asked openly how the Badgie family was doing so well. The women from other compounds, and asked quietly, among themselves, when sorting the tiny stones from rice, or winnowing the rice, or braiding each other's hair while they lay on mats under the large mango tree. They would never actually ask, more likely they made statements. 'The Badgies are having another celebration.' 'Arake Badgie has a new bed.' 'Momadou Badgie has a new donkey cart. Big and new.' Then the group would in unison respond with a 'hmmmm.' That is how it was done. Never an overt open question of 'Where is the money coming from?'

Adama was the proud mother of a handsome, lively, happy one year old, and Mustafa was giving his son a big party. Adama watched

Mustafa-boy as he stood, holding onto Adama's knee with one hand, bouncing up and down to the beat of the drums. He swung his free arm in circles and moved his whole chubby little frame keeping in perfect time. He had scrunched a piece of sweet bread in his free hand as the melted glaze drizzled down to his elbow. He smiled at everyone who watched him show off his dance style. He wore a bright blue shirt and nothing more. His face was full of grins and bare gums. Big eyes and a wide nose. Full lips, smiling.

Mustafa and Masanneh arrived late in the afternoon to join the celebration. They had been away most of the night and had slept late into the morning. Because these two men apparently had work someplace other than Sukata, and were bringing home money to their families, they were treated with great respect. No one questioned them about anything. They slept as late as they wished and ate whenever they were hungry or ready to eat. The mothers, wives, aunts, and sisters cooked for them and fetched whatever they spoke for.

Life was good for Mustafa and Masanneh.

The party went on into the late evening, well after Mustafa-boy had fallen asleep on his mother's breast. Adama took him to her room and placed him on the bed. Leaving him there, she changed her clothes for the third time that day into a bright red taffeta skirt and top. She put on the big gold loop earrings Mustafa had given her last week when he returned from a long absence. He had not been home for three days and nights. Masanneh also had been away that same time.

"Your mother worries when you are away for more than one night. Mustafa, where do you go on these nights?"

"You, Adama Darboe, do not ask me questions. Do you hear? If you do not like what I am doing, I do not care. You can go home to your compound in Jambanjelly anytime you wish. You can go there and stay. I do not care. You will, however, leave Mustafa-boy with me, here in this compound. I do not have the time or patience to listen to you. You are not my choice, so do not ask me questions about anything I do. Ya Moi?"

"I hear," Adama had decided that she would not waste her mind on him. She would wait and see how much longer before someone would find out what Mustafa and Masanneh were doing to get their money. She would wait a bit before she asked Arake to ask Momadou, father of Mustafa, to allow her to go for a visit to Jambanjelly. She missed her family and had not been home for several moons. She knew her parents wanted to see their grandson near the time of his first birthday. She would be careful and wait for a few days, then ask Arake for her help.

CHAPTER 28

Mustafa's Misadventures

They met Lamin and Abduli at the Gunjuir seaside with Buba, the boatman. Buba had been waiting for Mansanneh and Mustafa since sunrise. Standing by his dugout, holding a long pole taller than himself, he leaned his head against it and watched the men approach.

"Cousin, you are here," he said to Masanneh.

Buba shook hands with each of the men, smiling, chuckling in a deep throated gurgle, he slapped his cousins back. *Long time.* he murmured.

"Yes, it's a long time that I don't see you, Buba. How have you been, and how is the family?" Masanneh pushed at his cousins' shoulder gently.

The five of them stood in a rough circle shuffling their feet in the white, hot sand. They spoke of family and what ceremonies they had attended in the past few weeks.

Finally, Buba took a deep breath and started to move to his boat. "Come, we best be on our way." he said as he placed one foot into the dugout.

"You are familiar with the place where we wish to land, Buba?" Masanneh asked.

"Of course. I know every place hidden, or in the open of this seashore," Buba smiled slightly as he nodded to the men. They stepped into the dugout and sat on the bottom, cross legged. The dugout was narrow and long. The men sat, one in front of the other. Buba, who stood at the back with the pole planted into the floor of the sea, he pushed off. Buba knew exactly where Masanneh wished to be dropped. A few miles down the coast toward the Casamance, was a forested area where he would leave them.

It was a beautiful morning as they set out. Buba poled his dugout smoothly only a bit off shore, moving south. The four men lit up their tobacco simultaneously. Cigarettes had been rolled at the beachside in preparation of this bonus trip along the coast. Relaxed, they felt content and excited.

"You boys are going hunting I understand," Buba grinned at them. "You will be borrowing guns on the way?"

Buba suspected the mission of his cousin and his vue, but their secret was safe with any relative of these men.

Pure white beaches stretched as far as they could see. At one spot, fishermen were putting out their boats for the days catch. Dozens of boats were lined up along the beach, like so many beached whales. Each one a huge dory, painted in bright colors. The men in Buba's dugout watched the fishermen moving their boats down the beach toward the sea; pushing them over logs which acted as rollers as the men heaved and pushed them over the logs beneath. Picking up the log, which had been left behind at the back of the boat, they would run it to the front, again it would be rolled over. Men pushing and heaving and yelling encouragement to each other.

"Masanneh,. see there," Buba was pointing toward a tip of land which jutted out into the sea. "That is where I will drop you off. I will land on this side of the point where the sea is calm. Not much surf, nor many rocks there."

The men strained to see the place where they would be dropped off. They knew a long walk ensued from there to where the cattle grazed.

Masanneh paid Buba and told him to meet them in four days, sometime in the afternoon.

"If we do not arrive, just wait for us. We will return as soon as possible," Masanneh shook his cousin's hand, then trekked up the beach following his vue.

At the tree line they turned and watched Buba moving smoothly back toward Gunjuir. He waved and grinned.

They walked through miles of forests where narrow paths made by animals and people intertwined. Tall palms reached to the sky. Mango and breadfruit trees grew into the deep bush. It was nearly dark where they walked as the tallest trees reached over the paths blocking out the natural light of the day.

Sometimes they would walk into an open area where trees had been clear cut, leaving a stump filled field. Then, the sun would beat onto their heads, leaving the four men in need of rest and water.

"I have to stop, Masanneh," Mustafa called. "Give me some water. When do we have some rice? How much longer before we reach the cattle?"

The four of them sat together, as close as newly hatched chicks, under a coconut palm tree.

Mustafa collected four coconuts and pulled his knife from its sheath. He found a rock nearby and pounded the knife into the coconut. He passed one coconut to Masanneh, and one to Lamin, and one to Abduli. The men tipped the coconuts to their dry parched lips and drank like babies who had not nursed for hours.

They cracked the coconuts open wide and cut the meat from each one. Eating a few pieces of the meat, they then wrapped the remainder in one of Masanneh's pieces of material.

They smoked.

They stood, stretched, and moved on down the path and into the forest.

"We'll walk a few more miles, then take a break from the heat until the sun begins to go down," Masanneh moved forward followed by the others. "My contact will meet us before we get to the cattle. He will help us collect them and move them to the new place by the border."

****

It all went wrong.

As the sun was setting, they were met by several herdsmen who blocked the path where Mustafa and his vue walked. The herdsmen were tall and fierce looking. They stood in a line across the path, totally blocking the way. They stood with legs spread wide. Each held a spear a staff, with the other hand against his hip. They wore ragged tunics and trousers of hand woven cloth. Dirty and ragged. They appeared not to have bathed for several days. They were unshaven.

The most rugged man who stood in the middle of the five appeared to be the leader. He stepped forward and cleared his throat.

"We do not believe you should be journeying any further on this way."

"And, why do you believe that?" Masanneh asked.

"We have been told men are on this path with the intention of stealing our cattle. We are not allowing anyone to walk further than where we stand," the spokesman growled.

"But we are on our way to the Casamance, and do not intend to disturb anyone or anything between here and there," Masanneh lied.

The five laughed. They shook their heads and sucked at their teeth.

"Why then are you taking this path? Why are you not using the roadway to Casamance? We do not believe you and therefore are taking you to our camp for the night. We will lead you there, and if you cause any problem we will have to tie your hands behind your back and your legs at the ankles. Do you hear?"

"We hear," Masanneh mumbled.

They walked in single file with the boss leading. Two men followed the last of Massaneh's men, and the remaining two walked on each side of the path where the four men walked.

Mustafa was terrified as were the other three, including Masanneh. They tried to speak to each other but the boss growled.

"No talking. You are prisoners now and will be treated as such. Until you can prove you are not here to steal our cattle, you will remain so."

They smelled the cattle before they heard or saw them. They grazed in an open pasture area. It looked like a large herd milling about.

Three men sat by a small fire at the edge of the pasture, smoking and drinking tea. They looked up as Masanneh and his men walked into the clearing surrounded by their compatriots.

"So, you were right, Adam, there are rustlers out tonight. You are good at this mystical visioning! I'm sure our boss will keep you around for many moons!"

The herdsman chuckled as he watched the new group being jostled and pushed down to squat around the fire.

The herdsman fed Masanneh's vue rice and sauce. They then tied each one at their hands and ankles.

"For sleeping. We do not want to lose you," Boss muttered.

"You cannot tie me up for this whole night!" Mustafa yelled. He thrashed about, trying to stand, one of the men pushed him down and another sat on him.

They tied him using torn strips of material. They tied his ankles and his hands behind his back.

"Tie the others, Alkali. They cannot be trusted for the night," Adam ordered.

The night was long and cold. Mustafa's vue did not sleep. They were not able to move well with ties restraining them.

Lying on the ground next to the others Mustafa yelled, "I need to go to the bush! Untie me now!"

Adam shook his head then scratched it. He poked the man beside him where he lay, and said., "Take this man to the bush."

"What will become of us when daylight comes? Are you moving the cattle? Will we be allowed to return to our homes?" Mustafa asked the man who untied his hands and stood with his spear at Mustafa's back while he relieved himself.

"I am not allowed to talk to you, man. Don't ask me anymore questions," Mustafa's guard tapped him on the shoulder and beckoned him to lie down again.

When the sun peeked over the line of mango trees at the east end of the clearing, the herdsman drank tea, rose from their haunches,and led the herd away toward the west.

"Hey! Hey! You! You can't leave us this way! We are tied here. We'll die. We'll be eaten buy insects, hyenas, lions!! Help us! Don't leave us this way!"

The herdsman walked away.

CHAPTER 29

A Time of Wonderment

Two weeks passed since Mustafa and Masanneh left the village. Usually, they returned in four or five days. Never more than seven days were they ever away from the village. Adama clung to Arake, mother of Mustafa. Adama needed to follow the mother of Mustafa, in order to determine how worried Arake was feeling about her missing son, Mustafa. Adama watched every expression on Arake's face. Each furrow on her brow meant something to Adama, and she listened carefully as Arake spoke with her vue. Her sisters. For sisters always knew the truth of the others.

Arake was anxiously awaiting her son's return and watched every time the gate door swung open, holding her breath and watching, watching. It must be Mustafa, her favorite son. He must come through that gate, now. He did not.

Adama watched her mother-in-law for clues of how she herself should feel and act. The mysterious absence of Mustafa and Masanneh caused unrest in the two family compounds. And Adama was now part of the Badgie compound.

One evening during the second week of Mustafa's absence Arake went to her husband earlier than the usual time to go to him for the night. She sat at the far end of the veranda while her husband, Momadou smoked and chatted with the other elders. She hoped by sitting there it would be a hint for those men to go home and leave her with her husband. Arake knew that was not the way it worked, but she continued to hope for a miracle. That she would be able to caste a spell on them and they would run away to their homes frightened of this magical woman, wife of Momadou. But, of course that did not happen.

As she sat waiting, she shelled groundnuts in a huge agateware bowl for the planting of the next seasons crop. She did not look at the men, nor did she glance at the children or youth who walked past them through the compounds' dry dirt yard. She did not want to attract the attention of anyone because she wanted only to have time with her husband before the evening turned into night, and Momadou would retire to his room, tired and without the desire to talk about his missing son, or to do anything other than sleep.

Finally, the men rose and said their goodnights. 'Allah ma suto dialah.' *May God go with you tonight.*

They had gone to evening prayer earlier, and now they were going home to their respective compounds.

Momadou, already standing having said goodnight to his vue, began to turn toward the door of his room.

"Husband, I need to speak with you this night. Now," Arake's voice trembled slightly, as she cracked the last groundnut.

"Are you not coming into this room for the night?," he asked, looking perplexed and tired.

"I am afraid that before what I have to say is out of my mouth you will be asleep," She spoke in a quiet voice, looking down into the pot of nuts.

"So, I am to sit here with you, instead of going to my room and removing these clothes I have been wearing all day? And I am not to refresh myself with bath? I am not to put on my caftan for sleeping, but I am to remain here in the night air, tired and needing a change, so you can talk to me? I do not understand. Why can you not come into my room as it is your duty to do as I say. So, carry this pot of groundnuts into my room, place it where it will be safe from the rodents, take your shower, put on your sleeping gown and talk with me before we sleep!"

Sometimes Arake would argue with Momadou when he became so unreasonable. Sometimes it worked and she was able to achieve her goal, by speaking out and holding fast. She did not scream like some of the wives she knew. They invariably were sorry for such impertinence. It was according to how serious Arake's wishes were as to how stubborn or determined she would become.

This time she was afraid she would lose, if she became combatant and stubborn. She needed desperately to speak with her husband about their missing son. So, she nodded, grasped the agateware bowl, rose and walked with smooth gliding steps into her husband's room. He followed, scowling slightly, and at the same time admiring the movement of her backsides.

Momadou took his shower while Arake took hers in the nearby women and children's shower area. They met at the same time in Momadou's room. They did not speak or look at each other.

Spreading their prayer mats in the nearest corner facing the east, they said the last prayer of the night. Momadou in front of Arake, nearest to the east,

Momadou gave a deep, satisfied sigh as he lay on his side of the bed. He spread a piece of lightweight material over his shoulders and rolled onto his side, facing the wall. Arake noticed this settling in of Momadou and felt a twinge of anger. *He is surely going to sleep before I can speak of my fear and concern.*

She slipped into the bed. Facing his back she pushed against him with her hands, gently, yet firmly. No response came from Momadou. She repeated her gentle push against one of his broad shoulders. She sensed he was still awake by his body tensing.

He rolled over onto his back and looked at the ceiling.

"You are making me very unhappy, Arake Badgie. I am trying to be patient with you. I am tired. I will sleep now." He rolled, once more, onto his side and closed his eyes.

Arake held her breath for fear she would explode. She held her breath and bit her lower lip until she feared it would draw blood. She sat up abruptly, placed her feet on the floor and, in a loud whisper she said.

"If I were not a good wife. If I were a lazy, untrustworthy wife. If I were not a good mother to our children, I would not sit here and go against your wishes, Momadou Badgie. But, it is because I am worried, to the point of near sickness, about our missing son, Mustafa, that I wish to speak."

She lowered her head as far as it would go into her chest. A tear dropped onto her lap. Then another. She did not sob or cry aloud. Tears dropped silently.

Momadou drew in another deep sigh as he rolled over onto his back. He moved his arm around her and lay his hand on her lap. He patted her lap and tucked his fingers between her legs.

"You are worried about your oldest son, as am I. I believe I need to go to the compound of Masanneh's cousin. Maybe I will learn where Mustafa might be. Lamine is the one who Masanneh and Mustafa are working for. He should be able to tell me what is keeping them away from their village so much longer than usual. So, tomorrow I will go to Masanneh's family compound to find if they have any news, and also, if anyone would want to travel with me to Lamine Cooley."

Arake turned and threw her arms around Momadou, and rolled onto him and kissed him violently on his mouth. She straddled him and tucked herself into him and cried and laughed and said, "Abaraka, Abaraka, my husband." Thank you, thank you.

CHAPTER 30

Adama Visits Jambanjelly

Adama and Arake rose early and went to the garden. The sun had just peeked over the horizon as they walked through the narrow path leading to their garden just outside of the village. The women's' garden was less than a half mile from the village where there was enough cleared land to plow, plant and grow their food for the season. Each year as soon as the rainy season began the village women pooled their money and hired the old man well digger. He would strip down to his ragged trousers and, with an ancient shovel, commence to hack away at the still rock hard earth. The arrival of the rain allowed the dry earth to soften. Wells were dug a few feet deep when water rushed in and filled the shallow hole. Water buckets tied with rope or rags were dropped into the wells by the women and girls. The gardens were watered twice a day for about six moons, until the rains stopped and dryness returned. Nothing grew during the dry season.

It had been one whole moon cycle since Mustafa and Masanneh had been missing. During that time, Momadou, father of Mustafa, along with Amadou, the father of Masanneh, traveled to Gunjuir and met with Buba, cousin of Masanneh. They inquired if he had seen the young men. Buba confirmed he had given them a boat ride to the southern shore. He said Lamine Cooley had made the arrangements for the boys to be taken to that place. The fathers asked if he knew where they were going and what they were going to be doing. Buba said he did not know any of those things. Buba suggested the fathers call on Lamine Cooley. The fathers agreed to do that. They returned to Jambanjelly and the next day went to Lamine Cooley's compound in Sanyang.

Lamine Cooley's compound showed signs of improvement during the past recent moons. His father had a new house, made from newly made local bricks, and had been skimmed and whitewashed. It looked to be large enough to have a sitting room and perhaps two sleeping rooms. He, Lamine, had a new house, smaller than his father's. It was new and neat, with a veranda.

Once the men shook hands with Lamine, they settled onto stools under the old mango tree. Lamine stood in front of the two men, his elders. He was uncomfortable about this visit. He, himself was concerned that Mustafa and Mansanneh had not returned. He waited in the village and continued to direct and join some of the other young men who were rustling cattle for Lamine and his boss.

Momadou addressed Lamine. He asked Lamine if he could tell them anything about their missing sons. Lamine shrugged and said, "I made arrangements for them to go to their new work place where they would working as herdsmen for the same man I work for. He is a rich cattleman who is expanding his herd and he may have sent them to a far off place that I do not even know.

I have not seen nor heard from him, my boss, for a few weeks. He said he may be on travel for some time and his boys would keep the cattle safe and well looked after,"

Lamine Cooley shifted his weight from his left foot to his right foot. Clearing his throat, he gazed into the earth.

"Is there no way you can check on the boys whereabouts?" Momadou grumbled, perplexed.

"I'm afraid until my boss returns I have no idea where they may have taken the cattle. There is a great deal of grazing land in that area south of here," Lamine Cooley began to sweat. He pulled off his shirt and swiped it under his arms. "It is too hot today," he said, trying to change the subject.

"Hmm," Amadou, father to Masanneh, muttered. "Then we shall be on our way. We ask only that you inform us of any news about our boys as soon as you hear."

The two men returned to their compounds where the wives waited. The mothers of the two boys waited by their open kitchen fires. Stirring the iron pots full of rice, tomatoes and chicken. Watching the gate to their respective compounds. Nearly breathless, they waited.

Adama sat beside Arake. She had not let Arake out of her sight for days. She wanted desperately to go home to her family in Jambanjelly. She worried a bit about her missing husband, Mustafa. After all, her life was depending on his life. Aside from that, she was not particular concerned about him being in danger, or hurt, or sick, or gone forever. She wanted to go to home to Jambanjelly, and, with any luck from Allah, never return to this compound. She wanted to be with her mother and sisters and her vue. She was lonely and lost. And, above all, she wanted a glimpse of Modu the boy she loved. Across the way in his compound she would be able to catch a glimpse of him. Or, when he walked out of his gate and down the corridor. Oh, how she longed to see him. Now, their son, Mustafa-boy was over a year old, and looked exactly like Modu. How Mustafa could not see that was amusing and amazing to Adama.

He is a stupid man not to see how 'his' son looks nothing like him, Adama thought such things when she lay in her bed, blessedly alone, except for her baby, Mustafa-boy.

One morning while she sat with Arake by the cooking pot she decided to ask the question.

"Arake, I am thinking of my mother, Binta Darboe. I am missing her too much, and I want her to see her grandson, Mustafa boy. It has been too long since she has seen him. Do you think Momadou will allow me to go for a visit to my family?"

"Your family is here in Badgie compound, Adama Darboe," Arake sat calmly, staring into the cooking pot. Her eyes watered from the wood smoke. Her face was fixed in calmness, yet worry wrinkles spread across her forehead. Arake's high cheekbones caused her eyes to be almond shaped. Her wide lips were soft and supple. Although she was considered old, having sons in their twenties, and a grandchild, she did not look old. She always wore a brightly colored head wrap, and a loose blouse and long skirt. Sometimes the blouse, the long skirt and the head wrap would each be of different designs and colors. It gave the impression of a wild flower garden.

"And, what about your missing husband? Do you not want to be here when he returns? Are you not worried about his absence enough to await his safe return?" Arake slowly turned her head, looking directly at Adama.

Adama bowed her head into her neck. She felt ashamed that Arake was asking her a question that she would have to lie about.

"Yes, I know I should be here when Mustafa returns. And, I will be. I will only stay for a few days. If Mustafa comes home the drums will tell me, and my father will bring me back at once. Within a few hours I will be here! I promise, Arake. Please ask Momadou if I may go home just for a few days.

"I will think about it,' Arake tossed a piece of wood onto the fire, which was down to embers burning a brilliant orange glow.

****

That night, just before darkness set into the village and the sun was about to fall off the earth, Adama put Mustafa boy on her back and slid out the back door, through the gap in the fence by the latrine. She walked quickly, her short legs moving in a near run. Her round hips rolled from side to side as Mustafa boy bounced on her back. His head lay between her shoulder blades, being rocked to sleep as the sun was setting.

It only took a few minutes walking down the path to the garden for Adama to reach the tree where Owl now lived. She had not seen him to speak with for two weeks, as she seemed to always be with some member of the Badgie family on their way to the garden or to fetch wood in the bush. She, however had seen him perched on his chosen limb many times. No one else saw him when they passed. Adama knew Owl was only for her eyes. Adama understood magic and mysterious events, as did most of the people in that place.

Adama stopped in front of the big old mango tree and said nothing to Owl who perched there looking at her. He blinked, ruffled his feathers and made a sound deep in his throat.

Mustafa-boy opened his eyes and stiffened at what he saw. He grabbed his mother's hair, which had sprung from her head wrap at the nap of her neck. He kicked his feet, which hung from his sling.

"You have brought your son, Adama Darboe. He is a big boy. And, it seems he can see me. That means he understands the magic of Owl and Adama. Is that the reason you brought him today?"

"Well, I actually could not leave him unattended while I left the compound, and I needed to see you, Owl. So, I brought him with me. I did not think about whether he would recognize you, or not. What does that mean, Owl? Is he to be a mystic?"

"It would appear that way to me, Adama Darboe. So, what brings you here today when the darkness is nearly upon us? I have often seen you coming and going with your new family. Passing by on this path and it seems that you are being very brave and learning to accept your life as it is. I have heard the conversations about your husband, Mustafa and his friend, Mansanneh being absent for a longer time than expected. Is that why you have come?"

"I am not here to ask for help concerning the absence of Mustafa Badgie. He is not my main concern. I do not even miss him, Owl. I do not wish him harm, but I am not overly worried about him and his friend, Masanneh. I am here to ask your advice about how I can convince Momadou Badgie, head of the compound, to allow me to return to my family compound in Jambanjelly. Just for a visit. Please, how can I convince him it is all right for me to go to my family for a short visit?"

"You are wanting to see the boy across the way from your family compound, also, are you not? The father of the boy who kicks at your back and stares at me with eyes as big as the mangoes in my tree."

Adama's eyes began to show tears. She lowered her head and scuffed the path with her slipper.

"Yes, I do. I long to see him. Owl, why can I not forget him? Why can I not become adjusted to my new family and the man I am married to? Why can I not let Modu, the boy I love fade from my daily thoughts?"

"These are questions with no answers for quite some time. Maybe you will not learn the answer to these questions even in this lifetime. There are reasons your spirit has been attached to Modu Barrow. Perhaps from another time in another life. You know we are all growing from one spirit to another. Moving through the ways of the old spirits and the new. Even though the religions of today are foremost in our knowledge, the past, old traditional spirits continue in us."

Adama did not want to listen to this deep, confusing, meaningless conversation from Owl. Adama wanted to hear simple, immediate answers to her quandary. She stood with her head bowed gazing into the earth. Mustafa-boy pulled her hair and kicked her hips. He did not take his eyes from Owl.

"You have no suggestions how I might convince Arake or Momadou that I could go home to Jambanjelly?" she asked in a quivering voice.

"I do not. You must figure this one out for yourself. I believe I am your spirit animal to give you meaningful answers to questions of value. I have just given you that, but your feet are too rooted to the earth, which you presently stare at. Go now and be patient with yourself. I am sure you will go to your Jambanjelly family soon. I will tell you no more about this. You must try your own methods and see what happens. You will grow with each accomplishment. And, you will grow as you learn from each misfortune."

Adama turned slowly on the path heading home. She mumbled a goodbye to Owl, and moved slowly. Mustafa-boy continued to stare at Owl until he could no longer twist his neck. He shuddered as he looked around his mother's head toward the path in front them.

CHAPTER 31

The Missing Men

The four men lay tethered, unable to release the ties from around their wrists and ankles. They had strained and pulled making the knots even tighter. They had thrashed like caterpillars placed on their sides; wriggling toward each other. Back to back, they tried to untie the others binding knots. They searched, unable to move, yet by lifting their heads and casting about with their eyes, they looked for anything that might be sharp enough to cut the ties. In that dry, sandy earth stones are scarce.

Time wore on and night came upon them.

"I do not think we can stay alive without water. My mouth is barely able to open. It sticks from the dryness. It will be very cold here on the ground throughout the night." Mustafa muttered this to himself more than to the others. But, the others heard.

"I think we will not live through the night," Abduli, youngest of the four and youngest of his family of seven siblings, his mother's favorite, began to sob quietly.

His brother, Bardara, kicked at him. His shackled ankles allowed him to barely hit Abduli's heels.

"Ouch, why are you kicking me, Bardara? I believe, for many reasons, we will not live through this night."

As the night sounds of the bush surrounded them, the men were silent. Chatters, chirps and screams resounded throughout the tall trees and the low bush. The barn owl, the plain nightjar, the pied crow, the redstart all with whistles, hoots, and sweet song filled the cooling air. Monkeys yelped and hyenas barked. The tree frogs and cicadas dominated the chorus as the sun began to leave the earth.

Each man turned his head away from the setting sun, toward the east and said his prayers.

It seemed they floated into a semi-conscious state. They began to feel the earth turn cool, then cooler and finally by midnight they were shivering, teeth chattering and bodies shaking.

As dawn began to allow lightness to break through the savage night cold, the men became unaware of their surroundings. They had not had water for two nights and a full day. They were used to going without much food. They did not seem to suffer from a lack of nourishment, but they knew they were becoming dehydrated.

****

They did not have the strength to react when they heard footsteps approaching. Footsteps approached, coming from the direction their captors had walked, yesterday.

Mustafa squinted, lifting his head toward the sound. As best he could, he saw three men coming toward them. He was too weak to react. As he began to respond he thought,

Allah be Praised! Please let these men untie us and allow us to be on our way.

"You are still here, but suffering, I see," Seiny Cooley and Fabara stood over them, legs spread and staffs planted into the ground.

"Thank Allah you have returned. Please help us. We can barely speak. Water. We need water," Mustafa's voice was dry and weak, nearly impossible to understand.

They men were lifting their heads like hungry baby birds in their nest. Begging for food, but even more, begging for water. They needed water.

Fabara, the older and larger of the two captors shook his head as he sucked his teeth.

"We have returned to complete what we were told to do yesterday. We hoped we would not see you here. But, you are still here. We told our boss you were dead. That we killed you as he had ordered us to do should we find any one on the path yesterday. He had been told cattle rustlers were on the way and that is why we were here to stop you. We do not want to do this, but we have a good job. If we do not do what we were told to do we will no longer have a job."

"No, no!" Mustafa yelled as loudly as he could through his dry, scratchy throat. "We will return home. Just untie us, give us water, and we will run back to our homes. As Allah is my witness, we will run home, and say nothing."

Fahbara nodded to Seiny Coolie. Seiny raised his staff and began to beat the four men who lay defenseless. Fabara joined him. The men on the ground wiggled like caterpillars, screaming and thrashing until they were unconscious. Fahbara and Seiny continued beating the tethered men until they could not raise their arms any longer. The ground was wet and red with blood. The men on the ground were not recognizable. Screams from the monkeys and birds in the trees stopped. An eerie silence reigned.

The men were breathing in rapid gasps. Sweat covered their faces, pouring in streams and dripping onto the path. They stared at the corpses. The silence of the bush surrounded them.

"We need to go to that small well down near the old garden, and wash this from ourselves," Fabara said to Seiny. Seiny stepped to the side of the path and vomited. The two of them did not look at each other. They walked away in silence.

****

Late that afternoon, a stranger passed by the four bodies lying beside the path. Feet and hands tied and bound. Dead and bloody, with flies creeping around their eyes, noses and mouths.

The stranger began to pray as he looked down at the grotesque sight. His knees became weak and shaking. His prayers became louder. He fell to his knees and wept. He stayed in that position for what seemed to him a long time. He needed to determine what to do.

He was on his way to a small village tucked in the bush where his rice farm stood. He was carrying a machete to use at the farm. It was not the rainy season yet, but he, Bardara Sowe, liked to go to the farm and inspect the hut he lived in during the rice season. Also, he liked to see if he needed to dig a well in a different spot or if last years well could be repaired. Now, here was a problem. He could not walk past these bodies without burying them, or learning in some way who they were. Or both. But, how could he bury these bodies without knowing who they were? He stood, confused and sick to his stomach. Bardara was a good, caring man. He had never seen such a sight.

His face was long and full of wrinkles. He wore a short white beard. His skin as black as the moonless midnight sky. Large slightly slanted eyes were set between a fine nose which flared at the nostrils. He was a handsome old Jola man.

Bardara decided he must, before the night came, cover these bodies to protect them from the animals. But, he wanted not to bury them too deeply into the earth because he must somehow learn who they were and find their families. Once he learned who they were he wanted to be able to remember where he had buried them.

The spot where they had been moved off the path was on a flat piece of vegetation. Ivy and weeds grew between a cluster of tall palms and coconut trees. As Bardara scrutinized the area, he knew he would remember the spot where he would cover these unfortunate men.

Taking a deep breath he bent and grasped the shoulders of the first man. He rolled the body off the side of the path and placed it so there would be room for each of the four to be lying side by side. Leaving enough room between each of them to dig a hole. As he grabbed the shoulder of the last man a groan came from the body. Bardara dropped the man's shoulders and stepped back, tripped over the third body and landed on the remaining two. He scrambled off the bodies and tried to stand. He staggered and clambered about. Brushing leaves and weeds and sticks from his clothing he stared at the man. He walked closer and bent cautiously toward him. Another sound like a sigh or a groan ushered from the man's throat. Bardara reached down and touched the man's chest. *If he is alive his chest should reveal it. The thumping in the chest always means a man is living.* Bardara trembled as he reached to place a gentle hand on Mustafa's chest. Surely a thread of a thump was felt. Bardara knelt beside Mustafa, and placed the palm of his hand directly on his chest, keeping it there for several seconds. The thumping became more pronounced. Bardara looked into the face of Mustafa. He was not ashen like the other three were. In fact the color of his face was as clear and dark as Bardara's. It was not the face of a dead man like the other three. And, he could feel a slight breath coming from this man's nostrils.

This man is alive! Now, he must live so he can tell me the names of these others.

Mustafa's face was swollen; dark purple lumps protruded around his right eye and his cheek. His lower lip was split open and had been bleeding profusely. Blood, now black and crusty, stuck to Mustafas' lip and chin. He had three long open wounds on his head, which also had been bleeding. One arm was loose at the shoulder and lay limply at an odd angle.

Bardara knelt on one knee next to Mustafa, staring intently into his face, waiting to see if he would open his eyes. He knew only to stare at him and wait for some further response from this man.

Maybe he is not quite dead, yet not quite alive. Bardara thought. Mustafa's breathing became more evident and his lips began to move through the gross swelling. Bardara wanted to see the man's eyes open.

"Water," Mustafa whispered. "Water."

Bardara reached for his goatskin flask, lifted the flap and dropped a bit of water into the man's mouth. Mustafa's swollen lips opened like a fat fish, gasping for air. His tongue filled his mouth. He choked, and coughed and gradually swallowed the water. His eyes fluttered. With his good arm he tried to reach, weakly, shakily for the flask. Bardara dropped more water into the man's open mouth.

Mustafa looked through swollen eyelids into the sky and trees. He glanced closer and could see a hazy vision hovering over him. Mustafa did not know what this vision was. Mustafa, in fact did not know who he himself was. He was full of pain, and fear, and exhaustion.

"Who are you?" Mustafa asked Bardara. "I am confused. What has happened to me?"

It took Mustafa a great deal of time to say those few words. He had to stop and carefully lick his cracked lips. He motioned for the goat flask of water three times before he was able to complete the two questions.

"You do not remember what happened?" Bardara asked. "I am Bardara Sowe. I was passing by on my way to my rice farm when I came upon you and your companions."

"Where are my companions?" Mustafa asked. He tried to lift his head searching for these unknown companions, but he was unable to.

He lay quietly for a few seconds feeling not only full of pain, but full of bewilderment, and fear.

He closed his eyes and appeared to drift off, unable to further respond.

Bardara touched his shoulder gently. "Do not go to sleep. I fear you will not awaken again. Please, I have to tell you sad news of your compatriots. They too were beaten and were not as fortunate as you. They lie beside you, here, and I must bury them before darkness."

Mustafa's eyes flickered, but did not open. It was as if he was trying to open them, to react and awaken, but he could not.

"Whoever you are, please let me help you. I will take you to the farm and there I will clean your wounds, and provide you with rest and nourishment. But, first I must bury these three men. Please, can you cling to your life for just a small amount more time? Bardara spoke into Mustafa's face.

"What do you bury?" Mustafa asked, eyes still closed.

Startled by the question, Bardara regained himself and said; "We will talk about it once we go to my farm. Now, please rest and become well," Mustafa nodded.

It took Bardara some time, using the machete to dig into the earth and bury Masanneh, Abduli, and the boy, Bardara. Once he was finished, he sat on the ground with a hard thump, like a toddler who stumbles backwards and lands onto the floor. Sweat pored from his face; his caftan stuck to his back and chest. His breath came in quick gasps. *I am too old to be required to do this sort of thing,* he thought.

Three mounds of earth were lined neatly side by side in the flat area next to the path, surrounded on three sides by tall palms and coconut trees. Mustafa lay between two of the three mounds. Bardara must now figure a way to transport Mustafa to his farm. He sat for some time restoring his energy and thoughts. Darkness was coming very soon. He could see the sun leaning on the earth. The birds and cicadas were beginning their evening songs, and clatter.

If I cut two poles from the small trees and weave vines across them I will be able to place this man on this stretcher and drag him to the farm.

Darkness fell as Bardara, dragging Mustafa on the stretcher reached his farm. He came to his small round hut. A thatched roof had rotted over the past season allowing moonlight to peak through in the one room house. Dapples of gold danced on the dirt floor. A small window looked onto the back yard of the hut. The door faced a circular space that needed to be cleared of tall grass. Other small round huts stood in a semi circle facing the front yard. These belonged to Bardara's village friends. They would eventually come to plant the rice. But, not necessarily in the near future. It was early for rice planting.

Bardara placed the stretcher on the ground while he went inside to inspect the condition of the hut. Three rats scampered out the door as Bardara entered. He tried to catch them, but they scampered too fast. They would have provided Bardara with at least one meal for himself and this new person. Mohammed.

A short handled broom lay on the floor by the door. Barbara swept the floor clean of debris; dust, animal droppings, and twigs. He then pulled Mustafa inside and placed him away from the door and window. Mustafa stirred and asked for water. Bardara again dropped water into Mustafa's mouth.

I pray the well has a bit of water left. Our water is nearly finished.

Mustafa said 'Abarraka' Thank you. He opened his eyes, swollen slits, and gazed about. "I do not know what this is. My arm is paining me greatly."

Bardara untied Mustafa and left him on the stretcher which made a good bed for him. He used one of the vines to tie around Mustafa's wrist, placing it across his waist. Mustafa winced and tried not to show the severe pain that caused. Once Bardara had the arm in that position, he tied one end of a vine around the wrist, and extended it around his neck returning the vine to the wrist once again. The arm could not move, and hopefully would begin to heal. Tears were running down Mustafa's face, he was shivering in spite of the warm night. Bardara took his shirt off himself and lay it over Mustafa.

"I do not know what to call you. I am Bardara Sowe and I will call you Mohammed until you can remember your real name. Now you must try to sleep. I am going to find water. I will not go far from sight. I will keep the house in my view. All right, Mohammed?"

Mustafa nodded, shivered and wept.

As he walked through the bush just off the front yard Bardara gathered leaves of the seno tree for Mustafa's pain. He headed toward the location of the well. It was dark therefore he did not dare to go too deeply into the bush. He stumbled onto a rise in the earth and stopped quickly. Looking down, he saw the mound of stones and dirt he'd gathered last year to finish off the top of the well. Kneeling, he reached into the hole searching for the level of water, if any. He looked into it and saw blackness. He lay on his stomach, in spite of the darkness and awareness of insects or snakes. He reached again, and felt water, at the tip of his middle finger.

Praise be to Allah. God is good. Bardara stood, brushing dirt from his caftan. Now he must find something to hold the water. It was too dark and threatening to spend much time at the edge of this forest. He had brought the goatskin flask with him and it had twine attached to it which was long enough to reach the water, but he knew it would be very difficult to capture water into the flask. He lowered the flask until it landed on the water. He then jiggled the flask quickly, up and down, up and down. He was aware of the flask feeling a bit heavier as he continued to jiggle it up and down. In a few minutes Bardara pulled the flask up to him and checked how much, if any, water he had captured. It was disappointing to feel the minut amount that sat at the bottom of the flask. Bardara sighed and stood. He could not remain any longer in the dark forest. He could only hope that early in the morning he could find a container of some sort so he could gather water for this stranger for whom he had become responsible.

Bardara entered the hut and spoke softly to Mustafa. "I have brought you some leaves from the seno trees. Chew them and they will relieve your pain. You know these leaves?" he asked Mustafa as he broke them into smaller pieces.

"Yes, I know them," Mustafa was still shivering. He opened his mouth and allowed Bardara to place two or three pieces of the leaves through his broken lips. He winced as the leaves brushed through them. He cautiously chewed them for a very long time. "They will help me sleep?" he asked Bardara.

"They will make you sleep and relieve your pain. I was not able to obtain much water, but I did find the well, and tomorrow I will search for something to hold the water, like a gourd or an old bucket that has been left behind as no longer usable, although that is unlikely. We will find something now that we have found water, we have solved the major problem, right, Mohammed?"

Mustafa did not respond. He did not recognize his new name. He also was beginning to feel the effect of the seno leaves Bardara had given him.

"May I have water?" Mustafa slurred the question.

"Yes, Mohammed, drink before you sleep. 'Allah ma suto de Allah,':" May God be with you tonight.

Bardara said his prayers directly beside Mohammed, facing the east. He gathered branches, leaves, and twigs which he weaved together and then pulled it all into the doorway, creating a door and blocking the outside. He stood over Mohammed and felt a great swelling of concern and sympathy for this young man who has a story and is unable to share it.

Who is very damaged and in a great deal of pain. And, who may not survive.

Bardara felt overwhelmed with responsibility.

I alone am in charge of this man's life. I am in fear of this responsibility. But because Allah has given it to me, then I will do my best. But, I am very tired, hungry and thirsty.

Bardara fell asleep immediately. He lay on the dirt floor beside Mohammed. Close enough that he could hear his breathing. Mohammed slept in a deep drugged state. Bardara slept as an old man in great need of rest.

****

Seven sunrises came to pass and Mohammed-Mustafa was greatly improved. He sat outside in the shade of the round house on a bantaba made by Bardara. He felled a small tree and cut it into four short lengths for the legs of the bantaba, he then stripped bark in narrow widths from another tree. After making a frame four by eight feet he wove the narrow strips over and through it. It was a comfortable resting place for Mohammed.

His arm no longer caused him pain, but without the seno leaves he was afraid the pain would return. Bardara had found an old gourd in one of the other houses and was able to pull as much water as needed to drink and to wash their bodies, sparingly. Bardara caught several of the scampering rats, which had taken over the other houses. He made a fire late afternoons and roasted one or two for their dinner. It was the only meal they had each day. Some days Bardara brought mangos he picked from the orchard down near the rice fields.

Still Mustafa could remember nothing of what had happened the day of his attack, or anything before that. He spent many hours trying to bring about a breakthrough. He looked up into the sky of this strange, new place. He gazed into the dry blue of it. He did not recognize anything. He appreciated Bardara and was becoming very attached to the kind, old man. He would, now and then, slip and call him Da. Then he would sheepishly smile and say '*Sorry.*'

Finally, one day Bardara said "Do not be sorry. I guess I am your father until you remember who you are. My problem is, I have done all the work I came here to my farm to do. The well is cleaned and the house has a new roof of straw. And the yard is cleared of grasses. Everything here is fine. When the rains come for rice planting we are prepared for it. My friends will be coming sometime, but I do not need to wait for them before I return to my village. I have a compound there to oversee. I have two wives. Did I tell you that?"

Mohammed shook his head,"No, I did not know that. How many children do you have?"

"I am blessed with eight children. Five by my first wife Mariama, and three by my second wife, Aiminetta. But, Aminetta is very young and beautiful. I expect she will have several more children before she finishes.," he grinned a wide, old man grin.

"Then what is your problem, Da?" Mohammed asked.

"I cannot leave you in this condition. You are not strong enough to be left alone, and even if you were strong enough to walk to your home, you do not know where that is,"

Bardara scratched his head.

Mohammed remained silent. He did not feel strong enough even to help Bardara decide what to do with him.

He was able to say, "I could try being here by myself. You need to return to your home. Is it a day's distance to your home?"

"It is a over a day's walk to my home in Someta. I have family living between this place and Someta. I will stay overnight with them on my journey back home."

Quietness fell on them as they sat in the late afternoon shade of the bantaba. They watched the family of monkeys living in the bush close by the clearing. They watched six vultures soar overhead.

"I think you must come with me. We will travel slowly and rest often. There is no other choice. I can no longer stay here and desert my family with no good reason. We will leave tomorrow early," Bardara slapped his knee and stood.

Somehow Mohammed felt great relief when Bardara made this statement. He was Mohammed, a new man. Someone who no one knew. Not even he, himself. He must get stronger and his arm must heal before he can take care of himself. He must wait and hope his memory returned. He was becoming very attached to this old man who saved him. In amazement, he thought of how a few days ago when he regained consciousness from an attack, which killed three other people, this man Bardara was there to rescue him.

"I am happy to go with you, Da. I will try to be strong and not hold you back. When I am well I will work for you as long as you will have me. God allowed you to save and care for me. God is good."

It was again quiet as the sun came closer to the top of the palm trees surrounding the compound yard. Bardara sat beside Mohammed until late afternoon prayer time was due. And, even with Mohammed's broken arm and bruised face and scarred head, he knelt with Bardara for that sacred time.

"Sleep well, my friend, for tomorrow we will begin our journey. I will wake you at dawn for first prayer of the day. Then we will walk toward your new home. Toward my home, which will be yours for as long as you wish it to be." With his gnarled and wrinkled hand, Bardara patted Mohammed on his good shoulder.

CHAPTER 32

Haddy Touray - A New Life

Haddy Touray walked down the familiar lane where she had lived as a child. Leaving her family compound she strolled through the wide path lined on both sides with bamboo fencing. She knew every member of each of the compounds behind those fences. She called to two women who were in the back yard of their house were pounding rice. They returned her greetings, waving between strikes of the pestle into the huge wooden mortar.

I could have stayed with Ebrima Darboe and become a Kanyalenga, but Ebrima Darboe would not allow that. He said he could not bear to see me become a clown. He said he cared too much for me to see me dancing like a fool in front of all of the village people during the naming ceremonies, the weddings, and other holiday celebrations. Nor did he want his compound having a Kanyalenga living in it. So, now I am here in my father's compound and beginning a new life as a barren woman, or a woman in disgrace, or a woman who may one day have a child if Allah permits. I must become a Kanyalenga to show Allah I am willing to wait for my turn to have a child, or not. For Allah will decide when the time is right. Or not.

Haddy kept her head held high as she walked. Tears were swimming in her eyes. She was glad to be home, yet she was missing Ebrima. She was glad to be rid of the wives and children of Darboe compound, yet she was wanting to look upon Ebrima Darboe right now! He was the man who made her smile. He was her husband. He was not in this village.

She turned into the compound of the eldest Kanyalenga of the region, Awa Jara. Haddy was spending a great deal of time in that compound since she had moved back to Sukita. Many women lived there, as well as Awa Jara's husband, brothers, and three children, ages six, seven, and eight. Awa was one of the most prominent Kanyalengas in the western division. She had had five miscarriages from the age of fourteen to the age of twenty. It was then she became a Kanyalenga, and joined the many women who danced as clowns and buffoons for the celebrations in the area.

She joined the Kanyalengas in their gardening, rice growing, and soap making projects. These infertile women shared the work and the money they made from these projects. They sometimes lived together in the same compound. Sometimes they returned to their family compounds or their husbands compounds.

A Kanyalinga was to ask Allah to forgive her for losing her babies, and to allow her to become a mother of healthy, live babies one day. Babies who would survive the first few years of their lives. Awa did, seven years later, have a baby. And the next year she had another baby. And the next year she had another baby. One each year for three years! All were still living and healthy.

She, however, continued to be the leader of the Kanyalinga in the area.

Haddy liked being among all these women. In less than three weeks she had found several women who became her closest, dearest friends. Most of them were her age, and had similar problems.

Tida Jarju ran to the gate as Haddy entered. She clapped her hands and dragged her feet in a foot dragging, hand clapping happy greeting.

"Haddy Touray is here! Haddy Touray is here!" Tida called. Her tall, large body moved toward Haddy. She bent over with laughter. Haddy could not help but laugh also.

"You have come to dance with us this afternoon. To practice for the ceremony tomorrow, right? We will help you with your costume. I have found a hat that came from a fisherman who carried it from the Casamance. It is made of straw and has many holes. It is a ragged mess! It will be yours. And we have an extra gourd already with seeds inside and the outside has twine of many colors wrapped around it. You will be wearing ragged clothes and looking very sad!" Tida hugged Haddy and then slapped her playfully on her bottom.

Haddy blushed. She nodded as Tida took her hand and dragged her to the house where many of the women lived. She pulled her inside and faced her toward Mynima Jobe and Fatou Conteh who were resting on two of the six iron beds in a large, otherwise empty room.

"Look who I have found! Our sister! Haddy has come to practice with us this afternoon after we return from the garden. Right, Haddy?"

Haddy smiled and nodded. "I am afraid to dance tomorrow. I am shy to dance in front of all the people." She sat down on the bed nearest the door. The other women rolled over onto their stomachs in unison, propped up on their elbows, looking toward Haddy, their hands cupping their chins. "You will love it when you become accustomed to it." Mynima Jobe said. "We have a great deal of fun. And we get money to share amongst all of us. You see the clothes we wear when going to mosque and to family events and when we are not dancing? They are made using the money we earned being a Kanyalinga. We have more money than any of the other women."

"And no one can tell us what to do with our money. We can give it to whoever we want to or spend it on ourselves," Fatou Conteh said.

Tida Jarju sat closely next to Haddy. She patted Haddy's hands, which were folded in her lap. In a quiet, breathless voice she said, "You will dance with us this afternoon, here in this compound and then you will be ready to celebrate tomorrow at the Koolio. I promise you will be very happy."

"I will try," Haddy Touray said.

Six women walked to the garden outside the village, down a lane and into the bush, and out of the bush and into a large open field full of separate garden plots. Each woman carried a large agateware bowl on her head containing a short handled hoe, a bucket for pulling water from the well, a small bowl of cooked rice, material for cleaning herself after the work, and fresh clothes to change into for her return to the village.

They walked one behind the other, backs erect, gliding as if they were floating an inch above the dry dirt path. The line looked like a rainbow walking. Skirts and loose tops were of vivid reds like the sunrise of Sukita; yellows like the weaver birds by the river; blues like the sky of the dry season; greens like the leaves of the mango trees during rainy season. They laughed and bantered and told stories of what was going on in their compounds.

It had been a long time since Haddy Touray felt at home with a large group of women such as these she walked with to the garden.

Awa Jara called Haddy to come to her garden plot, "Come and let me show you the best tomatoes in this land! I save and store the biggest and healthiest seeds around! Come, help me weed and transplant them, Haddy Touray."

Tida Jarju grabbed at Haddy's wrist and held it. "Don't go. Stay with me. I will make you very happy," she pulled Tida's arm close against her body and looked pleadingly into her eyes.

Haddy did not resist, but laughed at Tida's actions. "I must go to Awa. She is our boss, you know. I will walk back to the village with you."

"Behind, or in front of me?" Tida asked.

"Oh, I don't know. Why do you ask, Tida? What is the difference?" Haddy giggled at the question.

"Because if you walk in front of me I can look at you all the way."

"You are too funny! You are a *si-si,* Tida Jarju!" Haddy slapped her own thigh, smartly and turned to go to Awa's garden spot a few parcels away from Tida's.

As the women worked, they sang in harmony. When they weren't singing they were chatting back and forth. Or, taking a break in the shade of one of the few trees scattered among the garden plots. The sun beat down unmercifully on their bent, tired backs.

They worked several hours as the day was coming to an end.

Awa straightened, stretched her back and sighed, "It is time to finish. Let's clean ourselves and go home." She called across the garden lots spanning several hundred feet of neat and tidy plots of vegetables.

Greens, okra, tomatoes, onions, and peppers all looking freshly watered and weeded.

The women stood by the well where they pulled calabashes full of water for bathing. They didn't expose their bodies as they bathed. Laughing, chatting, bathing, and dressing together everyday of the growing season was part of their lives. This was not new to Haddy. In every village in Gambia the ritual was the same.

"I must go to the Touray compound before I dance," Haddy called to Awa who walked some distance behind Haddy on the path entering the village.

"Then go, but come back soon, so we can dance before we cook dinner," Awa called.

Haddy stepped inside her father's compound, and called to the people there. Three men were sitting on the bantaba. One brother and two cousins were resting from their work in the field. Now they would wait for dinner which was being cooked in back of the houses in the cook area. She greeted them a bit shyly as she walked past them. They mumbled a greeting in return. Haddy did not feel comfortable yet in this compound, but knew it would get better as time passed.

She shared a house with two nieces. One, Ndey was preparing for marriage, which had been arranged by the nieces parents and Haddy's father who was the eldest of his generation, therefore he made or approved all decisions for the clan. They all lived in this compound, worked in the fields together, and kept the compound and clan together.

Haddy's father owned a small herd of cattle that was pastured in a clearing in the bush outside the village. Some of the young men and boys of the clan watched the cattle there taking turns living in the bush.

The second niece who shared a room with Haddy was about Haddy's age. Fanta was married to one of the herdsman who spent many nights in the bush with the cattle. When he came to the compound for an overnight, the couple would go to the men's rooms and find a place to spend those nights together.

"You are going to dance tonight, Haddy. That will be exciting. We are all going to watch you. Are you ready?" Ndey asked, as she pulled a basket from under her bed where she kept her clothes. Water dripped from her body as she had just come from the shower in back of the women's house. A piece of material was wrapped around her ample waist. Breasts hung loose and free as she fumbled for the dress she was going to wear that evening.

"I am too nervous to even think of it, Ndey. Please, dance with me. No one will mind if you do. Please, Ndey, dance with me."

"Well, all right. If it will make you feel better, then I will dance at the same time you do. But, I will wear my new dress, not the funny one you will wear. You hear?" Ndey stood holding and shaking out her newly pressed and carefully packed dress of bright red and gold shiny material coming from a traveling salesman, down from Mali.

"It will make me feel much better, Ndey, even if you are dressed like that, and I am dressed like this, it will be of help to me," Haddy said as she put on a ragged, faded brown skirt, with a worn, ugly multi colored top hanging loose over her torso.

That night Haddy danced her first dance as a Kanyalingo. She walked into the middle of the circle, surrounded by women who clapped, and sang in absolute harmony. Two drummers stood to the side, whistles in their mouths, drumming steady beats, fast and furious beats, and slow sensuous beats.

And the women wearing clown-like costumes, silly straw hats, ragged skirts, and bare feet slapped and contested face-to-face dancing. Arms flung out like a chicken about to fly, then abruptly stopped. Marching out of the circle, strutting out of the circle Haddy was a true Kanyalinga. She felt an accomplishment she didn't expect to feel. She felt proud she had met the expectations of her sister Kanyalingas. She felt surrounded by sisterly love from her new family.

****

Four weeks had passed when Ebrima Darboe unexpectedly arrived at Haddy Touray's father's compound. He had caught a ride with a tradesman who was traveling through the countryside, selling assorted goods from Mali. His horse and buggy was in good condition. He was a successful tradesman. He had stopped in Jambanjelly and visited his friend, Ebrima Darobe for an overnight. His next stop was Sukita, and Ebrima thought it would be a great opportunity to visit the Touray compound. He had not seen Haddy Touray, his third and beautiful wife for several weeks. He missed her, but knew he had done the right thing by sending her back to her family in Sukita.

Binta Darboe nodded slightly as she sorted the rice for dinner and as Ebrima told her he was going to Sukita to visit the Touray compound. Ebrima Darboe always conferred with Binta Darboe when making a decision. He never asked permission, but he always respectfully conferred.

****

As Haddy was stepping out of the Touray compound, closing the gate and turning toward the lane, she saw a horse and buggy coming toward her. She did not recognize it nor the two men who sat on the buggy seat. But, as they came closer, she gasped and put her hand to her mouth. It was Ebrima Darboe in the seat beside the stranger! Her husband was there in front of her and her heart leaped to her throat. She clapped her hands, and showed a broad blissful smile.

"Ebrima Darboe is here," she called as she ran toward the cart, clapping and singing.

Ebrima chuckled a low and throaty sound. He stepped down and held his hand out to her. She took it, bowed her head, and bent her knee ever so slightly. There was no eye contact. No touching beyond a quick clasp of their hands.

"You are here," she said.

"I am here. How is the family?" he asked.

"They are there. How are the people of your compound?" she asked.

"They are there," he answered. The greetings continued until Ebrima turned and walked into the Touray compound. Haddy followed behind the tradesman and Ebrima. She was overjoyed to see her husband, but she also felt torn because she was expected to meet the women at the garden. Thinking quickly, she called to one of the children who was carrying water to the next compound. The girl put the large bucket of water down and ran to Haddy who told her to go tell Awa Jara that Haddy's husband had come from Jambanjelly and she would not be able to go to the garden. The little girl picked up the bucket of water and scurried off to deliver the water to her compound, then run to the Jara compound and deliver the message.

The nieces left Haddy's room and found other places to sleep that night. Ebrima visited with the men all evening, having the attire, tea ritual, smoking cigarette after cigarette, chatting and laughing and telling tales of the past. The women cooked special goat and tomatoes sauce over rice as is the custom when company arrives. The men ate first and the women and the children ate last.

Haddy went to her room alone late in the evening after helping with the cooking and cleaning up from the meal. She showered and put on her most beautiful bright blue sleeping gown, and slipped into bed. She was very tired, yet excited to be expecting her husband into her bed for the first time in many weeks. She tried not to fall asleep, and succeeded in staying awake until Ebrima quietly entered her room. She pretended to be asleep, and heard him removing his clothes slowly.

He slid under the piece of material, which covered Haddy and lay quietly on his back next to her.

A few minutes passed before Haddy turned toward him and put her arm across his chest. Ebrima placed a hand on her forearm and patted it.

"I have missed you, Haddy Touray. Are you alright here?"

"I have tears in my eyes, Ebrima Darboe. I am missing you too much. I am happy here, but I am missing you too much. Must I stay here forever?" She put her hand on his cheek and rubbed it.

"We will see," he answered.

CHAPTER 33

Adama Moves Home

Eight moons passed over Sukita. Mustafa did not return. Nor did the other three men who traveled with him. The village folks spoke very rarely of them now. The mothers cried when alone in their private times. There were not many places for mothers to be alone and cry. But, when taking their shower, or when walking back from the garden, a bit behind the other mothers and wives, they would shed a few precious tears. Their sons did not return.

Mustafa was the only one of the four who was married. It was nearing time for each of them to marry, but because Mustafa was urged to take Adama as his wife quickly and unexpectedly, he was married sooner than the other men who had traveled with him.

After eight months, Adama could wait no longer. Earlier she had asked Arake, Mustafa's mother if she could travel and visit her mother, Binta. Arake had conferred with her husband, Momadou, father of Mustafa and he had allowed Adama to go to visit her family in Jambanjelly for two weeks. Momadou told Adama she would be alerted by the talking drums should Mustafa return before she, Adama, came back to Sukita. All this happened six moons ago. Adama now longed to be back in Jambanjelly with her family and to remain there. She no longer cared if Mustafa ever returned. In fact, she had never cared if Mustafa returned, even though she had begun to feel a kinship to him as time progressed in their marriage. But, it was not strong and deep; just a bit of closeness in her heart. It was fading into a memory. She was not even sure that any caring for this man was ever there. It was still only Modu, the boy she loved, that filled her heart. No room for anyone else.

One evening as Arake and Adama sat on the veranda of the women's house, Momadou, husband of Arake stepped up onto the veranda and greeted the two. He sat on a stool facing them and drew in on his pipe. Puffing several short pulls and watching the smoke float up into the still night air, he began to speak.

"Adama, you are the mother of Mustafa-boy, who is the son of our missing Mustafa Badgie. This means that Mustafa-boy's family lives here in this compound. This means that Mustafa-boy and his mother, you, Adama, live here. My son, Mustafa is missing and no one knows where he is or what has become of him and his vue. It has been too long that they have been missing, and we do not know what Allah has chosen for them. Allah be praised. I know you want to go to your family, Adama, in Jambanjelly, perhaps to remain there. I am not able and do not wish to give you permission for such a thing. But, I will allow you to go back to your family for a lengthy visit, with the understanding that as soon as Mustafa returns, you will return to him and us in this compound. You will remain faithful to your husband while you are away and continue to raise Mustafa-boy as the son of Mustafa. YaMoi?"

Adama fell from the bench and, on her knees, grasped the hand of Momadou and kissed it. Weeping, she thanked him many times, until Momadou, chuckling, pulled her up and placed her on the bench beside Arake.

"Alla ma suto di allah," *May God go with you tonight,* Momodou said to the two women as he stepped off the veranda and went to his house next door.

CHAPTER 34

Ebrima Darboe - Father of Adama

Adama arrived on a donkey cart driven by her brother, Ishmial. She came with all her belongings, cooking pot and spoon, bed linens, her clothes, and the clothes of her son, Mustafa-boy. The Badgie family lined up by their front gate to say goodbye, as did the people of the compounds surrounding the Badgies. The women wept with sobs and great tears. The men stood back, watching the drama. Adama waved and held Mustafa-boy tightly as they bounced down the lane heading toward Jambanjelly. Her heart thumped in her chest. Her face felt flushed as she wiped the drops of perspiration from her forehead. Mustafa-boy sat between Ishmial, his uncle and his mother, Adama. He watched intently as his uncle cracked the whip onto the rump of the slow moving donkey. He laughed at the lazy donkey as it startled forward, responding to the snap of the whip. He looked around in fascination as they moved through the village of Sukita. He saw the open market where women sold their vegetables; onions, okra, and tomatoes. All selling the same items. The women sitting side by side on benches behind the rickety tables that held their items.

Not many words were said between the brother and sister as they ambled toward Jambanjelly. As they approached Jambanjelly, she heard the call to prayer coming from the old man who walks through the corridors of the village. And then she saw the crossroads where the center of Jambanjelly intersects.

She was home. After nearly three years in another village, another compound filled with different family, another clan, she was home. She would not return if she could possibly manage that. And she would never allow Mustafa-boy to be taken away from her and returned to the Badgie clan. He was not a Badgie. If necessary she would inform the world that Mustafa-boy was not a Badgie. But, she realized that it would be a very serious problem should she ever do that.

At the gate of the Darboe compound her mother, Binta Darboe stood waiting for her daughter and grandson to arrive. The greeting was reserved and welcoming at the same time. A joyous hugging for Mustafa-boy as he dashed off to find his cousins and friends. He was as at home here as he was at the Badgie compound.

Adama directed Ishmial where to move her belongings. She was returning to the girls' room with her sisters. Mustafa-boy would be in any of the houses he wished to be in. Always looked after, always in the place where the food was, or the beds were, or the action was. Boys the age of Mustafa-boy owned the compound and the corridor where their compound stood. It was indeed a boys world.

****

Ebrima, father of Adama, stepped onto the veranda of the girls' house, and muttered "konk, konk" by the doorway. A piece of material hanging in the doorway provided privacy to the room. Adama was spreading material onto a mattress in the corner of the bedroom.

"Come," she said, as she walked toward the door. Her father greeted her with a broad smile and a brief hug.

"You are here. Welcome. This is your home. You will stay here until your husband returns. Ya Moi?"

"N Moi," Adama answered her father, eyes cast to the floor. "I am very happy to be here, da. I want to be with my family."

"You are welcome," Ebrima cleared his throat as he stepped out of the room. He was going to say goodbye to first wife, Binta Darboe, now as he was leaving to visit his wife, Haddy Touray, who presently lived in her family compound in Sukita. Ebrima had sent her home to her family because she had not given him any children for the three years they had been together. He loved his youngest wife, and mourned the fact he had to let her go, but he visited her each week and they were together then. In the Touray compound Ebrima and Haddy were happy together. Her father, Ebe Touray highly respected Ebrima and wanted his daughter to be part of a marriage no matter what the circumstance.

Since Haddy had returned to her father's compound, she had become part of the Kanyalengas, an appreciated, yet questionably devalued group of women who cannot deliver live, well babies. The Kanyalenga women act as clowns at events like naming ceremonies and weddings. They collect money for their antics. Haddy was still a married woman, and she was sent from her husband's family compound and therefore felt abandoned and displaced. Haddy felt at home with these women, and loved being with them. She also loved that Ebrima came to be with her often, and they spent time together, more time than they did when she was in his compound doing the bidding of Binta Darboe. Haddy felt she had the best of both worlds now and was quite happy. She had learned to shuck off the feeling of embarrassment when doing the antics of the Kanyalengas such as wild dances wearing funny costumes. All of the other women made it fun and frivolous, and the fact they were paid for the show they put on was worth a bit of embarrassment. They had money of their own. More than when they were living with husbands and the wives of their husbands. More than when they were married.

****

Ebrima sat on the bedside looking down at his bare feet. His trousers still on, his chest and back glistened from his shower. He waited for Haddy to come from the women's house to be with him for the night. Ebrima always used the strangers house when he visited the Touray compound.

As he stared at his feet; hands on knobby knees, he practiced what he would say to Haddy. He had already discussed this proposition with Binta Darboe.

"Binta Darboe," he had said as he sat on her veranda, "I am going to bring Haddy Touray back to this compound. Ya Moi?"

A silence reigned. A long, silence interrupted only by the usual noise of an active compound: children crying or laughing, donkeys braying, cocks crowing, and adults calling to one another. It seemed like an eternity before Binta Darboe exhaled and cleared her throat.

"It is your compound, Ebrima Darboe," she shifted her big body.

"I am aware of that, but it is also your compound, because you are my first wife. You know I want to, and always will, give you the information that I have in my head and heart. I am telling you that Haddy Touray will return and she will provide you with much help around the compound."

Binta Darboe's wide lips smirked, very slightly.

"I cannot remember why Haddy Touray was sent back to her family compound," Binta Darboe mused.

"I think you do," Ebrima Darboe retorted. "And I no longer wish to consider the fact she may never have babies. It is not that important to me. At times I do not wish to adhere to the customs of this tribe."

Binta Darboe raised both eyebrows as high as she had ever tried. They shot half way up, and made two black arches, in the middle of her broad forehead.

"You are not speaking," Ebrima said.

"I am thinking.," Binta responded

"I wish you to speak," Ebrima said in a deep, quiet voice.

"You are the leader of this compound. You will do whatever you deem fit for the good of this compound. I will adhere to your wishes. I am your wife who keeps this compound together. Your wish is my command. I am quite tired, Ebrima. Are we finished with this conversation?"

He sighed a deep, long sigh. He wrinkled his forehead in a scowl and rose to leave.

"I am going tomorrow to propose to Haddy's father that he allow her to return to this compound. I hope you will respect my wishes and greet her back into the family. Goodnight, Binta Darboe."

It took a great deal to move Binta Darboe from being a stable, strong, and good natured woman. She steered the Darboe compound in directions that proved best for all members. She had her daughter,

Adama, and grandson, Mustafa-boy, returned to her. Now, on the same day she is informed that Haddy Touray, the youngest wife of Ebrima Darboe was re-entering this compound, also. Being young and fresh is very good while it lasts. Haddy was nearing the end of that time in her life, and Binta knew that within a few years Haddy would be the same as the others, plus she would be without babies. Binta wondered if Ebrima Darboe would, like so many of the others, take another wife after Haddy was no longer as fresh and beautiful and as flirtatious as she presently was.

I am not happy with Ebrima Darboe. I would like to tell him so. I, however, will not. Ebrima Darboe knows I am not happy with him. He also knows I am as much the leader of this compound, and even this corridor where we live, as he is. I will allow him to think I do not realize this.

It was not Binta Darboe's night to go to Ebrima, so she was able to cool her anger with him. Ebrima was with only one wife, now days, so he had many nights to sit up late and chat with his vue. He also was going to Haddy Touray's village nearly every week for at least two days and nights.

****

Ebrima Darboe left early the next day, taking the donkey and wagon. His son Ishmial drove the wagon for the second time in two days to Sukita. This time arriving at a different compound than the day before. This time it was the Touray compound where his other mother, Haddy Touray, now lived. Yesterday it was at the Badgie compound where his sister, Adama Darboe had been living for several years. Now, she was home in the Darboe compound and Ishmial was happy to have his sister and his nephew, Mustafa-boy with them in Jambanjelly.

Ishmial was about seventeen years of age now and was working with his father in the ground nut and cassava fields.

Ishmial had the urge to see more of the world but was not even aware of how far that world stretched out beyond Jambanjelly. He had heard the men who worked for the cattle owners talk about the Casamance, a place beyond the river and the sea. He knew the men who were now missing, who had gone beyond the land that Ishmial knew. He knew Gunjuir, Sukita, and Brikama. He knew some of the up river villages, but only by wandering the paths which wended their way through the forests. He loved wandering within a days time, to and from. But, someday, Ishmial was determined to search the end of the world, wherever that may be.

In the meantime, Ishmial made himself available and anxious to drive the donkey cart to places his mother and father wished to go. And this day it was again to Sukita. Ishmial especially liked to go to Sukita because he had spotted a very beautiful girl who lived in the center of Sukita, fortunately close by both compounds where the Darboes were related.

This girl was probably a few years younger than Ishmial. He always found her in the same corridor where Haddy Touray lived. He would see her when she was on her way to the market. Or, carrying one of her baby sisters or brothers on her back. She was slight of build, yet one could see ripeness on her chest. Tiny bumps, already pushing through. Her shoulders were wide. Her neck was long and elegantly held. Her hair was worn close to her head in tight little braids. She had a sharp face with high cheek bones and piercing black eyes. A timid smile played on her lips. Ishmial pretended not to even see her the first time he noticed her walking along the side of the corridor by the Touray compound. But, on the third time he delivered his father to the Touray compound, he stopped for a courtesy visit. Within an hours time he said his goodbyes and set out for Jambanjelly, he spotted her as he turned the corner at the end of the corridor. He drove the donkey into the fence and stopped it so the girl was trapped between the fence and the donkey cart. He looked down at her standing there with her arms clutched over her chest and he smiled.

"A salam mali cum," he muttered.

"Mali cum salam," She meekly responded without looking up.

"My name is Ishmial Darboe. I live in Jambanjelly, and my other mother is Haddy Touray. What is your name, or do you not have one?"

She giggled. Still she did not look up.

"I'll let you go, if you will tell me your name," Ishmial liked the way he could control this girl so easily.

"Mariama Conteh," she whispered. Not moving her head, eyes glanced up slyly, through long black eyelashes.

"When I come back to collect my father in two sunrises I will find you at in this corridor. Where is your compound?" Ishmial asked the girl.

"It is the one on the other side of the Ebe Touray's compound. It is the Ousman Touray compound. They are brothers. Haddy Touray is my auntie."

"And that makes us relatives somehow. Isn't it?" Ishmial felt some concern for his feelings toward this girl who may be too close to his blood to care for her in this way.

"I do not think so," Mariama continued to look any place but Ishmial.

"I will go now. You will look for me in two sunrises and I will sit with you and we will ka-cha," Ishmial snapped the whip onto the donkey's rump, making him jump forward and run a few steps, soon to move into a slow, lazy walk.

****

Haddy Touray ran toward the Touray compound when she saw Ishmial leaving the corridor, too late to greet him, yet happy to see him and his donkey because that meant Ebrima was at her father's compound. She was excited that he was there waiting for her. Her life was good these days. She liked having Ebrima all to herself when he came here to be with her. And, lately she especially liked being with the women who were the Kanyalengas of the village. The one she spent as much time as possible with, Tida Jarju made Haddy strangely happy. She had grown to depend on seeing and being with Tida everyday, and if she did not, then Haddy had an empty spot inside herself she did not understand. She liked to watch Tida while she weeded her large plot of peppers which grew next to Haddy's garden spot. Tida would bend with knees as straight as the palm trees' trunk. She would lean down until her head nearly touched the ground and then she'd push her short handled hoe into the earth on each side of the plant and pull the weeds out of the earth. Sometimes in the heat of the day, the women worked wearing no tops, and Haddy would caste a sidelong glance at Tida's breasts. Haddy wondered why she loved to see Tida's breasts, long and full swaying in the intense heat. She had grown up with women's breasts often free of covering. Every day of her life she had seen the women feeding their young. She was somewhat puzzled at the pleasure she felt when looking at Tida's breasts. But life went on and she was happy to be here in this place, being with Ebrima at least two nights a week, not having to be where she was a second wife, but being with her blood family and also being with these women who had great fun where she worked hard, and played hard. All of this and most of all, she had this wonderful new friend, Tida Jarju who gave her immense delight.

Instead of going to greet Ebrima where he sat with her father, Ebe Touray, she stepped inside the women's house to quickly shower and change into clean clothes.

That night after the men had had their dinner, and women had also eaten, and cleared away the pots and pans, Haddy went to her room, expecting Ebrima to come as soon as he and her father and some of the other men finished their endless chuckling and smoking. He stepped into the room through the curtain and smiled down on her where she lay.

"You are here," she said.

"Yes, I am here and I have something I wish to discuss with you."

"What!" she asked quickly, clutching the piece of material that covered her. "What have I done? Why must you discuss something with me, Ebrima Darboe? I have done nothing!"

He smiled as he pulled his caftan off and stepped out of his trousers, at the same time sitting on the bedside where she lay.

"Easy, Haddy Touray. I am only going to explain what is to happen soon. It's a good thing. Listen and I will explain." At that he slid in beside her, pulling the material over himself.

"Oh," Haddy rolled on her side and moved against his side. Ebrima lay on his back, one arm covering his eyes.

"How would you like to move back to Jambanjelly and be my wife?" he asked her looking up at the ceiling.

Haddy felt her body stiffen, like a wooden stick. She tried to soften her stiffness. She found herself not breathing.

Ebrima wrinkled his forehead, blinked several times, and glancesd over at her.

"Why are you not breathing? Why are you lying like a stiff piece of rotten meat? What is wrong? Do you not want to return to me and be my wife, again?" He moved away from her, nearly falling off the narrow bed.

"Oh, yes, yes, Ebrima. I want to be your wife. I _am_ your wife. I love to be with you here. I wait for you to come to me every day. I am so happy you are my husband. I like this. This being together here," she stopped, knowing she must stop talking, or she would say too much.

He was quiet for some time. Haddy found herself holding her breath again.

"Then you would rather be here than at the Darboe compound?" he asked

She breathed. "No, Ebrima, I want to be with you,." she conceded. There was no easy way out of this, she thought. She could not exist without the assurance that Ebrima would come to her weekly. Her father would be unhappy with her if she had no man attending to her. And, she did love Ebrima. Very much. And yet. And yet.

Time slipped by as the two lay quietly with no more conversation between them. They dozed. They woke at the same time and made love at the end of the night just as the cocks began to crow.

The next morning Haddy crept out of the room and showered, dressed and went to help the women with the preparation of breakfast, sweeping the compound dirt floor, and tend to the little ones.

Ebrima rose and went to sit with the men.

The day wore on and neither Haddy or Ebrima attempted to be in the same area.

That night Ebrima sat up late into the night with the men. Haddy pretended to be sleeping when he came into the room. Ebrima did not attempt to wake her, and she continued to pretend sleep.

****

The next day Ishmial arrived mid-morning to take his father home. He had already cornered Mariama at the entrance of the corridor. She pretended to be looking for something in her basket as she headed to the market. He pulled up beside her and grinned.

"You are here," he said.

"I am on my way to the market," she smiled up at him with a brilliant wide, white toothed smile. She fluttered her eye lashes and giggled.

"I will be outside the gate at the Ebe Touray compound when you return from the market. "We can sit on that bench there and ka-cha. All right?"

"I will have to take the goods from the market to my mother. Perhaps I can pretend I forgot something and will have to return," she looked to him for his response.

"Very good! You are a very clever girl! Go then and I will be waiting for you at the bench."

They chatted for an hour before Ebrima stepped out from the compound looking for Ishmial who was expected to arrive much earlier.

"How long have you been sitting here, and why have you not let me know you had arrived? I am waiting for you! We need to be on our way. We will be late getting home now! What is the matter with you?!" Ebrima was obviously in no mood for this kind of dilly dallying.

He glanced quickly at Mariama, who ducked her head, looking away, down the corridor.

"Sorry Da, I am here. I have been sitting here for a few minutes. I am ready to return whenever you want to leave."

Mariama casually stood, took her basket and walked away, murmuring goodbye to whomever was listening.

Ishmial watched her walk away admiring the way she swayed her supple hips and her rounded bottom.

Ebrima shook his head and tried to hide his smile as he watched his son watch the girl.

They left within the hour.

Earlier that morning before Ebrima left the bed, Haddy had stepped back into the room, water dripping from her shower, towel wrapped around her waist. She stood over Ebrima, looking down at him. Sensing her presence, he opened his eyes, and looked into hers.

"You are dripping water on me. Why?" He brushed a few drops from his chest.

She smiled. "Because you give me problems, Ebrima. You are leaving and we have not solved our problem."

"And, you are sounding like you are in charge of this problem, Haddy Touray. What has gotten into you? You are not the boss. You are the woman. The wife. When I say there is a problem, that is when there is a problem." He reached up and grabbed her arm and pulled her down onto him. She squealed. He put his hand over her mouth, not wanting the people to hear them. He tickled her bare wet ribs and slapped her bottom gently.

She rolled off him and stood. She shook her head and opened her towel shaking her body for him to see her whole self. Then she turned and ran to the shower room where her clean clothes waited.

Ebrima lay there staring at the ceiling. He drew in a deep, long breath, and at the same time moved off the bed preparing to bathe, dress, pray, and return to Jambanjelly.

When he walked toward the donkey cart, Haddy followed him.

"When am I to come with you to Jambanjelly?" she asked.

"When you are truly ready," Ebrima said as he stepped up onto the cart and sat beside Ishmial.

"But, I am truly ready this day, Ebrima Darboe," Haddy's voice quivered.

"No, you are not. Perhaps I should say, when I am truly ready for you to return. I will see you at next prayer day, or sometime near that day, Haddy Touray. Goodbye," he nodded for Ishmial to go.

CHAPTER 35

A Time to Grow

A year passed since Adama had moved back to the Darboe compound in Jambanjelly. Mustafa-boy was now four, nearly five years old. A healthy boy. He played with his cousins and the neighbors, running the corridors in that part of the village. He was happy and settled into his family.

Adama infrequently visited the Badjie family, only because her father insisted she maintain that relationship.

"As long as we do not know what has become of Mustafa Badgie, we will assume he is alive someplace and you remain his wife. You and Mustafa-boy must go, at least once each big moon to visit a few days with them," Ebrima, father of Adama said as he, Binta Darboe and Adama sat on Binta's verandah.

"Do you understand what I am telling you, Adama Darboe?"

"I understand, da. I will take Mustafa-boy to see '*his* family, as you insist.," Adama stood and walked to the edge of the verandah and hugged one of the posts. She looked out across the compound and over the buildings on the other side. Smoke from cooking pots of the neighboring compounds cast a foggy haze everywhere. Darkness was creeping in along the edges of the village. The sun was lying on the rim of the earth. She felt the need to move.

"I am going for a walk.," she said as she stepped off the veranda. "Mustafa-boy is with Mariama at the garden."

"Where are you walking?" Binta Darboe asked.

"Just down the lane a bit. I will return very soon. In time to help with dinner," She waved to the two of them as she moved from the compound and headed down the magic path toward the river.

She found Owl on his perch. Adama had not seen Owl for several weeks. He was not present many times when she walked to the river. Yet, she had seen him several times since her return.

"You are here," he said. "It is good to see you, Adama Darobe. What have you heard concerning your missing husband?"

"Nothing. I have heard nothing. It has been many, many moons, all the seasons have come and gone at least one time since he and his friends left. I think I will never see him again. That is not the reason I have come to see you, Owl."

"Then, speak up, child. What is your reason?" Owl stretched his claws, and settled into a comfortable position.

"I am tired of going to Sukita to visit the Badgie family. I want to remain here in my village with my family. I want you to help me know how to convince my father that I need not continue to travel there."

"Why is it so important that you do not go there? Do you not care for any of the people of that compound? Do you not think it important that your son maintain a relationship with his other family?" Owl cleared his throat.

Adama stared at Owl with eyebrows arched. "Excuse me, Owl. If you are my wise spirit animal, why are you asking me such a question? I am sure you remember that Mustafa-boy's other family lives closer than Sukita to our family compound. I am not interested in continuing this lie. I will not be able to reveal the truth of Mustafa-boy's parentage, but I do not wish to continue this pretense."

Owl sighed, "How often do you see Modu Barrow?"

"I do not see him alone, if that is what you are asking me, Owl," she dipped her head into her chest. "I try not to see him at all, but that is impossible because all I need to do is look across the corridor and see him coming and going. My heart does not stay still."

"You are longing for him, still." Owl murmured.

"My heart will not let him go. I think I was born with him sitting there in my heart. I have his child. I see Modu every day. He is without a wife, for now. I could be that wife. But, here I am, without a husband. A husband whom I do not even like, even when I had him. And Modu is there, alone. I know he watches for me when I go to the market."

"What is it you want from me, Adama Darboe?" Owl asked.

Adama looked at her spirit animal and shrugged her shoulders. "I do not know. I depend on you to help me with problems no on else can help me with. Give me advice, even though I may not want to hear it, Owl, please. First, how can I convince my father I need not go to the Badgie compound? Next, help my heart to release Modu the boy I love, or help me have him."

"I will think on your request, Adama Darboe. I see you growing in wisdom and patience. It is good to see. I will help you with your problems when you next come to this place. Go now, or someone will see you standing here speaking to no one and no thing. They will think you have lost your mind."

Adama smiled slightly, turned her body facing home and sprinted away from Owl.

****

Mustafa-boy walked into the Barrow compound on his daily route of wandering. Each day, after breakfast he would leave his grandfather's compound and step out into the corridor. He visited every compound on the corridor. Sometimes he would simply walk around the front of the houses greeting everyone, looking for some of his friends, or food, or something with which to make a sling.

This day he ran into Modu Barrow. As Mustafa-boy ran around a corner of the men's' house at the Barrow compound, Modu stepped off the last step onto the ground. Mustafa-boy smacked into Modu's thigh, nose-first so hard he fell with a thud onto his bottom. Hard. His nose began to bleed. Mustafa-boy hated blood. He had a great fear of blood. He screamed whenever he saw it, which was a great inconvenience here in this land where people often bleed, and animals often bleed, for various reasons.

Chuckling, Modu reached down and picked Mustafa-boy off the ground. He swung the boy onto his hip and, with his farm shirt wiped the blood from Mustafa-boys face. Mustafa-boy's loud cries subsided to sniffles and sobs.

"You run fast, Mustafa-boy. Fast and hard. You must be careful, or you will hit something harder than my leg, and then you will have much blood and a broken nose. Shall I take you home to your mother? She may want to know you are bleeding. Your eyes are swelling. Maybe from the crying. Maybe from the bump you just received. What do you say? Should I take you across the way to your compound?"

Mustafa-boy nodded his head, wiping the blood from his face. Shaking, he tried not to cry.

Modu pushed the Darboe gate open and called 'Salam'. It was mid-morning, the breakfast fire was in coals; the yard had been swept, no one was to be seen. Most of the women had either gone to the gardens, or were selling their produce at the small market place, or resting before beginning to cook lunch.

He called again and this time Adama stepped from the girls room, rubbing her eyes as if from sleep.

"What is it?" she asked. Too stunned to say anything she stared at Modu holding his son, Mustafa-boy in his arms. He had a bloody face and tears. "What happened to you, boy?" she demanded. Stepping quickly off the veranda, she took the few paces to reach them. She held her arms out for Mustafa-boy, but Modu swung his arm holding Mustafa-boy away from Adama.

Smiling, he said, "He must tell you what happened before I release him to you."

"Oh.," Adama pulled her arms to her chest. Her heart was racing. Her boy (their boy) had a bloody, dirty face, and a little smile on his lips. "What happened, boy?" she said once more.

"I ran into Modu when I came around the corner." he ducked his head into his chest, and wiped his face with his grimy hand.

"Let me have him, Modu, he needs to wash his face and go about his day. He is a strong boy," she grabbed him from Modu.

"Now, go to the wash basin and finish cleaning yourself. And watch where you are going, henceforth. Because, if you do not you will not live to be a grown man. Ya Moi?"

"N'Moi," he said as he headed toward the wash basin by the shower room.

They stood facing each other like carvings of themselves. Looking down into the red dirt of their land. Like ancient carvings of this place. Like stories yet untold. For many seconds they stood, Modu looking to his right and Adama looking to her right into the ground. They both sighed and looked up into the face of the other.

"Hello, Adama Darboe," he said.

"Hello, Modu Barrow. Thank you for bringing Mustafa-boy home. He is a wandering boy."

A silence reigned for a bit of time.

"He is *my* boy." Modu whispered.

"I know," she answered. "People will see us standing here, Modu.," she said in a low voice.

"He is *my* boy, Adama. What are we to do about that?"

At that moment Binta Darboe swung her big body through the gate, opening it and entering it and closing it in one fell swoop. Coming in from the garden she carried a huge basket of tomatoes. She hesitated as she noticed the two of them standing there. She did not stop. She made a little noise in her throat and walked past them. As she passed, she said, "Modu Barrow, are you lost?"

"No, maBinta, I am on my way. Mustafa-boy ran into my leg as I stepped down from my room. He hit his nose and fell on his rump. I brought him home, bleeding and crying. He is cleaning his face, there by the wash basin."

They all looked toward the wash basin. Mustafa-boy was not to be seen.

Adama stepped away from Modu and moved onto her veranda. "He washed his face quickly. He will be back, Binta and you will see a bruise around his eyes. Thank you, Modu, for bringing him to me. I must prepare to cook," She nearly ran to her room and stood with her back to the curtained doorway.

****

As the days wore on, Mustafa-boy made a habit of being at the corner of Modu's veranda the same time each morning. He and Modu would greet one another and Modu would sit on his heels, pick up a stick, and make pictures in the red dirt. Mustafa-boy would ask him 'what is that?' and Modu would say 'what does it look like to you?' and Mustafa-boy would guess. *"a deer, or rat, or a lion? What?"* And Modu would pass the stick to Mustafa-boy who would draw a fish, or a bird, and Modu would guess what it was.

Then Modu would take Mustafa-boy's hand and lead him out of the Barrow compound, across the corridor, and into the Darboe compound. Modu would then greet whoever was there and wave goodbye as he left for the farm, or market, or to find his vue.

Mustafa-boy would look longingly at Modu as he closed the Darboe gate. Then he would dash off to find *his* vue.

****

Binta Darboe, mother of Adama Darboe, wife of Ebrima Darboe, thought as she picked tiny stones from the rice in the flat bottomed basket. She thought of what she had seen a few days ago when she entered the Darboe compound. Modu Barrow and Adama Darboe standing there, face to face, looking down into the earth. What had they been saying? What were they planning? She didn't trust the two of them since they ran away together all those years ago. She could see they still cared for each other, but that was not to be. Adama was married until proven otherwise. Modu need not assume otherwise. Adama need not assume otherwise. But, Binta was a wise enough woman; the mother of this young woman, Adama, to know that if one has ever gone to ask a marabou for help in loving someone then you can never undo that wish. Binta was sure a marabou had answered Adama's prayers long ago, and still the answered prayer stands.

****

When Mustafa-boy turned nine, and Adama turned twenty -three they took one of their annual trips to the Badgie family compound in Sukita. It was a pleasant enough trip. On the second day there, Momodou, head of the compound, father of Mustafa called Adama to come to his house. Arake, wife of Momodou, mother to Mustafa, collected Adama at the girls house and walked with her two houses up to Momodou's house.

Momodou wore a light blue embossed caftan. He greeted Adama warmly and asked her to sit. Arake sat beside Adama, facing Momodou.

"How was your trip?" Momodou asked.

"It was fine. My father and mother send their greetings," Adama replied.

"They are well?" he replied.

"Yes, they are well."

A moment of silence reigned once the long greetings was finished. Then Momodou drew in a deep breath and began.

"Adama Darboe, we have been waiting for our son to return to us, as you know. He left many many moons ago, to work with the cattle. He left with three of his coworkers and they have not returned either. Each of the families has searched for the missing men, with nothing to show for it. It has been long enough that Mustafa-boy has grown from a baby to a grown boy. It has been too long. Therefore, we want you to know that we release you from your marriage to our son, Mustafa Badgie.

"I must speak with your father as soon as possible to give him this information, so I will return with you when Ishmial Darboe comes to collect you in a day or two. I will remain there for an overnight and have one of my boys come to collect me."

Adama sat quietly listening to this news. She was completely surprised and numb at the thought of what this meant. She could stay in Jambanjelly as an unmarried woman. Her life had made a huge change. She looked up at Momodou and smiled slightly.

"YaMoi?" he asked.

"N'Moi," she replied. "A Baraka," *Thank you.*

Momodou stood, thus releasing the two women. They stood, nodded to one another, and the women walked out onto the veranda, down the steps and into the compound yard.

Arake, mother of Mustafa, took Adama's hand as they walked from the house of Momodou. They strolled across the yard and stepped up onto the wives' house verandah. Sitting on a bench they remained silent for several minutes. Then Arake spoke.

"It is finished. You are free, Adama Darboe. I am sad to think that my son may never return to us. Although it has been far too long since we have seen my son alive. I still pray he will return to us. Although it is only right you should be released from you marriage vows. Will you still bring Mustafa-boy to visit his relatives, please?"

Adama wanted to say, *No, I will never bring him to you all because he is not your relative.* But she could not do that. She only looked at her hand which was still being held by Arake and nodded.

"You are a good woman, Adama Darboe. You will always be my daughter, no matter what."

Adama squeezed the hand of Arake, and said in a whisper, "Mother."

CHAPTER 36

Mustafa Now Mohammad

It took Bardara Sowe and Mohammad two days and two nights to reach Bardara's village of Someta. A beautiful village sitting at the edge of the sea, nestled in a cove on the southwest border of Gambia near the border of Casamas, Senegal. Just a few round houses with walls of pink from the bricks made of the red earth, and with pointed roofs of straw. Sitting in a semi circle, they were tucked back from the beach into the palm trees. Long-boats sprawled like wildly painted beached whales, waiting to be launched for fishing.

Bardara walked, tall and proud, carrying a long stick, he followed the path through the forest that led directly into a cluster of houses. Children played at the edge of the path leading to the beach. They looked up to see Bardara coming briskly toward the houses. In spite of being hungry and old, tired and ragged he took long, great strides into the center yard where the homes of his village stood facing the sea. The children screamed and clapped their hands and ran toward him. They called *da*, and *Bardara*, and *nfama* (my father)! Mohammad wondered if all of these children belonged to Bardara. There were at least ten of them, ages ranging from two to twelve. They dashed against him and tried to crawl up into his arms. Bardara bent, staggering a bit as he swung them up into his arms, onto his back and allowed some to hug his legs as he staggered along toward his home.

A woman stepped from the door of the house where Bardara headed. She was brushing her hands together, throwing off her outside work shirt, and fixing her head wrap, all at the same time. She was a big woman, round and bouncing with joy, as she ran toward Bardara. Stopping one foot from where Bardara had stopped walking and was shaking off his appendages, he held out his hands to her. She grasped them and the greetings between laughter and tears began, ending after many minutes.

Mohammad stood back and watched this ecstatic, electric scene. Older girls and boys had gathered by now, and were watching. They smiled as they watched the children milling about while the two elders greeted each other.

Mohammad wondered who all these people were. He wondered who *he* was. He felt baffled and confused. He felt as if his life began only a few prayer days ago when Bardara made the stretcher and pulled him to Bardara's hut in the bush. That was all Mohammad knew. And now other people were surrounding the only person he could remember. What a great deal he had to learn and understand. He noticed young men and women, older girls and boys, all beginning to move away from the welcoming scene, and some of them casting sidelong glances in his direction. Mohammad could only look down onto the ground. He did not know what else to do. He stood as close to Bardara as possible.

Bardara swung around looking for Mohammad, and nearly fell over him.

"Oh, Mohammad, come I want you to meet my wife, Mariama. Mariama, this is Mohammad, he has come to live with us. He is our son until he finds his own family. YaMoi?"

Mariama extended her hand to Mohammad and clutched his wrist with her other hand, shaking with all her strength.

"Another son! Allah be praised," she beamed.

Mohammad stood silently and tried to speak. He eventually murmured a response. Mariama led him into a small house and said, "This is the men's house. Bardara will tell you where you will sleep. The women's house is a bit behind this one, near the cooking area. You will see it soon. Welcome to our family, Mohammad. What is your last name?"

Mohammad swung his head toward the door, looking for Barbara who was not there. Mohammad felt panic and did not know what to say to this new mother of his. This kind and pleasant woman.

"I have been ill. I do not remember many things. Bardara will tell you my story, I am sure," Mohammad blushed as he said this to Mariama.

"Then we will give you our name. You are now Mohammad Sowe. I believe that would be Bardara's intent. And, if it is not his intent I am sure we both will hear a loud voice come from your new father!" She slapped Mohammad's shoulder, and led him to a jardinière full of water. Handing him a dipper full she said, "Drink."

That afternoon Mohammad slept in his new home. The boys and single men had a house of their own that set amongst the houses of Bardara. It consisted of one room with four iron bed frames with double sized straw mattresses. Under the beds were large baskets for their clothes. There were two doors with tie dye curtains hanging, one for the back entry to the latrine and wash area, and the other facing the center of the communal compound.

He slept through the afternoon and woke as he began to smell food being cooked and the light of the day leaving. He stretched and looked for the door to the latrine. When he returned, fresh clothes lay on his bed. He wanted to bathe before he put on the new clothes, so he peeked out of the front door, and came face to face with a young girl about to leave a jardinière of water by his front door. She startled and stepped back. She looked afraid as he spoke to her. She murmured a greeting and began to leave the veranda.

"Wait" he said. "Where do I take a shower?"

She turned, brushed past him, flicked the curtain out of his hand, marched into his room, crossed the room, and stepped out of the other door. He lost her as quickly as he found her, but decided he would go quickly across the room and chase her until he found her again. And he did. As he stepped out of the back door, she stood facing the latrine and wash area, looking at it.

She pointed to the wash area. "Water is there in the bucket." she said and turned back toward the door to his room.

He watched her disappear into his room and he wished he could follow her once more, but was afraid to do something inappropriate in his new world. She was quite beautiful, and because he could not really remember anything about his past life, found it difficult to form opinions. He had been depending on Bardara to make all his decisions and answer all his questions, but he knew he must begin to trust himself about some things. After all, he had had a life before Bardara, and he must have known other people, and made decisions of his own. Seeing this girl, and feeling attracted to her, helped him know he was able to feel and think and he must learn to make the correct decisions as his life continued.

****

Time passed for Mohammed with this new family and village. The tiny village consisted of five families, all fishermen and tradesmen. He learned how to fish, and found it an exciting, challenging work. Going out into the sea on the longboats with the other men was exhilarating. He learned how to cast the nets and how to pull in the catch. He learned how to row the big cumbersome boats; to skull, and row and hunker down when a wind and rain came from out of nowhere while they were still out beyond the sight of land. Sometimes a storm would come upon them and waves higher than the men themselves came crashing over their boats. The men would flatten themselves over their catch, mainly because there was no other place to lie, but also to protect the catch from sliding from the bottom of the boat back into the sea.

He grew strong and healthy once again. He had strength in his arms and legs he could not know if he ever had before. He felt good, even happy. He had made friends with the young men his age, and had learned which young women were married and those who were still single, most already saved for some of the men. He learned that there were several small villages nestled along the coast nearby to this village of Someta. It was less than a half day walk from one village to the next.

He found that the families arranged the marriages of the children throughout these different clans and families in order to keep the clans healthy and in accord. He learned this over a period of two rainy and dry seasons.

For two full years he lived in this village and knew he loved it here. He was worried about the life he could still not remember, but felt removed from anything other than this kind place where fish and rice was available, and the women's gardens provided them with the other foods necessary to eat well. Also, the wells were always full of good clean water. He liked this place.

Several days after his first day in the village he had met the girl who showed him the latrine and wash area. She was visiting Bardara's compound from the next village of Kartunding. Mariama Sowe, wife of Bardara was very fond of this girl, Jabu. Yet, there was no arrangement made for a marriage between Jabu and any of the boys in the Sowe family. Mariama harbored a wish that she could change some of the arrangements already made for her sons' marriages. But this is not usually an option once the families have agreed on the plans for their children. Her boys had already been committed to girls from the other families in the villages, thus it was fixed.

When Mohammed arrived and Mariama took him in as an additional son, she was very pleased to see him looking at Jabu, smiling at her, teasing her, and Jabu appearing to like it.

"Bardara," she said one night as they were preparing for bed. "I think our son, Mohammed is fond of Jabu. Have you noticed?"

"I am not paying attention to the actions of our young ones, Mariama. I have other things to think of and attend to. Why are you asking me such a question?" Bardara sat on the edge of the bed with his back to Mariama as she pushed a basket of clothes under her side of the bed.

Mariama sat on her side of the bed and turned toward him. She reached for his shoulder and squeezed it with her strong hand. Bardara expelled a sign of relief and pleasure.

"That feels good. My head and neck give me pain, today."

Mariama smiled, and squeezed the other side of his neck and shoulder.

"That is why I am touching you. You think a good wife does not see pain in the eyes of her husband?" Mariama's smile remained on her aging, yet beautiful, round face.

"You do palaver, Mariama," he chuckled as he lay on his back and pulled her to him.

****

Mohammad and Jabu were married the following dry season. Jabu was young and fresh. She was however not too young to love Mohammad.

"I will always be good to you, Jabu Cooley," Mohammad said to her as he lay beside her for the first time. You will be happy I chose you for my first wife. You will be the number one wife for me, Jabu. Will that make you pleased?" he snuggled his face into her neck. Jabu lay on her back, stiff and holding her breath. She clutched the bed linen to her chin.

"I will not hurt you, Jabu." he whispered into her ear.

****

Jabu had their first son nine moons later. Her pains were severe and it took a day and a night for the baby to be born. She bled for two days after the baby came, and she was so weak she slept, only. The baby was cared for by Mariama and Aiminetta, Bardara's second wife. The little one was nursed by one of the brother's wives, Marang, who had more milk than her new baby could consume. Sometimes Marang would be holding the two of them, nursing them at the same time, and beaming. What was better than feeding two new lives at the same time? *Allah is great.*

Mohammad was the proud father of a son. Once the women had cleaned Jabu and the baby, he entered her room and looked down at her sleeping face and felt tears come into his eyes. The baby was lying in her arms, also sleeping. Fat round face with enormous amounts of hair sticking out in all directions from his huge head. His face was dark red. He was not a beautiful baby, but he made Mohammad smile through his tears.

He sat for a long time on an old trunk beside the bed and gazed at Jabu. He felt a warmth he could not understand. A feeling of wonder at this young girl who loved him. She had given him a son, and his heart was full of caring for the two who lay there in that bed. *God is good*, he thought. *I do not know, nor do I care where I came from, nor who I was before Bardara found me. This is who I am now, and I have a wife and son. I have a family and a village. I am a fisherman. I am Mohammad Sowe. It is final.*

Jabu woke to see Bardara sitting on the old trunk, staring at her and her baby now nestled in her arms.

"Why are you looking at me?" she asked.

"I am looking at our son. I look at you many times, but now I am looking at our son. He is quite ugly. Look at him.," Mohammed smiled as he said this to Jabu. In this country it is bad luck to say a baby is beautiful or handsome. Although, truth be told, in this case it was a fact; this baby of Jabu and Mohammed's was not beautiful or handsome. He was a baby who made people want to smile because he looked comical. A comical looking infant boy.

Seven sunrises after Jabu and Mohammed's baby boy was born, a naming ceremony was given. Everybody from surrounding villages came.

The women of the village pounded rice as the sun was rising.

A goat was slaughtered.

A small piece of hair was cut from each side of the boy's forehead where the hair stuck out in massive curls. Cut by one of the elders, who whispered the child's name into the ear of the eldest woman who sat next to Jabu.

His name is Lamin Omar Sowe.

****

Each year when Bardara walked the two days trip to the rice fields to stay during the rainy season, Mohammed would go with him along with eight other men from the village. It was now four years since Mohammed had made his first journey to his present home from this place. Each time he took this walk a stirring of darkness came over him. Bardara was aware of this and not surprised because Bardara remembered how he had found Mohammed lying near death surrounded by the other men who were in fact already dead. The path led directly through the place where Bardara found him, and buried the others, and rescued Mohammed. Mohammed would not talk about how he was feeling to Bardara, or the others, he simply became very quiet and withdrawn for several hours, until they arrived at the small cluster of huts where they would stay for a few weeks until the rice was planted and harvested. Once they had finished and headed home, and they walked again past the graves, Mohammed felt a relief come over him. He was excited to be on his way home to his son and his village.

But, this time was different. As he strolled along the path preparing to leave this place that caused him darkness, he stopped in the middle of the path, which was adjacent to the graves.

He heard a voice. A quiet whisper coming from off the path, in the ground. A voice that sounded somewhat familiar. He cocked his head toward the place the whisper came. Bardara looked back toward Mohammed in time to see him standing directly adjacent to the graves with his head cocked as if listening.

"Mohammed, come. The rest are going to be too far ahead of us. We must keep together. Why are you stopping here?"

Mohammed shook his head and started walking toward Bardara. "It's nothing, Da,I thought I heard a voice, but it was nothing. Let us walk quickly and catch up with the rest."

Bardara did not sleep well that night where they stayed with family members in the next village. He was afraid a ghost was calling Mohammed. He did not want to say anything to Mohammed about his concern as he was sure Mohammed still did not remember anything about his past. He wanted Mohammed to be Mohammed and married to Jabu and be a father to Omar, and soon to be a father to a second child. He wanted it to be the same always. Mohammed was very dear to Bardara, like his other sons, perhaps even more so than some of the others.

****

Mohammed began to hear the same whispers rising from the sea when he was fishing and the wind was high. He thought the voice was familiar, but really could not place it. He could not understand what it was saying. Only one word, but the word was not a word he recognized. It made him nervous and jumpy. He heard it more often as time went on. He could not speak of it to anyone because they would think he had become bewitched, or a ghost was following him. Mohammed was afraid that it was true. Perhaps a ghost had come up from the ground on the path which always made him feel dark and sad whenever he walked that path. Maybe he should not go to the rice farm again. Perhaps there was a ghost there in that path waiting for him, even following him here and living in the sea.

Mohammed was sleeping and eating less. He carried a worried expression, and was becoming thin and old in appearance.

Their new baby arrived and it was a girl. Jabu was in labor for four hours and Bassin was born after a few hard thrusts. She was small with a tiny heart shaped face, little round nose, and high cheekbones. Mohammed tried to become excited and happy about this new addition to his family.

The naming ceremony was not as large nor did it go on into the night with drumming and dancing as when Omar was born. Jabu could see that Mohammed was not well and the fishing was not as good as usual so there was not enough money for a big, expensive koolio.

Mohammed named her Bassin. "She is most ugly," Mohammed said, yet knowing she was the most beautiful thing he had ever seen. Sadness overtook him as he held her and at the same time heard the whispering in his ear. Every time he thought he was free of the whispering, it would return. He could nearly understand the one word it was saying, but still not sure. Something like *Mustafa* Or, was it definitely *"Mustafa?"* And why did that word make Mohammed so frightened?

Mohammed began to have nightmares where he would be walking in a dark forest with limbs of trees reaching out to grab him as he ran through them. Long limbs with fingers on the ends were reaching out to grasp him through the darkness. He ran as fast as he could to escape the fingers of the limbs which scratched him and made him bleed. The faster he ran the more scratches he would receive and the bleeding began to run down his arm and onto the path. Pools of blood softened the earth and hands reached up from the earth grabbing at him. Finally, Jabu would shake his shoulder and push at his arm to waken him.

"Mohammed, my husband, wake up! Wake up! You are having a dream that is upsetting you! The children will hear you and they too will wake. Please! Quickly, wake up!" Jabu pleaded each time he had this dream to awaken and to tell her about the dream.

"We can go to the marabou and he will help you with your frightening dream, Mohammed. But you must be willing to go and tell him what the dream is about. Please, husband, for the sake of your peace of mind and our children go to the marabou."

"I will go when I am ready to go, Jabu. You are not to tell me what to do. You are my wife. You do not tell me what to do. You are too young to be giving me advice, or orders."

Mohammed went to Bardara that morning. Sitting on a stump at the edge of the beach they talked.

"Bardara, you have watched me change from a strong young man to a thin, aging man, have you not?" Mohammed murmured.

"Yes, my son. Your mother and I are worried about you. I believe something deep inside you is trying to come out. Tell me what you think it may be. I may be able to help you with this."

"I wonder if I should be going to a marabou. What do you think, Bardara? Perhaps you can help me with my bad dreams and dark feelings without going to a marabou."

"I think you should go to your mother and she will help you reach our marabou. She knows more about where to find him and when you should go to him. As for me, I recommend you do go and ask him to help you with your dreams and pain." Bardara smoked a cigarette as he sat one leg crossed over the other, on the stump, looking out to the sea.

"Bardara, I have been afraid to fish these past days because there are voices coming from the sea. None of the other men hear the voices. But, I hear them constantly when we are out at sea. I do not know what is happening to me," Mohammed began to weep silently, shivering, his arms folded against his chest.

Bardara put his arm around Mohammed's shoulder and pulled him close."You must go to the marabou, Mohammed. You need the voices to be cast away. I believe he can help you."

"Do you know who those voices belong to?" Mohammed asked?

"I cannot tell you something I am not sure of. I want you first to see our marabou. I am worried for you, and I want you to do the right thing."

Mariama came to Mohammed the next day once Bardara had informed her of Mohammed's problem. "The marabou lives in the Casamas, which is a long journey from here. I must travel with you as we will walk for a day to reach the village where our clan lives. We will stay overnight with them and then hire a donkey cart to carry us to Kabadio, where the marabou, Alaji Sonko lives. You will stay with him for some time, Mohammed and he will cure you of your problem. I will return before you. YaMoi?" she asked.

"NMoi," Mohammed muttered.

****

She left him in a dark room with no windows and a metal door, locked from the outside. The marabou told him to go there, into the one room of the red brick house and Mariama was to say goodbye to him as she closed the door and locked it. Alaji Sonko, the marabou told her it was part of the healing process. The marabou, who Mariama trusted as much as she trusted Allah.

"You must then contact your driver and go immediately back to your village. When Mohammed is ready to return, the drums will let you know."

Mariama wept as she stepped onto the cart beside the driver. He did not look at her face. He looked only at her feet as she stepped into the cart. He did not speak until they were out of the town of Kabadio. A busy, bustling town with a few motor vehicles, which made the donkey buck and jump.

"The horse does not like these loud machines with wheels," the driver said to Mariama, who wiped her tears and tried to smile.

CHAPTER 37

Mohammed Leaves Mustafa Behind

Mohammed felt his way along the wall of the small windowless room until he reached a corner and lowered himself to the floor. The room was as dark as a witches heart. He sat quietly and prayed.

Marabou, Alaji Sonko said,"You will go into a room where darkness reigns, Mohammed. Food will be handed to you through the door two times a day. The latrine is a hole at the corner of the room across from the wall with the door. A jardinière of water for drinking, and for performing ablutions is in the room. You will remain there and pray. You will be with us for some time, but you will be brought out of the black room in a few days. I will know when it is time. The voices will be taken out of you. You must trust me and Allah to take the voices away. They are demons, you know."

Mohammed nodded. He was terrified of what was to become of him. He wanted to go home to his wife and children. He wanted the voices to cease without having to go into that dark room. But, he knew the voices were only a part of his problem. Until he could remember who he really was, things like strange voices would continue. Somehow he knew this to be true.

He stayed in that particular corner for five days. He prayed every prayer he had been taught since childhood. He made up new prayers.

"Allah, hear my call from this dark room. Help me. Take these demon's voices away. I beseech you, good Allah, help me!"

The voices screamed at him and he screamed the prayers over them. He shivered from the cold and from the fear.

He ate the rice handed into him by various strangers. He drank the water from the jardinière and he used the latrine, only by feeling his way along the wall until he felt the edge of the hole with his toe.

He slept fitfully and dreamed of a place that looked familiar, but was not his village by the sea. It was a peaceful place where a woman holding a child was looking over the fence of a compound.

He cried out during his fitful sleep. The people of the marabou's compound were accustomed to cries coming from the black room. That was what happened to those who entered it, and who eventually came out having accomplished the first step to the cure, of killing the demons.

Six days had passed and as he lay half asleep, Mohammad felt something brush past him, lightly, like the feathers of a large bird, it touched his face, his hands and his feet. He did not dare move although he wanted to stand up and throw his arms and hands all about him, pushing whatever it was away. But, he held his breath and closed his eyes even against the darkness. The thing brushed past him. The door opened a crack, and the thing slithered out into the African air. He saw nothing except the door open with no help from the outside. Then he watched a wispy, smoke like thing disappear into the compound yard. The door closed. Mohammad stood and quickly went to the door thinking he could open it and get some fresh air, and even step out of this black room. But, the door was locked.

Mohammad sighed and felt tears coming. He was exhausted. He moved along, feeling the wall and sat in his corner. Mohammad listened for the voices. He heard nothing. No voices came from his head, or from within the room, or any place. The silence was stark. He held his breath, expecting to hear at least a whispering.

Nothing. Only beautiful quietness existed. He held his breath and prayed to Allah. *Please Allah, do not let this be a dream. Please let me thank you for driving the demons away. Allah be praised!*

He waited for some time, quietly, hardly daring to breathe. Were the voices really gone? Was it they that opened the door and slithered out into the light of day? Somehow he knew that the voices were gone and that it was they who brushed past him and out the open door.

Mohammed remembered Alaji, the marabou telling him that he would know when it was time for Mohammed to come out from the dark room. Alaji would know when the demons had left, and he would come to lead Mohammed out of the room.

Mohammed fell asleep soon after he had watched the aberration slither out the open door, and he had said his prayer of thanks. He slept most of the day and was awakened by the sound of the door opening. His thought first was that dinner was being brought to him. When he looked up he saw marabou Alaji looking down at him, smiling.

"Now you may come with me and begin the next phase of your work toward wellness. The most difficult part is behind you, Mohammed. Now we will talk, and pray together, and you will share with the compound's work load. Come now."

Mohammed had not bathed for six days. Nor had he seen daylight, except for the times that food was slipped through the door. Nor had he walked much in that dark, scary room. So, Mohammed was weak, and thin, and dirty. But, a weight had been lifted from him knowing the demons were gone.

****

For the next two weeks Mohammed met with the marabou each day for several hours. Much of the time they prayed, and the remainder of the time Mohammed and Alaji talked quietly about Mohammed.

"You came to know Bardara, your present father on a path by the rice field, correct?" Alaji prompted.

Mohammed sat at the feet of Alaji in Alaji's bare cement room, which had one window and two doors. Alaji sat in a large, hardwood chair. The arms and legs were hand carved with geometric designs. He always wore an elegant caftan of satin brocade. He was old now, and wore a beard of salt and pepper. His hair was cropped close to his head and matched his beard in color. He wore a round cap with a flat top made of the same satin material as his caftan. His face was round, very black, with features as perfect as a king.

"I only remember Bardara pulling me on a carrier he made from trees and vines. I remember him being in front of me. I lay, not sure if I was alive or dead, and not knowing who I was, or where I was being taken, or who was taking me there. It was a very frightening time, Alaji Sonko. I remember nothing before that."

"Has Bardara talked with you about how he found you and if you were alone?"

"No, he told me only that what I remembered was correct."

"I think then, while you are here you will work with the men bringing wood from the bush, building and repairing the houses where necessary. You will help with the care of the cattle in the bush, and the ground nut farms. You and I will meet each day and pray, discuss anything you may begin to remember. Try to remember your past. It is important for your future. To keep the demons from returning. Now, this is enough for this day. It is nearly time for prayer, then dinner. You may go now, Mohammed Sowe."

Mohammed excused himself by rising from the floor and stepping backwards towards the door; never turning his back to Alaji Sonko, marabou.

****

A big moon had come and gone and Mohammed's new mother, Mariama Sowe was fretting about Mohammed's long absence. Her new daughter in law, Jabu Sowe, was left with two babies and no man to account for her. Jabu was lonely and often followed Mariama around so closely that Mariama would trip over her when she, Mariama, turned to go in another direction.

"Jabu! I not only nearly knocked you down, but this baby you are holding! You must stop following me so closely. I know you are missing your husband, but you must help with the work here! Do you understand? YaMoi?!

"NMoi!" I will go help Marang with the laundry. It is my turn to help her. I was going there. But, first I wanted to ask you if you know when Mohammed is coming home. Have you heard the drums, yet?" Jabu looked meekly into Mariama's eyes.

"If and when the drums are heard, you too will hear them. Who has the younger ears? Are my ears stronger than yours? I do not need to ask this question. You will hear the drums sooner than I, and you know it. Now, go do the laundry with your sister."

As Jabu began to turn, Mariama reached for her shoulder and patted her.

****

Four more big moons passed since Mohammed had been living in the marabou's compound. During that time he grew stronger, gaining muscles back from hard work and good food. He liked the family and they were kind and patient with him. He played with the little ones, and learned how to win the hearts of the four wives of marabou Alaji Sonko. He flirted with the single girls, but remained faithful to his wife, Jabu. He looked forward to going home. The demon voices had been gone for at least six big moons. So, now he was physically healthy, and strong. The voices had left, surely for good. The only problem remaining was his forgotten past.

He went to the marabou one day for his usual time, but this time Mohammed was determined to convince marabou that he was ready to go home. Marabou nodded as Mohammed gave his reasons for wanting to return to his family and village. Marabou drew in a long sigh and thought for sometime before he released his breath.

"I think you are correct, Mohammed. I think returning to your family at this time will be what you must do. I believe your memory will return when the time comes. We have done the best we can do for you. Your demons have left you. Your Allah is with you. Your body is strong and there is only one unfinished problem, and that will be solved when Allah chooses. Go, my son. I will have the drummers send their message to your village this evening. Praise Allah with me now."

Mariama came the very next day and took her boy in her arms and wept large wet tears on his shoulder. Mohammed wept with her. He was ready with his few clothes wrapped in a piece of material. He had visited all of the marabou's family and said his goodbyes. At least twenty family members lined the street to wave a farewell as the donkey cart clomped down the lane and into the bush toward home.

Home.

Alaji Sonko stood with the family and watched Mohammed disappear around the corner and into the bush. In his heart he knew the next thing to happen would be the return of his memory and that will change his life, once more.

Only when some unknown key unlocks the mystery. Even I as a spirit healer can not solve all problems. I have told Mohammed to return with his mother, and kill a goat, obtain three tomatoes and six onions from the garden and take them to the eldest man and woman in his village. This will help him continue to heal.

****

For three hours Jabu stood by the gate of their compound with their children, Omar and Bassin. She was dressed in her very best dress and the children were freshly bathed. Bassin, on the back of Jabu and Omar skittering around the area with his cousins and friends. Jabu trying to keep him in sight. She sat on the bench by the gate at times, then stood and craned her neck to see as much as possible around the corner. She listened for the arrival of the donkey cart. Finally, one of the boys came running around the corner of the fence by the road and yelled, "They are coming! They are coming!"

And there they were. Mohammed jumped from the cart before it had reached the gate and Jabu. Jabu rushed toward him and they met with a quick bounding hug. Laughing and crying.

"Jabu. The voices are gone," he said.

"I am happy, Mohammed. You look well. It has been too long."

Bassin was pulled from Jabu's back and Mohammed clutched her to his chest. Bassin screamed and braced herself against him. Mohammed laughed. "She does not remember me, but she will. You will remember me!" he laughed and snuggled her into his neck. "Come, we must greet the family."

And so they were all again in the compound of Bardara Sowe in their village by the sea.

CHAPTER 38

Bardara Saves His Son

Bardara walked from the tiny mosque at the center of his village, Someta, and continued past the round houses sitting in a semi circle, facing the sea. He strolled past his own compound nestled between other homes protected by fences of sticks and vines. Palm trees hovered, tall and graceful over them.

He ignored as much as possible the children playing and the adults sitting on the stoops of the shops. He wanted to sit by the sea and think, undisturbed. He had a problem he wanted to think through before acting on it.

The problem was Mohammed, his adopted son. Mohammed had returned from his lengthy stay at the marabou's village. He looked healthy. He was very happy to be back with his son and daughter, and of course with his wife, Jabu. The demons had left him and he had done as the marabou had told him he must do in order for the demons to never return. He killed a goat, and harvested tomatoes and onions. He then distributed this to the eldest man and woman in the village. It was done.

But, there was yet remaining the problem of Mohammed's life before Bardara found him on the path, nearly dead. Lying among his dead companions. Mohammed remembered nothing before that.

Bardara wanted his son, Mohammed, to remain here in his village with his family whom Mohammed truly loved and wanted to be with forever. Bardara knew this to be true. Bardara worried that should Mohammed walk with him to the rice field, through the path where he was attacked and nearly killed, his memory may return and then Mohammed would no longer be Mohammed. Bardara did not know who this other young man was. He knew only that he would not be Mohammed Sowe of Someta.

After what seemed a long time, Bardara came to this thought, *If I were to encourage Mohammed to stay here with the fishermen while others of us go to the rice fields, Mohammed will not have to pass through the path where he was nearly killed, and where he lost his memory. Perhaps then, his memory will not return and Mohammed will remain here with us in our village forever.*

That evening Bardara called Mohammed to come to his house and to sit on his verandah with him. Bardara had suggested to his vue of elders that he needed to speak with Mohammed for a short time and would they join him when he sent a boy for them.

"Bardara has called for me to come to him this evening. I think he has something important to tell me," Mohammed said to Jabu at lunch. Mohammed had just come in from fishing and was bathing in the shower room. Jabu was sitting in the kitchen area adjacent to it, with a fence separating the two spaces.

"What could it be?" Jabu wondered out loud.

"We will scc," Mohammed stepped out of the shower area of natural fencing, and wiped his body quickly with a piece of material. He stood naked, looking for a pair of trousers, the sun drying his body in the meantime. With a sidelong glance, Jabu watched her husband. She quickly looked down at the cooking pot when Mohammed saw her looking at him where he stood at the open doorway of the shower room. He grinned like a young boy. "You are looking at me."

"I am not!" she blushed.

"You like what you see?" Mohammed stood in the doorway and stepped into his clean, ragged pants.

Jabu shrugged, looking down into the steaming pot of porridge

****

After dinner, Mohammed stepped up onto Bardara's veranda. The two men greeted, shaking hands, as is the custom. They then asked how the work was going this day, and if the fields are ready for planting cassava, and if the fish are running as expected, and if the rain is coming.

Then Bardara spoke, "Mohammed, I have decided that this year, and henceforth I want you to stay here in Someta and watch the village with the other fishermen during the time we go to the rice field. We have plenty of men who walk with us to the rice fields when the season comes. I feel we need more men to stay here and fish as well as protect the village and make decisions. I trust you to be one of them. I have already made this decision and will tell my vue this evening of my decision. I needed only to tell you, first. YaMoi?"

Mohammed thought carefully and slowly before he responded to Bardara. He at first wondered why Bardara had made this decision. He was concerned that it may have something to do with the fact that he, Mohammed, had gone through this fight with his demons. He wondered if he really trusted him over some of his other sons, or if he needed some of them to go with him to the fields, instead of Mohammed.

He then thought of how happy he would be not having to leave his children and Jabu for that time. How happy his life was, and full of contentment.

Whatever Bardara's reasons were, Mohammed decided he would not worry about it. He would accept with graciousness, this decision of Bardara's.

"I will do your bidding, Bardara. I am pleased to fish and watch over the village while you and your men are away at the rice fields. Thank you for trusting me to do this."

CHAPTER 39

The Three Graves

Adama heard the women at the market speaking of graves discovered in a place far away. She listened as they chatted, at the same time passing change to their customers. She pretended to be selecting a tomato. She took one and rolled it over in her hands, checking for blight or worms. She listened to the women talk of graves far away. Her mother, Binta Darboe was there selling onions and pumpkin. Adama went to Binta's stall to greet her.

"Ma, what are the women saying about graves?" she asked.

"I will tell you when we are in our compound. Where is Mustafa-boy?"

"He is with the other boys helping Ebrima Darboe harvest the cassava."

Mustafa-boy was now ten years old. He was strong and full of life. He loved working with his cousins and his grandfather, Ebrima Darboe. Ebrima did not work as many hours each day as when he was younger. He had sons and grandsons to do the men's work. He now was among the revered elders of the village.

Adama anxiously waited for Binta to return from the market.

She warmed the porridge from breakfast for lunch, and began to pound rice in preparation for dinner.

She swept the compound yard.

She gathered laundry to be washed the next day. She put it in a large metal basin.

She pulled water from the well.

Finally, because the other women had not returned from the garden, and the children were all someplace else, she ran down the lane toward Owl.

He sat on his branch as if waiting for her.

"You are in a hurry, Adama Darboe. What brings you here in the middle of your work day?" Owl moved slowly on one claw, then the other. Stretching his toes, curling them tightly around a branch where he perched.

"Owl, I have heard the women at the market speaking of graves that have been discovered someplace far from here. I know no more than this. Have you knowledge of such?"

"I know about the graves. I have known about them since they were dug. I know and see many things."

"I do not understand, but please tell me what you know of these graves, and why they are important to the women at the market," Adama wiped perspiration from her forehead using an edge of her loosely fitting blouse.

"You will learn from your mother, Binta Darboe what she knows and wants you to be aware of. I will not reveal what I know until your people learn the truth."

Adama stamped her foot onto the solid, red earth. She forcefully clamped her fists on her hips and glowered at Owl.

"You are not fair, Owl. I need to know what this is all about. Does it have to do with Mustafa Badgie? I must know. I have not known for years of Mustafa Badgie's whereabouts or even if he is alive. If this is about him, I truly should know. Please tell me!" Tears were brimming the edges of Adama's limpid black eyes.

"Adama Darboe, you have been through a great deal of problems in your young life, and there is more to come. You must trust me to guide you through these times. And, know that I am your spirit guide who will protect you. Now, go back to your compound and feed lunch to the family. Wait for Binta Darboe to return from the market. She will then tell you the news of the graves."

Adama turned slowly toward the village. Looking sadly into the huge white feathered face of Owl, she turned the corners of her full lips up and nodded.

****

When Binta Darboe walked into the compound she was hot, tired, and hungry. She wanted to take a shower, eat, and lie down in her room where it was dark and cool. Instead, she was met at the gate by her difficult daughter, Adama.

"It is you," Binta said as she brusquely sidled around Adama.

"Ma! You told me to wait until you come home to tell me about the graves. I did that, and now you walk past me as if you will not talk to me! Please tell me. I will not take up your time once you tell me about the graves!" Adama wrung her hands as she followed Binta into her room.

Binta swung around and faced her daughter. "Sit down on that bed and I will tell you very quickly. I am tired and hot and hungry. I do not want to be gabbing about anything before I bathe. But, here you are on my heels like a little girl. Will you never grow up? You take more of my time than the remainder of the people in this compound!

Here it is. Three graves have been found beside a path. A path that is used by the herdsmen who watch the cattle owned by the man that four boys worked for. Some animals had dug into the graves. Pieces of material and a juju was recognized. They belong to our boys who have been missing all these many seasons. Only three graves, and there were four boys. We do not know who avoided death. We probably will never know, because it has been a very long time since these boys went missing. The one who did not die would have returned by this time if he had so desired.

That is the story. I am now going to shower, eat, and sleep. Good day, Adama Darboe. Go do your work."

Adama stood stunned into total silence. She stepped out of Binta's room onto the veranda. Her heart was racing. She could hear it pounding in her chest. She did not know what next to think. She did not know who to speak with about this striking news.

She ran to the compound across the corridor and stopped in the middle of it. No one was there. It was just before lunch time, and everyone was either at work in the gardens, or cassava fields, or at the market.

As she was about to turn and leave the compound, Modu, the boy she loved, stepped out of the men's house. He blinked into the sun, and stared at Adama standing there in the middle of his compound.

"Adama?" he said.

"Yes,." she could say no more. She stood transfixed, feeling nothing, yet everything.

"Are you all right? Is Mustafa-boy all right?" He stepped off the veranda and took several great strides toward her. "What is wrong? You are shaking. Is Mustafa-boy all right?!"

"Mustafa-boy is fine," she murmured, looking down at her hands clutched in a tight knot. The midday air was without movement. The heat of the day simmered into the earth and onto the tops of their heads.

"Then what is it?" Modu touched her shoulders with his long slender hands. A light touch, then released quickly.

"Have you heard about the graves?" She looked into his eyes. *Do not look into his eyes.*

She looked into his eyes.

"Yes. Just now at the market. The women are ka-char, ka-char (talking, talking) about it. Why does that make you shake and shiver this way?"

She said nothing.

"Oh, of course. You are thinking of who may be buried there. Of course. Adama, what if one of them is Mustafa Badgie?"

"What if the one who is *not* buried there is Mustafa Badgie?" she flung back at him.

"He would have returned to his compound in Sukita many moons ago." Modu felt lost. Unable to ease Adama's confusion because his was as great. He wanted to hold her and comfort her, but he could not even touch her.

He touched her lightly.

"I should not have come here. I will return to my compound. I do not know why I came here," she turned to go and Modu caught her wrist. They stood, neither moving.

"You know why you came here," he whispered.

She pulled her arm away and ran to the gate.

****

Young Mustafa-boy came to his mother's room and knocked, "Konk konk," he said.

"Come." Adama murmured from the bed where she lay trying to rest and relieve her aching head.

"Ma, I do not understand what my vue is saying to me. They are telling me about my father, Mustafa Badgie. They are saying graves have been found far from here, and they belong to my father and his vue. What is this story about? Why did you not tell me of this?"

His dirty face was streaked with tears. His long skinny legs were bare, sticking out of ragged short pants. A piece of old rope tied around the waist of the pants kept them from falling. His bare feet were broad and cracked. He had been running from one end of the village to the other in order to reach his mother.

Mustafa-boy did not remember his father, but when staying with the Badgie family they spoke of him, often. They told stories about Mustafa when he was growing up, and what a great hunter he was, and how much the girls loved him! They would laugh, lovingly about Mustafa and his charm.

"I only learned of the graves this morning at the market, Mustafa-boy. I have not been hiding anything from you. You know your father, Mustafa went away when you were a little boy, and did not return. We now suspect three of the four boys who left to work with the cattle are buried in those graves. We do not know which of the four is still alive. And, we may never know." Adama reached for the hand of her son,

Mustafa-boy. He let her pull him to her bedside. He lay beside her, his back cupped into her belly. She snuggled her warm mouth into the back of his head and wiped his wet face with the palm of her hand.

They both fell into a sleep of retreat.

****

Modu-the boy she loved, followed Adama down the path to the river. Adama did not go as far as the river. She always stopped half way to the river and stood on the path facing a very large mango tree. Modu would watch her stand and gaze at the tree. She would speak to the tree at times. Some of the time she seemed relaxed and nearly happy when she spoke to the tree. Other times she would stamp her feet and wheel about, returning to the village. When that happened Modu would slip quickly back into the bush where Adama could not see him as she ran past his place of hiding.

Modu knew the facts of ghosts, witches, and animal spirits so he was not overly concerned about Adama's actions. He was, howeve, very curious about what this unseen aberration of Adama's mission was. Was it helping her through her life, or was it hindering her?

Modu knew he had no control over this situation. He knew he needed to be patient and wait it out. He knew that regardless whether Mustafa Badgie was in one of the three graves, or if he was the one *not* in any of the graves in mattered not. Mustafa Badgie would not return to Sukita or Jambanjelly.

Modu made a plan. He would wait for the next big moon. If no one had any more news about the three graves, he would go to Ebrima Darboe and ask for Adama to become his wife and Mustafa-boy to be his son. After all, Ebrima Darboe knew the truth about the boy, Mustafa. He was the one who came to his father and settled what was to become of Adama and her pregnancy those many years ago. Modu knew he must speak with his father first about his plan.

Modu knew he had resisted marriage a second time after the loss of his wife, Mimuna and the death of their newborn son, because he longed for the return of his girl, Adama, and now their son, Mustafa-boy.

Time did not change his feelings. If anything his love for her increased as he saw her in the village on a daily basis. He woke every day thinking of his time with Mustafa-boy at the corner of the men's house where they would meet, chat and visit. They would draw pictures of animals on the ground of the compound yard. There was a strong bond between the two of them now. Mustafa-boy spent as much time in the Barrow compound as he did in the Darboe compound these days. It came naturally and gradually. It was not unusual for children to be involved and attached to two or three compounds. It was the way when families lived close and cousins, aunts and uncles nearly filled a whole section of a village.

One day when Binta Darboe, grandmother to Mustafa-boy was sitting in her seat at the market she chatted with Fatou Jammeh, wife to Ousman Barrow and mother of Modu Barrow. They sat side by side every day during the season when vegetables were ready to be sold and eaten. It was the beginning of the dry season, after the planting and growing of the rainy season. For years they were members of the same vue. They grew up in the same village and went to the bush for circumcision when they were ten years of age. They watched their two children become close; Modu and Adama. Then Adama's twin sister Jola passed away with sickness and heat. Sometime after Adama came out from her long sickness Modu and Adama ran away and were missing for many moons. These two mothers saw them return to the village and be separated by their parents. Soon, Adama left Jambanjelly to marry a stranger. Within several moons Adama delivered a baby boy, Mustafa-boy.

None of this is mentioned during the days the two mothers sit side by side and chat about life in the village. Who is having a naming ceremony, who is preparing for a wedding, who is having a baby. Who had died. How is the harvest of the ground nuts, this season. Never asking or discussing what is to become of Modu, Adama and Mustafa-boy?

Which boy is *not* in the grave?

But, one day, Binta spoke in a quiet voice to Fatou as they sat closely together. She wanted only Fatou to hear what she was about to say.

The other women were lined up along the long wooden tables at the marketplace. They talked and laughed in loud voices.

Binta leaned forward toward Fatou, and whispered, "I think Adama should marry, soon. She needs to have a husband. She must have more babies before it is too late."

Fatou did not respond. She knew what Binta Darboe was hinting at. She knew it made sense that finally Modu and Adama should be married and unite their family. Mustafa-boy should have a new name. He was not from a Badgie. He was from the clan of Barrow.

"What do you plan to do about it?" Fatou spoke in a low deep voice. Now, several women sitting along the row of tables were looking toward the two women who were speaking to each other in low voices.

"I will talk to Ebrima Darboe, tonight,." Binta murmured.

"And what will you say to him?" Fatou asked.

"I do not know.," Binta said to Fatou directly and in a clear voice.

CHAPTER 40

Husbands and Wives

Binta Darboe walked directly to her husband's house when returning from the market. She stepped up onto the veranda and cleared her throat before she knocked on the wall next to the curtained door. A breeze was ruffling the tie-dye curtain covering the doorway.

"Yes?" Ebrima's voice came from inside. It was the middle of the day heat, and Ebrima always took a rest during that time.

"Ebrima Darboe, I wish to speak with you sometime today," Binta used her business voice.

"I will inform you when the time is correct, Binta Darboe," Binta could tell he was not in a good mood.

As she walked across the dry, parched compound yard to her house she thought, *He is still wanting Haddy Touray in this compound. It is not my concern or responsibility to decide that. If Haddy Touray does not return, I guess Ebrima Darboe will be in a bad mood at times.*

Ebrima Darboe had been feeling angry and sad at the same time recently because Haddy Touray was wanting him to be with her in her father's compound in Sukata. She was resisting the return to Jambanjelly. Ebrima wanted Haddy in any way he could have her, so he traveled two times each week to be with her. Yet, it disturbed him that she would not obey him and come back where she belonged. She was in control of this matter, it seemed, and that concerned him more than anything. He knew he made a mistake when he sent her back to her family compound. He relished Haddy Touray. He wanted her to have his babies, and as is the custom, women can be sent back to their family compound if they do not have babies. However, he would now be most happy if she would return, regardless.

After Ebrima showered and put on a clean blue kaftan, he stepped out of his room and searched the yard for Binta Darboe. She was sitting there by the cooking pot, adding wood to the fire. Tears ran down her cheeks as the smoke surrounded her. Through the smoke and tears she noticed movement on the verandah of Ebrima Darboe's house. She straightened on her stool and looked through he smoke directly at him.

He motioned with his head, slightly, for her to come.

Binta called Adama to come tend the fire as she walked toward Ebrima.

"What is it?" Ebrima abruptly asked as he sat.

"You are not feeling well, Ebrima?" she asked as she sat on a bench across from him.

"I am well. What do you wish to speak about?" he looked out onto the compound yard, not at Binta Darboe, but past her, into nothing specific.

"I would like to speak of Adama Darboe and her future. I am thinking that Adama Darboe is becoming older each moon and she does not have a husband and she has a son who needs a father. Adama is a woman who should have a husband and maybe more babies."

Ebrima smoked his pipe, folded his arms and crossed his legs. He squinted as he looked through the smoke from his pipe.

"What brought these thoughts to your head now, Binta Darboe?" he asked in a more gentle voice.

"It is not a new thought, Ebrima. For a great deal of time I have been worried about Adama's situation and until recently she was still a married woman. She has been released from that marriage by her father-in-law, as you know. Yet, I believe we all have felt obligated to wait a bit longer to learn of Mustafa Badgie's fate."

"We are still not clear about Mustafa Badgie's fate. He may be the one of the four who was not buried. He may have been injured and able to escape the fatal beating the others endured. He may have become lost or captured and still may return for his wife and son."

"But, his father, Momadou Badgie, determined the fate of Adama Darboe and Mustafa-boy. He released them, as you know. Even if Mustafa Badgie returns some day he has no claim to her. And, it is not as if Adama was pleased with the marriage which was arranged those many years ago to accommodate the situation she found herself in," Binta Darboe spoke in her deepest voice, displaying her seriousness.

Ebrima Darboe looked down into Binta Darboe's lap. He sucked on his pipe and thought; *This woman is the most stubborn woman in the village, yet she is also very wise. I'm not sorry she is my wife. I guess letting her win this issue is not the worst thing that could happen. Maybe I can get her to help me bring Haddy Touray back to this compound. After all, if Adama Darboe marries Modu Barrow she will move to her husband's compound. That means without Adama, Binta will have even more work here in this compound. Hmmmm. Let me think.*

Binta Darboe waited for Ebrima Darboe to speak. She knew her husband well enough to know he was thinking, plotting how to make the best of this request. She wondered what would come from his mouth next. She was wary, but prepared for whatever it would be.

Ebrima cleared his throat, "I will speak with Ousman Barrow soon. I am not in a hurry to make decisions such as this. We must think about the consequences of such a serious move."

Binta suspected Ebrima already was making a plan that would benefit himself.

"I agree, Ebrima Darboe, it is a serious move. But, we will not be losing Adama and Mustafa-boy to people we do not know well, and they will be in our corridor, with little difference in how it is now, am I not correct?"

"You are correct," Ebrima said as he rose to leave. Without saying one more word, he stepped off the veranda and walked toward his son, Ishmial Darboe, who was giving water to the donkey by the well.

"Ishmial," he called with a voice loud enough for Binta to hear. "I am going to Sukuta before lunch, so do not go anyplace with the donkey. You will be driving me there, very soon."

And then Binta knew the strategy of her husband, Ebrima Darboe. She would be expected to encourage Haddy Touray to return to this compound and her husband. In exchange, Ebrima would encourage the marriage of Adama Darboe to Modu Barrow.

Binta smiled and shook her head in appreciation of her husband's cleverness.

****

Ebrima Darboe had not planned on going to Haddy Touray that day, but found he must. He didn't mind going, but had made plans to visit his cassava field where his boys and others were working. He decided that could wait until day after tomorrow, and in the meantime, have his youngest son, Ousamanie, act on his behalf. It was time Ouamanie began to take on more responsibility. He already was at the fields working, so it would be an addition to his role; to watch that all goes well with the harvesting of the cassava.

He knew Haddy Touray may be with the Kanalingas either gardening, or performing at a ceremony. Whatever she was doing he would wait at her father's compound for her return. He and Ebe Touray, Haddy's father, could sit, have attire (tea), smoke and chat. It was a very fine way to spend the day.

****

When Ishmial delivered his father to Haddy Touray's compound, he walked to Ebe Touray's house with him. He greeted Ebe Touray and several of the vue who were sitting on the veranda. It was mid-afternoon and attire would soon commence. Charcoal fire would be lit, and while it burned to the red coals and the pot of water sat on it, the men chatted, sat and rested. But, Ishmial was not anxious to sit with these old men. He would be staying overnight this time, as Ebrima planned to return to Jambanjelly early the next morning. Ishmial would be sleeping in the men's house of the Touray compound. But, until it was time to eat or sleep Ishmial would be free to do as he pleased. The donkey would rest there in the compound. Ishmial would find this girl, Miriama Conteh, who took up most of his thoughts recently.

Ebrima Darboe settled in for the afternoon on Ebe Touray's veranda where he would wait for the return of Haddy Touray.

****

Haddy Touray was with Tida Jaru walking slowly back from the garden. The other women in their group, the Kanalingas, had walked in their usual briskness. They were on their way to the village, and then prepare for the evening's celebration where they were to dance.

Tida took Haddy's hand and smiled at her. "Your hand is strong," Tida says in an unusually soft voice.

"No, it is not," Haddy murmured. "It is rough and dirty."

"It is strong and beautiful," Tida pulled their clasped hands to her lips and kissed the back of Haddy's.

"My hand is dirty. Do not do that" Haddy laughed, nervously.

"Then what should I do?" Tida asked and let their hands separate.

"Walk with me to the village," Haddy said.

They were silent the remainder of the short walk to the village. The path passed the Touray compound and Haddy could hear Ebrima laughing loudly along with the other men. She then knew Ebrima was here, again. Sooner than she expected. She felt something inside her flutter and fall. It was a nice fluttering and falling. She smiled excitedly and hugged Tida.

"Ebrima Darboe is here I will see you later when we go to the celebration. Ebrima will wait for me in my room, I am sure," she ran around the fence and entered the gate of the compound.

Tida Jaru waved and smiled broadly at the men on the veranda. All except Ebrima Darboe returned her greeting. Ebrima Darboe's gaze was fixed on Haddy Touray as she strolled toward them.

Tida watched Haddy's wide hips, supple and undulating, as she approached the men. Tida felt a pang of sadness and anger at the same time. Tida was used to these feelings. Tida expected that all her vue had these feeling, also. But, now that Haddy Touray was her friend, she felt it more often than ever. She did not understand so many things. One thing she understood now was that Haddy Touray made her excited and happy. She did not even question why.

**

Haddy had purchased perfume made by women in the neighboring village that smelled like the loudest smelling beautiful flowers in the bush. It smelled red and orange. She splashed some between her breasts and between her legs just after her bath and before Ebrima would be coming into her room.

After dinner was served, Ebrima Darboe excused himself from the men on the veranda. He went to bathe in the men's shower area. He put on his green night kaftan, which would be shed immediately before he slid under the cloth that covered the two of them.

They lay on their backs side by side. Ebrima drew in his breath and expelled it slowly.

"What smells like flowers?" he asked.

Haddy giggled, "I do."

"Are you now a flower?" He rolled onto his side and put his nose into her neck.

Haddy giggled again,."No, I am Haddy," His breath tickled her neck.

"I will find where the smell is coming from, then." He moved his face down and between her breasts. Haddy held her breath. She closed her eyes and waited for Ebrima to kiss her there.

**

Ishmial found Mariama at their usual meeting place behind the prayer ground. Tall trees and bush surrounded the prayer ground. It was a place where lovers met. Mariama was very young. Ishmial was nearly a man. He looked on Mariama as '*fresh*. Ripe. Pure and yet ready for advances. Mariama knew she must remain pure until her wedding night. Ishmial also knew the rules, but he knew how boys break the rules and unless parents wanted to make an issue of it, the rules could be broken.

"You are beautiful," Ishmial pressed Mariama against the fence that lined the path to the village from the prayer ground. She was much shorter than he, which gave him a great feeling of power. Mariama felt afraid of Ishmial's pressing against her. She cringed and ducked her chin into her neck as he tried to kiss her. He took her chin in his hand and lifted her face to his. She tried to move her face, but his grasp was too firm. She stopped trying to resist and let him put his lips on hers. He pulled her loose shirt up and fondled her young breast. Ishmial chuckled as he did this. She moved quickly and darted out around him. He grabbed the back of her neck as she nearly escaped from him.

He pulled her back and pushed her onto the fence once more. Mariama stood quietly.

"There, that is better, Mariama. I am not going to hurt you. I like you. I want you to be my girl. I am sorry if I frightened you. I forget you are a little girl, only. Maybe I should find a girl who will let me kiss her. Yes, I think I will do that. Should I do that, Mariama?"

Mariama shook her head, vigorously. She looked pleadingly at him through her long black lashes and smiled a tiny, sad smile.

"All right, then. I will not find another girl, because it is you who I really want to kiss. I will let you go now. I will be back to Sukatia in a few days with my father. I will meet you here. All right?" He had moved a few inches from her, yet contained her by holding her wrists against the fence.

Mariama nodded, moved her face to his cheek and pecked it very briefly, like a day old chick picks at seeds. She then wrenched her wrists from his grasp and flew down the path toward home.

****

The following prayer day, Binta Darboe decided to inform Ebrima Darboe that she would like to visit Haddy Touray. After all, she had not seen her for a great deal of time. She missed her, and she would say that to Ebrima. Ebrima would know why Binta Darboe was instigating the first move of their unspoken deal.

Binta would get Haddy back to the Darboe compound, and Ebrima would go to Ousman Barrow to initiate the marriage of Adama Darboe and Modu Barrow.

Binta sent Mustafa-boy to find Ishmial. She would have him take her the next day to the Touray compound. She would have Ishmial also contact Buba Cham to send a message with his drums to the Tourays that she was coming tomorrow for an overnight visit.

The visit went better than Binta expected. Ebe Touray was very happy to have Binta Darboe visit his compound. He was very pleased when Binta spoke with him about her desire to have Haddy Touray return to the Darboe compound in Jambanjelly.

"I have been expecting Ebrima Darboe to ask Haddy Touray to return with him. This is very good. We will speak with Haddy Touray when she returns from the garden. She is busy with her vue. She seems to be happy here, but she needs to be with her husband, Ebrima Darboe."

Haddy Touray returned from the garden and was very surprised and happy to see Binta Darboe waiting on the men's veranda with her father, Ebe, and her mother, Fatumata.

They greeted with smiles, and laughs and hand shaking. Minutes of asking for each member of each of the families took place. Haddy excused herself to shower and change into clean clothes.

When she returned the adults were having attire and she joined them. Dinner would be ready in a few hours.

That night after dinner, Haddy and Binta Darboe sat together on the veranda of the women's house. They sat side by side on an old wooden bench. Looking out over the compound they watched the stars begin to pop out of the dark sky. Several of the children sat on the floor at their feet, quietly speaking to one another and listening to sounds of the bush.

"I will be leaving tomorrow early, Haddy, and I want to inform you before I leave that we are missing you in the Darboe compound and wishing you to return."

"Did Ebrima Darboe send you with this message?" Haddy asked. "Because if he did and you are not wanting the same thing, Binta Darboe, then I will not even consider it. You do know he comes each week asking me to return with him, correct?"

"I do know that, Haddy. I know he misses you and is not in a very good mood much of the time. I am missing you, too. I would love to have you be part of our compound. There is always much to do. Sometimes I think about the time you left our compound and how full of children and adults it was that time. There was much work to be done, and you did a great deal of it, back then. There is less work now.

Think about it, Haddy. Your father wants you to return to Ebrima Darboe, but will not demand it. I think it would please him if you did. And, I am sure Ebrima Darboe will be very good to you."

"But, I can have no babies," she said in a sad, longing voice.

"We have plenty of babies," Binta slapped Haddy's thigh, bent over and laughed. Then she stood to take her shower and go to bed.

****

Binta Darboe returned to Jambanjelly thinking it may not take more than one more visit to Sukuta to convince Haddy she should come home with her to Jambanjelly. Haddy had come to Binta the next morning before Binta left with Ishmial. Haddy was on her way to the garden with her friend, Tida Jaru.

"Binta Darboe, this is my friend, Tida Jaru. We are with the Kanalingas. We dance for the celebrations. We also share a garden in the women's garden. She is my good friend." She grinned a wide, happy smile and pushed against Tida's large full frame. Tida pushed back and said to Binta, "Salam male cum, Binta Darboe. I have heard much about you and it is all good, kind words from Haddy Touray."

Binta shook Tida Jaru's hand and clasped her elbow, smiling as only Binta could light up the day. "It is good to meet a friend of Haddy Touray's. I am happy she has found a friend in this village."

Haddy stepped between the two of them and said, "Binta Darboe, I will return to the Darboc compound and Ebrima Darboe if I can bring my good friend, Tida. We will work together in the compound and the garden. Tida has no family except for the Kanalingas, here. She would love to come and be part of the Darobe compound, correct, Tida?"

Binta sat, legs sprawled, arms folded over her belly, she finally said, "I will need to speak with Ebrima Darboe about this, but I think it would be fine to have an extra person to help with the work."

Binta chuckled most of the way back to Jambanjelly.

Ishmial was not concerned about his mother's chuckling. He thought of Mariama backed against the fence and the excitement it gave him.

CHAPTER 41

The Return of Haddy Touray

Ebrima Darboe was elated when Binta Darboe brought the good news from Sukita. He was always amazed at Binta's ability to make things happen. To make things better for him and his compound. No matter what was the case, Binta Darboe was his first and most clever wife.

Haddy Touray returned to the Darboe compound along with her friend, Tida Jaru. Arrangements were made by her father, Ebe Touray and by her husband, Ebrima Darboe. The Touray donkey cart carried them and their belongings to Jambanjelly.

The Darboe family greeted them by the gate at the entrance of the Darboe compound. Some of the children had been waiting for what seemed a long time. They stood watch for most of the day, in great anticipation. And, when the two women, along with one of Haddy's brothers turned the corner into the corridor of the Darboe compound, a great cheer rose.

Only Ebrima Darboe was not present. The custom being thus, he waited until Haddy walked to his house and stood at the bottom of the steps. He then stepped from his room and greeted her.

Tida stood back in the crowd and watched. Two drummers had appeared just as Haddy and Tida arrived. Their joyfully loud noise added to the celebration. Some of the women in the group began to dance. Ebrima watched from the veranda. He gestured for Haddy to join him. She stepped up beside him quickly and watched the dancing and drumming. One of the neighbors grabbed Tida's hand and pulled her into the group of women dancing. Tida flew into a frenzied dance along with three other women. The people gathered there were delighted. Haddy was home and with her was a new and interesting person.

Binta Darboe welcomed the two women to the compound and had two of the girls show them to the women's room. Carrying the baskets on their heads, the girls entered the room. They slid the baskets under each of the two beds. Two other double beds filled the room. Adama Darboe and Mariama Darboe also shared this women's room. Binta Darboe, being the eldest wife, had a small house of her own. Her bedroom had two double beds. Female family from other villages used the extra bed when visiting the Darboe compound.

They settled in and quickly became part of the compound's activities. When Haddy and Tida walked to the garden, they walked with other members of the family. They became good friends. Binta did not go to the garden as often as she used to. She stayed behind and directed the activities of the compound. Adama Darboe and her sister Mariama Darboe went to the garden daily, often twice a day to weed and water. Life was busy and good for the Darboe compound, except for the constant struggle to survive in the land where drought or rain determined how hungry one was. How much water one had to carry and to use for cooking and to use for laundry. How far the women had to go to fetch water during the dry season determined how much strength they had to keep from becoming ill. And in the rainy season the children and adults dealt with malaria. Some died. Some lived.

Regardless, at this particular time in their lives, life was good.

It was at this time that Ebrima decided to go to Ousman Barrow and discuss the possible marriage of his daughter, Adama Darboe, to Ousman Barrow's son, Modu Barrow.

They sat on the veranda of Ousman Barrow. They smoked their pipes. They crossed their legs and folded their arms in a familiar manner. They stared out into the heat of the day.

"Ousman, my friend, I have something that has been on my mind for many moons, and now I think it is time to discuss it with you.," Ebrima blew a healthy puff of smoke into the air.

"I am listening.," Ousman murmured.

"We both know Adama Darboe has been left without a husband, and for a great deal of time has waited to learn of his fate. And, as you and I both know, she has a son, Mustafa-boy who belongs to many families. And, as you and I both know, your son, Modu Barrow is without a wife or son.

I am interested to hear your view of the future of our two grown children. Are you feeling they may make a good marriage? I see how attached Mustafa -boy is to Modu, and how Adama and Modu have always had a fondness for one another. I am in favor of the marriage. And, I would like your opinion."

Ousman hesitated for only a few seconds before he spoke. "I am aware of all you have said, and in agreement with your proposal. The boy belongs to these two clans, and I am pleased that conditions allow for a union between his two parents. If you are in agreement, I suggest we share this with Adama and Modu, and allow the mothers to make the plans."

Ousman extended his hand to Ebrima who took it and shook it firmly.

*****

Adama Darboe ran down the lane where Owl lived. He saw her running towards him like an impala runs through the bush toward safety. When she reached him she was out of breath. Bending forward, she clutched her knees and gasped for air.

"My, my, what causes this racing toward your spirit animal until you are out of breath?" Owl blinked his huge eyes and ruffled his pure white feathers.

"Owl, I am unable to understand what is taking place in the compounds of Barrow and Darboe! I am afraid I have dreamed a magic dream and I need you to help me know the truth."

"Then you must tell me what you think is taking place at the two compounds," Owl always knew what was happening in those two compounds, but he needed to know what Adama was hearing and understanding.

"Binta Darboe came to me yesterday and said Ebrima Darboe and Ousman Barrow have agreed that Modu-the-boy-I-love and I will be married, soon! Owl! I am afraid I have lost my mind and am dreaming this! Tell me please what must I do?"

"Did you not see your mother when she gave you this information?"

"Yes, I did."

"Did you see the compound around you as you and Binta Darboe spoke?" Owl asked.

"Yes, I did," Adama's eyes were opened wide and shining.

"Then, Adama Darboe, you must relax and realize this is not a dream. This is actual. Your fathers and mothers know what should be done, and they are allowing it to be done.

Now, return to your compound and act like a grown woman who will at last have her dream come true," Owl spoke firmly and in a deep owl voice."

"Will you be with me always, Owl?" Adama asked with a voice of hope.

"I am your spirit animal. I will be with you not only in this life, but all the lives and travels you may have henceforth, Adama Darboe. Now, go!"

*****

Adama and Modu met by the market and sat under the baobab tree on the ancient root worn shiny by the years of village rumps. They looked down into the dry, dusty dirt.

"I want to bring Mustafa-boy to the place we lived those many rainy seasons ago. I want you and I, when we are married next moon to take him in the Barrow donkey cart and go to that place. We will stay in our little house, the three of us, and we will show Mustafa-boy our well, and the path that took us to our garden, and we will tell him that that is the place where we were together as young people and that is why he is here. We will change his name to Young Modu Barrow at that time. YaMoi?"

She felt tears coming to her eyes. She knew people passing by them, nodding and greeting, were glad to see the two of them in public, together. It made her weep from gladness.

"NMoi.," she replied, still looking into the dusty yard.

"Your uncle brought the kola nuts to my father two nights ago, so we will be finally married once they have gone to the mosque this prayer day. We will plan to take Mustafa-boy to our special place the following day."

Modu stretched, clutched his knees and looked at Adama for the first time since sitting there in public.

"I must go," she said. She rose and walked away from him. She could not believe her great good fortune. She could not believe after all these long years she still loved this man as much as she did when she was ten years old. She did not know if other women loved their men as she loved Modu Barrow. She knew only that Owl had made this happen and she was ever grateful to this animal spirit of hers.

****

Adama told Binta Darboe of their plans to take Mustafa-boy to the place where Modu and she lived when they ran away. She explained that this was what Modu wanted to do, and she too wanted it.

Binta Darboe, when told, shrugged her massive shoulders and said, "That is what you will do, then."

****

The Barrow donkey and wagon waited in front of the Darboe compound. Adama and Mustafa-boy stepped out of Binta's house and walked toward the gate. Everyone had wished them well and expected to see them within a few days. Food and water was packed. A straw mattress hung out over the sides of the wagon. A bucket, a cooking pot, a small container of oil and a bag of rice sat under the mattress.

The couple knew where fruit and perhaps even okra was growing at that place.

Mustafa-boy looked as if he was the happiest boy in the world as he sat between his parents on the seat of the wagon.

They waved to the few family members who stood by the gate to see them off. The two clans stood mingled together, having known each other since time began in this place.

****

Owl spread his wings, flapped them slowly, then with more zest, and finally, jumped into the air. He took off from his beloved limb and flew up and out of the tall palm trees. He winged over the forest, and then dropped down into the place where Modu and Adama and Mustafa-boy would be settling in for a short time.

Mustafa-boy would become Young Modu Barrow and Owl needed to be close by when this new family finally came together.

THE END

Lightning Source UK Ltd.
Milton Keynes UK
UKHW012014070422
401263UK00007B/294/J